Praise for *Gentlemen of Space*

"A wonderfully tender and imaginative first novel, filled with a cast of quirky yet believable characters . . . the trickiness and slippery nature of memory and all of our protective self-deceptions are really the subject of Sher's delightful and memorable novel."

—*The Beat*, National Public Radio (Seattle)

"You'll remember Sher's metaphors . . . the overriding sense of loss and melancholy . . . its Fellini-esque sense of the absurd."

—"Chris Watson's Book Ends"

"Sher's inventive *Gentlemen of Space* . . . [confronts] the moment when a national infatuation with conquest and adventure slides irretrievably into confusion and despair."

—*The Washington Post Book World*

"Sher's affection for his characters is clear, and they shine with softly absurd humor and a DeLillo-like nostalgia for Americana and belief. This is a beautiful, eloquent first novel that dares one to use clever phrases like 'rising star' and 'out of this world.'"

—*Booklist*

"The novel's meticulous structuring and Sher's graceful writing, tinged with sadness and humor, mark this author as a bright star indeed."

—*BookPage*

"A first-rate work."

—*Library Journal*

"A ghostly and quiet story, quite marvelously done for a first outing, that makes an absurd-sounding scenario surprisingly moving by the end. A mysterious and gentle tale of loss conjured out of a more optimistic generation's shattered dreams."

—*Kirkus Reviews*

"Astonishing . . . blasts us directly into the longing and loss at the center of America and our relationship with American history. This is a novel told with genuine invention, its authority achieved absolutely and plaintively in the landscape of the moon and the father and storytelling itself."

—Victoria Redel, author of *Loverboy*

"In his wondrous first novel, Ira Sher takes us on a Pynchonesque odyssey to the moon, passing along the way through memory itself."

—Jenny McPhee, author of *The Center of Things*

"*Gentlemen of Space* is a parable of the tension between the desire to escape and the terror of being lost—a parable of America itself."

—Nick Flynn, author of *Some Ether* and *Blind Huber*

Gentlemen
of Space

IRA SHER

FREE PRESS

New York • London • Toronto • Sydney

FREE PRESS
A Division of Simon & Schuster, Inc.
1230 Avenue of the Americas
New York, NY 10020

First Free Press trade paperback edition 2004

FREE PRESS and colophon are trademarks of
Simon & Schuster, Inc.

For information about special discounts for bulk purchases,
please contact Simon & Schuster Special Sales: 1-800-456-6798 or
business@simonandschuster.com

Designed by Dana Sloan

Manufactured in the United States of America

1   3   5   7   9   10   8   6   4   2

Library of Congress Cataloging-in-Publication Data
Sher, Ira.
Gentlemen of space / Ira Sher.
p.   cm.
1. Children of celebrities—Fiction. 2. Manned space flight—
Fiction. 3. Fathers and sons—Fiction. 4. Astronauts—Fiction. 5.
Florida—Fiction. 6. Boys—Fiction. I. Title.
PS3619.H463G4 2003
813'.6—dc21
2002192807

ISBN 978-0-7432-4219-6

For Rebecca

Gentlemen of Space

*   *

*   *   *

*   *

Fate has ordained that the men who went to the moon to explore in peace will stay on the moon to rest in peace.

These brave men, Neil Armstrong and Edwin Aldrin, know that there is no hope for their recovery. But they also know that there is hope for mankind in their sacrifice.

These two men are laying down their lives in mankind's most noble goal: the search for truth and understanding.

They will be mourned by their families and friends; they will be mourned by their nation; they will be mourned by the people of the world; they will be mourned by a Mother Earth that dared send two of her sons into the unknown.

In their exploration, they stirred the people of the world to feel as one; in their sacrifice, they bind more tightly the brotherhood of man.

In ancient days, men looked at stars and saw their heroes in the constellations. In modern times, we do much the same, but our heroes are epic men of flesh and blood.

Others will follow, and surely find their way home. Man's search will not be denied. But these men were the first, and they will remain the foremost in our hearts.

For every human being who looks up at the moon in the nights to come will know that there is some corner of another world that is forever mankind.

—William Safire, 1969

To be read to the nation by President Richard M. Nixon in the event the Apollo 11 *mission failed, and the astronauts were stranded on the moon*

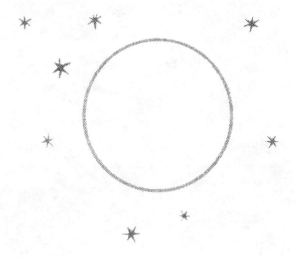

Prologue

Sometimes I wonder: Who's there, floating above the brick stars of the apartment complex? Who is it, always breathing, listening so carefully to his breath? Who loves his breath so much?

Perhaps you're old enough to have followed that momentous summer on TV, or maybe you've since read about the *Apollo 19* launch and the brief carnival of Americana that was to flourish around the apartment building my family called home. You might have seen newspaper photos of Magnolia Court during the weeks surrounding the moon landing; and you may even have flipped through Mr. Robert Nightly's hagiography of my father's days, in which case you will likely recognize from those pages, so dim and refracted as to seem almost submarine, my mother, Uncle Lyle, Mr. Nightly himself—all those people without whom this story wouldn't have been possible—including my father, Jerry Finch. Of course, Jerry Finch, for this is, after all, his story.

It is, though, the occasion of my father's return to earth that people seem most to recall. The still frames from those last hours are nearly as common to seventies iconography as photos of an embattled Richard Nixon, Kent State, or the airlifts from Hanoi. I suppose that's the danger of modern media: how it boils a long chain of events, an entire lifetime, down to snapshots—pictures both more and less true. When I see images of the burning police barricades and fountains of tear gas that would have greeted my father's homecoming, it is tempting to forget that the court wasn't always this way, but it's also a forcible reminder of what must have surrounded me as I ran through the deepening spiral of that night, aware now that I was being followed.

Illuminated by flares and searchlights, Magnolia Court seemed a place between advancing and retreating armies, the police laying into the flank of the crowd like gentle threshers as men and women hurriedly collected the last of their belongings from abandoned tents. It was, I recall, while we retreated with these straggling patriots from the strenuous call of the state trooper and the National Guard serviceman that my young friend and companion Fauna indicated the astronaut in the doorway of a building. We watched as he came outside, skirting the dark hedges behind us. In his soiled suit, he looked like a homeless person.

I've often marveled that we decided to flee from this sad and lonely man. In any grade school primer from this era, we should have discovered pictures of such a figure, grouped scenically with the police officer and fireman, as a member of that select social body in which little boys or girls seek refuge on dark and stormy nights; but it's also true that by now it was clear to me that the ruin of the Apollo team was in no small part my doing. Inasmuch as my silence regarding my father's plans had destroyed their hopes for both this world and the one they'd left behind, I shuddered to reflect—or reflect twenty-some years later—that such creatures are drawn to their destroyers nearly as a child to its mother. Grasping Fauna's hand, I ducked back into the lobby of the central apartment building.

Due to the construction of these high-rises, we couldn't see whether the astronaut had followed us, though after a moment we heard his shoes crunching across the linoleum and shattered glass. Even this late, it's possible we might have evaded him, but when I eased against the back door, it squealed, and as we entered the placidity and darkness of South Court, his long strides rang through the building in pursuit.

The instant the door closed behind us, the sirens and amplified voices in the North Court receded to nothing, just the greenhouse awake amongst the looming and undisturbed magnolias. Bubbling above the dark shapes of bushes, the structure seemed like an organism, green shell pulsing with the silent seethings of some transparent and microscopic life. I don't believe either of us even considered another destination, and we stumbled toward its shelter, little thinking that we must have been silhouetted against those glowing walls for the astronaut to see. When I heard the muffled report of my name, I was already following Fauna through the window beneath the exhaust vent. As I clutched her hand again, saying, "How do we get out of here? He's seen us—" the girl's answer could only crush me with its simplicity: "There is no way out. You need a key for the doors."

And so, I thought, it was to be as I'd always envisioned my demise in nightmare, where I'd climb into a tall house or tower, the body of a rocket ship, and find—my pursuer's footsteps upon me like the beating of my own heart—that there was no place to go but forward, into diminishing space. It was, I realize now, probably not unlike my father's dreams. Barely catching my breath, holding tight to her hand, I fled with her inward, through flowers and leaves, blundering into trees, the lash of fronds and branches only exaggerating our confusion.

All I could conceive of doing was hurrying toward the inner, desert room and, once there, hurrying through the final door to crawl beneath the tables of seedling trays, behind sacks of earth and stacks of green plastic pots. Even if I realized by then that we'd reached that ultimate cul-de-sac of nightmares, I could only reflect ruefully upon this, enfolded in shadow and cut off from my companion where I waited, scarcely breathing, until with a start I heard the door to the desert room slam open, then a grave, expansive silence.

The astronaut's first impressions upon entering that starlit plateau of sands, so fertile, if only to the mind, aren't difficult to imagine. No doubt he recognized in this place the fragile allure of space. The glossy black night beyond the glass walls must have seemed the moon's dark cradle— a shore that vends on a night so solid it hardly appears an effect of light. I know that in these first moments he'd also have noted any footprints, trained as the Apollo team had become to seek evidence of the passage of life on the lunar face; and so we may imagine him pausing there, drawn to an astronomical oddity: the footsteps of children.

It was in this way, I believe, that he came to open the door at the end of the moon and find the room in which we'd concealed ourselves, with its rows of seedlings, the long table at its center, glittering with vermiculite.

I heard in my bunker the twist of a knob, the creak of a hinge, feeling all over the cold formication of sweat as the tread of those great, silver shoes across gravel began. The footsteps drifted up and down the aisles, stopping sometimes, but always accompanied by deep drawn breaths; and though after ten minutes he seemed little closer to discovering me, I found myself more and more alive to a fear familiar to anyone who's ever hidden in earnest—whether in earnest play or earnest fear—that a body cannot possibly keep silent; that, beyond my control, my pursuer would hear me where I lived.

There was, however, something else I'd begun worrying where I crouched, inhaling earth and bark and imagining destruction. For bowed down as I was, watching these Mylar legs toil among table trestles and upended wheelbarrows, the thought had dawned upon me: what if this was my father?

Yes—my father. Certainly, if such a thing was ever possible, it was possible tonight. I'd just wandered through a place still echoing with his passage, like a fairground in the wake of a comet. I had seen those faces alight with rage and glory; I'd heard the air teem with his name.

Hadn't more than a hundred people watched him waver, on the verge of rejoining the world? And afterward, if he had walked as Fauna and I in the milling crowd, unremarked among his brethren, wouldn't he have awaited just this moment—the moment he might have spoken to me alone—when our reunion would be not an entertainment on the nightly news but the relenting of a deep silence, a light switched on by a bed, when we wipe a dream from our eyes?

*   *

*   *   *

*   *

Yet I see I'm forgetting myself: there will be those of you who don't remember this night, who are perhaps too young to recall the *Apollo 19* mission at all. *You've got to care for things,* my father once told me. *You've got to care for everything*—and I see I haven't been careful.

I promise that we will return to the greenhouse, but first we must look in on other rooms, and other nights. It was an age of moonlight, I remind you, when we saw ourselves, each of us, briefly reflected in that great, calm eye. Even today, I hear, sometimes, in those deep summer skies like the world holding all the light of the sun in its lungs, the breath of a man, and I look for the moon then, laid gently in the blue—a flower on the wallpaper in the kitchen hall, when I was just a boy.

ONE

About the Author

Memory passes below, like clouds over the earth, the winking lights of cities. Florida slipping into the color of oceans; the little figure eight near the shore of the green peninsula, double loop of seven asterisks, like stars drawn by some childish hand. Small stars full of lives, lives full of those small stars that make up a life: the *taste* of wallpaper, cornflower blue, patterned like a woman's dress in the slender hall between kitchen and living room; the iron crust of water beneath a sink; oily linoleum slipping and burning against my knees—a playland for trucks without the endless snagging and unsnagging of wheels from shiny loops of nylon carpet.

A world of carpet—or so I imagined the moon, mirror of earthly lands: beige, woolly, resilient.

One day my father would inform me, voice full of space and static, of how the moon is in fact stony, dusty, brilliant bright—but that lay in the future. This particular morning arrived with the bleary sound of the radio above the stove instead of his voice. My father had landed, we were told, and was taking turns with his fellow traveler, looking out the window of the lunar module.

I was kneeling, rolling a silver moon buggy from the hall onto the linoleum, looking up at my mother. She wore a long white nurse's coat, as she did every day. Behind her, the sky out the kitchen window had the bloodless look of full-on July. She yanked at her gloves, beckoned, and stooped to pick my shoes out from under the chair by the front door. She was going to be late. My father was placing his foot upon an astronomical body, like a god mounting a tiny silver throne, but she would be late for work, because the baby-sitter was sick and wouldn't be coming this morning.

Taking my hand, she led me down the tobacco-stained hall of the fourth floor to the elevator, where an elderly couple by the name of Stern, tiny American flag pins rippling upon their Hawaiian lapels, had taken up residence several weeks ago, graciously pushing the buttons for passengers even though the elevator was fully automated. They were the tip of a great iceberg of fans and enthusiasts who'd traveled from near and far to be near us during my father's odyssey, and had erected lawn chairs around a small table set with a red Thermos and two plastic cups of lemonade. "It's a scorcher out there," Mr. Stern said, clasping his paper to his chest so we might squeeze inside.

My mother adjusted her sunglasses.

"You're looking especially glamorous this morning, Mrs. Finch," he added, and his wife, reaching into her purse, said, "You must be so excited, Georgie," handing me a worn scrap of candy.

I'd met the Sterns before, but today their eyes burned as if in each of us they recognized a secret grandchild. The candy had the metallic taste of fear, and when the old woman plucked at my sleeve, muttering, "Can you keep a secret, Georgie?" I hid in the folds of my mother's coat, trying to focus all my attention on the shiny moon buggy I still held in one hand. I knew that outside there would be cameras, an atmosphere of carnival and balloons, where my name would be repeated until it lost all meaning.

My mother, for her part, only smiled. "Thank you," she said, her thank-yous generous, conscious of their public like queens, though at this moment she felt only beleaguered. If she considered asking these people to watch me for the afternoon—there was no doubt they'd have agreed—she did so only as one revolves any number of familiar and flawed endgame options: the Sterns belonged to that broad category we loosely term fanatics; it would be like giving her child to gypsies. Pursing her lips, she recalled Doris Fitzpatrick's voice on the phone this morning—the voice that had begun this series of revolutions, even as it elaborated her daughter's illness.

"Again?" my mother had broken in, noting that this would be the third day running.

"She was fine last night—we thought she was fixed," the woman chirped into the frustrated pause. "Have you heard your husband's landed? On the moon, I mean. I do hope they're OK with everything."

My mother shuddered once more, now, at the thought of these men paddling around in their space suits, playing golf—the ridiculous pretenses of normalcy they would set up in their oxygenless world; and then we emerged from the elevator, and saw the crowd beyond the smoked glass doors of the lobby. Just inside, Lyle Barnes, Uncle Lyle, as I called him, handsome as a cereal-box hero, was lounging in a suit, chatting with a security guard.

He turned his boyish eyes—blue with the slightest tremble—upon us, saying, "It's great, great, bringing the spud with you to work—bravo, Barb. We've got NBC, ABC, CBS, PBS, the *Post,* the *Times*"—he counted them back to himself, glanced toward the doors, where the crowd, catching sight of us, pressed forward like a wet nose against the glass. "It's a rodeo out there."

"Lyle," my mother said quietly, "I don't want to talk to anyone now, do you understand? I *cannot* talk to anyone."

He paused a moment, moving his square jaw from side to side, realigning himself behind this proposition.

"Sure—absolutely"—he nodded—"I understand completely." But, pushing through the doors, he seemed to rethink matters. Glancing around, he said, "We have to give them something, Barb. Should I say this evening? Should I offer CBS the exclusive?" until he saw the firm set of her mouth and turned sadly back.

The guard squeezed outside. Police were there already, shaping the mass of people, and the effect of the crowd, seeing not ourselves but my father as they gazed through the glass, was ferocious, like an animal snapping at a reflection; years later I would recognize a perhaps truer likeness in the desperate clinging of a newborn chimp to a terry cloth–wrapped mannequin.

As the doors hinged open all the way, and the light and heat and noise poured over us, I was sick on the worn, pink tiles of the lobby, in the smiling eye of the crowd. The moon buggy slipped from my hand and careened across the floor to come to rest against one of my mother's heels. I watched myself as if from above as Lyle bent to retrieve the fallen vehicle, the crowd made its distant roar, and my mother, giving me a handkerchief from her pocket, hauled me out by the arm into the light.

*   *

*   *   *

*   *

In the safety of her car, Barbara Finch took off her sunglasses. Beneath the brown bob of the day, she had, you might remember from newspapers or television, one of those angular faces that wear sunglasses well. Perhaps, if you recall her at all, you've confused her with Jackie Onassis in your shoe box of memories; but perhaps you also remember, from those few public photos of my mother without sunglasses, that she had a wandering right eye. She was quite vain about it, and the gesture of removing her dark glasses and revealing that pale face with its single defect always had the quality of an admission.

"I suppose you have what Angie has," she said, pulling out of the parking lot.

My mother probably had little conception of the state into which I'd been plunged, only moments ago, confronted with that wild, unseeing crowd; she was—and is—a fearless person, much more so than her husband the astronaut. Noticing, however, that I was still turned, staring back behind us for signs of pursuit, she added, "They love this, don't they? There's really nothing they'd rather do." At the corner traffic light she gazed in the rearview, pressing her lips tight before she said, "But then again, if your father didn't exist, Georgie, someone would have to invent him."

People make such pronouncements all the time, on subjects ranging from hairpins to divinity. I recognized in these words, nonetheless, a parody of my father's own, and suspected that she, too, was thinking now of the night of the parent-teacher conference, one week before Jerry Finch wrote his entry for the astronaut contest, months before his name would be announced in the newspapers, nearly a year before this day, the day the lunar module touched down in a cloud of pulverized glass and rock.

You've probably forgotten Jerry Finch. He wasn't among the famous astronauts, and really, in every respect except the one, crucial point of traveling above and beyond the earth's atmosphere, of walking the surface of the moon, my father wasn't an astronaut at all. Until that summer he left the world behind he was an earth science teacher in central Florida for the Ashtrakan Normal School. If you lived in Ashtrakan or the Greater Titusville area, you might have seen him: a deliberator at the register at McDonald's, a collector of *National Geographics* at yard sales, a passable swimmer at the local YMCA, and, what is less known, an amateur bird-watcher, populating my earliest memories with impressions of tall grass, ourselves crouching within the still heart of the world, binoculars in hand, following with infinite voyeuristic care the distant domestic scene of a creature the size of a heart.

But you do at least remember the year—1975, nearly twelve months before his voyage—when our elected officials gathered in our televisions to concede that the space program was errant, had forgotten its roots. My mother, seated between my father and me that evening, was putting on her shoes for parent-teacher night, paying little attention, but her brows arched perceptibly, as if what had been implied by this concession was that the astronauts had departed forgetting their lunch. She didn't realize at what future cost to herself these pronouncements were being made, and the nation's trusted representatives, for their part, were as yet blind to my mother, even as she rose, terrifying, to turn off the television.

My father, on this occasion, stayed her hand, and for a moment we listened together to the sentiments of our president, that great man of words. His logic was deductive, potent: after all, he reminded us, strip away from the Apollo space program the glamour, the secrecy; strip away the military-scientific complex; yes, strip away even the spaceships—and what *is* space travel about?

People, surely. People, like you and me.

The president hesitated, mouth modest, eyes dreamy, because for this one moment of his brief term, the representatives of our nation had laid aside partisanship and tendered to him their loyalty and trust. They may have tendered these things as children do, or perhaps, as my mother pointed out, as devious men of politics tender all wares—this was immaterial. I do not claim that the following actually occurred, but it was as if each senator, as the curtain went down on the Vietnam Era, as the oil crisis hovered in the wings of the decade, took advantage of this caesura to kindle a butane lighter to a single cause.

And even if there was no such stadium drama, and the decision arose through a simple counting of votes, a weary shaking of hands, the outcome was the same: the thing to do, clearly, was send an ordinary man to the moon.

I think by "ordinary," our representatives imagined someone a lot like my father but made of some solid, wholesome fiber, like flame-retardant pajamas. A write-in contest appeared in major magazines, and I remember him reading his entry aloud to us one night—the scorn with which my mother received his suggestion that the moon might have something to teach us. "The moon," she said, "is a veritable palace of idiots."

My father, drawing his onion-shaped head further into his collar, persevered in his monologue. It was well for him that he did. His essay was entitled "Gentlemen of Space" and would be reprinted in every major paper in the country.

"Gentlemen of Space," in its quiet way, has become a modern classic of the middle school civics class, no doubt because whatever my father wanted for himself, this man who wrote in "Gentlemen" of the beautiful things he'd bring back from the moon, it's clear he'd grasped, even seated there amidst his family, in the comfort of his Florida living room, that people prefer to love their fugitives. They crave *human* astronauts, not hard, hairless men with weathered faces, those faces with weathers so strange and distant only other astronauts can understand. In the closing remarks of his essay, my father vowed to humanize space; and in retrospect, arguably, he did. My father, with his small chin and broad hips—he would appear as incongruous on the moon as any ordinary man. Visitors to our home who'd never met him exclaimed over the framed photos in the kitchen hall of his face frozen behind the curved glass of his visor. They sat in his yellow chair, worn in the seat from years of service; they noted the deposit of gray hairs on the fabric; and the visitors, understanding only so much, knew my father, then, as a fellow traveler. If they grew strident and indignant when they next spoke, if the country as a whole would forget at times that space had been not imposed on him but chosen, it was because they felt for him not as an astronaut but as a human being.

Glancing back with my mother to that distant parent-teacher night, however, I see this was all just beginning. The October dark smelled of gasoline as we drove across suburban Ashtrakan's palm-lined avenues in our Country Squire, the yellow butt of the car hanging low above the ground, a rash of fumes condensing behind us beneath the streetlamps. My father was driving, one hand on the wheel, the other sifting slowly through the woolly shadow of his hair, massed against the sweeping headlights of passing cars. He'd been preoccupied ever since the announcement of the astronaut contest a few hours ago, but his brown eyes, until then loitering upon the road, suddenly reflected back at me.

"Do you know where we're going?" he asked, a slyness in his voice.

"The secret night school," I replied.

He winked. "That's right. Your mother doesn't know that yet—"

"Oh, I've heard all about it, thank you—"

"Or at least she doesn't *really* know," my father added, speaking in his "old cowboy" voice culled from Westerns. "Barbara, I don't recall seeing you at the secret night school before."

"I was too busy making the secret night dinner for the secret night husband."

He gave my mother a crestfallen glance, and she reached and took his hand out of his hair. Stealing a look in the mirror again, he winked at me.

The secret night school was something I'd inherited from my father's own childhood mythology. I didn't believe in it, the way he once truly had, but I don't think he wanted me to—he wanted us to laugh with him, at himself and this invention of his earliest years. For he'd believed for a long time that there really was a secret school the other kids went to after dark, when he was in bed. It was here that everyone learned the answers not to the ordinary questions that could be handled in a multiple-choice fashion—state capitals, spelling, arithmetic—but to the true questions: who to pick for your team, which movies were destined for popularity, how to address girls—all those impossible distinctions everyone else seemed to divine automatically.

He was, I see now, the kind of man who often impressed his students as a well-meaning crank. His hair, despite my mother's best efforts, rose in a peppery fountain as if from some youthful trauma. He had the bad habit of beginning stories in the middle. He had a blue felt-tip drawing of a watch on his wrist at the moment, left over from some classroom science demonstration.

Twiddling with the dial on the car radio, from which the word *moon* gently and periodically lowed, my mother said, "Why this fuss all of a sudden about the moon? We've been to the moon, and there was nothing there."

It was a question my father was frequently forced to counter over the next months, and to which he never grew accustomed. He could only marvel that anyone, given the same chance as himself, wouldn't do the same. "Barbara, it's not like a trip to Dallas. It's—well, it's hardly a place at all. It's like being allowed to speak with the dead."

She looked at him with distaste, and he stuttered, "Just think of it. Any person who's ever walked the earth—if you could talk to anyone, who would it be?"

My mother, as my father seemed momentarily to have forgotten, was a hospice care nurse and from her slender stock of romantic notions had long since excised anything related to death or dying. She said, "I don't want to meet any dead people, Jerry."

With a baroque rattling, the car turned a corner at this point, and ahead, limp above the avenue, trembling in the fronds of the palms, was the controversial satellite.

"But just *look* at it," he said, brown eyes flickering between the moon and the road. "It nourishes us, I think. It's as necessary as mother's milk"—intercepting my mother's protest—"because if the moon didn't exist," my father insisted, a satisfaction entering his eye now, "we would have to invent it."

There was a palpable silence in the car, ruminative or dismissive, as you will.

"Can you imagine the night sky without the moon, day after day? We'd go mad, not even realizing what was missing—" He held his hand over it so we'd see what he meant. "And it's just sitting there. It's a whole continent, waiting for us.

"Do you know—do you know," he continued, noticing he was speeding up, "when Jim and Kay—Jay and Kim—came back from their vacation—"

My mother's gaze focused for a moment. She smiled. "Georgie," she asked in the mirror, "when was the last time we went on a vacation?"

It's the look I associate with her—this pained amusement. If one could lay claim to such a thing, she could certainly be said to own it. It washed in and out of her face, gone the next moment as she turned around in her seat, wet her thumb, and adjusted my hair. Behind her, the school loomed like a toy prison, and then we were pulling into the parking lot.

Parents milled on the front steps, smoking or loitering in the evening heat. A large woman in a red sarong—I recognized her as a classmate's mother, Kitty Shank—touched my mother's shoulder at the door, and for a moment the two women confabulated. There weren't many other children around, but Mr. Rectin had especially asked my parents to bring me, which didn't bode well—like the crowd. Whenever there was a crowd outside in warm weather, it meant the air-conditioning was down; and, sure enough, inside it was a greenhouse.

Adults in the halls said hello because my father taught middle sections here—his parent-teacher night would be next week. He ambled from friendly face to friendly face, stopping to pick a crumpled piece of paper off the floor, as if he were in his own home.

Mr. Rectin, two damp patches under the arms of his shirt, was standing at the darkened windows when we came into my classroom. He was middle-aged and fond of sweater-vests, and with his wife, Kim, would sometimes go bowling with my folks on weekday nights.

"Jerry, Barb," he said, coming forward, "sorry about the heat."

Everyone shook hands. My mother gazed around the room with its party-colored pictures and letters spelling out things like "Congratulations" and "Welcome Back," and then my father sat down, patting the knees of his pants. "Before we start, Jay, I want to know what you think about something."

Probably sensing the turn the conversation was about to take, Barbara wandered toward the back of the room and the drawings the students had made during the first weeks of class. Mr. Rectin fussed with his papers and nodded. He had a small mustache with which he dusted his lower lip.

"If you had the chance to go to the moon—" my father began.

"We were just talking about that in the lounge." Mr. Rectin smiled, sitting down on a desk as my mother rolled her eyes.

"Yes, yes—but what did you *think*?" my father asked, sitting forward a bit and rolling up his plaid sleeves. "Would you go?"

Jay Rectin picked up a pencil and was about to draw a parallel between lunar exploration and some famous historical moment, the way he would in class, bobbing the pencil up and down between thumb and forefinger. But he looked from my father to my mother, pressed too attentively toward the pictures on the back wall, and saw there was a disparity of views. He put the pencil behind his ear. His mustache nibbled. "Well, it doesn't really matter—it's not like they're going to pick one of us."

"There," my father said, turning to his wife.

"He didn't say anything," she protested.

"But the point is you *would* go," my father pressed as the man looked at my mother apologetically.

"Thank you, Jay," she said, her eyes trailing over the drawings on the wall. "Though I admit it would be a real kindness to me—when you two finish filling out your applications, of course—if we might talk for a few minutes about Georgie. I presume there's some reason you asked us to bring him here tonight?"

It's true that the request for my presence there was remarkable: I was quiet, not given to raising trouble or even my voice. "Barbara," Mr. Rectin remonstrated.

She shot a glance across the room at the two men, slumped on the tiny children's desks. "Georgie," she said, "come show Mother your pictures."

The mustache lifted delicately and brought itself down. "Georgie's pictures aren't up." Clearing his throat he added, "I have them over here, Barb. I think you should have a look."

Mr. Rectin removed from his yellow briefcase a blue vinyl folder in which he kept his attendance rolls, and from this he extracted a handful of papers. He laid the drawings out on the desk, and it's true there was something immediately striking to them. There were four in all, and I was pleased, primarily, with my mastery of the conventions of realism: specific details, such as the upturned head of a dinosaur, its great eye rolled toward the sky as if staring at the viewer; a whorl of hair upon my father's own head, his binoculars like a capital H before his face; the seven asterisks of the Magnolia complex scattered in their figure eight on a green field; a blue and green sheet of water, with a man inside, silhouetted like a chalk outline as he swam or slept amongst aquarium fishes.

My parents drew back before bending forward to inspect them more carefully, the silence in the room palpable.

"They're quite well done," Mr. Rectin suggested, to which no one seemed willing to add anything until my mother said, "Georgie—why are they all drawn this way?"

Every image, you see, was drawn as if viewed from above, from a greater or lesser height—I didn't know why. I didn't remember, even then, making any of these pictures. Not that I doubted they were mine— I know they were.

The adults waited briefly for a reply and then turned to one another.

I remember the conversation falling around me, above me, like gray rain; Mr. Rectin asking, "Does he have many friends outside of school? Does he show affection?" I felt myself fading into a set of abstract and anomalous behaviors, fixed to some impulse or action whose origin I didn't even recall. When I looked at my mother, I saw she thought my father was somehow to blame.

We all, I think, saw that these were pictures drawn from a point of view that orbited, rather than rested upon, the earth. That my father had only on this very day voiced more than a passing fascination with things lunar didn't matter: we'd sensed in him for months now a nascent fantasy life, a dreaminess that my mother recalled from his previous forays into crop circles and the language of whales, but of which I, like an animal living above a fault line, had registered the larger significance far in advance of human auditors.

It was, she must have felt, as if I were channeling his manias—things invisible to us before tonight; and it could only have seemed frightful and irrational that, before my father's desires were even articulated, they would loom up here, inside me.

"I think he spends too much time alone," Mr. Rectin said. Someone murmured the word *psychologist,* and for a moment it bubbled around, my father following the whole thing with the habitual expression of panic he wore for practical situations.

When my mother brought the conversation up short, at last, she placed her hand on my head, grown warm and perspiring brightly. "But it's probably nothing," she murmured. "Isn't it? We can talk about psychology until we're blue in the face, but it's much simpler, I think—"

Jay's mustache quivered. "I didn't mean to alarm you—"

"No, no, thank you," my mother said, standing. "You did the right thing." She couldn't explain to this man that the root of the problem was in fact quite clear. Or perhaps she didn't have to. We all glanced at my father.

He had the pictures in his hands still, marveling at the accuracy with which his own sparse yet electric hair was depicted; and my mother was walking toward the door, turning and reaching back her hand to say something to him. She would explain to him that he was setting a poor example with his spongy, inarticulate fantasy life—that it could affect his students in the science classes; that it was the kind of thing that acted subliminally, without anyone meaning anything. If he would just put away the idea, for a little while, of some cowboyish escapade in space— But she slipped just then and skidded on her feet. Looking down, thinking one of her heels had given out, she let out a short scream.

We followed her eyes between the desks, and there on the tiles was a brown starfish the size of a hand, one of its appendages—probably the one just trod on—curling slowly back.

"Damn it," Mr. Rectin said, blushing as he stooped to retrieve the animal. "They do this whenever the air-conditioning fails. We have an aquarium full of stuff for the kids, and they just crawl out when it gets too hot . . ."

I came over and stared at the little creature, of whom I'd never taken much notice in its tank beside the geraniums. It was harmless, blind with a vegetal life; but my mother looked as if she'd seen a ghost.

*   *

*   *   *

*   *

I know there are those amongst you who might wonder at a grown man remembering so much of his early childhood, presuming at all to know the minds of his parents at so tender an age; but imagine for a moment the story that overwhelmed my family, and you will understand that these events were part of the great central myth of our lives that we told amongst ourselves again and again.

All the same, perhaps this isn't the place to begin. There are lives, like shoelaces, which require only a single strand to work themselves into complex, mathematical knots; but my father's is not such a life. There are strands here I cannot touch yet—I don't want to touch.

So let's start anew. Let us leap forward, out of the dark of that parent-teacher evening. And while we could return to the side of my mother, driving silently through the bright Ashtrakan morning—and we will again, soon; I promise we will make good on all our false beginnings—let us now begin anew entirely:

"—I can still perfectly picture North Court, like a mirage of light cast against the wall of my study: the sunburnt grass between the brick towers, the brightly colored lawn chairs; the huffing, red faces with their white plastic visors, tipped up toward our window.

"I would be there, looking out, chin crooked against my hand, and the phone would ring—"

Let us begin, then, on *this* day, between the parents' night and the morning of the moon landing. My father had risen long before us to go to the NASA training camp, and my mother would have gone to work. We were driving together with her a moment ago, and we will leave her in her car, alone now, as she goes to visit the dying. From the window, I'd watched her depart, reflecting that every place she worked had the name of a person, or of people—the Roberts', Mrs. Morris's, Mr. Osseau's, the Ludens'—and when at that age I imagined her in these places with people's names, I saw the name ghostly in a blue glass, like a set of teeth, bubbles striving over the enamel letters, the name growing deeper, more luminous, most perfect.

It was already summer, and I was out of school, but this was during the infancy of my father's fame, and the court contained just two or three local reporters and a handful of elderly, heatstroke-prone gentlemen hoping to point my father or a member of his family out to their grandchildren. Let us begin here, then, safely on earth, where we can breathe.

TWO

The Astronaut

I'd lift the phone on the kitchen wall to my ear, and there'd be a noise: a trembling, crackling heat, like fur rising along a dog's back; or a different sound, like the sound—that delicate, incredible sound, a field of flowers opening—of just-poured cereal popping in milk. And then my father's voice: "Do you know what that is?" he'd say, the phone flooding with the crackle of coral growing through its own bones, elaborating the reef.

"It's cereal," I'd tell him. "It's that rice cereal."

I could hear, through the phone, the yawn of his smile. Long since he'd given up actually trying to fool me.

"That's right," he'd say. "That's it, exactly."

In these months prior to takeoff he was learning so much to prepare him for the rigors and pleasures of space: not just the protocols of NASA manuals but the stock of oral experience, the personal folklore of Neil Armstrong and Buzz Aldrin, his experienced mission companions. Of all things scientific or anecdotal, it was sound, more than anything, that captured my father's imagination.

Space, as he conceived it, hissed with the pressure of underwater, like the soft scratch of sand against itself in a current, or the sound—rarity in Florida—of snow and ice polishing a window at night. It pulsed and hushed like dry leaves stirring at the approach of winter; or like our own heartbeats, amplified between our ears and pillows, soft and endless as the slow tread of feet through autumnal groves.

"Georgie"—my father's voice would flare through this static of earthly things—"what does that sound like to you?"

I hesitated. A fine spray danced above the receiver, a noise prickly with stars, but I knew it didn't originate in space—there was too much rushing and striving. Space, I felt, would be an effortless place, full of the milk of dissolving suns, without friction, only atoms waking and sleeping, winking gently in their clouds.

"It's soda," I said at last. "It's a can of soda."

"Well, OK, Mr. Know-It-All. Are we talking Coke, Pepsi?"

Now it was my turn to smile. "Neither. It's too carbonated. It's tonic."

"Good enough for government work," he said, and I heard a harsh, rasping laugh near the phone—the laugh a large bird would make if it could do such things.

"When are you coming home?" I asked.

"We're just catching some lunch, here. Armstrong said he'd give me a lift after training."

*   *

*   *   *

*   *

I remember hanging up the phone and gazing down at the court, a little patch of green between the four brick buildings at this end of the complex. The only window of my family's apartment that faced the picturesque North Court was the kitchen window, while the living room and bedrooms stared abruptly, if obliquely, through curtains at other living rooms and bedrooms on the adjacent arm of the asterisk-shaped building. I'd been sitting there for more than an hour now, as I did each morning after my mother went to work, when I accompanied Angie, my baby-sitter, to the kitchen, and we waved down to the loose crowd of patriots and cameramen gathered among the scrappy magnolias. A parched cheer would rise as they spotted us, and then my mother would emerge from the lobby, dividing the crowd like a starlet.

We watched them beat excitedly around her cold glow, Angie's gaze sticky with jealousy as she followed the flash of my mother's heels down the walk toward the front gate, the rush and recession of this sea of faces—Angie, with her pouting mouth, herself suddenly a faint star, as all of us were now, by association. For a moment, she lingered, then she retired sleepily down the hall, toward the television.

We were in the season of summer thunder, the sky bellied blue-black over the rooftops. A boy not much younger than myself waved up at me, his other hand clutched in that of an aged guardian. The wind from the encroaching storm tugged at their hair, and then the first rain streaked the glass. I waved back and stood away from the window, watching the drops multiply and swim before I went to tell Angie what my father had said.

Like those of most sixteen-year-olds, Angie Fitzpatrick's place in the world—her individuality and its locus in the honeycomb of life—vacillated wildly between the poles of the macro- and microscopic; but she lay very close to the center of *my* world this year. I had the sort of heart-racing-fourth-grade-teacher infatuation in which, as I would hide each morning when she came to the house, I would understand once again why the word *crush* was applied to such situations. She would walk through the apartment calling my name as my mother, savaging her handbag for the car keys, followed her muttering, "The brains of a lamb . . . No brains at all in that child . . ."

I loved her with a vague, warm tenderness residing mostly in her hair, which was, of course, long and blond, and her breath, which smelled of the liquor she filched from our liquor cabinet and of cigarettes—acrid, burned, and golden. Her breath reminded me of movies. I loved even the freckles on her nose, those poor, earthbound constellations she despised.

When I came into the living room, she was watching the TV with astonishment on her face. It was a program about the *Apollo 11* mission.

"Is *that* where they're sending him?" she asked. There was an astronaut on a pure, white ground bounding slowly into the distance as if he'd lost his mind.

"He thinks the moon sounds like soda," I told her, and she turned to me with the benign look of incomprehension adults so often bestow upon children.

"What? Jerry? Walter Cronkite said the moon's totally silent." She looked at the barren territory on the television. "Cronkite said it's empty, actually. It would probably be really boring—if it wasn't so cool."

I should point out here that astronauts and things astronautical permeated our lives, lived, as they were, so close to Cape Canaveral, in a way different than they did the rest of the country. My father's adventures would become, in a handful of weeks, a national drama, but in the shadow of the launchpad, so to speak, we'd always followed the exploits of the Apollo teams as if they were local football stars. High school kids would drive dates the twenty minutes to the causeway on a Friday night to watch the molten light pour out over the earth as the rockets rose. It was of these men we dreamed at night: pale, nocturnal scars of the men we'd see around town or, more often, on the beach, where you might discover one or two of these sharp, athletic-looking lads held in a crescent of faces, talking to a girl on a blanket.

Angie glanced over my shoulder as lightning illuminated the white drapes in the living room. The sound of rain nuzzled the building, like the fuzz of an old record, surging and delicately surging. She picked up a pillow from the couch and hugged it to her chest.

"You know, when he was my earth science teacher in junior high, everyone thought he was kind of a dork. I didn't think so," she hastened to say. "*I* didn't, you know. I always thought he was sort of brave, not to say cool—he wasn't cool, then—but brave, saying all those things about the earth, and the moon and stuff. But who would have thought that he'd become, you know, an *astronaut*."

She might as well have said *rock star* or *lifeguard*. She turned to the TV again, and I thought of Jerry Finch, suddenly risen phoenixlike from his inglorious life. This sloughed-off, discarded man—my father, actually, as he'd always been to me—was a different animal to Angie than the man she knew now, and her recollections of him brought me back to a time I'd come with my mother to his classroom.

We'd watched through a window in the hall door, unseen, as my father, in a red plaid shirt, held a model of the Saturn V rocket out to the restless room. He was waiting on the results of the NASA contest, and his hands became sweaty whenever he held the tantalizing object. His face, too, was bathed in the glow of perspiration as he pointed the black nose of the craft to a map of the moon he'd pulled down over the chalkboard and said, "It is those things we love most that are most changeable, most fleeting. And so, perhaps because the moon is always changing, revealing and concealing herself from our eyes, we find her beautiful." He shook the model in his hand till some plastic part clacked gently inside.

"Beautiful, but also deceptive.

"Mare Imbrium, the Sea of Rains, for example—a misnomer, as are the names of all of the various sinuses—Latin, for bays—and canals, those lines we see here"—he pointed—"and here, extending like their earthly counterparts from what we once believed were oceans and lakes.

"It's true—men have walked the moon now, and found her dry, fruitless, and lonely. And yet," he said above the gentle snicker of the girls, turning their heads from side to side to display their hair, "and yet, just these names are capable of breathing life again into a world of cold stone and dust."

Outside in the schoolyard, someone was laughing, a blunt sound like two books banged together that carried through the open window, causing everyone to look.

My father waited until the class gave him its attention again.

"Perhaps this seems sentimental to you," he acknowledged, catching the eye of a chestnut-haired girl who'd inadvertently fallen into the droning chasm of his voice. She looked away, perhaps fearing she might find something wonderful, enchanting even, in this least auspicious place—my father's eyes—but he was undeterred. Jerry Finch was an indefatigable man who could work for hours with the weariest spark of interest; in fact, this atmosphere of semiprivate musings was the only one in which he seemed truly at home.

"What, then, of this—this unsentimental affair of steel and ceramic —this vessel of our modern explorers?" he asked, holding against the silvery map of the moon the model of the Saturn V rocket tipped with its space capsule. The model was white, twice as large as his hand, and inside the plastic windows at the top a tiny astronaut was visible clutching a steering wheel. He opened the doors of the lunar module.

"Normally, of course, there would be equipment in here," he said.

"What kind of equipment?" the class asked, startling him.

"Scientific equipment," he returned.

"What is the equipment to be used for?" they asked in that unstable, middle school voice. A boy in a baseball cap spoke up from the back row: "Are astronauts still, by and large, homosexuals?"

My father turned his face stoically away as the girls leaned eagerly forward with their ill-conceived cleavages. The class turned its acne-scarred head to the boy.

"What is the equipment to be used for?" the class repeated; and the boy, encouraged, said, "Is it homosexual equipment?"

I felt a rush of pity for my father, just as he glanced up into the door at us, his features suddenly becoming unfathomably happy; and sitting in my own living room that day with Angie, I wondered if such an image of Jerry Finch persisted at all in her mind, or if it had long since been overwhelmed by the splendor of his new identity.

On TV, on the moon, the astronauts were bounding in the gentle, breathing sound of rain. Angie got up and changed the channel. With her head tipped to one side, her hair scintillated before the images on the screen. I wonder if she sensed any of the tenderness I felt for her; that while she was, in her quasi-maternal role as baby-sitter, a surrogate-mother figure to me, she was also a first departure into that deeper ocean of more mature longings. She twisted the dial to local weather, and we watched gray and white clouds swirling above Florida, a man's voice cheerfully explaining the shapes and patterns of the storm. Lightning flashed again. There was a distant, shifting sound as the plates of the sky ground together, then a startling knock at the door.

When your father is planning a trip to the moon, people make a point of dropping by. We received care packages, requests for things to be said on television or personally endorsed while standing on the earth's only natural satellite, and, not least of all, we were shadowed, even at this early date, by a cunning trickle of journalists masquerading as fire marshals, house cleaners, or exterminators. Rather than answer the door every time such an enterprising individual knocked, Angie would sneak into the vestibule and put her eye to the peephole.

After she'd looked for a moment, I tugged at her denim dress, awkwardly aware of wanting to protect this woman who was, technically, my baby-sitter. Shrugging my hand off, she whispered, "It's a guy in a suit," applying her eye to the door again. "I think he's a cop."

"Does he have a badge?" I asked.

"Of course not—he doesn't *look* like a cop."

"What does he look like?"

"He's wearing a light blue suit . . . with white stitching. He looks . . . like a bible salesman. And"—catching her breath—"he has something behind his back—"

The knock was repeated. For a tense moment we waited. Perhaps it was a gun. Or a bible. My mind slued with scenarios as Angie pressed against the door, and I, beside her, pressed into her dress.

"Georgie," she whispered.

"Yes?"

"I want you to go to the kitchen and get a knife"—the thought shooting through me with a thrill—"I don't like the look of this guy."

Slipping down the hall, I discovered a very large, incidentally dull, serrated knife laying on the counter by the sink. Admittedly, my choice of weapons might have been more inspired, but we'd just used it to make peanut butter sandwiches and, dirty as it was, I reflected, it would leave a nasty, septic wound.

Angie received the weapon with a mixture of curiosity and concern. "What's he doing?" she murmured, pressing her eye to the door again.

It seemed that the man outside kept looking up and down the hall. He was, as they say, casing things out. Anyone who's ever watched a police movie from this era, however, will recognize in this brief sketch not so much the sleuthful cautiousness of the cop as the furtive depravity of the cat burglar: this methodical site checking, followed by a sudden burst of criminality.

The handle of the door twisted and strained against the lock. Angie's hand gripped my shoulder. Adrenaline sloshed back and forth, leaving my mouth dry, my hands damp and cold.

"Let's call 911," she whispered; and I, surging with young chemicals, thought, What would my father do now? What would *Jerry Finch* do?

The answer leapt to mind almost instantly, and more: I think in my discovery I captured the very essence of my father's mode of being. Never particularly good at solving the problems that life handed him— one might even say constitutionally crippled in that part of the brain where the reality principle and its functional minions dwell—my father survived by reimagining problems in forms that they themselves hadn't thought to take but that he might meet with more success. While my mother had somewhat narrowly labeled this as avoidant behavior, it enabled me, in a single, decisive stroke, to reinterpret the scenario.

After all, if Angie and I decided to assume the role of predator, rather than that of prey, all other circumstances favored us: (1) surprise: because the stranger didn't know that we were there, behind the door; (2) boundary control: the locks all being, of course, on this side of the partition; and, finally, (3) armaments: in that whatever the stranger concealed behind his back, I was confident we could use the preceding points, above, to bring our weapon more quickly into play.

Granted, as I was nine, my train of thought was simpler—contained, perhaps, none of these elements—still, the end result was something any father would have been proud of. As Angie turned to lay the sticky knife down on the little table by the umbrella stand, presumably intending to phone for help, I flung the door wide and, grasping the weapon, launched myself at the belly of this unsuspecting man.

You may say it seems a brutal and violent act for a child to undertake. I had intended, brandishing the knife and shouting wildly, to scare away the enemy—perhaps, at most, to wound him superficially. But, instead, I found myself immediately buried in his chest.

"Georgie," a voice grunted from above. "You little rascal you," he said as I struggled in the lapels of a blue blazer, the slippery knife having gotten away from me.

"What a little dynamo you are," the voice ambled. "I just got into town, myself. I thought I'd look you guys up and"—I arched my back in the grip of two strong arms—"well, it's pretty crazy out there. I mean, with the rain, and then these people mooning around with cameras, and telescopes, and microphones," the voice said, before I was placed gently back on the ground. It was one of those moments—another filmic moment—where, in the trenches of a man's private wars, he recognizes in the face of his enemy a long-lost friend. Lyle Barnes—Uncle Lyle—stared down at me from beneath the brim of a white hat. I hadn't seen him in almost two years.

"I don't know what I'd have done if you weren't home," he said, plucking the knife from where it stuck to his shirt and returning it to me—"You've got to carry these things point down"—before he took his hat off and slapped the water out against his leg, smiling his shy, midwestern smile. "These folks picked a helluva day for a picnic, unless they're here to see you, champ?" he teased and then, catching my expression, saw he wasn't so far off the mark.

Lyle Barnes, aftershave hero: in his robin's egg blue suit, hat in hand, he might have been our protagonist had this been a different tale—perhaps the narrative of a musical such as *Oklahoma*. His broad, tanned face appealed to me with no more conception of guile than someone who's heard of it as a ritual practiced by city folk, far away.

"Your dad around?" he asked, as Angie came up behind me.

I should add that I hadn't seen or heard her approach but it was a shift in Lyle's demeanor alone that told me she was there. Had he drawn a shallow breath? Stood just a bit taller? I may be inventing the details, but I saw suddenly, in certain physical tokens, how a grown man—albeit a very particular man—might look at Angie. My own gaze was young, anatomically incorrect, and I studied Lyle as his eyes swept over this girl that even my mother, in her dismissive way, would admit was pretty. His attention tripped down the soft line of her figure—a dress ending at her knees, knees red from kneeling in front of the TV—then leapt to her face—her hair parted down the middle, slipped back behind her ears; the blue gaze with which she'd fixed him. There were pleasures in this room I didn't know, pleasures I couldn't admit to myself. And then, just as quickly, the moment passed. Angie's eyes drifted to the hand still kept behind his back.

"Friend of the family?" Lyle hemmed, hat wafting gently. Perhaps noticing he was staring, becoming embarrassed, he sprang with the concealed hand a bouquet of daisies, obviously picked from some curbside garden. Angie's short scream subsided into a long "Ohh."

"What about Barbara?" he asked, and when we just stared at the flowers as if they were broken, he added, "But seriously," gesturing behind himself as he closed the door and lowered his voice to a whisper, "what's with the long faces? And what's with the guy with the camera hanging out down the hall? I didn't know what to do out there."

"Don't you watch TV?" I said. "My dad's going to the moon. He's going to be the first ordinary man in space."

Lyle glanced for confirmation at Angie, who stared back with ill-concealed hostility.

"The moon? No kidding—" He turned again to her, then me. "I guess I've been on the road a lot. Missed this one entirely," he admitted, seeming lost for a moment in an amusement that made him blink. "I guess I should congratulate him."

"You had no idea," Angie said.

"No. I was just in town, you know—"

"And your horse broke down in the rain?" she asked, retrieving the knife from me with a frown and heading toward the kitchen.

"Hey," he called, "I'm from Michigan, not Colorado. I thought I'd just look in on Jerry and Barb, and Georgie." He hunkered beside me, pointing toward her receding back and wringing one hand painfully. "Look, give your mom the daisies when she gets home. I'll come by again in a bit, OK?"

*　　　*

*　　　*　　　*

*　　　*

Even after I'd locked the door, my heart still pounded. I found Angie standing at the sink, and from the set of her shoulders I could see she was angry with me—the cause, insofar as we could both imagine where it lay, being self-evident.

It might surprise you that a man of Lyle's relentless amity should begin his tenure in our community with such a hostile reception—not mine so much as hers; but as the servants of the famous are often more wary of social climbers than the famous themselves, perhaps Angie was merely cautious of all our relations above and beyond the call of duty. Whatever the cause, when I offered her the flowers, I saw there had arisen now a flaw in our imagined, or perhaps not imagined, intimacy, and where before a light seemed to me to pass between us, she'd drawn away. Throwing the bouquet down on the table, she pretended to examine the dirty dishes, submerged and colorful. She had a little longer to clean them. My mother—who cared about such things—wouldn't be home for hours.

"Look at you," she said, glancing at me. "You've got peanut butter all over yourself."

We went into the living room, and she sat down on the couch, gazing off absently as she scrubbed a Madagascar-shaped patch with a napkin. For a person who usually evidenced little power of attention, she was certainly concentrating on something.

"What are you thinking?" I asked.

"About Uncle Lyle there. What's his deal?"

"He's my uncle."

"But is he a fireman uncle, a lawyer uncle?"

"He's a football star," I said, because this was what he figured as in every story my father told about him or he'd told about himself.

She snorted and continued to rub at the spot until she grew tired and went out into the hall to smoke. Pleased she was angry with someone besides myself, I followed, watching as she put on the older, harder face she always did when she angled the cigarette up to the flame. I guiltily hoped she'd say something more about Lyle, and I wasn't disappointed.

"Your uncle's a creep," she finally announced, blowing out a deep cloud of blue. "He shouldn't stare at women like that—it's disgusting."

Admittedly, I'd been jealous of the way he'd looked at her—a way I didn't even understand—but it was wonderful now to appear, instead, magnanimous. I had the pleasure of trying to defend him and also, almost immediately, the pleasure of hearing her dismiss any kind words said on his behalf. We were able to commiserate, and she could forget she'd been angry with me at all.

"He's exactly the kind of goon my mom would like," she said, blowing out another cloud. "My mom's such an idiot. Can you believe she wants me to work at the K-drug with *her*?"

"But you've got a job—the best job," I suggested, cozying back into her affections.

"That's what I said," she responded, waving the cigarette. "She says she wants me to work there so K will pay my college tuition. But it's not like they're going to pay me to do just *anything*. It's job training—as if I wanted to be a *pharmacist*. She's gotten it into her head just because your mom's a nurse it's some kind of a *cool job*. I don't think she even knows the difference. She's such a reject."

I knew my mother had initially met Mrs. Fitzpatrick picking up medication for her clients at the drugstore, where Doris worked. Doris had, in fact, volunteered her daughter when my mother had asked to put up flyers to find a baby-sitter.

"I know the job here won't last forever," Angie said, knocking her hair back behind her ear. "*Obviously* it's temporary, while your dad's in space. But does that mean the only other thing to do in this town is what she does?"

She sucked at the cigarette. "How do people grow up to be such retards? My mother, that guy . . . he should have the word *retard* written in velvet letters on his back. I can't believe they're *related* to us."

"Uncle Lyle's not related to me," I replied.

She glanced at me bemusedly. "Well, anyway—you're lucky. Your dad is so cool—"

And just then there was a chime down the hall. The elevator door opened, and for a moment Jerry Finch paused, silhouetted in fluorescent light.

As it turned out, the storm had disrupted power at Cape Canaveral, shutting down everything but the most necessary systems. Neil Armstrong had dropped him off, and now he stood in the fourth-floor lobby, gathering the world to himself. We could feel, in the fluttering tubes on the ceiling, the cracked paint of the walls, green giving way to past pinks and yellows, that he was in some way choosing these things—making our ordinary world beautiful because he was choosing it, the way we constellate the sky with its stock of stars.

"Oh, shit," Angie said under her breath, dropping the cigarette behind her—"Hi"—as I darted toward him, launching myself into his arms so I was carried over his head, borne this way into the apartment, trembling up in the yellow glow of the stippled ceiling, where he'd glued glow-in-the-dark constellations. He recited the names to me as I rode across that tiny sky on his shoulders: Hercules, Orion, the Big W, the Bear.

"Hey, Angie," he said as he put me down, "I ran into your mom in the court." He withdrew carefully from a shoulder bag two cupcakes, upon each of which was a pink, frosted astronaut, curled like a shrimp.

She shuddered, preparing to say something crude—something to impress him—but my father was already talking, showing us pictures and diagrams he'd made in class, holding his glasses to the bridge of his nose as he climbed tables and chairs to give us a sense of what he'd experienced, arms bowed above him like Atlas in increasing sections of sky. He began at a stutter, reminded no doubt of his own science lectures, but when he saw us following him without reserve or boredom, he spoke low, intimately:

"I hadn't thought I'd ever get to know these astronauts," he confided. "They're strange men, Georgie, like strangers to their own planet, but I like them.

"Just today, for example, I shared my lunch with Neil because he'd forgotten his. We were all famished after being sick in the flight simulators, and I was so hungry I didn't notice until I was finished with my half sandwich that he hadn't touched his at all. He was just watching me.

"Now, I gotta tell you—astronauts are hard to read. For a long time I wondered if they even went to the bathroom," my father said, realizing he was getting sidetracked. "But the point is, I was starting to wonder, so I said, 'What's the matter, Neil—don't like bologna?'

"Well, Armstrong just kept staring at me with those steely little eyes of his. And then"—he glanced at us both to make sure we were listening—"he said that he envied me. Can you beat that? He told me he *envied my humanity*. 'There are habits,' he said, 'acquired in space, which are difficult to shake.' And before I could say anything—this really surprised me—he put his half sandwich back in its baggie and mashed it up. Until it was just pulp, Georgie."

My father had been moving a little closer the whole time, and now his face was right next to mine.

"Well, I was beginning to think there was something really wrong with old Neil. But he gave me just the hint of a smile"—bending closer as I began giggling—"and he took out a straw"—grasping me—"stuck it in the baggie, and sucked it down, just like that"—blowing on my belly button until I howled "No, no, no," because I didn't believe him and because I was terrified with delight.

He lifted me then, raising my feet from the ground and twirling me as he said he had been twirled, during the day, in the great gravitational machines and the "vomit rocket" of the training camp. The world dissolved into banded colors, the thoughts of the day collecting at the back of my head, pressed there by the force of acceleration.

Afterward, while I closed my eyes and lay on the floor, inwardly spinning, my father reached for Angie's hands, grunting at her weight as he began to turn, straining but determined to drag her from the carpet into the weightless world.

"Mr. Finch—" she said, caught off guard.

"And so you've escaped the earth," he interrupted, not allowing her embarrassment, as, with a heave, her legs coasted into the room, over-turning lampshades and the television antenna.

"Mr. Finch—"

"It's our heaviest chain." He huffed, closing his eyes as he strained.

"Mr. Finch," she said, looking wildly around, one of her shoes resounding against a wall, "I feel sick."

"But look how beautiful you are . . . without the anchors of the earth." And while she looked down at herself, streaming out in the room, he opened his eyes and grunted, more hopefully, "Haven't you always felt . . . this could happen to you?"

She looked back at him, and something serious came and went from her face. "I always felt," she said, giving in to the delicious unwinding that is space, "that I was different . . . from people."

"Oh?"

"Like—I don't think my mother . . . could be my mother," she said, catching her breath. "I mean . . . they have hospital mix-ups."

"People make terrible mistakes," he said, "all the time. Now close your eyes. This is something . . . Neil taught me: I want you to imagine all the things . . . you'd fill the moon with, given the chance."

"Things?" she asked, a bit distracted; and then a flush crept over her, as if one could imagine with the skin alone.

"What would you like to find, if *you* went to the moon?"

Sick from weightlessness, exhausted where I lay in a heap on the floor, I watched her spinning, her dress a bright cone opening into the room.

The beautiful thoughts of that day were peeling, sifting from the wall of consciousness like flecks of gold into the deep of sleep. I thought of Lyle again, and in my mind I heard Angie's voice, a soft giggle, then the vast gulf I'd felt earlier that afternoon, when Lyle and Angie stood above me in the doorway. There were pleasures, I recalled with a shudder, sliding with relief from those dark dreams to other, light-flecked chambers.

As my head lolled back, their voices blurring, I blinked heavily into the blue waters of the television. It was upside down, and I saw, upside down, soldiers—American soldiers—standing in the doorway of a makeshift lean-to, in the night, beneath the boughs of a forest.

"—It isn't that we don't want to go home. None of us wants to live here," one of them explained, arm resting across an automatic rifle. "We have families, and lives down there." The camera panned back, across a steep pine bluff, overlooking a valley dappled with the lamps of a town. "But each of us knows we've got men on the ground, right now, who can't come home," he said, glancing at his fellows. "And I can't go home, as long as I know that's true."

Fireworks flared and melted into the sky. The soldiers squinted in the changing light, and I wondered at these men, who'd become strangers to their own country, to themselves, even, until I was carried by the rising camera above the valley, toward the fireworks again, and the wondrous globe of the moon. I closed my eyes to the sound of laughter, and whispers.

Who among us can resist the astronaut? What astronaut can resist the comfort of the human hand? It was nap time—I felt it inside me like a warm, inner day contained in the hot walls of the outer day. And I slept, even as my father carried me to my bed.

THREE

The Candidate

L yle Barnes, for those of you wondering what became of him, didn't return that day. More than a week would go by, the moon swelling from half empty to a nearly full disk in the sky—a circle just blurred to one side where the earth's shadow slipped through lunar mountains— before he knocked again at our door.

My parents had, by this time, decided that his rain-soaked visitation had been an invention of my bored afternoons; and their conclusion, though erroneous and belied by a now-wilted vase of daisies on the cof- fee table, wasn't entirely surprising: my summers were dull, and in case it isn't already clear, I was a boy with few friends. My best friend—in fact my only friend in the neighborhood—Fauna Shank, was away at camp. In several weeks I'd go to camp myself, but until then, there was hardly anyone around to play with besides Angie. It was as if all the children in a normal community had been replaced, in Ashtrakan, Florida, with elderly people, and so when Angie wasn't baby-sitting, I spent a great deal of time by myself, staring out the window into North Court.

Face crushed into the open palm of one hand, I was watching, on this particular evening, as a middle-aged couple struggled to stake a tarp on the dry soil beneath a luxurious magnolia, leaves trembling whenever he struck a plastic peg with the rock he clutched in his hand. The court was filling with shadows now the sun had sunk beneath the rim of the buildings; it was an intimate time of day, the lights of the buildings across the way just winking on; from this distance, even the blows of the rock seeming muted, kind.

There was, I noticed, another tent on the opposite side of the court, and as this was still during the infancy of my father's fame, and people weren't yet literally camped out on our doorstep, I was just going to find my mother to ask what was going on when there was a knock at the door, and I heard her crossing the apartment to answer. Looking through the peephole, she let out a little cry of surprise: there stood Mr. Barnes, wearing a dark wool suit that gave him some of the size and sleekness of a limousine.

"Hello, Barb," he said as she opened the door, his broad face shining.

"Lyle Barnes"—she gasped—"what are you doing here?"

"Just thought I'd stop by, say hi."

My mother straightened her hair and did her best to look pleased. "You're so . . . dressy. Didn't anyone tell you it was summer?"

"What? This?" he asked, winking at me and looking over our shoulders.

"Well, as much as I'd like to, I can't keep you out there. Come in," she said, turning on her heels and marching us into the living room.

"You'll have to wait a moment for Jerry—I think he's asleep—but he'll be so happy to see you."

"I'm sure he's a busy man," Lyle said affably, his eye roving the coffee table stacked with fashion magazines and books on astrophysics. He spotted his own flowers and was reaching for one of these faded offerings when my mother, misunderstanding, intercepted his hand and snatched up a crumpled napkin.

"Our baby-sitter—fresh from the trailer park you'd think. Can I get you something to drink?"

Lyle shook his head and turned to examine a photograph of my father in a camouflaged birding costume. "I'm a teetotaler now, Barb, didn't you know?"

She thought he was joking but decided not to press. "Go wake your dad," she told me as I lingered at the edge of the living room.

Lyle hitched at his pants and sat slowly on the plaid couch, facing my mother. "What *I* want to know," he said, "is what's all this Georgie was telling me about astronauts."

"Oh, now really, Mr. Barnes—"

"Honest. I had no idea before I got into town last week. Of course, I've heard all about it, since. Still, thought I'd stop by and get it from the horse's mouth. As we're going to be neighbors."

He let this fall casually, but my mother caught it. "What do you mean?" she asked, perhaps not sounding entirely thrilled.

"Well, I've been thinking of settling in Florida for a while. And what better place to go than where you've already *got* friends." He smiled and blinked at us, stroking the cushions on either side with his hands. "I thought maybe I'd pick your brains about it."

His eye continued to rove the brown and green furniture, the orange floor lamps of the room—it made my mother uneasy, as if he was preparing to move in—until he came up short against the irregular shape of a telescope tarped under a white cloth in a corner. "Hey there, is that a P-38?" he asked.

"It's a Zeiss 5300," I said.

"It's broken," said my mother, and to me, more emphatically, "*Go* get your father."

The telescope, the result of a swap Jerry had made of some stroboscopic equipment with a fellow ornithologist, had never worked properly. It was the size of a motorcycle, and nearly as complex to understand. My mother referred to it as the German Machine.

Lyle slipped across the room and drew the tarp from the telescope's long, tubular body. It was angled up into a dark corner, but he pressed his face to the eyepiece and, after fooling with a mass of knobs that rose from the knuckle where the viewer and the body joined, he surprised us both by taking off his jacket, getting down on the floor, and squirreling beneath it on his back.

"Jesus, Lyle," my mother said, a bit appalled. A terrible fear came over her that he'd notice how long it had been since that part of the house was dusted. "Georgie, get him out of there, will you? Where the hell *is* Jerry?"

"What are you doing?" I asked, kneeling by his legs.

From deep within the guts of the machine his voice throbbed: "I just need to move the oil pan aside. I think . . . I think . . ."

My mother, who'd begun pacing, stopped and stared at us. "Thank you, Lyle," she said.

"I think—"

"Thank you, but I would be much more comfortable—"

"It's the refraction shutter—she's stuck—and if I could—"

"Please, Mr. Barnes," my mother fairly shouted.

He popped up from behind the telescope. "Do you have a hairpin?" he asked; and it was right then that my father emerged from the bedroom, where he'd been, as supposed, asleep.

"Get the man a hairpin," he said, massaging his head and suddenly freezing as his face seized up and he sneezed. "Sure"—turning to Lyle—"we've got a hairpin around here someplace."

Looking back, I don't think the two men even shook hands. It was right there, you might say, that Lyle entered, or reentered, our lives, in the easy way he entered all things—with a kind of half glance behind him, a slight smile, as if entering at every turn the glorious supper club of life.

If I had to guess what was actually happening *behind* that trembling eye, that slightly sloped smile—if I had to reduplicate in this man the revolutions of the last week—I'd submit that Lyle had arrived at Magnolia Court with one humble mission: that of borrowing money. I do not mean to paint him as an adventurer or schemer—nothing could be further from the truth—it's just that he must have remembered my father, from their shared years in high school, as the kind of on-the-square guy who would always have something put away, and would never begrudge a friend if he could manage it. This might be a less-than-glorious way in which to enter our tale, but it should be no reflection on Lyle Barnes. It was, I remind you, an honest enough hand he was prepared to hold open. Let us instead pause for a moment to beam—as we were beaming, or merely staring, at his brawny shoulders, bent over the German Machine—at the eureka, the true exclamation point, that this day was to be in the new life of Lyle Barnes. Because while he hadn't entirely abandoned his monetary concerns, he'd had a glorious idea—a far more glorious idea—a week ago, driving through the rain from our apartment.

Lyle, you see, came from an old Michigan political family. And while it is natural for some, when at loose ends in their lives, to turn to waitering or waitressing, and for others simply to slip deeper within their white or blue collars, Lyle's mind had turned to what seemed to him the most natural career: that of politics. More precisely, seeing that he was to enter the political fray here, in Florida, beginning his campaign so far from the nourishing roots of what he might otherwise call his electorate, a few days of canvasing Ashtrakan, listening to the word on the street, told him that success could be his merely by asking my father for an endorsement.

No mention had been made yet to anyone of this idea, but a few minutes later he'd dragged the telescope to the kitchen window, where we were all being treated to the first serviceable demonstration of its functioning.

"If you move a few degrees to the left," Lyle suggested from the sink, where he'd washed the oil from his hands, "you'll note the steppes descending to the Sea of Tranquillity. That's the proposed landing site, isn't it, Jerry?"

"That's right," my father said, standing and gazing at the object the size of a dime risen over the opposite buildings of the court. Everyone was silent for a moment.

"You must be so . . . excited," Lyle said quietly. We looked at the moon there, inscrutable and mottled with silver scabs, and then Lyle looked again at my father.

In a random lineup of men, chances are Lyle Barnes would always have been chosen most likely to pursue an astronautical career: his figure was softened now but still clearly molded by a youthful environment of team sports; and he shared with the astronauts a face of mild disposition, from which strong emotions were easily cleansed. "I'm an optimist, basically," he was fond of saying. Yet here he was, standing beside this slope-shouldered man in a plaid shirt who in a few days would rise above the shackles of the earth and join the chosen few.

"I can't explain how it is," my father said, as he ducked his eyes and looked again through the telescope. My mother, who had no interest in the moon and a limited interest in Mr. Barnes, left the room.

"Lyle," my father asked without getting up, "do you have a lot that's holding you here?"

"What," Lyle said, "on earth? If you're wondering if I ever got married after my rough-and-tumble days"—he chuckled—"I'd have to say no. But"—he sobered—"that's all pretty much behind me, that stuff. I'll even admit that recently—quite recently—I've been thinking, if I was going to run for some sort of political office"—perhaps he believed this was his chance to take the subject of the *glorious idea* by the horns—"if I was going to represent the people of this country in some way—or any country, I imagine, when you get right down to it—it might be prudent—"

"I have a lot," my father cut in. He was normally an attentive listener, but in this instance he was preoccupied; Lyle, for his part, returned again to the *glorious idea:*

"And it's good," said the nascent politician, "for a man, as I mentioned, in the *public* eye. You see, as you might have overheard me saying to Barb, I'm settling down here in town for a while, and, frankly, I'm thinking of running for local office. Now, you're going to laugh, I know—maybe it's just my old man talking—"

"These things act on me," my father said, his voice suddenly thickening, "like the moon on the sea, driving me back and forth. Do you understand?" He paused and Lyle looked at him, unsure whether to jump in. "Maybe," my father added, "I'm just falling back on the metaphors closest at hand. Have you ever been terrified of the earth, Lyle?"

Lyle Barnes hadn't expected the discussion to take this turn. He'd always considered my father a meditative man, but Jerry's ruminations had been confined in the past to scientific speculation—the migration patterns of birds and such—and although he'd rehearsed over the last few days a number of possible exchanges in which he overcame varying degrees of reticence on my father's part, he found his resources useless to him now and said simply, "No, I like it all right."

"Yet I know I love the earth better"—my father nodded—"than any man I ever met, until I met these astronauts"—which otherwise might have made an excellent segue for Lyle and his own personal love of the people of Ashtrakan County, if his ideas hadn't been so entirely routed by my father's use of unprecedented oratorical strategies.

"You were a wildcat when we were young, weren't you?" my father asked.

"I guess—"

"But you're not sorry, are you? It's better to just get it out . . ."

The two men stared at each other for a moment, and then my father's face darkened, seized up, and for a moment I thought he was going to say something awful, for which none of us could be prepared.

He sneezed.

"Because you're free now," he went on, sniffing, standing and resting his hand on the large shoulder of his classmate, who was in this way being driven from the house. "I admire that. And I'm glad you're joining us here, Lyle. If I can help in any way— It can be expensive starting out in a new town, I know . . ."

This was, as I mentioned, something Lyle probably planned to ask for, himself, but Jerry had outmaneuvered him: sometimes a notion is more embarrassing when you hear it articulated by others. Instead he said, "I was actually hoping to maybe offer you some help, by way of my political expertise"—nearly forty years, in fact, beneath the thumb of his father, the Michigan senator—"because you're going to need a press guy, if it's already this bad"—though before the stunned politician could rally his forces further, my father spoke again.

"There will be people," he said, "who won't understand what I've done." He shook his head. "But I would go to the ends of the earth— look, even beyond—for the ones I love—" This was a bit cryptic, even backward, for Lyle; still, when my father held out his hand to his former classmate and said, "You believe in me, don't you?" Lyle Barnes could only put on his best smile and grasp that hand, saying, "Sure, Jerry—I'm with you all the way."

It's odd how sentiments voiced just once can take on so much life. Lyle was a man of his word, and I knew even then his own words would haunt him. As they left his mouth, he was already worrying over them, delicate children that they were. I could see, too, that night, that he found in my father's questions something ominous. Perhaps men like this were never meant for the political arena.

My mother, for her part, had come into the hall in time to catch my father's last words, and they rang in her mind—would ring for a long time, resonating with other things he said in these days approaching his departure. They became part of a fund she could draw from when her husband was far away—a vocabulary of such moments she possessed and could refer to, sometimes for others and sometimes for herself.

At first, it must have been fortifying to possess this shorthand, even to recall those elements that most reminded her of what a feeble sense of reality her husband possessed; however, as with all languages of limited scope, when she was forced to reconcile these few available words with the unfolding of new and unexpected conditions, the lexicon had to serve double duty; and, in retrospect, she was less and less certain of what her husband's words had really meant. Perhaps this is why, as the days wore on, her memories all acquired multiple meanings, and even the simplest phrases became strange and full of worms.

FOUR

The Astronaut's Wife

I will never know if it was these words of my father's that weighed on my mother's mind as we drove across town on the morning of the moon landing. Perhaps she was still back at the parent-teacher conference, or perhaps she'd moved ahead, to things as yet untouched by this narrative. She herself was silent as the air-conditionless wagon rattled from intersection to intersection, windows wide open. On the radio, there was nothing in the news besides lunar reports, and she twirled the dial until she found some faint twinge of music.

"It's really not such a long time to be gone," she mused at last, "a week and a half. I mean—it is and it isn't, you know, but if it wasn't for the television and radio you might think this was just one of his bird-watching holidays."

We were skirting, now, a more affluent neighborhood, the houses set like jewels in strict arrangements of lawn and foliage. Before plunging within this more generous world we pulled into a strip mall, beneath the shadow of a gigantic steel and plastic sign.

"I think," she said, "I prefer to think of him that way—just driving across the states somewhere, binoculars on the seat beside him, listening to the radio, like us," she added, glancing gently at me as she cut the engine.

It was true that my father took such trips occasionally, usually to meet up with fellow members of birding societies. What humble tourists they must have been, crouched in marshes on the Michigan shore or along the sullen flanks of Galveston, Texas. Still, she'd surprised me. It was an admission of sorts, a fantasy from a person who allowed herself few; and it made the danger of everything—something we only glanced at, awry—seem less, as much a way of thinking as a genuine, physical state.

When we got out of the car, I didn't immediately recognize where we were, until, looking skyward, I saw the red K-drug insignia upon a white ground, and then, behind automatic doors, we were inside the cool and familiar timelessness of the store. We were drawn naturally up the central aisle of seasonal products—the showcase for a venue's talents—passing between lawn chairs and stands of suntan lotion, novelty sunglasses and small dioramas composed of shells and plastic googly eyes; finding, in the very back, as if crowning this promenade, a toothy monument of a woman, waving to me from behind the prescription drug counter.

I never entirely understood Angie's objections to her mother—a person who, to me, had always been kind and sweet and reminiscent of a large, frosted cake left out in the sun too long. In her white and yellow uniform, the comparison seemed only more reasonable.

Doris Fitzpatrick was forty-two, forty-three, but already her red hair had gone to rust, her frame blossomed from what was once, apparently, something statuesque into a caricature of Florida living. She was letting herself go, as they say. She'd moved to Magnolia Court in 1962, when it was as pristine as an architect's vision; and though things had changed here—especially of late—she wasn't sorry to have left central Massachusetts, where she'd grown up, and married, and from where she'd always dreamed of escaping.

Her husband had died some years back, but Florida had remained largely undimmed in her eye. Even after all these years, in 1976, when she got out of her car at the Astro Mall, humble home of K-drug, the sky was an answer to a childhood prayer; and the moon, just a splinter shaved from a cloud—it was closer to the earth, a streetlamp hung over all the curving lanes of suburbia.

"Georgie porgie," she said, mouth elaborate and full as an éclair, "you handsome devil, you." Mr. Spinnicker, the pharmacist, gave us his watery eye from the other end of the counter, where he was measuring out pills. After beaming at me for a moment, Doris turned her attention to my mother. "Don't be mad with Angie, Mrs. Finch, she was puking like a sailor this morning. I couldn't send her out of the house like that."

"Have you thought of taking the girl to the doctor?" my mother asked, handing over her slips to be filled.

"Well, you're a doctor . . ."

"Or a nurse," my mother suggested.

"Do you think it's serious?" Doris asked, wandering back to the shelves. "I thought maybe it was nerves, on account of your husband."

"On account of my husband," my mother repeated. "Georgie seems to have that. The entire nation, actually, may be vomiting this morning on account of my husband. I'm not sure how serious that is."

"Well, what do you think, Mrs. Finch?" she said.

"Have you considered that your daughter might be . . . in a family way?" my mother asked. She was, I think, pleased to be able to say this, having felt tortured by the Fitzpatricks for the past seventy-two hours. The two previous days, she'd persuaded Kitty Shank to take me in, but today, left without support, she must have been delighted by the opportunity to terrify her torturer. Mr. Spinnicker, having never been pregnant himself, coughed and drew his chin impossibly far up inside his face.

"Mrs. Finch—don't say such things." Doris lowered her voice, handing the little bottles of pills and elixirs back across the counter. "You have no idea what it's like bringing up a teenage girl these days. She's my third child, and they just get worse, every year—"

"Sorry—"

"She doesn't listen to me as it is, you know—"

"Really, Mrs. Fitzpatrick, I'm sorry."

The woman turned to me again. "As for you, little gentleman. I know she misses you. You're her favorite little boy—and no wonder." She held a dish of candies down to me from the counter. "Why don't you have something nice?"

A thrill went through me, an intense pleasure, more like that of opening a love letter than that of selecting a bonbon. I cherished the candy in a fist in my pocket, crinkling the cellophane; and so it was that we climbed back into the car, each silently nursing whatever delights and injuries we owned until we arrived at Mrs. Morris's house.

Mrs. Morris was a silvery haired former actress, supposedly dying but possessed of eerie, supernatural health; she was also largely deaf and remained almost entirely in the dark regarding Jerry Finch and his adventures. We pulled into her driveway and found the old woman standing in the yard like a snowman. My mother, leading her back inside, asked if she was feeling better today, and she replied, "Yes, I just had something removed— No, I feel infinitely worse today. Much, much worse, thank you," as they went off together to arrange the elaborate details of her medication. I was left to my own devices in the large, partially decayed parlor.

I remember rolling the lunar buggy across the gardens of an Oriental rug, like an island in a sea of wood. Furniture made lacquered, Chinese mountains. An indefinite quantity of time passed, in which I'd just begun to understand Mrs. Morris's peculiar state of preservation in this place, when I knocked a round, white vase from an end table. It fell soundlessly into the wooden waters. I was surprised it broke at all.

"Little boy," Mrs. Morris said, appearing above me. And then I was lifted away to the kitchen, where Barbara stood bowed at the sink, sanitizing an array of plastic shapes that seemed to be molds of the human body. For the rest of the morning I didn't leave her sight. I remember my mother making these cups and bowls, which must have normally contained parts of Mrs. Morris's body, brighter, harder, and myself beside her, on my knees, driving around and around through ammonia clouds. Mrs. Morris sat a few feet away with her friends, who appeared now and then with their postage-stamp faces in the windows of the back door— to each of whom she said only, "Much, much worse"—watching and smoking. Her friends, who were neither deaf nor shy, asked my mother questions about what it was like, being married to an astronaut:

"So, well, tell us, Barbara, what do astronauts eat?" said a nasal woman who didn't look like she ate at all. "I bet they like their steak rare—"

"*Rahr*," suggested another lady, crumpling her nose.

And my mother, poised behind a sponge and a fistful of needles, drawing all darkness from the world into a steel pan, would make something up.

"Do you have a favorite perfume? Does space have a smell? Does he have allergies?" they chorused, coughing, eyes moist with cataracts.

"I bet he's a hopeless romantic, your astronaut. I bet he's just bald with virility. Oh, I just bet . . ." And they looked at one another, these laughing ladies, eagerly turning to my mother and holding out hands crowded with rings.

Barbara wasn't amused by these requests for romantic confidences. She had no desire to talk about her husband, and found their interest in the lives of younger, healthy people ghoulish. But if the women sensed anything amiss in my mother's silences, they remained doggedly unoffended.

"Of course, he's lucky to have such a lovely wife. You weren't ever an actress, now, Mrs. Finch . . . ?"

"No, thank you, Dalia," my mother said, flinching at the compliment. Mrs. Morris, who had retained only the word *actress,* added, "There aren't any real actresses anymore. It's just one long ordeal between the sheets these days—just torrid." Then she recalled that I was there beside her, crawling around a piece of overturned Tupperware beneath which my butterscotch candy loomed faint gold. It was, if she had asked, the enviro-tent my father's mission would set up in a day or two, after establishing their base camp. She placed a finger over her own lips.

Dalia, raising a trembling cigarette, sighed. "Gorgeous lady like you, and your husband takes up with the moon. She's quite the rival, isn't she?"

"No, Dalia, not at all." My mother smiled at last. "She's four and a half billion years old, and a quarter million miles away."

And Mrs. Morris, in a moment of realization, murmured, "Why, you're serious with this astronaut business. Just sending a man to the moon like that—you must be terrified for him. He's probably struggling for his life, so to speak."

My mother would have replied, but the phone began to ring. It sat in the hall, just outside the room; and although a small red light was flashing on the top, I imagine unless Mrs. Morris was looking directly at it she would never have noticed. The old woman seemed very sad to me, her face in profile as she sat musing about my father, a tight rubber sheath around one arm as my mother took her blood pressure.

"Are you expecting a call?" my mother asked.

Mrs. Morris shook her head vaguely. "Yes, call. Tell him to give me a ring—if he wants to speak to someone, I'd be happy to offer any advice." And then, as an afterthought: "I was in India, once, as a girl. No telephones there at all, of course."

"Do they have telephones in space?" inquired a guest.

My mother glanced at the woman, decided it was better to say nothing, and then turned to me where I crouched on the floor, driving the moon buggy from the enviro-tent toward the phone's flashing beacon.

FIVE

The Voice of Space

Memory passes below, like clouds over the earth, the winking lights of cities. I'd lift the phone to my ear, and there'd be that noise, like the inside of a shell, like talking to someone in the shower.

We're riding over the Pacific now, he'd say, voice lyric and bitter as an old cowboy's. *It's dark down there—just islands chained and twinkling. Up here, though—she's full of dust up here tonight, boy. This is what happens when you never clean something, Georgie. You've got to care for things. You've got to care for everything.*

Think of the moon, caring for the earth, cleaning him with all of her tides, he said before he laughed or the static moved in. When his voice returned he said, *I was never more aware of the world than up here, tonight. The earth fills the whole sky, Georgie. We've been sitting in the capsule—me, Buzz, Neil— watching it turn and listening to the sound as it moves through space—"ahhhhh,"* like that, and he made the noise.

Glory upon glory.

*　　*　　*
*　　*　　*
*　　*

I will never forget that first time, his voice crinkling open like cellophane:

Georgie, he said through the rasp of a quarter million miles, *Can you hear it? That sound? What does it sound like to you?*

For a moment we both leaned into the crepitant dark.

"Space," I said, knowing it as if I always had, glancing down the hall at Angie, absorbed in television. "Do they really have telephones in space?"

Can you imagine a place, anywhere, you might want one more? It's like nothing I've even dreamed. How could I have dreamed of such a place, so different from anyplace I'd ever seen?

He spoke for several minutes of the wonders that surrounded him, but we were never destined to finish this first conversation between worlds: a great, turbulent roar rose up between us, as if we were separated by lanes of highway or train track instead of hundreds of thousands of miles. When I hung up the phone, the world I'd reentered seemed frozen and unreal. I went into the living room.

A terrible drama involving plants was happening on public television. The tendril of a vine had reached the top of some surface and was now sweeping back and forth in arcs, seeking to climb, as insistent on overcoming its blindness as anything with an actual consciousness of vision. Angie looked up at me.

"That was him," I said, sitting down beside her on the sofa.

"Who?"

"That was my dad."

"Let me know," she said, "if you get a call from mine." And although her father was long dead, our conversation had been, I reflected, what I imagined it would be to commune with ghosts: they would speak to us through a breach of physics, urgently, fearing at any moment they'd be discovered in their trespass and deported to gray lands.

We turned back to the drama on the screen, and then Angie got up and flipped the dial until my father's face appeared, abashed, eyes flitting over the camera as he jerkily waved inside the padded space suit, looked down and away. Sitting back on the couch and opening a pack of gum, she placed her feet on the coffee table, unbearably uninterested in asking after my strange and wonderful conversation.

I'd just spoken with my father, who could look down upon the earth as I might stare at a ball lying on the ground. There's a sense, I'm reminded, in which such an event—any event—doesn't exist unless we can share it. We do not, after all, live in a world of singular realities—even our most cherished beliefs survive only by the rules of something akin to a game of telephone.

Angie had a book in her lap, and when the next commercial arrived, she began to thumb through it idly.

"He said to say hi," I lied, wanting to resume our conversation.

"Oh, I bet he did."

"He said—"

She laid the book aside. "Georgie, can people make telephone calls from the moon?"

"That's what I asked—"

She broke a bubble between her teeth. "Well, they can't, you know. They can't just dial up the operator in Titusville," she said, grasping a pair of glasses—my father's—from the lamp stand beside her and perching them half down her nose the way my mother did when she borrowed them to read.

"The transition from childhood to adulthood is accomplished when one lays aside one's . . . childish daydreams. 'Reality testing,' my dear." Angie sighed in an impressive caricature of Barbara before lifting her book again and twiddling through the pages.

"What are you reading?" I asked.

She held up a blue hardcover with white writing: *Nation Indicted* by Robert Penwarren Nightly.

"Is it good?"

"It's great," she said; and then, with a glint of mischief in her eye, she asked, "Did you know that 'war is the wet dream of empire'?"

She smiled, and I smiled too, a bit uneasily.

"However, according to Mr. Nightly, 'in the coitus interruptus of the Vietnam Era' . . . do you know what that means, Georgie?"

I continued to smile at her, which meant no, and she flipped a few more pages.

"'Can mechanized warfare, then, even be compared to adult, genital love? We see here, in *Pnom-Din* most clearly, the anal gratification of the stratospheric bomber . . .'"

"Is this," I said, "the same Mr. Nightly who always walks home with you?"

She winked at me—or perhaps I imagined she winked at me—and read aloud another passage from the book.

I should instead have asked, hearing this bedroom chatter couched as political analysis, whether she believed Mr. Nightly had any ulterior motive for walking with her, as he did, each evening, from our house. She'd mentioned him to me on several occasions, in phrases typically beginning with "Well, Professor Nightly says" or "According to my friend Bob"; and though I didn't know at the time that Nightly, like my father, had been one of her schoolteachers, it wasn't hard to see she was flattered by the attentions of this man who, like Jerry Finch, had now reentered her life under a different system of rules and roles. Like a jealous lover, I had begun to look for him, late each afternoon, from the kitchen window.

I'd first noted Bob from this vantage several weeks ago: a squat little man in a green professor's jacket hurrying to her side as she emerged into the court, his hands clasped behind his back in an attitude of introspection as he escorted the girl, already an inch taller than himself. It was a short walk—the distance through a dozen tents to the next apartment building—but something boiled inside me every time I saw him, the sort of anchorless fury that had hurled me, on a previous occasion, upon Uncle Lyle's soft underbelly. I was in love, after all, as much as a nine-year-old boy can be. But I was nine. Recognizing in the author of *Nation Indicted* the same Nightly who haunted my beloved in the courtyard, I knew, as one intuits such things even at a tender age, that *Nation Indicted* was the product of a vulgar mind. Nonetheless, Bob's words were something that I understood only incompletely, that I found myself vaguely excited by; and most of all, for both of these reasons, in which I discovered an insurmountable wedge formed by the years between Angie and myself. This was a game in which, even against the diminutive Nightly, I had no chance—and it thrust me again into the skin of a nine-year-old boy who fell back on what was nearest to his heart:

"Do you know what Jerry said the earth looks like from space?" I asked.

"Cut it out, Georgie—"

"But he wanted me to tell you," I stammered, blushing at my increasingly transparent attempts to interest her.

She hesitated, a flicker and a pause before she said, "You're being a creep." And then—no one could have been more shocked than I—she stormed into the kitchen. The room went hollow, each of us as far from the other as solitary astronauts astride separate planets.

I understand, with hindsight, why she refused to believe me: space is, after all, a thing of which few have firsthand knowledge, which most probably expect to be both more exotic—infested with aliens; incapable of supporting telephones—and also more prosaic—a place to play golf—than it actually is. There are times when an adult's cognitive faculties are hampered by such expectations, against which a child, given only the pure fact of experience—in this case a phone call—does not have to struggle.

Still, I appeal to common sense: Can we not detect something more than mere dismissal in her tone? Would a person so vigorously deny what is to her no more than the logic of fairy tales? Stand so strictly in the way of a child's fancies—unless she sensed in these fancies something menacing? Something not at all childish? Angie's was the very gesture of pulling the covers up over one's head while disavowing the increasingly undeniable scratching of monsters beneath the bed.

I remember how, that evening as my father hurtled toward the moon, I waited for the phone to ring again, still carrying his voice inside my ear, so that whenever I closed my eyes the voice reopened. In bed, listening, my mother's kiss fading on my cheek, I wondered if I'd imagined the entire conversation, all my father's grand and sober words entering the house like a cold storm; all night as the phone remained silent his words moved through my head, the litanies of lunar mares and sinuses like coves in a garden of dreams: *Sea of Vapors, Sea of Rains, Bay of Seething, Lake of Sleep, Marsh of Disease, Ocean of Storms, Sea of Fecundity, Bay of Dew.*

My mother, in contrast, when informed of his communication, was entirely nonplussed by the suggestion that her husband had called from a point beyond the earth's atmosphere. And while this was somewhat surprising, it at least gave me the opportunity to discuss with someone the details of this wonderful event. For the last three days, in fact, I'd been elaborating for her my conversation with my moon-bound father. On the drive home from Mrs. Morris's—the day of the lunar landing— I'd returned to the subject once again:

"He said the moon was so close, now, that the earth seems like the satellite, not the other way—"

"While in fact they both are, after all," she pointed out. "But isn't this information a bit outmoded? Hasn't our correspondent in fact *reached* the moon?"

"I haven't talked to him since he called Monday."

"I see," she said.

"But when he *did* call, he said those were his first words all day, when he talked to me. Neil was on the radio with mission control, but him and Buzz had just been looking out the windows, watching the earth roll by, then the stars, then the moon—"

"I get the idea."

"I wish he would call again," I said. "I wish he would tell me more about the moon."

She glanced over and cocked one of her brows in mock anger. "This space voyaging is all very nice," she teased, "but it's no one's fault but his own if he insists on calling home during working hours. Don't you think I miss your daddy?

"If you should speak with him again, young man, I would hope you'd ask him to kindly call back in the evening, when his wife might also have a word with him."

The Magnolia Court apartment towers rose before us now, above a boulevard of brown palm trees. She put her sunglasses on, knowing that in a moment we'd be back among the cameras and crowds, and her face acquired, with its fine, wide mouth, sharp nose and chin, the severity and charm that millions of people around the country would recognize like a trademark in days to come in their newspapers and on their televisions.

I hadn't considered the shortcomings of my father's telephone tim- ing, but in light of what she'd just said, hastened to add, "He asked all about you," which was true. *You'll say hello to your mother, won't you?* He'd hesitated, the phone a vat of static. *If she was here, Georgie, I think she'd agree—it's just beautiful.*

"And he asked if you were mad at him, for leaving the world."

What does she say, when she says my name?

Reaching over, she laid her hand on my head. It occurred to me that she didn't actually believe it was my father I was talking about—perhaps she thought I was speaking of myself, as is the habit of children who want to air something personal but cannot bear the repercussions of revelation. It was natural for her to infer, I understood—or understand now—that it was I who was in need of comfort, who was perhaps confused by her moody silences, and was embodying these fears in the words of her absent husband.

"Well, has he done something wrong?" she asked, turning into the main parking lot. "Or is this just a little moon madness?" She smiled, pulling into her parking space. "Really—it's not such a big thing, the moon." Reaching out her hand as my father once had, she held it over the translucent shell of the satellite, rising in the pale evening sky. This time, however, I found the gesture frightening, and pulled her hand from the windshield.

My mother laughed but gave me an odd look.

There's a feeling of rootlessness, Georgie. Buzz tells me this is the worst time, when you're neither on the earth nor on the moon. We feel our loved ones behind us, holding our lives at the end of a long tether as we strive through space. Your voice, he said, is like the tug on the rope of a deep-sea diver for me. It orients. It is more powerful than perspective.

"Tell him," she said seriously, noticing how quiet I'd become, awash in memories, "that I'm sure whatever it is, everything will be fine."

*　　　*

*　　　*　　　*

*　　　*

Lyle Barnes, blue blazer flapping, met us halfway across the parking lot, two reporters at his heels. Some distance behind, blurred in the shiver of hot pavement, the crowd was emerging in a colorful stream from the complex's black iron gate.

"Barb, Georgie"—he panted, walking sideways beside us—"we've got a lot of people *very* happy to see you, and I guess what I need to know is, are we still on hold here? Should we go with CBS? Can we go with *Life*?"

My uncle Lyle had, you may have noticed, assumed a sort of managerial role regarding my father. Failing, I suspect, to broach directly the subject of his bid for political office to the now-departed astronaut, he had, instead, followed through with the offer for assistance he'd made, satisfying himself with the tacit endorsement such a relationship indicated. No one could say he didn't look pleased with his part as he signaled to the waiting press.

Two reporters approached my mother, we were joined by someone carrying a film camera, and then there were questions—a hail of questions from a third group, mostly parried by Lyle—until we hit the first wave. My mother's hand tightened around my own; her mouth assumed a neutral smile. Lyle took up his post on the other side of me, and together they formed a barrier against the sunburnt faces and the hands with various objects—pieces of paper, photographs, baseballs—to be autographed. As we passed into the court, a cheer went up, and I was reminded again of the transformation that had occurred in our once quiet home.

Barely a place remained to pitch a chair. Perhaps thirty tents dotted the grass, which had been worn into paths, now, between the magnolias. There was, I knew, in the rear visitor parking lot, an additional encampment of Winnebagos and trailers, where days ago the crowd of overnighters, or "patriots" as they called themselves, had overflowed the confines of the court. Beneath the first, pale stars, grills were being fired up for the evening, smoke drifted in thin, black columns between the buildings. As I watched, a small army of these patriots rose from aluminum lawn chairs, converging on us.

For a moment, in a rush of limbs reaching for coffee or sweets, I entirely lost sight of everything familiar except my mother's stockings and black flats. When I saw her face again, she was shaking hands with someone, sharing a microphone back and forth between them like a popsicle. Lyle was steering us toward a table he'd set up, past a succession of faces peeling back one after another to reveal other faces, equally expressive of whatever it was they expressed; above me, I heard my mother's murmured thank-yous, the concussion of our names, and periodic snatches of quibbling between herself and Lyle, who wanted us to give *Life* the OK.

"They're nice people, Barb. Here—have a donut, have some coffee," he said as we arrived at the table and he passed a styrofoam cup into her hand. "You seem tense." Disregarding the hot drinks, my fingers were moving out, instinctively, to a pile of crullers, when I heard above me a familiar voice, gruff but sweetened by a Caribbean lilt—"You're going to spoil your dinner, young man"—followed by a quick, deep chuckle I recognized as Kitty Shank's. Glancing up, I found all six feet and 250 pounds of her poised above me, eyeing the crowd.

"Mr. Barnes, is this zoo your responsibility?" she asked. Lyle smiled uneasily as she tightened a red sarong about herself, and her husband, Tom, frowned at his brown beverage.

The Shanks had always occupied a privileged place in my imagination. Besides being the parents of my friend Fauna they were the proprietors of the Toy Den—a toy and hobby shop—an occupation to a nine-year-old child beyond even the ambitions of presidents and firemen. In truth, until my father became an astronaut, I'd always been jealous of their daughter, who was not only the fortunate beneficiary of this wonder but also one of my few companions during the summers, when my entire social sphere collapsed down to the Magnolia apartments.

As if divining my thoughts, Kitty whispered to me, "Fauna's coming home from camp in just a couple days, and she is *excited* to see you—I'm sure she'll want to get all the goods on your dad."

"Which is fine with me," Barbara broke in, suddenly right next to us, "as long as she won't be requiring an exclusive."

The two women scowled in agreement, my mother obviously pleased to find Kitty here, among the reporters and onlookers. They'd originally met simply because their children were playmates, but they'd become, over the last year, occasional friends.

"Sorry I couldn't help you out today with Georgie," Kitty said. "But if I leave Tom alone in the store too long, he gives away all the money." Her husband glanced back into his coffee. "Why can't you put that Lyle fellow to use baby-sitting?" she asked, resting her hand on my head.

"Baby-sit Georgie?" My mother laughed. "Lyle would love that—the man is really no more than a gigantic child—"

"Yes," Kitty agreed. "I see what you mean—"

"—but can you imagine, with all this"—Barbara waved behind herself—"and Lyle's media-savvy, or whatever you want to call it—my son would be on the front page of every daily in the country the next morning."

She turned to me, then, an arch expression on her face. "Georgie, of course, would be perfectly pleased, wouldn't you? And I can only guess what sorts of fairy tales you'd make up for all these credulous reporters."

For a moment, she waited to see if I might have anything to say, until, noticing the cruller in my hand, she turned back to Kitty. "I'm afraid we really must get going, though, before he gorges himself. You want to come up for a drink?"

"Thanks," Kitty replied, watching Lyle, "but we have things to do, too, unlike some folks—"

"Yes, I'm sorry about all this—"

"Isn't your fault. It's just this kind of thing drives Tom *crazy*," she said, closing her eyes and grasping her husband's arm, pushing him forward as he gazed around with mild interest. "Which is why I'm going to extricate ourselves, before he loses his temper."

The two women waved good-bye, and my mother, taking my hand and turning to the politician, murmured, "Mr. Barnes—can you please cut me a path through this thicket?" Losing sight of everything, I held fast to that warm and familiar hand until I heard the squeal of our lobby doors.

*　　　　　*

*　　　　*　　　　*

*　　　　*

In the elevator, my mother removed her sunglasses. The Sterns, cheek by jowl beside us, pressed the button for our floor and regarded us with their accustomed kindness. They'd been playing Scrabble, idly reading magazines. It was almost possible to forget why they were here, except that in the woman's lap was a *Newsweek* with my father on the cover.

"You're looking very well today," Mrs. Stern said, pleased my mother had taken her sunglasses off, as for a moment they beamed at that vulnerable face with its divergent gaze.

I don't know if it was easier or more difficult for my mother to know that her husband was finally, actually *on* the moon; but there had been, she reflected, something soothing in catching a glimpse of the silvery satellite—reassuring as the sound of his voice. She was silent, perhaps thinking of Jerry Finch where he lay nestled now, probably asleep. When the elevator doors opened onto the fourth-floor hall, there was even something wistful in the way she waved good-bye to the old people. I don't know who heard the phone ringing first.

It was a gentle repetition, like an alarm clock nudging at the edge of a dream—but there was little doubt in my mind which apartment it came from. She unlocked our door slowly as the phone continued to ring. I must remind you, there were few answering machines at this time. Unlike the phone calls of subsequent decades, the calls of the nineteen seventies, if they arrived early or late, were not often preserved for posterity. It was as if they'd never been—and so people let the phone ring longer back then, before giving up. The phone had rung at least a dozen times. At that moment, I felt it had been ringing for weeks.

Was there some small part of Barbara Finch that felt as I did? That something extraordinary was happening? That she might hear on the other end of the line the voice she wanted to hear above every other? Placing her styrofoam cup deliberately down on the kitchen table, she lifted the receiver to her ear.

"Hello?" she said.

Had there been, when she spoke, a quaver? It was a moment that spread out like the sea, full of unfathomable possibility, in which I crouched to the ground and grasped in my hands the carpet, like swollen chunks of lunar silt.

But if she had entertained any hopes, when she spoke next, it was in the voice of everyday: "Oh, yes—very nice seeing you this morning, too."

She sighed, glancing at her watch. "I do miss him—but, you know, we get along. Lyle brings us groceries. Everyone, really—everyone's been so kind."

She caught her reflection in the door of the microwave oven, then tested her coffee, grimacing—her first beautiful frown lines. "Good. I'm glad you did.

"What I said?" She scrabbled with a spoon in the sugar bowl and began stirring her coffee, then stopped. "Really—she is?"

"Oh," she said, "Mrs. Fitzpatrick. You're quite sure—"

"Tests—she'd already been to the doctor? Yes, I see." She rubbed the lipstick from the rim of the cup, murmuring, "Oh."

And then another pause followed, the tiny warbling of Mrs. Fitzpatrick just audible. I'd begun to find this soothing, just about to close my eyes, when my mother, growing very red in the face, stood up. The coffee slued, the spoon rattled, a dark stain ate at the table. "Mrs. Fitzpatrick. Mrs.—If you mean to imply that my husband—"

Warbling. "If you mean—"

And then she sat back down. "Really," she said. "Written in his own hand," she repeated in a monotone of dictation, "on NASA stationery."

"I'll need to see for myself."

There was a long, strained interval before she said, "Mrs. Fitzpatrick, please, we all admire my husband very much, but—" And then she went to the sink and ran the water. It was like the sound of space, water flashing on steel, the sound that always accompanied my father now. She turned away from me, and the water hissed in the empty sink for a long time before I heard her say, "Nothing, nothing," and then, a moment later, "Yes. Thank you," as she hung up.

*   *
*   *   *
*   *

This is, for those who haven't yet remembered or aren't old enough to know, a story of disaster. But don't be disturbed: disasters, too, grow more perfect in the retelling. There are the disasters we outlive, and there are the disasters we become, growing into them with each visitation until we know them like a home, and we sense when a careless visitor, a Mr. Nightly, for example, has muddled the furniture, rearranged silverware in a drawer.

I realize, as of yet, Mr. Nightly has made but a faint impression on this narrative. He will, in time, furnish us with as near a villain as we're likely to find in these pages, and he was a man who, fittingly, appeared first to us through his books, and only subsequently as a speaking, breathing person. Already, though, even at this early date, I can sense him, looming like a darkness on the horizon, and it is to this figure I direct you.

Those of you familiar with Mr. Robert Nightly's account of my father's ill-fated journey might now remember some of Jerry Finch's public statements during his tenure on the moon. Perhaps, during that turbulent summer, you listened in on some of the *Apollo 19* radio broadcasts. While even a slight perusal of this material will reveal a man far more nuanced than the person discovered by Mr. Nightly in his noodlings—and who can ever discover a man more complex than himself?—it is in the confusions and humanity of his love for my mother and me that we truly see how little Jerry and the Finch family conform to Nightly's description of "this singularly guarded and ambitious clan crouched like vultures on the trust of the American people."

Which brings me to something difficult to omit from any memoir today: that is, a brief excursion into the relationship between reality and fiction. In Mr. Nightly's work we have a strong example of weak fiction. He was a man who barely knew his subjects, and thus who sketched my family in his book in the only way he could: as characters drawn from his own mind. For my part, I cannot answer as a historian for every word and gesture in this, my own history, but I can vouch for the genuine shape of my father's life as I will describe it in these pages.

I must admit, however, to a certain trepidation in continuing this treatment of a subject Mr. Nightly has already dressed in all the trappings of journalism, perhaps hopelessly prejudicing the reader. I am afraid that my father's life, as I will present it here, may seem incredible to you. Perhaps having read Nightly's fictitious account, you will even find the real life of Jerry Finch—the life of a real-life astronaut—hard to believe. I must ask you: bear with me.

Certainly, there is a blurriness where any biographer extracts to the best of his or her ability the essence of a life: it is the black serum that he or she hopes may function like a vaccine—those mummified diseases by which we educate our antibodies—the inanimate shape of the vaccinating matter fooling the reader's alarmed system into mounting a defense as if actually set upon by the living virus. True, this demi-creature, neither alive nor dead, is not so different from its larger cousin of antiquity, the Frankenstein golem of fiction; and perhaps approached in a lightless room, with only the assistance of a microscope, the two may appear indistinguishable from each other. Many a reader has delved within, in search of memory's vaccine, only to be discovered by the cold light of day dead from the blunt blows of golem; many a reader has entered the dark room, ready with club in hand for the embrace of the fictional monster, only to feel instead the sharp, awakening jab of the biographer's needle.

But worse, to further expand this metaphor, if we allow the astronaut—the man of science, exploring regions unknown to him—to stand in for the nonfiction reader, and liken the fiction reader, then, oppositely, to the deep-sea diver, wan lamp sweeping the submerged, inner truth; and if we grant how similar these persons must seem, glimpsed only in the darkened room of human consciousness, both readers masked in bulbous helmets and suits, breathing imported, terrestrial air, it shouldn't come as any surprise that the annals of literature are strewn with clubbed astronauts, howling divers stuck with needles, golems wearing flippers, and all kinds of aberration. It is exactly the scenario I've described that has led me to believe we must declare ourselves, loudly, whenever entering a dark chamber—"astronaut, golem, et cetera"—if we are to avoid havoc.

SIX

The Narrator's Baby-Sitter

That said, now comes what, for me, is perhaps the most difficult part of our odyssey, owing to the simple fact that despite everything I've asserted regarding fact, fiction, and in-between, we—all of us—obviously possess differing and therefore imperfect memories. It is what saves history from becoming a mere receptacle for numbers and names, the contents indifferently consumed by subsequent generations, like a bowl of salted nuts; but it also places me in the position of a man who's begun his speech at the head of a gathering with who knows what allegiances, whose memories pick up from who knows what point. If I nod and wink at you, and you return my glance, I cannot be sure whether you've done so as collaborator or through a perfunctory and confused reflex; when I tap my spoon against my glass and rise, my father's name upon my lips, I am uncertain, peering from face to face, to which man—which Jerry Finch—you believe I refer: we are, after all, each in his or her own way, a multitude, a tumult.

I also realize that many, given that Mr. Nightly's works are out of print, will never have read *The Secret Night School,* his cruelly titled biography of my father. It would appear in 1981, five years after the time in which our story takes place, and vanish into the nation's bathrooms and dustbins following a middling spell on the *New York Times* bestseller list. Blessedly, my father's persecutor would suffer from the same growing indifference to space that ultimately buried Jerry Finch and a generation of astronauts beneath subsequent strata of celebrity. If I forget this at times—if I envision the book forever upon the nightstand of America, as it remains, despised, on mine—please assign the fault to my own preoccupations.

But more to the point, it's time I admit the possibility that some of you may recall my father for other, less glorious events in his life. There are those of you now remembering—loyal paper readers, good grubbers of history—and a glimmer enters your eye. Jerry Finch, you say, squiring your mouth back and forth. The name stirs again at the periphery of that botanical hothouse, collective memory—a ripple of darkness; and then comes a glint, and something hard.

He was, you see, also this other man, the one you're thinking of now—the Jerry Finch who slept with sixteen-year-old Angie Fitzpatrick, my baby-sitter, so cross-eyed for the newspapers. Who the nation—that cummerbund of virtue—discovered high above itself in the moon's yellow searchlight, in all of his depravity, in scandal, in gracelessness. The same.

*   *

*   *   *

*   *

"Well, I feel terrible—for everyone—for you, too, of course, Mrs. Finch," Doris Fitzpatrick said, smoothing out her floral-print dress as she opened the door. She was a person my mother had never entertained any interest in—the entire Fitzpatrick family seemed to her to be the work of a less ambitious creator—but now there we were, in the heart of the Fitzpatrick residence, surrounded by those derided things most Fitzpatrick: ancient photos of the Fitzpatrick children, that chewed mass of reddish blond hair; photos of the sanguine Mr. Fitzpatrick, a uniformed person, eyes half-lidded, as if already in his coffin; the small porcelain objects with which the Fitzpatricks cemented their lives.

She tried to keep these things out of her voice when she said, "We both know why I'm here, Mrs. Fitzpatrick, and so there's no point, really, in—"

"Call me Doris, please," the woman suggested, taking my mother's hands in hers in a firm and feeling grip. This was undoubtedly intended to soothe my mother, but it had the opposite effect. "Can I get you anything? Some tea, maybe?"

"Before we go any further," announced my mother, folding her hands together so they couldn't be grasped a second time, "I'll need to see this letter you mentioned on the phone. I suppose you've referred it to a lawyer—"

"Angie has it in her scrapbook," Mrs. Fitzpatrick replied.

My mother looked at her. The words gave her some trouble. "Mrs. Fitzpatrick, you understand we aren't well off—particularly by the standards of astronauts," she said, although in truth she had little idea about the home economies of space travelers. Doris simply continued to watch her. The woman had probably been pretty, once, but it was all paint now; she was chewing something in her round, pink jaws, and this coupled with wide eyes, black and wrinkled all around, made her resemble of all things a stuffed horse; if intelligence lurked there, it would have to be lured with gifts of grass and refined sugar, my mother thought. "I suppose you've decided we lead a very glamorous life—I imagine it appears so, from the outside, with all this business in the courtyard. And it would come as no surprise if you yourself would like a moment in the sun, too . . ."

But these comments yielded no appreciable difference in this woman's demeanor. My mother adjusted her position slightly. "I should make clear that if it's compensation you're seeking—"

"Oh no, not at all," Doris said, looking pained. The two women regarded each other, both waiting for some additional information; and then Doris smiled, which was the most unbearable response my mother could have calculated.

"I think none of us wants to see this turn into a media circus," said my mother abruptly, grasping for a foothold on the slippery incline.

"Oh dear," Doris responded, rising, so that my mother was forced to rise with her.

"Mrs. Fitzpatrick," my mother inquired, then more sharply, "Mrs. Fitzpatrick," as they began walking, and I followed, hand locked in my mother's. We passed a glass cabinet full of bowling trophies and bicentennial cola bottles. We went through a doorway marked with the heights of children in various colors. My mother's heart hammered madly.

"Mrs. Finch," Doris said, knocking softly on a door at the end of a hall decorated with devotional weavings. An insistent, pounding music came from within. "I'm sure Angie will be happy to show you the letter if it makes you feel any better. We know how much this must mean to you, and I can say, from my own experience, my husband—rest his soul—would be the first to admit he's made mistakes in his life—"

She knocked louder, and the music faded. Angie, shirt raised over an entirely unremarkable belly wrapped with a yellow measuring tape, opened the door.

She'd been painting her nails, and the room reeked of acetone. The walls were papered with images of sweaty-chested men—or women, Barbara hesitated—playing guitar. My mother's nerves were drawn tight as wires, over which the slight details of candles, beads, and other trappings of youth trembled. Planted high on the wall in the midst of all this androgynous imagery, she couldn't help but note a large poster of John Glenn, gazing down at her at a forty-five-degree angle.

"Hi, Mrs. Finch," Angie said, unwinding the tape measure and walking back to her bed to sit down, selecting another bottle of nail polish.

Barbara's eyes roamed over the girl, who stared back equally candidly at this woman in a tweed coat, still in sunglasses, with a small child clinging to her arm. My mother mistook this gaze for fear, and reflected that she certainly dressed badly enough, the little tramp; but perhaps Jerry liked that sort of thing—the torn jeans and those tight shirts—it was part of a whole seamy heap of prurient desires she could see would be paraded now from his closet. He'd just been too embarrassed to admit the kind of trash he'd really wanted.

At this point she checked herself, remembering the girl was a schemer and likely simply a liar; and still, there was some fraction of this fury she couldn't rid her mind of. She wasn't sure why she kept drifting back to a tacit belief in what the girl claimed—it was, oddly, all tangled with the idea of phone calls, in itself ludicrous. Just the thought made her feel guilty, and as this new emotion touched her, she became angry all over again.

"Go on. I'll be fine," Angie said to Doris, and the door closed behind us. Immediately, Angie opened a pack of cigarettes, offering one to my mother, who with a flash recognized that this was why there was always that smell—

"You shouldn't, you know," she said, gesturing to the girl's belly.

Angie lit the cigarette from a candle on her bureau. "If you've come to make me apologize—" The words ran out as she took a drag, but it was clear what she'd meant to say. A flush of something like pleasure went through my mother. This was better, she thought. The child was at least intelligent enough to be angry. This she could get a handle on.

"You misunderstand. There's no point in discussing anything until I—"

"See the letter? Don't worry, I wouldn't dream of disappointing you," Angie replied, not even looking at me, as if I wouldn't divine the subject of conversation.

I'd seen her talk this way, above and around me, when she and my parents dealt with money, and I would feel then something cold steal into my chest: the possibility that no matter what we'd said and done that day, our friendship was no more than a contract. Without a doubt, I was the loneliest one in the room, lacking, as these two had, my own rage to keep me company.

Angie went over to her bureau again now, and for a moment wrangled among some large, bound diaries. When she came back she unfolded a letter on the familiar blue and white NASA stationery. Looking it over, scratching the nub of her nose, she handed it to my mother.

"You're how old?" Barbara said to her. "Sixteen? You think that this is just about you and him and me—a nice neat triangle—don't you?" A bit of color leapt into the girl's face. "You don't know anything."

My mother read the letter aloud, and I will do the same here—I have it sitting right in front of me. Written in blue ballpoint, with frequent crossings-out, it must have been posted on the eve of his departure and represents, no doubt, the fractured state of his thoughts:

> *Dearest Angie,*
> *When you read these words, believe that in the place where I lie tonight, every light that shines, shines from far away. The traveler who finds himself among the stars, naturally looks for some comfort, some reassurance, but in the*

end can only conclude with science that to look out into space is to look back into time, at old light; and there can be no comfort when peering into the past is like nothing so much as gazing back inside yourself.

In my childhood, I often imagined a room to which all my classmates went while I slept. In bed, I pictured them sitting with heads tipped skyward, staring through the roof of this chamber at the moon and an ocean of stars. I called it the secret night school, and it's a joke, really—it exists nowhere—but when I was seven or eight, I thought that this was where everyone I knew went, at night, to learn.

I grew up, as I've told you, in a small town near the Michigan shore— and it wasn't that my peers were endowed with any special knowledge, only that it was a knowledge I never possessed and that I couldn't seem to acquire during the day. They knew how to pretend to what they didn't know; they seemed in silent agreement about things I couldn't see. One extrapolated: they would guess when to hold hands, when to kiss; they'd drop the right names when they interviewed for jobs. They were like people written about in books—or even more, they were the authors of their own books, and I— somehow I had not paid attention at some crucial instant, some moment I'd deemed, at the time, of no significance—I had never seen the way to this secret school, and now I would never find it.

You may ask why I've led you here of all places, Angie, when there is so much more we might have said to each other tonight. Please don't mistake me—it's not that I still want to find this nonexistent school. Had I imagined, at one time, that Barbara would take me there, I recognize now how ridiculous that was. I can only tell you that even my students sensed as much about me on the first day: that they'd already graduated from a school I'd never been admitted to—or, I should say, everyone sensed this, except for you. I'd always hoped that there would be someone like you.

If I seem to contradict myself, if I make little sense, chalk it up to a childish evasion of responsibility—as a child admits some guilty action by ascribing it to another. Listen to me: a man hiding behind a child hiding behind a man.

Still, I remain,
Jerry Finch

I think there was little question in anyone's mind regarding the authenticity of this letter: it was full of my father's dictions and confusions, in themselves comforting to me, like his voice. Yet when I thought of what he was actually saying, the import was crushing.

It was as if everyone I loved was turning away. I'd listened throughout the letter for a mention of my name—even today, I scan the page in vain. Did he feel, I wondered, looking to my mother for some confirmation of what I felt, so distant even from *me*? But my mother only made a face, obviously disgusted by my father's prose. Angie, whose own journal writing wasn't dissimilar to my father's romances, was relieved to find Barbara just as coarse and insensitive as she'd always believed.

"I suppose," my mother said, folding the page in thirds again, "you used no birth control."

"He told me he was sterile." Angie shrugged, pretending to go back to her nails, but she saw how my mother shrank. "He told me you'd been trying to have a child for years."

My mother looked away and held out the letter for her to take, suddenly truly hating her husband. It was as if, at his invitation, someone had crept into her home late at night as she slept, cut open her body, and spat inside, over all those hidden things.

"I guess it wasn't him at all."

My mother continued to hold out the letter.

"He doesn't know," Angie said, and my mother shook the letter gently, refusing to speak—"but I'll tell him"—as my mother threw it on the bed and took my hand, her face gone stony. The only satisfaction the girl could be denied was that she'd have to imagine the extent of the devastation—it wouldn't be shown her. "I'll tell him," Angie repeated, screwing the cap back on the bottle. "And I'll tell him he doesn't have to be ashamed of me. I believe in him."

Angie looked at the letter, at me. She'd received it in the mail two days ago and read it a hundred times already; she certainly wasn't going to weaken now: her magnanimity, she'd instructed herself in her journal, was to be modeled on my father's, even if, through repeated applications of ink, it had become so firm it had made the subtle shift to righteousness.

"You're quite the queen," she said, "aren't you, Barbara?" We were in the doorway. She finished her cigarette and put it out in the waxy reservoir of a candle. "Well, he's gotten away from you, and that's enough for me. I don't want anything from you."

What she said next came almost as an afterthought, though it's true, she'd never had any other intention: "But don't worry yourself. I'm not telling anyone else. We won't tell anyone."

She was young and she wasn't very pregnant yet, and perhaps this is why my father's letter only made her more loyal, only gilded him in her eyes. Unfortunate that my mother, cast into an affair not of her choosing, had to play all the parts scorned by the other actors. She couldn't afford to be proud under the circumstances, and half-turned before she went down the hall.

"Thank you," she said, haggard, not wanting to thank anyone but feeling that only a bricolage of these two words kept further disasters at bay.

SEVEN

A History Lesson and a View of the Moon

It's to my mother's credit she didn't take this opportunity to humiliate her husband in my eyes—I, who understood indistinctly what infidelity was composed of, something akin to borrowing another woman's bicycle. Was she angry? Naturally. Bitter? Yes. The situation filled her—her, of all people—with shame. And then, of course, to be unable to confront him made it all dreamlike, unreal, as if everything might still be no more than a grotesque misunderstanding. We won't embark, however, on a discussion of how my mother felt. I perceived at the time only that she saw my father as something of a fool: he was, as far as she was concerned, the kind of person people used.

This is not to say she held him blameless—she would deal with that when he came home. But while she wasn't sure what she'd say to him—at the moment, she was nearly grateful for the space that kept them apart—she did know that even given the power of his new and glamorous life, his smart NASA uniform, her husband wasn't much of a seducer. No, she thought, striding angrily down the hall, away from the Fitzpatrick bunker, obviously that smug little frog had taken advantage of him.

Had my mother, herself, once taken advantage of Jerry Finch? While Mr. Nightly has insinuated as much—"marrying him as she committed all social acts: as if stepping down from a curb to catch a cab"—to suppose this would be unkind and, except in the most superficial sense, untrue. I believe that when she married him she was drawn by the same qualities that drew everyone to my father, finding his impracticality charming; his obliquity and scatterbrainedness appearing, to the untrained eye, as incipient marks of genius.

She'd continued to love him, but since that time had decided that her hopes had been a bit naïve: he'd been diverted from becoming a doctor or scientist into the easy employ of the public school system; fooled by the schools into coming to central Florida; gulled from practical ambition into dreamy complacence; and now, when he did, finally, have tangible ambitions, look what a wreck they made.

She already hated and envied the space agency as if it were a rapacious and reckless other woman. That there should really be an other woman—this one not even of legal consenting age; this one also, no doubt, out to use her husband—only muddied the waters. From her point of view, my father was the dupe of young Angie Fitzpatrick just as he'd been the dupe of NASA's PR machine and a few slick-haired congressmen riding the running boards of an election year. Perhaps, though, we should take a moment here to fully understand her concerns.

For the sake of those already familiar with the economic subbasement of the Apollo missions, I'll be brief, but even those better informed may find some useful lumber down here:

If you recall, the space program ran out of funding in 1973, four short years after the *Apollo 11* mission first placed a man on the moon. The nation had decided that it couldn't bankroll a space program no longer dedicated to spectacle; that the ordinary business of space was, alas, less exciting than the cold war hysteria previously filling the vacuum of national consciousness. Our men on the moon, even unchallenged as they were, had proved as strategically useful, and as fascinating to the public and its advertisers, as a national monopoly on dental floss, leaving us, after seven years, high and dry in the lee of a wave of patriotism and futurist nostalgia that had seemingly exhausted the feeble resources of its waters. But that is not the subject of this story.

What is important to grasp, or at least have within reach as you read on, like one of those furling maps in a classroom, is that this was the summer of '76: fireworks were melting in the sky. Vietnam veterans hiding in bunkers in the mountains pondered the sulfurous plumes of red, white, and blue that sagged above the populous cities of the eastern seaboard. And as the Roman candles dimmed to a retinal burn, as the cherry glow of two hundred years faded from the eyes of the nation, as we reawakened to the twin plagues of oil crisis and recession—biblical clouds of darkness that shrouded the land—there was a wondrous window that opened for gentlemen of space everywhere, such as my father.

At the time, no one perceived that we were at the apogee of an irregular orbit that would soon draw the moon hopelessly from human hands. The astronaut, strange creature of its day, was about to be, like the Paleolithic dinosaur, stranded by rising sea and encroaching snow; but this advancing ice age was stayed by the fervor for one, final American victory on the stage of space. Announcing the winner of their mail-in contest, NASA portrayed my father's journey as the first in a series of layman adventures, a kind of mirror of democracy in the twilight of the second millennium. That my father was to be the sole example of this new breed of democratic representatives is not, as Mr. Nightly maintains, to be laid entirely at his feet. You may discern within this story larger forces drawing earth and moon apart, lifting my father up even as they drove his dreams further and further from reach.

I think we've all felt such a thing at times. He was a remarkable man in his way, Jerry Finch, but his case may not be so unusual in this sense at least: once we have arrived at the land of our dreams, we will always be lucky to return from there alive.

* *

* * *

* *

It was dark when my mother and I emerged from the Fitzpatricks' building, and I remember seeing Lyle, standing in a circle of men and women, indicating with a flashlight various constellations. Barbara was trying to hustle through the periphery of the court, hoping that the carnival atmosphere of the night would allow her to slip by unseen, but it was not to be.

Lyle isn't, even by his own lights, a sensitive instrument. His emotions are large and comfortable enough to sit down in; and nestled among his fellow enthusiasts, arms crossed, nodding his head in time to something being said by an elderly man in golfing pants, he was capable of catching sight of my mother and me, fleeing willy-nilly across the furthest reach of the court, and perceiving absolutely nothing out of the ordinary. He was simply happy to see us, and ambled in our direction.

"Barb," he called, and then again, "Barb," as he drew near. She turned toward him and tried to smile without stopping, making an I-was-just-on-my-way gesture, but "Barb," he continued to bark, until at last she came to a halt.

"Hello, Lyle," she said.

"We were looking at Jerry," he said, breathing deeply of the night air. "Well, I mean, you couldn't really see much of the big man, but you could see the landing capsule pretty well. We're going to try to get our hands on a larger scope," he added hopefully, "so we can zoom in," but came up short when she turned her swollen eyes to him. She'd been weeping in the elevator on the way down from the Fitzpatricks'.

"Barb," he murmured, crouching beside me, "he'll be fine. Just fine—really. I have a great feeling, about everything."

Lyle gazed up at my mother. He truly loved helping other people and, as a result, was in the habit of believing, sometimes erroneously, that others wanted help. Most people are more than happy to participate in such an exchange, but my mother was not such a one—it was too much like being dug out of a snowbank by a dog, having this large, woolly brained man staring at her. Without adequate resources to defend herself, however, she allowed the soft laving of his attentions to thaw her slightly.

"It's nothing, Lyle," she faltered. "I was chopping onions, for Georgie's dinner . . ."

Her obvious fabrications ground to a halt, and Lyle smiled and stood.

"Let's go have a look at everyone's favorite astronaut," he said, motioning over his shoulder toward several clusters of people, arranged as if in football huddles. I realized that they were clumped around telescopes of various sizes and configurations. Glancing toward the closest group, I saw a man in a red hunting cap indicating some portion of the moon with his extended arm; another man held a large map out beside the body of the telescope, as if they were going for a drive, while a third person, a woman in curlers, aimed a flashlight carefully into the crinkled sheet of paper. My mother hesitated.

"Go on, Barb," he said. "I'd like you to meet some of these people. They'd *love* to meet you. It would thrill them. It would be the kind of thing they'd tell their grandchildren about."

Lyle took my hand in his, and the three of us walked over.

I'd grown accustomed to my mother's dismissive treatment of the large politician, but these folk were obviously pleased he'd dropped by. The court was one of those social spaces, like a psychotherapist's retreat or a short stint in prison, in which, isolated from the pressures and norms that drive men's lives, people meet and bond with unusual speed; people who might normally never give one another a second glance could feel as family here.

"Barnes," said the man in the red flannel cap at the telescope, "you've got an eye for these things—what do you make of this?"

The politician stooped and put his face to the eyepiece. He held still for a moment, then said, "It's a shadow cast from the rim of Copernicus. It's rippling that way, Dave, because, relative to the moon, the sun is highly oblique at this hour, shining across the face of the mare, pitted with meteors. Looks like water, doesn't it?"

Everyone smiled, having wrangled for the last few minutes about the possibility of lunar rain.

"The whole thing is amazing," Lyle said to my mother. "With all the fluctuations in temperature—a range between 135 degrees in the sun to minus 150 in the shade—viewed with strong magnification, the moon looks alive, just shimmering with heat and shadow.

"But I sound like your husband now." He chuckled, adding, "And I'm forgetting my manners," as he saw the expectant faces of the court dwellers. "Barbara, Georgie, this is David Moscowitz," he said of the gentleman holding the map; "Clyde Barnstable," of the flanneled man; "and Janet Barnstable," of the woman in curlers. They reached out their hands with care, as if afraid of damaging us.

"Would you like some chicken, or some corn—we've got corn on the grill," Clyde offered, taking off his cap. He had a pale, freckly face and lots of teeth.

My mother shook her head and smiled. In her gray linen and stockings, she looked quite glamorous—even her swollen eyes gave her a haunted beauty.

"We were looking at the boys a couple minutes ago," Dave said, wrinkling the map. "They just woke up and were out, you know, poking around."

"Would you like to have a look?" Janet asked, and Dave said, "Sure—have a look. It's an exceptional night."

"Thank you," my mother said, "but I can't, really. It would feel too strange—seeing him so far away. Do you understand? But maybe Georgie would like that—"

"Maybe?" Lyle laughed, orchestrating. "Why don't you step over here, champ, and we'll set you up."

Everyone looked relieved. Clyde began adjusting the telescope, carefully repositioning the viewfinder. While he searched again for the lunar lander, the others urged my mother to have a peek, but she declined firmly, thanking them again as Clyde waved me over and, holding my breath, I looked down into the eyepiece.

Before me, a tiny circle of light blazed, so bright it was impossible to distinguish detail. The telescope trembled, and then the scene dimmed—Lyle had screwed a filter in place—and I began to make out gradations in the brilliance. Dave guided my hands to the focus knobs. Everything granulated as I adjusted the objective lens, then blurred again; and finding that point of granulation once more, I realized that what I'd taken to be a fleck of deeper light, a point of refraction near the edge of my circle of vision, was in fact one reflecting, trapezoidal side of the moon lander. It was no bigger than a piece of glitter. Staring hard at it, my eyes began to swim, but then I also perceived that what appeared to be small specks and dots floating across the fluid sea of my eye—those ghostly swimmers we find when our eyes are dry and tired—were minute living creatures. There were two of them, the size of fleas—even smaller—leaping around beside the moon lander. With my head bent to the eyepiece, I felt as if I was looking at something not vastly far away but at something tiny, occurring right here, under my very nose.

"Do you see them?" Lyle said.

"Yes," I whispered, fearing the tremble of my voice would disturb the delicate focus. The scene, I realized, was already moving, dragged inexorably to one side by the rotation of the earth—a force invisible to us here but increasingly evident as we sweep our eyes out into space along the spokes of vision.

"Pretty good scope, heh?" he said, patting Dave on the back. "It's no 5300, but it's no slouch either." The middle-aged man blushed with pride and placed his hat over his bald head.

For a moment I watched the two astronauts, losing them among the craters and boulders, finding them again. Their movements, from this distance, seemed completely without logic.

"Which one is him?" I asked.

"What do you mean?"

"Which one is my father?"

"Well," Lyle said, "which one does he look like, Georgie?"

I stared again at the tiny creatures in the lens, not very much like human beings. I could choose either, I felt, selecting one and willing my father into this distant consciousness, and then, just as easily, selecting the other. There was nothing at this remove to distinguish the two, unless, perhaps, one of them had chosen to write his own name in giant letters on the ground. They seemed to lack the intelligence for even such a simple task.

"What's he doing?" my mother asked when I looked up again from the viewer.

"I don't know," I said.

Impatiently, she leaned her head over the machine, holding the hair out of her face. We waited as she groped at the knobs and dials governing the telescope, wanting to offer some assistance but kept silent by the irritation in her motions. And then, for a while, she was still, breaths coming in bursts, watching until the rotation of the earth dragged the astronauts from the circle of light and she was left staring at the empty, icy sheet of the moon.

When she finally stood up, she said, "Yes, that was a mistake."

EIGHT

Lost

I t's difficult to feel angry with a man so estranged, so endangered, that he seems to be tenuously molting toward life as an animal of another order. Or, for my mother, it might be better to say that it wasn't difficult to be angry so much as impossible to know in what way. We'd both seen him leaping on the brilliant lunar sand, but how was she to articulate rage, disappointment, fear for a person rendered no more substantial than a housefly? That night and the next, after coming home from work together, we watched television warily, expecting his crimes to be momentarily exposed, to hear him denounced by wrathful hoards, but the Fitzpatricks kept their word: there was only adulation, letters from mothers in Nebraska, interviews with bright-eyed grade school pupils.

And there was, on the other hand, no phone call from him either. I found this unbelievable at the time, expecting, as I was, some sequel to our first communication; but I understand now that, even without the knowledge that Angie was pregnant—enthusiastically pregnant with his child—ample room existed where he wandered to imagine all sorts of activity down below: I'm certain that, like most men of profound inner resources, he could be equally scourged as sustained by them. With Neil at his side—with these days spent in the company of people he admired so much—just the thought of his shallow frailties being revealed to his fellow astronauts must have been excruciating. He would have sought signs of his own downfall in every NASA communication and, as the phone rang unanswered at our house during the afternoon, he must have trembled.

In the end, more than anything, I think it was this—my absence from the apartment—that informed him of his unmasking. Something had disturbed the order of the world he'd left behind, and it could bode nothing but ill. Adrift in space, surely realizing a change had taken place in the chemistry of his home, he must have guessed during those silent nights, the days with their voluptuously repeating dial tones, that we'd found him out. Perhaps when he stood on the moon, collecting rocks, he saw the whole planet boiling before him.

For my mother and me, it was all unspoken, only an omission, a buildup of silence day after day, amounting to certainty.

You may point out, of course, that I can speak only for myself—perhaps my mother thought nothing of the dearth of correspondence from her husband. There had been, after all, just the one, solitary call, received by a child. Perhaps, you might say, she never believed.

I don't think so, however, and the reasons should be clear, shortly. Either way, all we could do was guess at what Jerry was thinking, what he might have told us, had he the opportunity.

And then came a particular moment, while we were at her work together, my mother injecting one of her clients, the immobile Mr. Josephine, with a baster of enriching juices, when we knew my father understood exactly how naked his position had become, and that he'd taken an irrevocable course. Along the catwalk of a single action, he'd opened up an entirely new world—one in which the previous world was scarcely conceivable, because it seemed too impossibly good.

I was lying on the carpet near my mother, looking up at a wedge of sky with its little crescent badge, the clatter of syringes in a tray like lights in my ear. The man she tended was absolutely still, like a part of the bed. All morning the radio had spoken in the other room, where Mrs. Josephine sat with her cats, combing them and following the incredible exploits of my father and Neil as they collected bag after bag of rocks from the moon's gleaming plains. "My God," she exclaimed at one point, coming to the doorway to share her delight. "He's so ordinary."

As each rock was lifted from the dust, they described it for the listening world, as if plucking the golden apples of the sun. Bursts of NASA broadcast broken by jocular commentary from news announcers have almost exactly the quality of sports reportage, and, eventually, my mother and I had ceased to listen. I'd begun to think of my father more as an athlete than as a navigator of space, and was coming to the conclusion that space was the perfect arena for sports of all sorts—save, of course, water sports—when Mrs. Josephine came clattering into the room, breathless, the comb still in her hand.

"Oh, little boy," she said, looking at my mother, then kneeling painfully beside me, stroking my cheek. Her face was plaster white, powdered and fine with wrinkles and the pocks of some long-ago ailment. Her mouth radiated tiny creases, along each of which red lipstick bled a narrow thread. My mother watched from where she sat, shaking down a thermometer.

"Little boy. He's lost, you know," she said, laying her small, waxen hand on mine, her mouth trembling with teeth impossibly white and new. "It's terrible, little boy," she said. "It's in all the news—they can't find him anywhere. Just terrible."

* *

* * *

* *

I'll be honest with you: I'm afraid my mother is escaping me. My father—do not be concerned, we will see him again—is a large, sloppy creature, backlit for a brief moment in American history so that his ordinary qualities appear unexpectedly large, significant; his domino game of disasters is as easy to follow as any grade school tragedy production.

But my mother sat with me in the living room that night, her husband a far-off flame lost in the constellations, her only companion a nine-year-old boy who idolized everything, at that moment, insane. She felt, most of all, unbearably alone. If my father was for the first time now finding the light of history to be a flat and oppressive glare, the only light history had and has ever allowed Barbara Finch is that reflected off her more illuminated husband.

I don't know how we made it home, the darkening summer city passing like a blue blizzard over the car. Perhaps she was weeping—I don't remember. I don't remember any sound at all.

The apartment seemed to have been deserted long ago, and not even by us, when we finally arrived. I can still remember her running her hand along the pictures in the hall; I realize now it was so that she wouldn't see them as she passed. She didn't want to look at anything, even me, and as soon as we reached the living room she clutched me tight against her so she wouldn't have to look into my eyes. Whenever I saw her eyes, she knew I could see that she believed him already dead.

"I wish he'd call," I volunteered at last, unable to stand the smothering silence. "Maybe he tried to call—"

"Stop," she said.

"But maybe—"

"Please." And when I persevered, when I explained how he might have tried again, even that day, she lost her temper with me. It was one of the few times she truly did.

"It's just *not true,* Georgie," she said, taking hold of my shoulders and shaking me. "There was *no phone call,* do you understand? There *never was* any phone call. It's *enough.* It's impossible, and it's cruel. And every time you say that," she started to whisper; but her voice crumpled up into nothing, as I, too, frightened, began to cry.

"It's too easy, just to disappear," she said when she could speak again, to me, to the television with its interminable news reports. "It's selfish"—closing her eyes—"It's not an accident—it can't be an accident. It's too easy for him . . ."

And then for a while she lapsed into the television's sad faces—the faces of people around the country reflecting back the deeper swells in which her anger could only thrash and sink.

"Ladies and gentlemen," the anchorman was saying—I recall Walter Cronkite's steely mustache, his own red-rimmed eyes glancing to where the moon hovered over the skyline of Washington. "A terrible drama is unfolding above our heads tonight, as we speak. The arena is the moon, there for anyone to see, but thus far, the events themselves, horrible to imagine, have remained only that—imaginary—eluding the brightest and best minds in America, in the entire watching world . . ."

"Am I supposed to feel sorry for him?" she began. "After he did so little—" She seemed to consider this for a moment, turning again to the television, its local anchorman now flickering in the North Court, just below our windows. "I can't expect you to understand, Georgie, but if I could wish one thing, I would wish you'd never said those words. I wish—I wish you'd never said he called.

"Christ"—she admitted to me, to the sad and silent phantom on the screen—"all I can think of is his stupid, stupid phone call."

Her face reddened and she turned away. The entire telephone scenario, I knew, resembled nothing so much as the daydreaming of a child already obsessed with space. Granted even the possibility of such a communication from a man who was, in theory, in constant contact with mission control, who may not even have had access to a private line, why would her husband place a call home at hours calculated to leave the least possibility of speaking with her? But it was exactly this question, I realize now, that she found most disturbing. Whether she believed it to be true or not, in the very oddity of the action itself—the terrible urge to speak entwined with the fear of speaking to her, with being too ashamed to speak to her—there was a seed of truth.

With a mumbled "Oh, shit, shit," she stalked out of the room, coming back with a blanket over her shoulders. "I'm sorry," she said as we huddled on the couch, ensconced in covers and air-conditioning, watching the news. We must have remained that way for hours, barely alive to the world, simply soaking up the endless repetition of onscreen facts, before my mother asked, "Did I ever tell you how I met your father?" Perhaps she wanted to give me something—something in exchange for the thing she didn't want to believe. She tried to catch my eye, but this time it was I who turned away. "I don't think so," she continued. "It was actually on a night like tonight, another night when he was lost."

NINE

Moonshine and Lion

H e had a face like yours—damp, a little wrong-haired, recently lifted from the embrace of a mother. Imagine such a face— your face—on a seventeen-year-old boy, Georgie, and you have your father."

I cannot pretend to use her words, but I think she would agree that when they were in high school, my parents were strangers to each other in every way. My father existed for my mother as badgers do for swans: without fanfare, without note. If she was leaving school late, after some stage project, she might pass him in the halls—an ordinary and determined boy in backpack and bottle glasses, leaving an extracurricular offering of the Birding Club.

He had, for his part, often taken note of her; but because he was a creature of a different species, his love for her, if you wish to call it that, was of the humble and puzzling sort displayed for children in illustrated tales, where one animal in boots with a guitar is serenading some other creature, usually up in a window, as if both have recently escaped the Island of Doctor Moreau.

Time has often been compared to a bog, or a sled lost in the snow; and if you find it difficult to imagine my teenage mother and father, doubly removed from us by these troubling analogies, it may be simplest to see them instead as swan and badger rather than the shadows of the adults you're beginning to know—adults who will need a substantial amount of carpentry to saw them back into adequate physical likenesses of seventeen. Even my mother, sitting beside me, had some difficulty in making the leap.

"I'd noticed him around," she said, "but only as furniture, you understand: he was awkward. You could tell he'd never kissed anyone he hadn't been told to."

In my hand I held the model of the Saturn V class rocket and lunar module, poised beside a tall glass of milk. I felt that perhaps I wasn't the true audience for this confession, but I was all she had. And I have sometimes, afterward, felt that my mother, probably far more intelligent than any other player in this drama, saw herself even then as appealing to someone like me now—a person sifting memories—and not a little boy with his feet banging the legs of his seat.

It was at a school dance, where my future parents moped beneath crepe streamers in opposite corners of the gymnasium. The room was dimly lit by an enormous paper lantern, shedding a tepid sort of moonlight, beneath which the backs of classmates swayed. Boys had taken off their jackets and danced in shirts; my mother's friends were dancing badly, but with eyes so bright that their clumsiness appeared for once not only capturable but desirable.

She'd had a fight with her date, and his last words—"You're a piece of wood, Barb. Use your imagination"—still rang in her ears. As if it was necessary fate draw my mother and father to similar stations so they might be joined, she was dissatisfied with everything about herself. She felt like a toddler in her prom dress, and whenever she caught a glimpse in a mirror of her own pale shoulders emerging from the ludicrous froth of green satin, she turned quickly away.

My mother had noticed my father early in the evening. He'd been drinking to keep up with the crowd, wandering out back of the school with his friends to a car full of bourbon, returning sweaty and skittery-eyed to the chaperoned hall. He wore his alcohol like he wore his clothes, like something someone else had dressed him in.

His companions were older and more experienced. He knew one of them—Lyle Barnes, son of the Michigan senator, our Lyle Barnes—only slightly and had attached himself to this group, who after years of tripping him and holding him down in locker rooms had finally acquired some affection for his soft but ineradicable presence. He was the weed in a white tuxedo: the Finch.

She'd even spoken to him, halfway through the night, beside the punch bowl. The boys he'd come with were stumbling a bit, and one of them, out on the floor, had just collided with an ice sculpture of some sort.

"God, your friends are dopes," she'd said, feeling wretched, a little cruel.

"They're not my friends," he'd replied, through either bravery or cowardice. The boy who destroyed the ice sculpture sat down holding a chunk of ice in a napkin against his head.

"Finch," he suddenly called. "Finch, you freak, get me a drink."

"Why do you hang out with these guys?" she asked. "They don't even like you."

He found her a bit out of his league. When he answered, he looked not so much at her face as at the marvelous double curve that ran between the tip of her nose and her upper lip.

"Moonshine and Lion are left to bury the dead," my father-to-be croaked nervously.

"What?" she asked, annoyance gilding her voice.

"You're in Shakespeare, aren't you?"

Yes, she was, although she couldn't recall anything about the class, and he was embarrassed now, having come out with his little quote.

They were quiet for a moment, watching the ice boy, who'd already forgotten about my father and was silently mouthing the words to a song. My mother, meanwhile, had decided she liked Jerry. He was the sort of boy you could play with without getting hurt.

"You want to kiss me, don't you?" she asked with that deadpan she still had twenty years later. It was hard to tell if he heard her correctly— in that tone of voice, she might have said anything.

There was a bank of mirrors behind the ballet bar in their corner of the gym. "That isn't an invitation. I'm just looking at you," she told his reflection, wanly illuminated by the pale lantern above the dance floor. "I can see it in your face, by the moonshine."

He glanced to the mirror, over the ice boy's shoulders. There they were: himself in his white shirt, like an office clerk, face slightly stupid with pleasure; and my mother, green gowned, her hands gloved, her wandering eye like a misgiving. He *was* a bit drunk. He knew she was teasing him, and was elated.

"Moonshine?" he repeated. "But there's no such thing," he said, through either humor or humorlessness, "as moonshine. The moon, after all, has no light: everything you take to be the moon's—all the world of moonlight—is only the light of an unseen but all-illuminating sun.

"The moon is a dark mirror," he concluded solemnly to her face turned toward his in the glass. "And in the mirror, it's all backward. Over there"—he indicated their reflections—"they envy us—those people. And over there, it's you who wants to kiss me."

He didn't know where the words came from, but after a startled moment, she laughed. It was the most ridiculous thing.

"That's enough *Shakespeare* for one night, Finch," she'd said, though she'd always remembered.

Much later, everyone drove to the Lake Erie shore. There'd been a storm in the last couple of days, and the coast was full of the shine of wreckage. Down the shingle a house was pulled into the lake, the plumbing gaping in the moonlight; a crippled dock slurred into the water among half-submerged timbers. Where the ten or so cars had parked on the beach, a long chain, links like fists, led from a massive anchor and snaked to the water.

It was Boris Gabbler—the ice sculpture boy—who announced that this chain was connected to a yacht sunk in the storm. He'd read about it in the paper—a pleasure boat belonging to some local money magnate. There were, he assured everyone, bodies unaccounted for.

"Boris, you rabble-rouser"—Lyle snickered—"trying to scare the ladies with your shipwreck adventure tales." In his expensive slacks and wool cardigan, he looked like a large, healthy incarnation of money— which he was. He was more fond of himself in those days, and harder than the man I'd begun to know—a cheerful alpha male with an oft-demonstrated ability to dispatch tender conjectures with the blow of an idle remark. The subject of the sunken yacht probably would have qui-etly tilted back toward the sandy bottom, uncelebrated, Boris's objections so much foam, except that on this particular night Lyle—normally not one to provide information on any topic—said, "Of course, I *could* tell you what that really is," although he didn't seem particularly inclined to do so.

There was a general murmur from the crowd—"Whatcha mean, Barnes?" "It your boat, Barnes?"—until, eventually, his eyes drifted over the rim of his beer can.

"My dad," he said—understood as *the senator*—"didn't want it all over the papers on account of gold diggers, but, you know— I might as well tell you now"—quietly, glancing around—"when a boat that size goes down and no one claims it, it generally means smuggling. Running goods to international waters, that sort of thing." He crumpled the can in his hand, as if for emphasis, and hurled it over his shoulder into the back of someone's pickup.

"Barnes," Davy Pullet said, wrestling an ice chest out of his Ford Fairlane, "we're almost out. Go slow there."

The crowd muttered, and a few people looked surreptitiously down in the sand, maybe thinking there'd be a gold doubloon or a diamond tiara washed up. They stared out over the slick back of the lake, but the water didn't look inviting in early spring, especially at this hour; and then, after a few seconds, there was a snicker, a laugh, and pretty soon the joke was clear to everyone.

Once again, the subject would have died, filled in with the cement of what may or may not have been knowledge, if Boris, a dogged, humorless boy, hadn't refused to relinquish the story that had originally animated this fascinating exchange of ideas.

"Right, right, sure—laugh it up, you fucking sausage heads. But the thing about the yacht was true—it was in the papers. There were bodies and everything."

Lyle patted Boris indulgently on the back. He liked Boris, and was amused and sorry to cause him grief. My mother, meanwhile, had listened with growing interest. Lyle was the boy she'd started out on a date with that night, and she longed to humiliate him in the midst of his grandstanding. They had been, until then, going steady.

"Of course, all this is neither here nor there," she yawned. "As everyone knows, Lyle has a way of *exaggerating everything*"—to a general truckle of laughter—"Doesn't matter how small the reality is, by the time he's done, it's a mountain in his own mind."

It was an unusual treat to see that bit of pink skin normally adhered closed between two people on intimate terms; even Lyle, good-natured fellow that he was, had to laugh. Only Boris was sulking—he wished he'd saved the newspaper article.

Had my mother wanted only to humiliate Lyle, this would have made an end to things; but there had been, more specifically, a slur made on her imagination. And although Lyle's definition of imagination was at the time composed almost entirely of sex acts, she went one step further now, "If you want to know what that anchor really is," she ventured, "there used to be a floating hotel that docked here during Prohibition, before it sank in the thirties. Lyle, you wouldn't have heard about it—it wasn't open to low-class folks like *your* daddy's people—but you've probably seen postcards. Anchor's been here for years."

Admittedly, this was fairly pale on the scales of invention; there was a touch of truth to what Lyle had said about her, she felt, and now, however neatly this sunken hotel yarn had rolled off her tongue, she felt embarrassed at the poverty of the idea.

Lyle's lips pursed, and it was clear he was seconds from turning on her with some caustic remark, when Boris blustered in, "God damn—you're all so full of shit. It was in the papers. It's a yacht—a yacht! What's the matter with you idiots?"

Years from then a similar outburst in a courtroom would sink his budding prospects as a lawyer in the state of Alaska; he was, however, rescued from a similar fate that night by my father, who'd been idling around the anchor. It wasn't like my father to get himself tangled in this sort of thing, but people weren't behaving as they should, and a small, almost entirely sublimated torch for my mother had been kindled in him. Perhaps he, like so many before and after, had conflated truth and beauty into one hybrid animal.

"Hang on a minute, Gabbler," he said, wanting to alienate no one but having taken the crucial step now. "Barbara's right. The hotel name's still on the anchor."

Boris, powerless with all the weight of journalism behind him, looked grimly at my father, no doubt reflecting that it is on such insectile men that empires rise and fall.

Lyle, however, wasn't paying attention to Boris anymore. "You don't say, Finch? What's it called?" One of his eyebrows climbed above the rim of a fresh can of beer.

"The Grand Hotel," said my father, quietly, because against all expectation everyone was listening. "She would slip out to international waters on weekends, so the hotel guests could gamble and drink, and then they would come back and dock up here, during the week."

The words traveled ponderously through the crowd as if they were pagan objects presented by South American explorers.

"Finch," someone said, "how'd you get so damn smart?" The crowd laughed, breaking open its beers in tiny gasps, until my father told them he came out there at 5:00 A.M. every Sunday to go bird-watching with his grandfather, who actually remembered finding pieces of silverware and such washed up on the beach even ten years after the wreck—at which point they all laughed harder.

Everything he'd said about what his grandfather told him was true, but it was only here, beneath the uncertain glow of Kentucky bourbon, Milwaukee brewing, and a newly awakened crush, that his perceptual apparatus had attained the crystalline state where his grandfather's words themselves began to seem true. After all, the old man had reminisced about a lot of personal experiences, many of them drawn from films or story anthologies, now too firmly woven into legitimate histories to be easily extracted without profound damage to the entire apparatus.

Lyle threw the empty over his shoulder, and a hand reached around and rested another sweaty beer in his palm. If he was riled that this young horsefly was trying to settle in on the affections of his girl, the sensation was easily banished by the thought that he was now a free man, and that Leslie Philopian had been eyeing him all evening.

"So she sunk at the dock, Finch, if I'm understanding you correctly."

My father, flattered the conversation was still going on, smiled. "Why, yes, I guess she did. She had an explosion in the boiler and sunk like a stone—there was no point trying to get her out."

"Know how it is with that, Finch. Takes a strong man," Lyle remarked, winking at Leslie.

My mother had followed this exchange with some confusion. On the one hand, she was pleased to have this hotel crap made so much of; but on the other, it was pure invention. Through whatever trick of memory, either she'd lighted on a true story or Finch was carrying the bluff forward for his own inexplicable reasons. She tried to catch his eye to detect some sly flirtation, but Lyle kept drawing him away into conversation.

And Boris had begun to take interest again, too. As he gazed at Lyle, something like intelligence entered his eye, the way it occasionally did after he'd squinted for long enough at the blackboard during halftime, giving tentative glances at Barnes and his other teammates, the dull concussion of the coach's words falling against his sweaty head. "Would you say, Finch," Boris asked, "a guy could follow that chain all the way out to the wreck of the Grand Hotel?"

My father blinked again, confused. "Sure, I imagine, Gabbler," he said.

Lyle handed my father a beer, and into his now empty and waiting hand appeared another, which he opened slowly, and did not immediately drink, as if deliberating on matters of importance. He winked at Boris, who stepped in again. "So a guy—guy like you, Finch—could follow that anchor chain out to the wreck of the Grand Hotel, if you wanted?"

My father opened his beer. Perhaps if he hadn't—if he hadn't raised to his lips this watery elixir, if he'd never accepted that gift of the underworld—the evening would have been entirely different. His life might have taken another shape; I, surely, would never have been born. But he did, and then he said, "Well, Boris, to be honest I don't know."

Boris threw his hands up. "You're full of shit, Finch. The both of you." He glanced around for Barbara, off looking at the anchor. "It was a yacht, everyone. A yacht." And he stalked away through the murmuring crowd.

At which point Lyle said, "Finch, I've heard you're quite the swimmer."

He could just as well have said, "You're quite the entrepreneur," or "You're quite the astronaut," for all it meant at the time. My father could swim, but no more than that. The crowd of students, however, received the news with enthusiasm. Even Boris paused on the edge of the swaying circle.

"Finch," they chanted as my father looked around, dazed and embarrassed to hear his name, hoping there was some praise intended, however defracted. He gulped down his beer, half simply to interpose the can between his eyes and the wall of spectators. The girls looked hard and inhospitable, older, their breasts assuming all kinds of violent and unexpected angles from backseat gropings beneath strapless dresses.

Leslie said, "Fish me out some earrings, Finch."

"Bring me back a human ear," someone heckled, and a squeal went up. Once again, the event threatened to decompose and become a collective fumble beneath the clear night.

"No," my father said, waving his hands, refreshed by his beverage, "no," trying to marshal the crowd through a strict adherence to fact, however secondhand. "It was forty years ago," he recalled, everyone looking out into the black traffic of wood and water. "Too long ago, I'm sure, for that, because, you know, human tissue—"

Lyle chucked another empty over his shoulder. "I'll be honest with you, Finch. I like Barb as well as the next guy, but I think this whole story of hers is going to be chalked up to chickenshit unless you're a pretty good swimmer."

And my father, impressionable youth that he was, perhaps thinking this was a question of a young woman's honor—a vast and amorphous term for him—took off his shirt and shoes and, to the cheers or jeers of the assembled crowd, waded into the chilly water, smiling and laughing with the rest. I don't know what he thought he was going to do.

The moon floated on the still surface of the lake that night, like a dinner plate floated up from the wreck of a sunken hotel. He just walked out, the voices growing distant behind him, holding the anchor chain, grasping it waist high and moving hand over hand into the dark water. When only his head was showing he looked back once, and the crowd roared his name wildly from the shore, and then his face sank from sight.

He would never tell any of them what happened during the long minutes he vanished under the lake. He would always say, afterward, that he didn't remember; but my mother, aware at the time that this situation had been in some way set in motion by herself, remembered each of those minutes with nightmarish clarity. About fifty feet further out he surfaced for a moment, and looked at the shore. Everyone expected him to swim back then, and no one really cared, until his head disappeared for a second time, and the night grew nervous. It erupted in confusion when Barbara came down to where Lyle stood staring over the water, scratching her head and saying, "I don't know what he's talking about with that anchor. It doesn't say anything at all."

Cursing, Barnes thundered into the lake with a few of the others, grappling the chain and following it, diving and wrestling in the black water for a body. Boys onshore began to take up the heavy thread of iron, tugging against the dead weight of metal. At the end of three minutes panic set in, people climbing into their cars and peeling out, secreting themselves from this terrible thing. The beach filled with the noise of engines and squealing tires, the struggling sound of boys pulling at the chain, and the splashing of divers. It was a hysterical flurry and seemed, even in its moment, like the prelude to a drowning. I think everyone was surprised when the chain began to draw back along the beach.

Derrick Parker, who started pulling first, said he didn't know why he was doing it: maybe just to let my father know he'd been down too long, as if he would have been conscious still and needed only a reminder—a tug from the surface—to come to his senses. There were five or six boys pulling, huffing and swimming on their feet in the sand, and when the chain first began to move, the noise died down considerably. Obviously, it was impossible they could dredge up something the size of a hotel, or even a yacht, but rather than causing them to cease their efforts, the realization only made them pull more furiously.

Working hand over hand, they hauled the iron links, slimy with weeds, growing lighter as the chain's water-bound length decreased, and soon everyone still left was standing on the beach in the moonlight, pulling, watching the chain coil. It took a few minutes to bring the whole thing in, and despite the impossibility that there might be a building or boat attached to the other end, the disappointment now was palpable as they saw how still the water remained—that there was no great hulk riding the floor of the lake toward them.

Goaded by this, gasping in the sand after his attempt to dive down after my father, Lyle crawled to the anchor and saw that Barbara was right: there was nothing written there, just inches of barnacles and calcified rot from years spent by the red iron in the lake. Hand gripping the metal, he grasped in a flash that, if this boy died at his instigation, it would destroy his father's career—it was the kind of thing that would be taken up by all the papers, scandalous and endless. He wasn't selfish—he wasn't afraid for himself or the things that would give way in his life— but he was wildly afraid for what he'd done, and for a moment my father became a precious thing to him, as he was to my mother.

People were weeping with indistinct fright at the proximity of death. Barbara and the remaining women milled around where Lyle lay on the beach. "I just made it up," she kept repeating to different people. "You knew that, didn't you? Was he fucking crazy? Everyone knew. There's nothing there. There's nothing"—her voice mounting.

And it was into this general lamentation that they dragged my father from the Lake Erie bed, clutching the last links of iron in one hand, his other clenched in a fist that seemed the rigid mark of death. Someone screamed. Lyle crawled over and pumped the boy's cold ribs until, when he was exhausted, someone else stepped in; and they took turns pounding on his lungs until the water rose out of his mouth like a snake and melted into the ground, the crowd by now too harrowed to feel much joy when Jerry coughed, turned on his side, and curled up, chest heaving.

When he opened his eyes a few minutes later, he looked around at everyone as if he'd never seen them before, his attention fastening finally upon my mother. He told me once that he'd looked for what seemed like hours that night, under the water, for her eyes. He opened his hand, the one clenched in a fist, and there was something there—a piece of ceramic, most of a white tea saucer. It was polished, the broken edge worn smooth with years of sand, but you could still see at its center an eroded silver monogram—"GH" for Grand Hotel—around the bleached logo of a starfish.

TEN

Messages

When my mother fell silent, it was just growing light out. The room was worn down to its foundations, but we felt more awake than we'd been in days, perhaps weeks, forced now into the indefatigable present, as when in a murder trial the jury realizes the dead man has truly embraced his death not from the revelation of the killer's motive, or from the narrative of fatal events, but only when the prosecutor stands and explains for the benefit of the court some tiny incident from the man's life that renders him alive again, human, and vulnerable to his fate.

Even so, we lacked my father's body, and so this present in which we found ourselves remained lit by the too-sharp, hallucinatory light of dreams; it seemed possible—to me, entirely probable—that he was still linked to us by some tenuous thread, a single wire.

For twenty-four hours we stayed in the apartment, watching fabulous television reenactments of his disappearance: scenarios in which my father was portrayed by a procession of strongmen, successively wrestling various darknesses that menaced the edge of the screen. Sometimes the darkness was tentacled, sometimes endowed with bold, Stalinist whiskers, and sometimes it was no more than the bulk of a large rock arresting his progress. In every situation, however, the moment came: the door shut, the cave was blocked off, the shadow of a hand reared, and the screen went black. As with all commercial programming promising to reveal the key to the afterlife, the genesis of the universe, or the night habits of ghosts, the narrative inevitably slipped: the announcer appeared with his well-fed face and in his fist some object—an ankh or pencil—that summed up the essence of man's relation to mystery. One was left with a tinny sound in the ear, decompression's bends.

My mother's feelings about her husband must have been hopelessly convoluted. She was like an actress made to play an impossible part in a B movie—one of those films with a touching romance, a jailbreak, a musical sequence, and space aliens—in which there was no way to remain in character; and still, she had to keep on with her lines, make supper for me in the evenings, answer the phone when it rang. Her smile had to remain hopeful or sad, not merely insane.

We knew little about my father's prospects, and what we knew was of scant assistance. According to official numbers, he had, between his primary and secondary life-support systems, depending on physical exertion, eleven or twelve hours of oxygen. These estimates were conservative and, as with all the overdesigned fail-safe systems in the space program, could be realistically stretched several hours more; if he was unconscious—a distinct possibility—then his breathing would be shallower, and he might last even longer.

There was another factor, however, which complicated these statistics and threw a blanket of conjecture over the otherwise firm realities of the oxygenless world. The astronauts had, on the second day, set up a tiny lunar enviro-tent with its pool of water and cloudy raft of blue-green biology. Scientists had hoped the tent, no larger than a Volkswagen, equipped with an air lock and solar panels to store heat during the day and regulate the nighttime freezes of the thin atmosphere, would provide a sustained environment, a toy world that might be monitored and visited by subsequent missions.

Was it possible that her husband had been able to gain some precious hours of oxygen here? If so, might his time not be reckoned in the more generous terms of sustenance—water, even, being present—rather than the brutal demands of his lungs?

Through a sense of delicacy, Science, though skeptical, withheld its musty claw. From above, the orbital craft, manned by Buzz Aldrin, surveyed the dark interiors of craters, looking for a sign of the missing man. My father's fellow moon walker, Neil Armstrong, made frequent trips to the little plastic bubble to determine if Jerry was visiting this potential oxygen reserve, perhaps, having lost his bearings, stumbling on the enviro-tent on some random trajectory across the lunar face. The Apollo men sent hourly updates, as on earth the nation crouched, watching the moon through telescopes.

It was a perfect season for our enterprise: cool nights winking with detail, a moon as clear to a boy standing in front of his apartment building as a lighted window across the court. The whole sky was full of colors and shapes we'd never noticed; a sky brought down to earth, as the meteorologists remarked—the sky in the movie theater with its constellated manes of animals and tracery of thrones, chariots, and other furniture—and the world was watching it.

Perhaps I exaggerate, but in the summer of '76 everyone in Magnolia Court, at least, was watching and seemed to have a stake in our well-being. People then didn't examine human tragedy as even the young do today, with the eyes of connoisseurs; down in the court, and at dinner tables throughout the seven asterisks of my young world, the topic of conversation was my father's salvation.

There was a considerable debate, for instance, about whether my father, on the moon, might also be equipped with a telescope.

One camp, largely supported by science and common sense—both of which in this instance Kitty Shank was the representative of—pointed out impatiently that, while the moon lander did contain telescopic equipment, it was nothing my father or Neil would have unbolted from the apparatus; and that even if they had, through a wild twist of events, done exactly this—removed the small lunar telescope from its housing—it was unlikely my father would or could have slipped away with such an object on what was, to all reports, a routine rock-collecting mission. Wouldn't the cumbersome shape of a telescope on his person be remarked by his fellow astronaut? Why would he have done such a thing, in advance? Wouldn't he be compelled to mention his decision, irregular in itself, to someone?

Yet however much dignity one gave to these assertions, voiced often and identically, there was an opposing faction, operating on the high wire of reason but playing closer to the bone of our hopes and imaginations, that suggested it was not only possible but even likely that my father, amateur birder that he was, had secreted away some observational equipment on his person, even if just a pair of binoculars or opera glasses. From the crystalline atmosphere of the moon, these optimists pointed out, he might easily view the earth, perhaps in some detail—didn't satellite technology already allow much the same thing?

They argued—and this group, I should note, included Lyle Barnes—they argued with some force that Magnolia Court would naturally be the focus of my father's interests, being the locus of everything he held dear in the universe, and in this light created large signs, turned toward the heavens and easily visible from the rooftops, with encouraging words and suggestions indicating how my father might draw attention to himself. I can still remember, for instance, leaning out the kitchen window and reading among the black backs of umbrellas WE WILL NEVER FORGET YOU in large, runny capitals.

It was raining that night, the end of our first twenty-four-hour vigil, the sky bedded with clouds reflecting back the city glow like a blaze. Periodic flashes of lightning and the red bur of ambulance lights thrown from some other, less celebrated tragedy, fired the air. I doubt that any telescope known to humanity could have penetrated such weather, but there they were, the most stalwart supporters, drawing beads on any suspected break in the storm; and perhaps because of this, my mother, wanting to distract herself and feeling grateful to the men and women camped below, made cookies that I brought downstairs by the trayfull.

I emerged into the warm, clinging rain in my yellow mac. The cookies—oatmeal crisps—steamed in the drizzle as I circulated. Bonfires had been built at intervals, throwing people into sudden relief as the flames guttered and strove. Someone was playing a guitar; a child was crying, unseen. The patriots huddled on the ground, some in the shelter of staked tarps, some in flimsy cardboard boxes. They looked up at me, these beleaguered men and women, with faces full of pity, determined faces, as if by the force of their collective wills they might save my father. I offered them cookies, which they took singly, with infinite care for their fellow petitioners.

"Your mother's a saint," an elderly lady said, clasping my arm. A lit-

tle girl showed me a drawing she'd made of my father either setting foot
again on the earth or crushing a large bean under his shoe. As I was bending with my tray toward an ancient gentleman, his body covered in
newspapers, I felt a strong hand on my shoulder and looked up to see
Lyle Barnes standing beside me.

Lyle was among the few still up walking in this weather, managing
his flock of loyal enthusiasts, bearing messages, hot drinks, comforting
words. He was in his element, a natural politician—not in the modern
sense of a person of weak moral conviction but in the sense that he didn't
think like a lone man: he was always a collection of people, of which he
was also, simultaneously, the reluctant representative. Beneath his
umbrella, his face appeared as clean shaven as ever as he shook my hand,
then removed an oatmeal crisp from the tray, tasted it, and held it up so
that others could see the value of these cookies.

He said, "Your father's testing us, Georgie. He'll come back—I know
he will—but it just isn't time."

I'm not aware of the moment when Lyle's sentiments for my father
shaded into the realm of devotion, but I saw a side of the man, suddenly,
that I'd never known. He said, "I've been thinking a lot about this,
Georgie, and I believe"—he stared off into the rain—"maybe I was a bit
selfish. Maybe I was looking for what was coming down the pike for me,
and I wasn't thinking what a debt we all owe to the big man. Your father's
a teacher, Georgie," he said with the undeniable conviction we give to all
things baldly true.

He smiled then, in a way that made it seem possible that he, too, was
in secret communication with Jerry Finch. I don't think this was Lyle's
intention, but one always felt that Lyle Barnes, public cipher that he was,
was privy to the same information, sentiments, collective history, as oneself. His eyes shone calmly from a face damp with rain.

"Have you spoken to him?" I asked, hope and anxiety flooding my
voice. I'd begun to doubt my own memory of the phone call, and while
I can see now that Lyle was referring to a spiritual rather than a physical
rapport, I remembered Lyle's own visit to me that rainy afternoon, and
how its existence had been thrown into question for some time. He
knelt, taking the tray quietly from my hands. "I guess I have," he said.

I looked around at the humble crowd, and my heart swelled with regret for my mother, who perhaps alone among us all had not. Up in the apartment, her silhouette loomed in the window as she cleaned something at the sink. I saw her in profile, raising a hand, wrist attenuated by light and distance, before she let it fall again, as if in blessing. Lyle followed my eyes, and tears rose inside me. I couldn't be angry with her for not believing, and I was about to run, leaving him crouched in the rain with the plate of cookies in his hands, when a voice startled me, and I turned.

At first there was just an occlusion of the bright clouds, the vague form of a man I half-recognized.

"You must be the Finch boy—Georgie," the man said, removing his hand from a soggy bag of chips and wiping it on his raincoat before offering it to me. Lyle held out the cookies.

"Don't have much of a sweet tooth," he declined, sucking his teeth as if to emphasize this before returning his attention to me. "Bob Nightly—American journalist."

For a moment I turned over name, face, and title. I was used to watching him from my window, at a distance, but up close there was some dissonance between these things; and then I realized that his face was to me not the face of a journalist but that of a schoolteacher. I'd passed him innumerable times in the pink linoleum halls of Ashtrakan Normal.

"Hello, Mr. Nightly," I said, as he squinched up his eyes.

"Please—call me Bob," he replied. "There's no room for misters in this world."

Since, I've often tried to imagine Bob in the trenches of Southeast Asia, where he apparently spent quite a few years. He must have been a terrifying sight, peeking up through the marsh grass. A preponderant quantity of him seems to be taken up by his head, made bullish by drooping, brown mustaches just beneath a bulbous nose. The nose, a sort of teardrop, runs straight from the top of his head, without any of the usual detours a nose takes in allowing room for brows and bridges. His eyes are drooping and expressive—his best feature, magnified and rightfully so by black, plastic glasses, but also aware that the nose has been spotted first, will always be spotted first—they seem hurt from the moment you catch sight of them. Add to this that he might have been a handsome man otherwise—he has a strong jaw and high temples and always wears his hair swept back—and as soon as you reach his eyes you see that he's already traveled the length of this description with you and, as you've practically insulted him, it's difficult to get things onto a better foot.

I shook his hand.

"Hell of a night," he said, "huh?"

Lyle, still crouched at my side, said, "Don't forget, Georgie, it makes no difference to the big guy: it's always dry where he's standing," he glanced skyward and meant well, I'm sure; but the spell we'd shared was broken. Bob looked at him with open alarm. "Hey," Lyle said to Nightly, "have you signed up for the pickup game tomorrow? Meet some new faces, get a little exercise . . ."

The journalist returned his attention to me. "Georgie, I'm doing a piece on your father—a book actually, as your mother probably told you. She's a great lady, very busy, I understand. But this is the thing, Georgie: I think your father's an important man, and I don't mean that in the sense that all men are, de facto, of value, or that he's important in the small sense of setting foot on an astronomical body other than the earth."

Lyle smiled at this, and Nightly, noticing, smiled at Barnes. He pushed his glasses up on his nose.

"Which reminds me. I spoke with your mother, the other day about, uh—an interview. But I lost the paper I wrote it down on—you know, about the time." He patted his pockets demonstratively, smiling again, all gums. "I think it was for tomorrow. Will she be around?"

I nodded.

He seemed to think of something and patted himself again. "Here, kid." Fumbling in the pocket of his rain slicker, he pulled up a damp paperback. We all looked at it together, and I saw it was *Nation Indicted*, the book Angie had read me passages from. "I don't have many copies left, but this is special. If we're to know each other, as I explain in the introduction, we must be prepared to bare ourselves . . ."

"Oh, I see—that's yours," said Lyle.

"You know it?" Nightly asked, but Lyle shook his head.

"Well, this is the thing," Nightly said to me. "I meant to give her a copy of this when I talked to her. Could you just leave it at home, say, on the kitchen table—something like that. Don't tell her—I want it to be a sort of surprise. She probably thought I forgot and—"

Barnes and I watched him. He was a new kind of man to both of us.

"Just leave it out for me, would you?" he said. "She could probably use a little surprise, a little pick-me-up—and if she forgets my name, it'll jog her memory: Nightly, you know, like the moon. It's there even when you don't see it." He smiled again, his teeth, illuminated by a flash of lightning, flecked with golden, fried food. I took the book.

"What're you going to do with it?" he asked chummily.

"Put it on the kitchen table," I said, placing it in the pocket of my mac.

"Bravo." And after shaking my hand and telling Barnes he'd see him at the game, he backed away and sank into the rain.

It was almost exactly as Bob Nightly vanished from view that Kitty materialized, her body gathering form out of the particulate dark where he'd disappeared, all six feet of her wrapped in a sarong that drew the eyes to where the cloth gathered and folded over itself just below her arms, above her massed bosom, like a still point in the universe. She swayed a bit side to side as she came on, lavender umbrella held high overhead, brown face twinkling behind a pair of swallowtail glasses.

"Young Georgie, Mr. Barnes," she said in her island patois. Lyle scrambled to his feet to shake hands as he did with all members of his electorate. "I hope you're not teaching this young man your bad habits," she added, letting go of his hand and taking mine. "Your mother asked if I could look out for you a bit. You know, all the excitement, and then those cookies"—her eyes went wide—"has her tired out."

"Has there been any news?" Lyle asked.

She shook her head, watching through fogged lenses to determine how much I'd made sense of this confusion; the tragedy would be halved, she was sure, if its true dimensions eluded me. Her face broke into a reassuring smile. "Of course, there's something will turn up. The other isn't possible." But a moment later she looked sternly at Lyle again, and he shrank.

Turning from the politician, she seemed to relegate him to the camp of children and half-wits, drawing me with her into the fold of like-minded adults.

"I thought you might like to pass the time with Fauna," she said, smiling once more as she saw my interest spark, "now that she's back from camp. She's been asking after you all day."

*   *

*   *   *

*   *

The rain had let up to a dull mist by the time we located Kitty's daughter in the seclusion of South Court, normally a near mirror of North Court—my domain—but become a relative backwater in recent weeks. The magnolias here, free from the gropings of children and the meddlings of Eagle Scout fathers making skewers for marshmallows, loomed like diminutive pagodas in the abraded air. Fauna Shank was playing with two other kids, Jen and Louis, who we collectively called the Cousins, not because they were related to either of us or because they were themselves cousins of each other—they were brother and sister—but because their last name, inexplicably, was Cousin. I knew the Cousins slenderly: I would have described them as well as I could by saying that they had straw-colored hair and, as my mother informed me once, they came from Connecticut.

Murmuring some final benediction, Kitty released my hand and nudged me forward by the seat of the pants; when the pressure of the hand receded, I turned to look for her, and she was gone.

I crept toward my playmates, who at the moment were navigating a game without discernible rules. I hadn't seen Fauna for a while, and we studied each other for a moment. Louis, crouching in tan safari shorts and a Winnie the Pooh oxford shirt, suddenly glanced up at me.

"What grade are you in?" he asked accusingly.

"Fourth," I said.

"All right!" Jen chimed in.

The Cousins went to a private school I assumed was full of other blond children like themselves; their enthusiasms were a mystery to me.

Louis squinted up again. "Do you want to see me destroy something?" he asked, staring into my face with his close-set eyes until Fauna rescued me.

"I've got a Neil Armstrong," she said. And, remarkably you might think, I knew just what she meant.

She was talking about the plastic action figures, about four inches tall, that NASA had licensed a toy company to make back when *Apollo 19* was a simple and glorious thing. She had, I knew, an extensive collection of NASA toy paraphernalia, greatly in demand and secured for her by her parents before it even went on the shelves.

"Neil's a faggot," Louis said. "I've got Buzz Aldrin and Cud Wilson." He produced the two astronauts from his pockets, both with their hands held over their clear plastic helmets, the only discernible difference between them being Cud's trademark thumbs-up.

"Cud's not even a real astronaut—he's Jerry's *second,*" Fauna informed him, taking out her own action figure and examining it critically before saying, "Anyway, he's not a faggot."

"A faggot takes cocks in the ass, right?" Louis said, with a certain logic. "Then he's a faggot." And, turning to me, he bragged, "I had a Jerry Finch, but he's dead, so I destroyed him."

It was like an explosion at the pillow factory. Everything got kind of quiet. And then Fauna said, "That's fucked up—he's Georgie's dad."

"Cool!" Jen said.

I think everyone was pretty surprised at how well I took this. If I hadn't been convinced to the contrary about my father's state of health, based on his phone call and bolstered by Lyle's encouraging remarks about his own alleged communications, I probably would have done the expected thing: scream and kick Louis in the balls. But as it was, given the evidence of my own ears, even these doubts expressed about my father's ability to make calls from the moon only honed my certainty that something remarkable could be expected from him. I thought of Lyle, of everyone who might share some secret correspondence with my father, and the prophecies of his destruction sounded like the naïve utterances of those characters in comic strips who, unable to believe that the superhero could be any better than themselves—that a superhero will, by def-

inition, always come through in the end—see the dire newspaper head-
lines and beat their breasts before the final act. I could afford to be calm,
and this won me a certain hard-boiled respect.

"Finch was pretty awesome," Louis admitted. "He had the secret
space compartment in his chest you could hide rocks and things to throw
at the bad guys."

The idea of "bad guys" on the moon might seem surprising, but in
the midst of the cold war and the race for space, the moon, as imagined
by children, and not a few adults, naturally sustained a colony of Russian
spies; however, as the Soviet Union had no cosmonaut expeditions slated
for 1976, and no lunar successes of its own to date, the toy company had
fallen back on the likenesses of the Soviet soccer team, who'd had an out-
standing showing at the Olympics a few weeks before and who, market-
ing demonstrated, had the highest recognition figures of any Soviet
celebrities. Six of their number were represented, all with diabolical grins
and tremendous calves.

We were each probably wrapped in thoughts of such foes, except me,
absorbed in memories of my father, when Louis concluded his eulogy
with the epigram "Shame he's dead."

Those of you already groaning inwardly, because you sense I'm
about to spill the secret truth about my father, keep in mind that, to my
nine-year-old brain, these miniature playmates with their soft, barely
formed faces were powerful men and women about town, agitators and
conspirators to be reckoned with. Also recall that I was lonely, with no
one to turn to besides my mother—not even Angie now. The admission
of certain information here, I knew, could be worth big points.

With this foremost in my thoughts, I glanced coolly around. "He's
not dead," I said.

"You faggot, of course he's dead. He's dead!" Louis screamed, starting to dance, glad my Bogart-like show of grace under pressure was
crumbling.

"He's not," I assured them. "I talked to him on the phone—" And
when Louis continued to bounce up and down, eyeballing me, I added,
"And Lyle Barnes talked to him, too."

"Lyle Barnes," Louis repeated, freezing in place, "is an athlete."

"Lyle Barnes talked to your father?" Fauna asked.

I put my finger to my lips. "It's a secret."

Jen, obviously unaware of the responsibilities that attend such things, said, "We've got a secret, too," before she added, "but yours is better," almost making up for everything she'd said before. We must all have looked very solemn at that moment, each of us having risen, standing in the quiet drizzle of South Court, feeling like movie stars. A secret can do that for you.

It was in this way that they led me, with ostentatious silence, to the far end of the court, where the greenhouse glowed lush in the night. Pushing at one of the bottom glass panels in the rear of the structure, under the roaring cover of the exhaust vents, we snuck inside.

The greenhouse was Magnolia Court's concession to organic existence. I'd been in it only once before, during the winter, savoring the delicious feeling of coming into the warm, damp breath made of the odors of wood and decay. My father had brought me there and introduced me to Mr. Pebbles, a fellow birding enthusiast and the caretaker of the greenhouse; and Mr. Pebbles, an old codger with a back like the bottom of a rowboat, had led me down the four aisles of the large, glass room, walls opaque with steam, naming everything for me like a retired Adam in his garden.

Yet, however wonderful that was, it paled in comparison with coming to such a place in secret, with only a fugitive desire to hide beneath everything, and nothing to absorb the wonder and strangeness of the unnamed: dense screen of rippled leaves; purple throats of water; red, liquid berry eyes; flowers waspish and blurred with the competing fiddles of ferns, the slow creep of moss. Yes, it was Florida July outside now, but under the constant greenhouse breezes, Mr. Pebbles had been at work all year, nurturing the coiled heart of summer.

Screened from the surrounding court by a protective shading of green plastic, we moved slowly down an aisle, brushing back palm fronds, fanned colors, tendrils hung from suspended pots. Our skins became wet and stuck with petals. No one spoke. The undergrowth was so dense the room seemed formless, and we lost all sense of direction.

Crossing a dark path of chipped wood to another section of the room, we came to an unexpected door that opened onto another space, within the greenhouse, fogged from view. I turned the knob carefully.

Inside, the light was dazzling, the floor silvery with sand. The air was so parched it seemed to hiss when it encountered the torrid tropics of the first room. I had forgotten about this place.

We closed the door behind us, and an otherworldly silence descended. Blinking in the dusty desert, our eyes relieved only by pale green fingerings of cacti, buttons of pearly pink, and stars of yellow on the floor, I saw my solitary footprint behind me in a sand drift. I noted tiny craters made by some predatory insect and breathed this thin, stripped oxygen.

"It's the moon," I said with certainty.

"Of course it's the moon." Louis sneered, walking past me as he produced his dolls and handed one to his sister. "That's what we always play here."

*   *
*   *   *
*   *

We knelt in the sand by the side of a little circular path, feeling the heat in our knees.

"Now he's OK, you can play Jerry Finch," Fauna suggested, as everyone had a doll except myself. And though Louis objected that I didn't have a Jerry Finch, he was soon shouted down by the gabble of girls.

"Of course he doesn't have a Jerry Finch, you idiot." Fauna sighed, looking around. "First we have to find him."

Louis sized me up. "All right," he acquiesced, obviously not understanding this train of thought. "Until then he can have Oblomov," producing one of the Russian soccer players from his back pocket: a small man in a red shirt, missing both arms, and with one foot perpetually affixed to a soccer ball. When he saw me staring at the armless holes, he said, "He's dead too—it was a counterstrike—but we can pretend he was saved by the radiation. He's a mutant now." I was equal to this.

So it was we wound up creeping around various corners of the greenhouse desert, crawling between the lugubrious cacti, solitary searchers calling to one another in voices garbled to simulate shortwave radios:

"This is Tranquillity Base to mission control—*pssht*—we've picked up the subject's tracks at 37°50'29" and are in pursuit."

"*Pssht*—this is Buzz Aldrin, mission control. The Russians have Finch—they're going to melt him down, the fuckers, they've torn up the Geneva Convention—*pssht*—I'm going in with my ray gun."

"Mission control—*pssht*—this is really beautiful. There are so many diamonds and—*pssht*—hey, Buzz Aldrin is hitting me—"

I watched from my lonely vantage point, my armless Russian soccer player probing a tall grove of lunar prickly pear with his athletic legs. There was a sniggering sound, then the distant *p-tchew, p-tchew* of ray-gun fire.

My position, I realized, was precarious: I was searching, like all the rest, for my father, but I knew if any of these others found me, I'd be destroyed. The actual blood nature of our relationship, though it should have transcended nationality, would mean nothing to these astronauts and, in my damaged state, I had no illusions about my chances of survival if I came into close quarters with the Americans: I lacked the means to pick things up or even bend at the waist, let alone fend off attackers.

On a nearby crest of yellow sand, Neil Armstrong came into view. Although I tried to flatten myself behind a stand of Mormon tea, he spotted me immediately and raised one arm in greeting. I could not reciprocate.

"I followed your tracks, Oblomov," Neil said. Looking behind me, I saw that the soccer ball had left a highway of telltale depressions in the low dunes.

Oblomov returned his attention to Neil, and they surveyed each other silently, a tremendous sense of moment in the air. I was outnumbered, practically a criminal in the eyes of these American astronauts, and yet, so far from the earth, our shared humanity became, instead of the dividing gulf it was usually perceived to be, a common sea. *Apollo 18* had linked with *Soyuz 19* only the year before, but that was a meeting in the cold arch of space, like two ships crossing at sea. How different, then, to meet here, on this shared field of dreams. The event we were witnessing now and, to an extent, taking part in, was unprecedented; we were moment by moment more keenly aware of how far on the one hand this American astronaut, and on the other this damaged Russian soccer player, had come to find each other in this most remote place—this fiddler's green of all history's fantasies.

The lunar atmosphere is exceptionally clear. We studied each other's faces. Did I catch a glint of some deeper emotion in the astronaut's eyes? I shuddered at what he perhaps felt for me. It was, I think, my mother coming through—this inability to be pitied. And I saw myself for a moment as others saw me: as a boy whom destiny had robbed, who would submerge himself in any delusion to escape the truth about his father. I doubted, suddenly, that Lyle had spoken to Jerry Finch at all.

"You don't think we're really going to find him," I said, "do you?"

Fauna watched me, her eyes dipping. Neil advanced a few feet, his features, behind a plastic bubble, a rigid mask of uncertainty.

"I know where my father is—he's coming back," I said as the Russian soccer player turned aside and withdrew, like the Venus de Milo, into Siberian stillness.

"I talked to him—" I began, but broke off beneath Neil's stern gaze. His face, if you recall from newspapers and television, is as inscrutable as the Midwest plains—nearly bald, skin hardened by weather—and you might at first believe the world could make no impression on his cold, blue eyes.

"He is," I insisted, a tremor in my voice, though I knew it was no use. Someone else had to say it, someone besides myself—I needed someone else to believe; and I thought, if only Lyle was there with us, on the moon, if one of those loyal men and women out in the court could hear us, and lend their faith.

"He is," I repeated, hearing the horrible quiet, now, in the room.

And it was then—just when that silence seemed most awful, like the emptiness of the very vacuum of space—that she said, "I believe you," words that no one can truly make any other human being say.

The Russian soccer player seesawed across the sand, stiff-legged like a cowboy, until the two lunar explorers were no more than a few inches apart. I think we both felt it: this great rapprochement of nations written here, isolate and small; that flush of feeling that leaps at times, like electricity, from life to life; but the sound of a nearby shout, unadulterated by radio and surprisingly adult in its register, brought us up short.

"Hey there—who's inside now? Who is that?"

Someone had obviously come into the greenhouse without our noticing and overheard our communications and gunfire. Instantly, we were on our feet, Fauna marshaling everyone military-style through another door in the rear of the desert room.

"Hold it right there" came the injunction of invisible authority, the gravelly voice growing closer as we quietly shut the door behind us, arriving in a third, dark chamber of long tables covered in seedling trays. Hearing the door slam open in the desert room, we dove for shelter beneath the tables, in the musty shadows of sacks of earth, spare pots, and garden implements. In the few moments left to us, we wormed through this twilit warren, quickly losing track of one another, hearing only the occasional squabble of voices when two people came at the same hiding place. There was a slatted wooden crate in the room's left rearmost corner, and I secreted myself behind this, staring out into a tiny portion of aisle.

I'd expected the man to burst in, full of fury, intent on flushing us the way a pack of dogs might flush ducks from a marsh; but his tack was different. I heard the door open, close gently, and then the slow scrunch of footsteps on gravel as he made his way down the right-hand side of the room.

A young trespasser caught in the midst of his crimes is likely to let a multitude of retributions kindle his imagination and, as the steps drew near, my heart thrashed with increasingly elaborate and half-formed dreads. Yet hidden and blind in my little bunker, I must admit to you that my feelings were, when I took the time to examine them, more complicated than simple fright: for I found, the realization at first taking me completely by surprise, that some small part of me instead insisted, however irrationally, that our pursuer was my father.

If you find yourself recoiling before this idea, as a canny traveler before the allure of a treacherous mirage, know that I did much the same; but it isn't, perhaps, of mirages that we should think: it was as if my conversation with Fauna had magnified my father, focusing him among us like a ghost. Certainly, as a being with a ghostly pull on our lives, he didn't seem bound by the same physical laws. Perhaps he'd even come *looking for me*. And while the voice hadn't sounded particularly like his, and his presence here—I knew—would be impossible, still, the thought of his sly and bashful face swept through me, nearly bringing me out from my hiding place.

I probably would have stood up right then, too, if fear hadn't retained exclusive control over my legs. Several long minutes passed in this state of deliberation, in which I knew, with increasing certainty, that sooner or later I would have to stand and look, because the thought of my father there in the room with me, the possibility that out of fear alone I might never see him—perhaps ever again—was the worst thing I could imagine. I had gone so far as to crawl forward a few feet on my hands and knees when, close by, I heard a grunt, a clatter, and a brief scuffle—"Let go of me, you old fart!"—followed by a swift, answering smack, and then quiet.

It was Mr. Pebbles, the gardener, I concluded, both disappointed and renewed in my panic. A moment later there was a second scampering, an "I knew you'd screw it up," Jen's tearful, "No, you," and then the return of sullen silence.

The steps began again now across the back aisle, toward me, this time accompanied by a reluctant shuffle. I watched a brown pair of boots come into view, flanked, on tiptoe, by two pairs of children's shoes.

My own inexorable unmasking rose like a sob. Already demoralized, I was on the verge of giving myself up, being a natural cooperator with an angry law, when there was a distant crash from somewhere in the area of the adjoining desert room. With a gruff curse, the booted feet wheeled inches from me and strode away, the Cousins mewling like kittens as they hurried alongside. The door opened at the far end of the chamber, I heard the remote door to the tropics bang shut, and then nothing.

Very slowly, I crawled from my hole. Fauna unexpectedly emerged from behind some fertilizer bags a few yards away, and we stared mutely at each other.

Finding the desert room empty, we crouched, listening to hear if Mr.

Pebbles was returning, staring at his large, grooved prints in the sand. "I thought it was you," I whispered of the noise that saved us. There was another distant slamming of doors, and then, after a bated minute, we stood and reentered the first room.

"I think he's gone," she whispered, obviously shaken.

"Where's the way out?" I asked, uninterested in discovering what had become of our companions, filled only with a sense of my own luckiness and failure. She led us back through the dripping hive of green.

The path seemed to have grown in just during the hour or so we were off exploring. With my hands held protectively before my face, I advanced through the jungle. Several times I lost sight of her. Peering into the shifting spectrum of foliage, I called her name in a whisper before, growing nervous, I called again, more loudly, and heard a rustling ahead.

By the time I reached the glass wall and the window that hinged open to the outside, Fauna had already scooted through and was waiting, watching for further trouble. It was unexpectedly bright out, I remember thinking, and I was about halfway through myself when something in the way the moonlight reflected on the glass caught my eye, and I saw the writing on the inside of the panel. Five words drawn with a finger in the dust, confirming what I'd always believed, electrifying as the signs of true religion:

I can never leave you.

"Fauna," I said again in a whisper, pointing to the words. I didn't want to understand how—it wasn't necessary. Had I invented every hope I ever felt, what hope could approach this, drawing earth and moon so near? Rising in me, all over again, was an unreasoning, marvelous belief.

I remembered those astronauts, leaping among the craters to the sound of rain. It was a joy like that I felt; and we read the words together, Fauna and I, glancing behind us, through a rift in the clouds, at the silvery trace of the moon.

ELEVEN

The Journalist

I'd arrived home, as you can imagine, in an excited state and, forgoing supper, unable to face my mother in my present condition, pretended to be ill. Only the following day did my trauma begin to abate, replaced by a mild euphoria. The fear I felt, and the subsequent giddiness—a return, really, to what I'd immediately understood, staring at those words scrawled on the glass—originated not in my own narrow escape from the clutches of Mr. Pebbles but in the realization that my father had been silent—had probably not spoken with another human being—for nearly seventy-two hours. Perhaps this point is obvious, but I had neither years nor wisdom, and as long as the Apollo crew continued to search the moon for him, delaying their return home, I'd been able to push from my mind the possibility that something truly final and terrible had occurred. The appearance of the message on the wall of the greenhouse had in effect allowed me to perceive the narrowness of the thread by which his life was suspended, because it was also his salvation; and the next day it was this same impossible feat that renewed my belief that my father's resources, so uncommon, so little reckoned by the lights of an ordinary world, were undepleted.

With this in mind—and the idea I might assist him somehow—I began paging through the massive manual for the Zeiss 5300. Written in army-ese, bound in olive drab vinyl, and kept on a high shelf in one corner of the living room, the book was full of thorny phrases and complex diagrams of lenses and mirrors reflecting black lines back and forth in cat's cradles. It was more grueling than any school text I could imagine, yet I knew this was the only way I could master the enormous telescope.

That said, I wasn't even supposed to touch the Zeiss, let alone actually employ it for scientific investigations. Like many other elements of these days, my efforts at study had to be conducted in secrecy, and so the next evening found me sprawled in bed, mystical diagrams replete with Greek letters and Roman numerals open before me, memorizing which knobs and dials operated the adjustments on the azimuth, which on altitude; which of the focuses applied to the objective lens and which to the viewfinder; how to calibrate the clock drive—a host of difficulties— when there was a loud, repeated ringing of the front doorbell.

Rising from my labors, I came into the kitchen to find Bob Nightly hemming and hawing at my mother. He wore the same green jacket that he'd worn under his raincoat the night before—that, as it would turn out, he wore every day during the brief compass of this memoir; and he was picking up in one ink-stained hand his book—the one I'd dutifully placed on the table beside a pile of old newspapers.

"It must have just slipped your mind," he was saying to my mother as she took the paperback from him, glancing at his name on the cover. "I understand—completely—you must have so much to think about these days, Mrs. Finch—"

"Yes, I am rather busy," she admitted, handling the book with some wonder.

"It's my first work—*Nation Indicted*," he explained, opening it helpfully for her. "A sort of treatise, you'll find, on the Vietnam War—really, an analysis of the psychology of a nation, an entire people that could abandon its own children, while being simultaneously a study of this same warlike progeny—among whom I lived," he added modestly, turning a few pages, "and who I found already perceived themselves, whether at home or abroad, driven now into exile from the very breast that gave them suck—"

"But you would think," my mother interrupted, as he followed her past me into the living room, "and this is really not a good time—we haven't had supper yet—"

"I understand, but even a few moments—" He paused beside the television, his glance boring into her until he caught her eye. "Have you perhaps heard of my work, Mrs. Finch?"

She shook her head.

"Perhaps"—he smiled—"you've heard of my column in *The Titusville Speculator*—" Her head continued to move slowly back and forth, his face grew perceptibly longer.

There's something about Bob Nightly on first encounters that gives one an impression of fragility—a defensive, somewhat neurotic fragility, perhaps, but a kind of vulnerability all the same. One resists contributing further to his oppressions, wanting—not unlike with my father—to feed that slim flicker of optimism leaping from time to time in his eye.

"I'm not a big reader, Mr. Nightly," Barbara was telling him, wishing she had something to offer, when she was suddenly buoyed by the realization that she *had* seen him before. "But haven't we met at a school Christmas party?" she asked. "Yes, it's all coming back. You're—"

"Right, right. I'm a colleague of your husband's at the middle school," he admitted; and, as if to draw some distinction from this admission, he added, "A history teacher, actually."

"Of course," she said, glad to have the riddle solved.

"One could say I'm writing a history in which your husband's significance will feature quite largely—"

"I see."

"Because if we consider your husband in the abstract—or, even prior to this, consider the fecundity of technology—" But he was brought up short by her raised hand, a request for a pause in conversation that reminded him so forcibly of the classroom gesture of volunteerism, he lost his train of thought.

"Mr. Nightly"—she smiled, handling the book again as the phone began ringing—"please consider my position. What is there, after all, to say at such a time?" She was dismayed as he returned her smile too eagerly. "If I asked you to come by, I'm sorry. I certainly seem to have forgotten all about *this*. And as for my husband's place in *history*, you probably know as much as I do. I really don't care to know anything more, to be honest. If he isn't coming home, what more is there?"

Nightly was somewhat surprised at my mother's position. I could hear them in the other room, his voice sweet, prying. "I had hoped, Mrs. Finch, to write the *authorized* biography—" And my mother's voice immovable, tired. "Obviously, you would have to ask my husband—" Followed by his confused and hesitant reply.

"Would you get that, Georgie, please?" my mother called at last.

I gazed grimly at the black, plastic device. These days, the phone rang dozens of times each morning and evening with false news of sightings—various objects, shadows mistaken for the motionless body of a man on the distant lunar surface—sympathy calls from everyone we'd ever met, and some we hadn't.

And in truth, as this hubbub surrounded us, not answering the phone accomplished little. Down in the courtyard, voices would erupt as one of the many telescope enthusiasts shouted a set of coordinates, and all the rest redirected their equipment. A burst of feverish adjustment would follow, at the end of which, after a chorus of curious grunts and cries, a collective sigh would go up, and someone would shout, "Good intuition, Doug," or "The light's a devil, isn't she?"

You might think so much activity would be cheering or distracting, but it only increased my loneliness. Reluctantly lifting the phone in both hands, I put my ear to the receiver, and recognized the frozen rush of space:

Georgie, my father said.

Both of us must have been overcome with relief, and for a long time we were silent, hearing nothing but the rolling wall of static. At last he asked, *Are you angry with me?*

There was really nothing to answer. I was too happy—it had eclipsed everything.

"Hold on," I told him. "I'll get Mom." But he asked me to wait.

It's a terrible embarrassment for everyone. The only man, the only ordinary man ever sent to the moon, and I've escaped.

The idea that he'd escaped was novel. "What do you mean?" I asked.

Don't worry, he said. *I'll figure it out—I just need space. Space and time.*

Time is on my side, you see. It's time I'm counting on, and there is so much, even on the moon. They can't wait forever—the air is running out, and I see Neil at night, even, hunting around behind rocks, searching for me. They'll have to leave soon, Georgie, and then I can begin to set everything right again.

We were quiet. I heard the bubble of my mother's voice, Nightly laughing theatrically in the other room.

"Georgie?" she called. "Who is it?" But her voice trickled away, and I heard the two of them drawing off to some cove of the house.

Georgie? he asked, and I said, "Yes?"

There are times, seeing Neil crouched in the shadow of a crater, resting in his search, hand held up against the sun, I'm reminded of days not so long ago, in the quivering heat of the Texas shore; of waiting in the dawn hours for the slightest motion, that moment in which the land seems to blink, before a great blue heron rises from the salt marsh.

But while it's true that we like to imagine similarities, he told me, *as when you awake in a strange room and through half-lidded eyes believe you've discovered a dozen familiar places, the moon isn't like the earth. Can you imagine seeing the blue world rise across the dusty plains? It's like watching your blood run out your body, knowing you're dying. I am terrified*—he paused—*just to think of it. There is no shame in this, though. I am not ashamed to love the world.*

We think about the earth all the time, up here—like the pictures of loved ones soldiers carry with them to the trenches. The earth, Georgie, is no calendar girl. When we see it, we are each again terrified, and we are warmed.

The sound of static poured in, and for a moment his voice ebbed to silence. I remembered the Zeiss, then, and thought he would like to know I was learning to use it.

"I'm going to find you," I said, "with the telescope."

I hope you do, he replied. *You're the only one I want to find me.*

I didn't understand why this was, entirely, but I was pleased all the same. There was a howling racket, like wind.

Georgie, he said, listening until he heard the sharp explosion of my breath. *I tried to call you the other day. I wanted to tell you—we played the game. It was the day before yesterday, in the evening, when the earth rose and covered the sun. We spun each other around, like I used to spin you around, in the apartment. We took each other's hands, Neil and I, and took turns spinning each other; and when you let go here, you sail off through space, away, far away.*

There was a long, gravelly pause, at the end of which he said, *I can still see Neil from here, poor fellow, collecting rocks—there's not much else to do, but his heart's not in it. He keeps looking up, shielding his eyes. I miss him already, Georgie.*

"Is it like a game?" I asked. "Does he know you're hiding?"

No, it's a game for no one but me. And you, Georgie—it can be a game for you, too.

I smiled at the thought of something we alone in all the world had in common—this secret life he was beginning. It's long ago now—imagining myself is like imagining another man—but even then, I understood my father well enough to know it was fitting that his destiny be tied to the moon, that most self-effacing of planets—not a planet at all, they would have us believe, but more an appliance among astronomical objects. He himself said it best, over the crackle of space:

Ask your mother to look at the moon tonight. Or better, say nothing, but casually draw her attention to the moon when you're together, talking about me. I'll be outside, collecting stones—they call them rocks up here. I want her to see me in the humbleness of my days, the insignificance and magnificence in which our lives unfold—all of us here—like mountains, or luxurious plants, or some very small creature, a mole, perhaps.

My word, he said, *will be flourish,* and then, in a welter of rising snow, a general wrinkling of sound, he hung up.

I listened to the dial tone and stared into the sky, purpling with approaching night. When I finally looked away from the window, I found Bob Nightly watching me from the hall.

"He never listens," my mother was saying. "It was probably the president, and he just stood there—" She hustled him to the door, where he peered at me one last time before giving his attention to my mother. I heard the door swing closed.

"How awkward." She sighed, stepping up beside me and untucking her blouse. "And you—you're no help at all. So, who was it?"

I didn't think about what I would say to her as my father talked, or as she stood, now, slipping off the shoes she'd slipped on in answering the door. The decision I was about to make would have momentous consequences, but I think I had only a sense that my mother didn't want these calls. They were galling, and seemed to accomplish the opposite of whatever gentle reconciliation my father believed he could orchestrate through this veiled exchange. Instead, I would do as he suggested—I would draw her attention tonight to the moon: our silent companion, our constant and humble friend.

"Well?" she asked, probably noticing that I looked flushed.

"Nobody," I said. "It was a wrong number."

TWELVE

Mirror of Earthly Lands

I t was on the afternoon following Nightly's visit, while my mother was out shopping, that Fauna came over to the apartment and suggested we practice "teloscopy" by training the Zeiss across the complex on the central building—her own—and, more specifically, on the apartment of a new neighbor just down her hall, on an arm of the asterisk facing, unlike hers, onto North instead of South Court. This person, she assured me, was a freak—massive and porcine—and, perhaps for this reason, emerged from the apartment only at night, paying neighboring children to run his daytime errands. Every large building complex contains its obligatory Elephant Man, and I admit I was playing on her belief that we were looking for a new such representative, now that Mrs. Pandalamb had moved out to some private retirement community or circus—the rumors varied. But when we'd dragged the machine into the kitchen, my true intentions quickly became apparent; and, as I expected, Fauna gave in to the allure of space.

"It's like looking under a big rock," she squealed, all of her interest in things terrestrial gone as she squinted through the eyepiece into the teaming soil of the heavens.

Laugh if you will, but have you ever looked through a high-powered telescope? I'm not speaking of one of your large, prosaic home models, set up like a newborn calf on its rickety tripod, casting a bleary eye little better than a magnifying glass over the sky; I'm speaking of the genuine instrument—the kind employed by the military and scientific community—capable of bringing space to the palm of your hand. Stars crumble, erode, and give up their tiny faces to the human eye; the tangled hair of comets is discovered twined through the corridors of galaxies, left like old Christmas tinsel on the counterpanes of planets and the baroque mantles of asteroids; there are strange bodies of dust and gas feeling tentatively through the more elusive portions of our universe, digesting suns; and the moon, so comparatively near, becomes like an object viewed beneath a microscope. The eye toils over fields of blazing silt and, adjusting the focal length, we climb the cones of craters, overwhelmed by solitary footprints, the broken equipment of past lunar endeavors rendered vast in the tiny window of glass, like whales drifting by the periscope of a submarine. Everywhere, over everything, is the trembling silence of 250,000 miles.

During the succeeding days, I followed in the lunar dust the detailed record of human passage, of lunar minutiae. On graph paper I drew elaborate plans of the routes taken by the astronauts, trying to capture my father's last hours of human companionship, and the possible avenues of his disappearance.

Down in the court there were many theories thrown around on the best way to track a man on the moon. Barnes and Nightly each had distinct notions on this subject, and as the days went by, and relations became more casual, sometimes one of these men would come upstairs and I would crouch beside him at the viewer—permitted, as they were, to handle the machine—soaking up suggestions about focal adjustments and lens diameters and such. With Lyle hunkered on the kitchen floor, a warm cologne of football and political anecdotes encircling us, it was sometimes possible to forget that the object of my search was, in fact, my own father. My mother could also momentarily join in this amnesia. She would lean in the hall, watching, Lyle's presence a welcome reprieve from the slow business of my father's dissolution.

"You have no idea how nice it is," I remember her saying, "to see two people doing something *ordinary* around here."

We, for our part, tried to believe her—to pursue our studies as if they existed in that timeless vacuum science is often misunderstood to be. It was in these days that we were informed by phone that the astronauts would be leaving the moon, giving up the search. President Ford made the difficult call. He was such a sad, earnest man that my mother found herself consoling him. "It is a blow to the nation, and I know," he said, voice like a lake covered in yellow leaves, "that each of us tonight, in our hearts, will pray with you at your bedside." The thought in itself was unnerving, but she thanked him. She'd taken the news calmly, having expected nothing else for days; relieved, even, that she might begin to accept that her husband was, by even the most generous standards, dead and not, more horribly, dying.

Her only source of immediate worry was how I would receive this information, which she imparted gently, seated on my bedside, staring into my eyes. That I didn't seem overwhelmed must have been taken by her, as it was by Kitty, to mean I hadn't grasped the enormity of the situation and was still holding out childish hopes for an impossible reversal.

And yet, if I refused what she took for bald reality, I was not alone— there was a whole court full of patriots gathered beneath our window who found the entire scenario being painted by NASA and "the bigwigs in Washington" a little too easy.

Lyle, for example, could often be found making the rounds among the magnolias, explaining some of the options available to a man stranded on the moon, shrugging off the imminent return of the *Apollo 19* crew as a minor impediment to my father. Those of you who remember as far back as the Gemini missions might recall the plans NASA had originally entertained for solitary, unassisted return trips from space; and it was to these plans that the politician now referred when asked about Jerry Finch's chances of survival following the departure of his peers.

As one can learn in any NASA manual, the space suit worn by each astronaut is, in itself, considered to be an independent spacecraft, capable of sustaining pressure and oxygen flow not only on the surface of the moon but in the pure vacuum of space. The only feature of a conventional spacecraft lacking in an astronaut's space suit is propulsion—and this, of course, is supplied by the astronaut himself.

Surprising as it may seem, NASA had originally devised that all the Gemini astronauts' reentries into the earth's atmosphere would take place without the protection of a larger ship, involving only space suits.

Several such schemes were developed in the 1960s for both emergency and routine scenarios, where the astronauts would literally leap from an orbiting capsule and fall to earth assisted only by parachute and some form of handheld rocket to slow and guide the descent through an increasingly frictious atmosphere.

While this information didn't entirely resolve my father's difficulties, it was true that the abandoned landing stage of the *Apollo 19* moon lander contained both small navigational rockets, whose fuel hadn't been entirely consumed during lunar entry, and an emergency parachute designed to accommodate the entire module in the event of rocket failure. In fact, with this in mind, it was clear that the only as yet unaddressed task faced by my father would be his initial escape from the moon's weak gravitational pull.

Speculation aside, I was delighted to discover in Uncle Lyle a man who approached astronomy as a boy my age approached all physical phenomena: as if a tiny door might at any moment spring open upon unexpected, uncharted worlds. When we were together at the telescope, he frequently became so excited at the sight of a broken radio antenna or the wing of a defunct satellite that he would completely upset the apparatus and have to start again from scratch.

"That was the one, there. That was our man," he'd say, hunkering over the eyepiece for another go while I made sandwiches. "I think we're on the edge of something *really big* here—something *huge.*"

Mr. Nightly also enjoyed house privileges for some time, his limited astronomical experience perhaps balanced by a paper he'd written on the use of helicopters in the rural tropics, "Aerial Invasion and Its Dependence upon Preconceived Notions of Transcendence in the Nuptial Rites of Nomadic Peoples," which finely honed theoretical skills he now brought to bear on this new situation.

"Optics and truth are different animals," he was fond of saying, "though we may use one to study the other as long as we recall that truth is a caustic—something which may only be introduced through the subliminal chords of a dream.

"You see," he told us earnestly, blinking first through one, then the other, soiled lens of his glasses, "I do not believe in accidents."

"Oh," my mother replied, unsure she herself believed in accidents, and disturbed at where Nightly's reasoning might lead.

"I've often wondered at the simplicity of this national exercise—the 'ordinary man' contest. Haven't you always thought it was, after all, a little too simple?" the journalist inquired, nodding in agreement with himself, regarding my rounded child's face. "You'll understand one day, Georgie, that it is precisely the simple we must learn to mistrust."

My mother, wary of this windy speculation, attempted to redirect him. "Mr. Nightly, if you'll kindly stop yammering a moment, would you consider assisting the boy with his telescope?" But grown comfortable with my mother's brusque manner, Bob merely smiled and drew his chair a bit closer, reaching into his pocket for a pad of paper. The outline of his book was taking shape for him from day to day, and he wanted to try it out on someone, practically anyone.

"Now, Barbara," he purred, "doesn't the entire tragedy seem like an obvious metaphor—the sociology of a nation writ so large even a child could understand?

"Even that Fitzpatrick girl—bless her simple heart—half-conceives the fact that something extraordinary is at stake here."

He merely smiled when my mother asked with unnoted fright: "Has she made any suggestions of her own?"

"It's more a matter of generous appreciation than generative apperception. But seriously—she seems like a bright enough girl in her way, doesn't she?"—as Barbara shrugged and tried to appear occupied—"And then, it's a wonder she's inherited even a grain of intelligence with that lampshade of a mother," he mused, before taking me up and sitting me on his knee—a large, bony affair. "Georgie, what do you make of all this? A father on the moon, so far from his family—lost to them," he intoned, watching me closely with his magnified eyes. "He gazes at his loved ones from afar, and from afar, they gaze back, searching. The nation as a whole sweeps the sky for the lost father, the missing common man, really." He grasped one of my shoes—they had pictures of race cars on them—for a better look.

"They wait for him, all their technologies brought to naught; they wait as man once awaited his Messiah—in a metaphorical sense, you see?"

At this moment, much to my relief, Lyle knocked on the front door. My mother rose gratefully to let him in, and when he entered the room, everyone stood up. A kind of trenches camaraderie had smoothed all intercourse between the supporters of my father down in the court, but already there was an electricity between these men—opposites even by physical standards—which at the time took the form of exaggerated politeness.

"Mrs. Finch, if I knew you had guests." Lyle bowed.

"Don't be an idiot," she said, and he stepped to where Bob was just setting up my telescope by the kitchen window. Lyle surveyed the scene as Nightly bent over the eyepiece, mumbling, "Yes, as men once awaited . . . that's it, exactly."

"How's it going, Bob?" Lyle murmured. "The old 5300." He nodded toward the telescope as if it was an elder statesman, coming up beside Nightly and placing his hand on the end of the long, tubular body.

"Jesus," Bob said, jumping up.

"I'm sorry—did I disturb the clock drive?" Lyle asked, using the opportunity to apply his face to the finder scope as Bob stared witheringly after him. For a moment no one moved, until Lyle said, "God, she's fierce today."

"It's an artifact of the Barlow lens," Bob offered.

Lyle fumbled at the face of the telescope until he'd screwed a dark round of glass across the aperture. "It's a better ride, for my money, if you use the lunar filter."

"But with a crescent moon, and considering the power is currently 1200x—"

"Yeah, but with a sixteen-inch aperture—" Lyle answered.

Mr. Nightly colored, glancing at me, then my mother. "I think it's just the nature of a reflective man, Lyle, to prefer the reflective scope, unfiltered and so undimmed, don't you think?" And he glanced again at my mother, who pretended to find a spot on her blouse.

"The 5300 isn't reflective, it's a compound, Bob," Barnes reminded him, collimating the finder scope in impressive silence.

"You have a bit of dust on the objective lens, Georgie. It can lead to refraction and maybe eventually some binding in the motor . . ." He trailed away. "But the resolving power in one of these babies . . ."

"Have you ever used a P-38?" Bob ventured after a minute, relighting his pipe.

"You say P-38? The Schmidt-Cassegrain machine? Why, sure. A true American classic."

"It's the bride for light."

"It is," Lyle said, standing up and taking a hard look at the moon. With his long jaw and a curling lock of fair hair on his brow, he seemed the very image of positivism.

"It resolves the moon down to its dimples."

"It does," Lyle admitted, as my mother glanced at him nervously. Lyle caught her glance, misunderstood, and smiled in what he probably considered an easy way—the smile he'd often reserved for that strategic moment in a game when the field is beyond dispute, only a question of finesse. Yes, she always was a finicky creature, he thought, and he would just set her heart at ease regarding the value of her own scope while offering the olive branch to Nightly—he wasn't about to alienate anyone. "Of course, this is all fumes, isn't it Bob?" He chuckled. "There's no better machine made anywhere in the world, Barb, than the old 5300."

"It's the bride," Bob affirmed, a little disappointed at the final turn of things.

My mother, who had no interest in telescopes and wanted to lie down, saw no point in protracting the discussion. "That's wonderful, Lyle," she said, glancing now at Bob, who evidently felt he'd come off second in the contest. "I'm glad to see you boys can be such adults about this, but if you would excuse me for a bit—" And she kissed me on the cheek and went off, down the hall, and out of the bright arena of scientific dispute.

*   *

*   *   *

*   *

This wasn't the first or last such exchange between these two scholars, who often found themselves at loggerheads over a thing they didn't yet fully comprehend, employing a language designed both to display knowledge and to draw out the weakness of fellow telescope enthusiasts.

But it's also important to understand that the telescope was certainly not as simple, or as rewarding, as the abundance of theories surrounding its use might have led us to believe: the telescope was no panacea and, as even Nightly understood in his own way, the search for Jerry Finch was more than simply a question of optics.

It was footprints we followed with our lenses and mirrors, a laborious process, especially when the steps of the astronauts—at times playfully hurling each other through the thin lunar atmosphere, if my father is to be believed—could be broken by gaps of hundreds of feet. In addition, even though Jerry Finch was a considerably smaller man than his companion, I found his and Neil's tracks nearly indistinguishable, so that my efforts to pursue his steps to their ultimate destination were constantly foiled by dead ends or false starts. My difficulties may best be demonstrated by the adventures of an evening in which, after several hours of intense and lonely scrutiny—Fauna having gone home—I traced my father's progress along a previously uncharted track, and accidentally lost focus navigating a steep incline. The moon dissolved to bright white and, like a pilot blacking out, I jerked my head up.

I think my first reaction was common to many school-age children: I was being thwarted—the deepest yearnings of my humanity, thwarted—by the indifferent mechanisms of physics. Uttering some grisly boyish curse, I reapplied my eye to the scope. After a moment, I realized I was gazing at the surface of a lens, deep inside the machine, granular with terrestrial dust, the great curl of a human lash; and then, with a shudder, darkness swept across my field of view, and I found myself staring at the reflected image of my own eye.

I blinked. I saw the blood wall of the eye, and the fluid sphere like an ocean through which all sight must pass. I saw the coiled veins clenched like windswept trees, and raised my head again.

When I restored the focus to its proper length, imagine my surprise to see that I'd been deposited, beyond all expectation, back at the shimmering footprint of dust I'd just, so I'd believed, irretrievably lost. At first I was jubilant, but something caught my attention there, and refocusing once more I noted a bent, white cylinder. I thought fleetingly it might be a gas cartridge, the kind used to scrub lunar silt from delicate equipment,

until I saw a band of gold near one crushed end, and a tiny crest of man-
ufacture, and I knew it was the stub of a cigarette pressed beneath the
heel of the broad, grooved print.

I don't wish to disturb the tenderhearted reader—Mr. Nightly in
his naïve eulogies to space has probably created some unreasonable
expectations—but more than a "veritable palace of idiots," the moon is
a palace of trash. It abounds with the detritus of past explorations, errant
satellites, and the quills of various scientific devices launched like har-
poons from earth to probe the white flanks. Objects like cigarettes,
however, are unusual in the oxygenless world—even a young boy knew
as much.

I continued following the shoe prints across uneven lunar silt until I
reached a broad slab of blue-black pebbly rock, stark and clean. And it
was in crossing this trackless void, rippling with heat, that I encountered
the yellow band of paint that made me return to the crumbled asphalt
edge, turbulent domain of ants, and search up and down the strip of
blown-out retreads and mufflers until I found a tilted road sign and realized, through some oddity of reflection from the moon's silver disk, vast
convex mirror ball, that I was staring not at any piece of that distant satellite but at Utah.

I was too confused to feel anything other than disappointment at the
time, but I have often wondered, since, if the hazy impressions of light
and dark, faces and shapes we see on the moon on very clear nights, are
not merely the ghostly mirrorings of earthly lands.

THIRTEEN

Grand Hotel

Approached from the silt bed of the lake, the lights of the Grand Hotel oil the water. The structure lists a little to one side, but it still invites the traveler, hands cold from gripping an anchor chain. The windows ripple six stories high, forty wide in the teeming green cliff. The name rests like fox fire on the mansard roof: letters of neon four feet tall, made to resist the worst winter winds to rip the lake. A shoal of lantern fish, mild fluorescence, emerges through the O and disperses above, as smoke, as stars.

Stopping to look back, behind himself, the traveler sees that his footprints have stirred up a clouded thread, a vapor trail rising sluggishly from the yellow floor. At a distance, mongrel fish hang like bells in the water. The mild glow from the dusty field of the lake shades to green and brown darkness, and the traveler shrugs and shivers on, grateful that the door is opening—the great, curving fin de siècle door like a mouth in the very center, nearly red within, shadowed by the glass awning—and he abandons the chain and climbs the bank of sand and bladder-weed, across the stove hull, onto the marble steps.

It's late, but there's still a little life. The porter's shoulders are braided gold. His face mirrors the traveler's face with mild surprise, as if astonished to see anyone climb from the silt floor at this hour. He smiles as the traveler smiles into the vaulted ceiling, at the chandelier, a fountain held upside down. The grand stairs sweep in hoops to the upper floors, red carpets melting into the lobby, and they advance together across the soft ground, traveler and porter, rising weightlessly with each step, coming down without a sound, past Second Empire chairs and brass spittoons, until they stand before the long mahogany desk and the mannered mouth of the concierge.

"Do you have a reservation?" the concierge asks, mouth diffident and humorous at the tips, before him the yellow registry, open and full of names.

"Finch," the traveler says, peering through his visor. "Jerry Finch."

The concierge turns down a smoky monocle, pages back, back, back, and then smiles, turning the book around in a single sweep for the traveler to sign.

"We thought you had forgotten us, Mr. Finch. Do you have anything with which you will require assistance?"

"No, just the room, thanks," the traveler says, accepting a pen. His freshly printed name coils from the page, like a burn.

The concierge turns to the bank of hooks and brass keys, nearly empty in this season, and takes down a number from the fifth-floor row. "Would the same room—?"

"Yes," the traveler says, "the same, please."

"Very good," the concierge replies, pace unvarying, turning and handing him the key.

The traveler rises and falls across the lobby with its curls of something milky—cigar smoke perhaps—beckoning from the parlor room where the old-timers are sitting out a last hand of whist. There is a noise of glasses and voices gurgling, but he doesn't stop to look.

The elevator moves up, slowly, as old elevators do when pushing a weight of water. The operator doesn't turn to him until the red carpet and brass sconces of the fifth floor have slid quietly into view beyond the rising metal grill, and they stop. "Five, please," he says, coming round, and the traveler wearily recognizes him—young, jutting jaw helped from beneath by the strap of his cap. The traveler has dimly recognized everyone here, and understands that while he has come and gone and grown older, no one here has changed. What should he have expected? Certainly he's dreamed of these men. He's seen them only once, but it was memorable, his visit to the hotel—just as the postcards promised.

The carpet is patterned with small gold crests bearing the olive branches, the starfish, the florid GH monogram. Looking behind him, once, toward the elevator bank, he sees someone crossing the hall with measured, loping strides, as he imagines he must be walking himself. A face appears in profile for an instant, a streak of polished hair like walnut, the gibbous flash of a monocle, but their eyes don't meet, and then he's at his room: 535.

He lights the lamp on the nightstand, and the chamber leaps into being: a single, queen-size bed with a brocaded spread, a row of windows opposite behind two chairs and a low table. Everything is vegetal with gold, even the paper on the wall. The window is black, setting the room against itself in murky, undersea attire. He sits down on the edge of the bed, bent forward in his portable life-support system. There is plenty of time. But there's one thing he wants to do before he closes his eyes for a while.

He rises and bounds slowly to one of the chairs, beside the table where he'll have his coffee in the morning. The detail comes back to him. He'll ask for a wake-up call from the front desk; but something else, first. On the table, near two cups with the hotel insignia, is a telephone, long-necked and lacquer black. It was a luxury item when the room was built—customers had to ask for it especially. It is the only concession here to the outside, save the windows, which he turns and looks into; and after sitting that way a long time, his face reflected back at himself, his helmet where his expressions swim like great, sad fish in a bowl, he reaches for the phone. As he lifts it, the cord coils rise behind the receiver, full of life, and with the same hand he swirls the rotary dial, then places the receiver against the curved glass by his ear and listens.

FOURTEEN

Fellow Travelers

There are regions of our lives we pass through, after which we may never again accept the world from which we came; and I recall a middle time, too, in which the worlds on either bank seemed equally unreal, and all that existed was the bridge—a long thread through the dark. For my mother, the days following my father's disappearance were this darkest period, when the moon, like her husband, first faded and then vanished from the sky.

Sometimes I would find her standing at the kitchen window, staring wistfully among the stars; but I know that if she were the one to tell the rest of this story, it would be different from here on—entirely, irrevocably different, because, for the first time in my life, I had a secret from her. Not the sort of small secret that we delight in telling, or keep to ourselves because we're merely ashamed. It was the kind of secret that shapes a life from within.

I looked from our window upon a landscape that my father had never entirely abandoned, in which he shone, latent, as the sun at night continues to shine and warm the back of the world. Yet, when she stared out at the same people and things—the tents and tangled magnolias beneath the starlit court—I know she saw only so many mourners who wouldn't depart after the funeral; people with lives desperately in need of direction; and a pregnant girl hidden among all these innocents, like a bomb wired inside a clock.

Lyle came frequently to the apartment, usually in the company of the Barnstables or some other members of the court. He didn't dwell on my father's situation but instead distracted us with the quotidian, with updates on his race for district representative. Much to our surprise we learned that he, himself, was ahead in the polls, owing largely to the quantities of public airtime with which my father's disaster had furnished him. It was even true that, within the past week, the incumbent representative, David Cabot, could sometimes be found below, in the very camp of his enemy, as it were, grasping warily for a moment in this luxurious spotlight of constantly rolling cameras. Lyle's star had certainly risen with my father's, and it was no surprise that he looked a little anxious on the day *Apollo 19* touched down amidst a flurry of helicopters in North Atlantic waters.

All morning I'd gazed over the campground, sensing a shift in the air: a mingling of relief and sadness, the low hum of life punctuated occasionally by a metallic clank, a dispirited shout, where three old men played horseshoes. Just after breakfast Kitty appeared at our door, wearing a palette of somber colors. She stroked my head and drew my mother off into the living room with the harsh shush of her voice: "I'm sorry to just drop in, but I've been calling for days, and there's nobody picking up the phone."

"It's best not to," Barbara admitted, turning down the television before she slumped in my father's yellow chair. "Besides, what could anyone tell me on the telephone that I wouldn't find out ten minutes later on TV?"

Kitty played with the rings on her hands. She was aware of having known my mother just long and well enough that she should be there, now—but no better; and certainly not well enough to escape a growing self-consciousness about what to do or say. She felt stuffy in her mourning attire, noticed a warm pressure to the whole house, so that after a moment, realizing the room was nearly dark, she was glad for the excuse to go to the window and open the curtains. Kitty herself had never experienced a loss like this but was sure that, if she did, she'd want someone nearby. She only wished they'd already had the chance to become closer friends—she was waiting for some sign on how to proceed.

"I'm not being much of a hostess, am I?" Barbara said. "It seems I made the mistake of turning on the news first thing, and now I've watched it all morning, until I can barely think." Erecting her pained smile, she saw me lingering in the hall, playing with the moon buggy, and beckoned. "I imagine myself to be such a rational person— When they left the moon, you know, I thought I could begin to put this all behind me. But I've discovered I need to see their faces. It might sound ridiculous, but I need to talk to someone who was there."

"It's the most natural thing in the world," Kitty soothed, lowering herself into a chair. "You just can't carry the whole thing around by yourself, in your head. How about this fellow?" she said, trying to get my attention. "How do you feel?"

"He doesn't like to talk about it," said my mother, drawing me to her side. "I'm not sure he believes the astronauts coming back even matters, do you?" To which I focused all the more attention on the little silver car.

"Barbara, if you don't mind," Kitty said after a pause, "I'd like to give Georgie something. Tom and I were saving it for Fauna's birthday, but I'm thinking maybe you could find some use for this—" She reached into her handbag. When she withdrew her hand, through the clear, plastic packaging, I recognized the smooth dome of a helmet, the gentle, reaching gesture of the arms; and then, with a warm intake of breath, I knew it was a Jerry Finch.

"Ooh," my mother said, enthusiastic though unaware of its specific identity. "What do you say?"

"Thank you, Mrs. Shank," I said, the wonder quivering in my voice as I caressed the laminated card stock against which the doll was sealed.

Of all the NASA action figures, none was so popular this season. People paid hundreds of dollars for them, stampedes occurred in toy stores when rumors of fresh shipments circulated. I myself had never actually held one, I'd only seen commercials in which some dramatic adventure was being staged by children in a sandbox; the close-up of my father's awestruck, plastic face.

Kitty smiled, and I smiled blearily in return, my interest in the toy already obliterating my gratitude; and then, as if embarrassed, we all turned away from one another: myself to the doll's painted eyes; the two adults to the television screen, filled with stiff, pale faces and hands nervously adjusting neckties. In the background was a diagram of the returning space capsule's trajectory from moon to earth. The moderator was posing a question of some sort, after which the faces glanced at one another. My mother turned the sound back up.

"Well, Dan," said an elder statesman in square glasses, lips pursed, "I'm not sure we're prepared to answer that right now. I mean, we've never had a situation like this."

"I think that's right, Dick," another offered. "If we deal strictly with the numbers, things don't look good. But as quite a few people have pointed out—"

"Mr. Barnes not the least of them," someone pitched in, and there was a chuckle.

"—let's be honest—these are *highly* resourceful men we're talking about—these Gentlemen of Space, if I might borrow Jerry's coinage— and the addition of any single factor—the so-called enviro-tent, the manual use of retro-rockets—there are a number of variables that could entirely alter the outcome . . ."

The moderator, rejoining them, thanked everyone, and then the station ushered us into footage of Magnolia Court, presumably live. None of us batted an eye to see our own front door, the lobby of the building shining wearily behind glass. There was a close-up of a couple in jeans and Hawaiian shirts crouched by a tent, a distant shot of Bob Nightly stroking his mustache as he talked across a wrought-iron railing to a cop.

I'd unwrapped the Jerry Finch from its plastic casing and, although it did little to remind me particularly of my father, by squinting my eyes, I was able to infuse the action figure's expressions and gestures with something animate—as I imagined an astronaut might appear when standing on the moon's shimmering, daylit plains. I knew my mother, too, wanted to look at the doll—perhaps now she was beginning to sense that it wasn't the likeness of just any astronaut—but I kept it from her, resentful of how easily she'd accepted my father's death when even the news correspondents held out hopes. I pitied her a little, in the way the religious pity the atheist, with his or her sad cart of reason and science and arithmetic.

The news had returned to footage of the court, a blond and bright-

eyed woman reporter leading us toward a crowd of blue NASA suits that
in turn parted to reveal Lyle Barnes, face confident and warm amongst
the tense bric-a-brac of government men and onlookers. He glanced at
his watch and shook his head. A smile touched his face—a Little League
smile—as he said, "We remain optimistic, Dana—"

Kitty peered across the room at my mother's profile, perhaps reflecting that it was just like Barbara, before she was even entirely awake that
morning, to have made herself up for the cameras; that while she hadn't
given herself a kind face, it was exactly the face she'd have wanted: one
meant to convey the minimum.

"Don't much like the look of those NASA folks," Mrs. Shank suggested, slipping back to the screen, the mirrored sunglasses of the men
hovering at Lyle's shoulder.

"NASA?" my mother said. "Oh yes—the National Ass-in-a-Suit
Administration. I meant to ask, can I get you some tea? Coffee?"

"Coffee's fine," Kitty replied, feeling that the conversation was being
kept deliberately on the surface. "I don't know about you, but NASA,
these patriots, the news crews—all these people make me nervous." The
reporter reappeared, earnest and thrilled—probably on her first major
assignment—to announce that she'd just received notification: we had
splashdown. It was, she explained for the benefit of the nation, a bittersweet moment.

"Bittersweet?" my mother remarked.

"*She* looks just as pleased as punch," added Kitty.

We watched Lyle lift a baby from a woman's arms and kiss it, that
slender smile haloing his face, her face, the face of the child swaddled in
blue as, with a strikingly childlike expression himself, he said something
about the promise of the future.

"Are you afraid for his life?" Kitty said quietly, thinking the mention
of fear might, as with her own children, precipitate a confession of such;
but my mother shook her head.

"No, I don't think I am." With little thought her husband was alive,
she had correspondingly few fears of his death. She felt, however, mildly
annoyed at the mental prodding Kitty was engaged in. On screen, Lyle
shook someone's hand and swept his broad palm toward the heavens.

My mother, noticing Kitty staring across the room at her, glanced over, and their eyes tangled for an awkward instant.

"Maybe someone could tell me what the hell's *he* smiling for?" Kitty blurted, perhaps simply to say *something* at first, but then deciding that this was exactly what she meant as she gathered herself forward in her seat.

"Lyle?" said Barbara, rising to make coffee or, as Kitty suspected, escape the room. "That's just the way he is. Lyle's not smiling at the bad news—the man doesn't even believe it. He's no better than Georgie when it comes to believing or not believing what he wants." My mother caught a slight *harumph* as Kitty narrowed her eyes at the screen.

"Looks to me," Mrs. Shank replied, gazing at that honest face wrapped in some tiny victory of the soul, "like Mr. Barnes is going to be smiling whichever way this works out for your husband."

My mother, I suspect, recognized in Kitty's words a verdict close to what she herself had hesitated so far to pronounce—not so much about Lyle as about the whole court. It wasn't that any of these people were indifferent to my father's fate—quite the opposite; it was just that, in my mother's eyes, her husband's fate was no longer an open question. And, given such a position, she had naturally begun to wonder what satisfaction so many people were gaining by continually, as it were, reopening this wound.

All the same, as she'd hesitated thus far to say anything overtly critical about these patriots so invested in her husband's well-being, her first reaction was to find such a critique disconcertingly crass, coming from someone else's mouth.

"Please," she said, "now you're just being cruel."

"Cruel?" Kitty asked. "Who am I being cruel to?"

"To Lyle, of course—"

"Well, and so what? Look how that man's gotten you all upset—"

"But *also* to me," my mother finished, exasperated and feeling she'd said the obvious thing but had been defused in her intentions. Kitty stared back in a pantomime of disbelief until, after a moment, her expression wavered, then fell.

"I've known Lyle since we were both fifteen," Barbara said, "and he's *not* perfect—he's as smart as a ham—but I'll give him this: he's grown up a lot. If he didn't mean everything he's doing down there, he'd be back home in Michigan right now, feet in a pool, living off his father—the *senator* of that state. It's certainly what the rest of his family does." She was angry and, as happens when one's angry, she felt herself getting into a passion over things she didn't care about. Honestly, she wanted Lyle to leave herself and her family alone as much as Kitty did, but she wanted everyone to go—and at this moment, that everyone included Mrs. Shank.

The silence that followed felt giddy. My mother removed herself to the kitchen while Kitty, beginning to wonder if she *had* been cruel, gave me a bewildered look and turned to the TV in a sulk.

As the station coordinated some late-breaking event, I held the astronaut against the blue expanse of screen. With his life-support backpack grasped in my fingers, he bounded across my knees, my lips forming a delicate plosive each time his feet launched up. The doll paused upon a promontory—the arm of my father's chair—backlit by television, gazing out over the wonderland that is our living room or, really, that any small place becomes writ large. Barbara, like some giantess, reentered the room with hot drinks in her hands. And then, as I caught upon the doll's face the first glimmer of my father's sad and sloppy smile, we found ourselves all unexpectedly staring at televised footage of real astronauts, weak and stooped as they were helped out of the helicopter that had collected them from the North Atlantic. We could already sense the pallor of the event from the way they turned like criminals from the cameras.

Thinking of Kitty, beginning to admit a guilty resonance in herself with the things the woman said, my mother gave her attention to the Apollo men arriving at Cape Canaveral, the cavalcade of vehicles that would bring them to Titusville and the press conference. She was struggling, swaying over the abyss of admitting Kitty, at this moment, into the very foyer of her heart; though beyond this, even as she began to speak, she knew that all doors, every stair, every window, must eventually lead to her husband and that girl—that wretched girl. As she glanced down at me, her mind swam in the question of who the unborn child would look like—if she would recognize Angie or her husband in that diminutive face, if it would at all resemble me. She knew that Kitty already sensed something amiss, that she was trying to help. And this is what people do, my mother told herself, taking a deep breath and looking at her friend: they tell each other things.

Television coverage had returned to the court, where Lyle, his face a simple rubble of hope and concern, was shaking someone's hand. A security guard opened the door to our building and, escorted by two people, he disappeared behind the reflective glass. The camera panned back to the blond reporter, speaking into a microphone: "We're outside the home of Barbara Finch, astronaut's wife," she was saying, breathless on this historic day; my mother, as if someone had just asked her a question, glanced again at the TV.

And I think right then, whatever she'd wanted to do a moment ago, Barbara knew that even here, in the shelter of her home, with one of the few people she might really call a friend, it was impossible to say anything—impossible to say that she was afraid her husband hadn't exactly "gotten lost"; impossible to say she suspected he'd been afraid to come home—impossible, because everything implied everything and, at least for the moment, the chance that no one would have to know remained.

Kitty could only mark my mother's agitation and wonder. She thought of her husband, that man of deep calm and forbearance; later she'd tell him what a mess she'd made of the morning, meaning only to help. She watched my mother stand and smooth her skirt, resigning herself to the TV as Barbara said to me, "Why don't you go let your uncle Lyle in? He'll be up in a minute."

*　　　　*

*　　　*　　　*

*　　　*

The politician took his seat in my father's vacated chair. Up close, removed from national television, he appeared deflated. His tie was loose, his hair rumpled. He pinched his eyes together and gazed into the lattice of his fingers, saying, "I'll be honest with you people. I can't pretend it doesn't depress me a little."

He was accompanied by Clyde and Janet Barnstable, seated now in their matching jogging sweats on the sofa, looking between the politician, my mother, and the news. The grainy screen showed an open limousine with two astronauts inside, waving slowly, faces bare though otherwise dressed in their silver-white suits, the car easing through a silent parade. The people lining the roadside stood practically still, like a film backdrop; and when the camera panned in, as it already had a dozen times this morning, all of us—the entire nation, most likely—saw the glimmer in Neil's eye.

"The poor man," my mother murmured. "My husband was lucky to know him."

Janet jerked her head tearfully, opening a small purse, from which she removed a smaller packet of tissues. She held them out to everyone.

Barbara got up and went to the window. Drawing aside the curtains, she made out the glow of television in apartments across the way; down below, the court pressed in a silent semicircle around a TV on a picnic bench. From coast to coast, people were gathered around this same scene and, reflecting, she decided this would be as good a time as any to broach a subject she believed to be on everyone's mind: "I guess the question," she said, "is what do we do *now*?"

She caught Kitty's glance as Lyle came and stood beside her at the window. "All we can do is be strong," he said. "We have each other, after all, and I think Jerry would agree that that's worth a lot." He looked older, Barbara thought, noting between his pale blue eyes a fresh crease dividing his brow. But then again, she told herself, we probably all do.

"I mean about everyone else—down there," she said after a moment. "What should we say to them, now that he's not returning? Should *I* say something?"

Lyle put his hand on her shoulder. "Put it out of your mind, Barb. I know things seem dark now—unbelievably dark. But it's important not to give in to despair."

The words washed over her as little more than sound. She gave him a quizzical glance, wanting to shake her head and say, No, you don't understand—it's not despair; but she wasn't entirely sure *what* he was talking about. She looked at Kitty, who was pretending to watch television, then at Janet and Clyde.

"What you're feeling is *natural,* Mrs. Finch, don't feel bad about it—" Janet began.

"You've just got to hold on a little longer, that's the thing," her husband concluded.

Lyle's eyes narrowed. He was giving her his earnest look, modeled on the faces of generations of athletics coaches; a face his father, the senator, displayed rarely, when he wanted to inculcate in his boy the meaning of an ideal, such as "sacrifice." "We're doing everything we can to turn this around as fast as possible." He nodded. "We've got congressmen on our side—the whole country's behind us."

She turned to him, feeling like a child stroked by his voice.

"That's right, Barb. I'm impatient too—you've got every right to be impatient. They can't just leave the man there, after all he's done."

Something flashed through her mind. "Would they do that?" she asked. "Send another mission to recover his body?"

Lyle shook his head. "That's what I mean. Don't *do* that to yourself. He needs us—he needs us to be strong."

My mother looked around the room, perplexed. Kitty glanced away—she'd had enough trouble for one day. To Barbara, though, it was as if they were all deliberately keeping whatever they meant just out of reach. Letting her eyes go from face to face, finding nothing of any utility, she could feel herself getting angry again—indignant might be a better word—about what it was they wanted her to endorse. What was she supposed to be *strong* about?

She was going to ask exactly this question—a tiny, petulant breath, the start of a nervous laugh, had already escaped her—but she found everyone was staring at the television; and, as she watched, the camera cut indoors, to the sober face of a news commentator, mouth moving silently at a press conference. Neil Armstrong suddenly appeared at a podium, speaking, and Lyle scrambled for the volume.

"Thank you, everyone, ladies and gentlemen of the press," the astronaut said, his face blurring into the room, small and ashen on the screen. "As you know, we are not gathered here at this time to congratulate or rejoice, and so I'm going to make this brief.

"Only a week ago, we believed that this would be an occasion for reunion, for loved ones and familiar voices; but having expected a kinder climate, we find ourselves now in a land peopled not by those we sought but by our sorrows." He stroked the thin stubble atop his head, studying the room, as if still searching for something. "People of America: tonight, as you're getting ready for bed, as you turn down the lamps of your homes and look up from your windows and porches at the starry sky, know that a part of us remains: the very conscience of the nation—of the world, if you will—watching."

There was a hail of flashbulbs, and the astronaut winced, unaccustomed as he was, without his visor, to bright light.

"While you must know by now that we've failed you, my friend," he continued, "if you're looking down upon us here, as I believe you are, from that lonely station, I want you to know that you haven't been forgotten. Quite the contrary: tonight you've soared into the hearts of millions"—his voice growing husky—"although I'm sure you already knew that for myself and Buzz, at least, you'd made your nest there long ago."

I could hear, I remember thinking, the vacuum of space between each syllable; and when at this point Neil paused, the last sounds seemed to resound amongst us, like the very speech of canyons in a weightless world. Perhaps this is why I was barely surprised when he reached beneath the podium and lifted his helmet up before the nation. Grasping it like a crown between his hands, he lowered it back onto his head, as Buzz stepped forward and slid the locking rings into place. Amidst the confusion and questions in the conference room, Neil then turned and did the same for his companion.

"What's going on?" my mother asked, the camera panning back from these two men standing now before the world as if they stood 250,000 miles away, until Neil's voice, miked from within the suit, leapt above the confusion.

"Please," he said. "Please, everyone take your seats. We mean no disrespect, to yourselves, to the people of this nation, or to the people of earth—" A chill settled over the room. "But there is a question, I'm convinced, on everyone's lips this day. *What do we do now?*—" The words pierced my mother as the astronaut's eyes pierced through his visor into the stunned space of the conference room. "And the answer, I would submit, is a simple one: We must return to the earth her own."

Exchanging glances with Buzz Aldrin, he continued: "Buzz and I see no other course but to resume, in solidarity with our fellow traveler, that uniform Jerry Finch cannot himself discard. We would each, I know, gladly trade fates with him, but as we cannot, we must instead share what we are able. And we will continue as we are until that hour we may again touch his hand, and hear his voice"—though as to what came afterward, my mother had no recollection.

She'd closed her eyes, trying to see herself from without. She tried to imagine the world as others saw it—those seated beside her, those hunkered in the midday Florida heat, the people in that conference room, watching with rapt attention as these men quarantined themselves from humanity. Had the entire nation gone mad? she wondered. Was this the sort of widespread hysteria one read about in books? A national, psychotic break in which witches are burned and men transformed into gods?

Or, she thought, was it herself? Was this her way of taking out the hurt she felt on the man who'd inflicted it, an act of recrimination hidden from the careful gardening of her own mind: to deny a truth—painful because it meant uncertainty, but psychologically necessary—that all these good, honest people held without question? That her husband was alive, in all likelihood; that he was depending on them; that he would still come home, if he could.

She saw a glint in even Kitty's eyes—a helplessness—and held me close against her, as she perhaps would have held her husband then, were she able.

*   *
*   *   *
*   *

We all, I'd like to think, felt this identical urge that day—to clasp my father to our collective breast, to admit to one another, simply, our love for him. But with the search still agonizingly fresh in our minds, people stopping us to ask questions in the halls—even a mission to recover the lost man thrown around Congress with a grim show of goodwill—the arrival of five astronauts at the apartment the next morning placed the situation in some perspective.

En route from their debriefing at Cape Canaveral, Buzz Aldrin and Neil Armstrong had been joined by the standby crew—earthbound seconds to the members of *Apollo 19*—men who'd trained and spent nearly every waking hour for the past three months with them and who, in the last week, had sympathetically undergone, like estranged twins, agonies identical to those endured by their counterparts in space. Pent up in Mission Control, Houston, they'd watched the drama unfold, powerless and guilty that these trials were not their own.

It was early when the astronauts rang the bell, quietly at first, then leaning on the buzzer. We hadn't known they were coming—the incessant ringing woke us from dreams of reconciliation. My mother opened the door and I heard her scream, and then they were inside, filling the house like balloons, arms canted away from their sides, gestures expansive with loss and space.

Everyone has his or her own vision of what an astronaut is like, drawn from photos and movies, assembled from blurry statements made over the nation's radios. Barbara had some ideas herself, based upon her own television viewing, augmented by my father's various accounts; and although you might say that her ideas had a great deal more substance than those of the average admirer, the astronauts gathered that day in our living room were a far cry from my mother's dreams. They smelled like sulfur. When they spoke from inside their helmets, it sounded like the ocean. Through an effect of static electricity, streamers and Styrofoam peanuts still clung to their silvery bodies from the parade of sad horns and gaunt faces that had greeted them upon their return to earth.

Led by Neil Armstrong, the group floated into our home, twisting delicately in their suits as they navigated the front hall, legs barely moving as if propelled by a silent current.

"Mrs. Finch?" Armstrong said over his radio. "Mrs. Finch, I'd like to apologize for disturbing you at this hour—" But his voice fell away when we fled before them. Following a brief consultation, he signaled for the others to remain behind as he advanced cautiously after us into the apartment, loping toward the corner of the living room where Barbara sat collecting herself, clutching me in the folds of her bathrobe.

"Please, Mrs. Finch," he said, extending a silvery hand as she began to rise. "I know this is a difficult moment—for all of us—and I know we must seem to you and your boy to be little more than the bearers of sad tidings . . ."

I watched at a distance as the astronauts silently began examining our home. Gary Sprine and Flek Davis paused before the pictures in the hall, and we heard them relaying to each other the discovery of my father's face. Buzz Aldrin and Cud Wilson entered the living room then, and while Cud stopped and rested his hand on my father's chair, bending close to the fabric as if to ascertain its reality, Buzz knelt on the floor by the sofa beside the toy moon buggy. There was something soothing in these scientific explorations, a gentleness of which I'm sure I wasn't the only one aware.

"I realize," Neil continued, "that our appearance at your home is irregular—perhaps seems unnecessary—but I don't think I exaggerate when I say we had to come here, to meet you, and Georgie. And most of all, I guess, to apologize."

The morning was so new it was still dark. The astronauts, absorbed in their purpose, had crept through the gantlet of sleeping people camped below, though looking out the window, my mother saw that her initial scream had awakened the crowd and, no longer feeling alone, she was able to regain some poise and recollect that, sadly, this was precisely what she'd wished for—to speak with these men with whom my father had spent his last hours.

"Sit down, please," she said to the crewmen spread through the rooms. "There's a seat for everyone. If you'll give me a minute, I'll make coffee, and then we can all be civilized to one another." She sensed, despite the analytic decorum of their activities, that the astronauts were perhaps as traumatized as herself; but though Neil prevailed upon them to put down our belongings, and my mother eventually got them seated, handing around cups that they held but could not drink from, there was nothing we could say to comfort them.

Perhaps this—this last assertion—isn't entirely true. Barbara, who possessed only limited information, and whose animosity toward NASA didn't extend to these servants of its designs, no doubt did her best.

I myself, however, was in a more complicated position, and can only reflect now that it is a great convenience at times to think of our heroes as otherwise-made than ourselves, not entirely human; in this case it might be better to say that because they seemed so unlike us—more like wonderful, talking animals—I was able to lie to them, by omission, when they took turns holding my mother and me in their pillowed arms. Even if I thought I would have to tell her, the next time our eyes met, everything I knew about my father and his continuing, fugitive existence, I had no such compunction with these astronauts. Neither dishonesty nor honesty had any place in my thoughts for them, because they seemed as distant from these concerns as cats or dogs.

Only once, during that first meeting, do I recall feeling for the Apollo crew anything like sympathy—and, even then, it was a sympathy hopelessly muted by awe and condescension. For when we were all drawn silently around our drinks, the astronauts bowed on the furniture, my mother at last broached the topic that so weighed on her mind:

"I suppose you've come to tell us what happened up there"—words murmured so deferentially they were barely spoken aloud but, despite their gentleness, which caused the astronauts each, one by one, to take hold of the question like a bit between his teeth. I watched Cud avert his face, heard their sad monologues—eulogies more than explanations— and remember feeling ashamed of my mother and myself, gazing at those gray and stubbly faces sealed in glass; ashamed to ask such a thing, whose answer, like the very circumstances of my father's disappearance, seemed beyond their control.

Afterward, when everyone had drawn together in the kitchen to gaze at the awakened patriots gaping up in the courtyard, Barbara waved down to indicate that it was all right.

"Have they found him?" Lyle called up, his words spreading through the crowd. "They've got him—they found him—" bubbled back excitedly until Buzz put his face out the window. "He just disappeared," he said, voice hoarse with emotion as he repeated the story he'd told us a moment before: "It was a routine rock-collecting mission, entirely within visual range, everything according to blueprint. I was watching Jerry from the command module, and mission control radioed to ask if I'd have a look at some data coming in on the monitors. There'd been a sensor failure, and we needed an OK. . . . I was watching him. . . . I just turned to confirm our coordinates. I just looked—"

Mr. Armstrong—tall and somber, meditative where others were likely to be carried away—stepped in and restrained him. His voice, terse as his words, humbled the crowd. "Jerry Finch was an eagle and a teacher. He saw farther, and flew further than our eyes could follow, and if he has now truly soared forever into the heavens, we will always remember him as a great, proud man."

Leaving off, Neil went to lie on the sofa while the others ambled distractedly around the rooms, eventually, as the morning drew on, slipping into the halls and elevators, sulking among the knots of reporters standing vigil in the magnolias. People in the court gave them lawn chairs in which to rest, but the large, bulkily padded men became tangled and fell slowly in the terrestrial furniture. They complained of terrible, unquenchable thirst, and were given lemonade and straws to drink through.

And I imagine it was around this time down below, during some frail moment of consolation, that the idea got started of throwing a potluck dinner in the court that night, in honor of the Apollo men.

FIFTEEN

Two Calls

Barbara was still vacuuming up the layer of lunar dust deposited on our counters and tabletops when the phone rang, and Mrs. Fitzpatrick's voice quavered into our lives once again. "I was just coming back from the K, with some chocolates for Angie," Doris explained, artlessly but no less effectively than if she'd brought a heavy shoe down on my mother's head, "and I heard Mr. Armstrong saying all those sad things to everyone about Jerry."

Barbara gazed through the window at the astronauts, lying in the midday sun beneath umbrellas or bushes. There was a great deal of activity going on, people running here and there, a space for the potluck being cleared of tents in the center of the court. She pressed a hand to her brow, where she felt the premonition of a headache; a sense that, rather than bringing things to a close, the return of the astronauts had only inaugurated a new chapter. Doris's voice brought her back.

"I haven't seen you in a few days now, at the K—"

"I've been taking some time to be with my family—"

"Oh, of course," Doris agreed and, after a barely perceptible hesitation, went on, "Barbara—I think of him like my own family. Not a day passes we don't say a prayer for his return."

My mother reflected on how near she'd come to forgetting Doris, who seemed prepared to accept any role for herself in the turmoil of events—even no role at all. It was this pliant, selfless quality that had allowed Barbara to push Mrs. Fitzpatrick from her mind but that was also, she found, unfathomable and therefore somewhat frightening. Had the woman no sense of indignation? No spark of outrage? Her daughter was pregnant with Jerry's child, for Christ's sake, and she had as much rancor as a puppy.

"I think," Barbara said, "that I and my family would just like to put the last few weeks behind us, get on with our lives—" to which there was an appreciative silence. She felt it incumbent upon herself to add, "And how is your daughter—progressing?"

"Thank you Mrs. Finch—Barbara—" Doris amended. "I know you probably think all kinds of things about her, you know, after the accident, but she really is a good girl—she just wants him to come back soon."

"I'll take your word," Barbara said, unpacking the thick cotton of euphemisms, unable to help herself from suggesting, "I'm sure she does just as she's told," though the irony had no perceptible effect.

Usually such a lack of response would have infuriated my mother, capable of entertaining herself in even the bitterest circumstances provided she had a small audience of intelligence. What was different, however, on this occasion, was the sense she had—a grim, dawning awareness like the onrush of fever—that Mrs. Fitzpatrick's indifference was only a rubbery crystallization of everything else that surrounded us. It was as if no genuine feelings were allowed my family, because they all ran into the gummed walls of other people's ludicrous dreams.

"I hope he's not lonely now, wherever he is," Mrs. Fitzpatrick offered, and Barbara, unsure whether Doris thought my father still living, or whether she was referring to some platitudinous afterlife, said, "I'm sure his thoughts are with us."

"I'm sure of that, dear. Why, I'm sure he's looking down at the world right now, all blue and green—they say it's very beautiful from there, you know. Only, you wish they didn't have to leave him, don't you? You wish someone could have stayed, or"—she fretted a moment—"left him something. Do you think they left him anything?"

"What do you mean? Like a book?" Barbara asked, finding herself imagining which book her husband would have wanted—it would have to have been ornithological.

"Or a telescope," Doris said. "I hope he's watching us. He loves you so much, and Georgie." She faltered, unable to go on.

Barbara listened to this unreasoning, superfluous kindness, so out of place coming from Mrs. Fitzpatrick it appeared mad; she wondered why it was here, greeting her at the end of a long chain of cruelties. And she felt some new feeling stir inside her.

Perhaps this feeling started with a rare moment of self-pity, but it quickly snowballed; because my mother, herself certainly the least to suspect it, found herself moved—grudgingly at first, and then with a deep resignation, as something welled up that was an alchemy of regret for herself and my father, where the feel of his hand and his childish desire to touch distant things like birds, the moon, particular stars, suddenly rushed in, full of life. It was all worse for being told by this woman who seemed to cling to the same inane hopes as Lyle—as everyone else in the deranged world outside her window—yet whose words at this moment exercised her in the same way we're swept up by the soundtracks of shamelessly sentimental movies; worse still, that much harder to contain because she was angry with her husband.

Mrs. Fitzpatrick was left to interpret the long silence on the phone as best she could. "You think I'm crazy," she said. "Oh dear."

And Barbara, staring out the window, confessed, "Yes, yes—completely—" feeling nearly happy as she added, "Doris, I'm coming over."

Hanging up the phone, she stood for a while, looking down into the court. They were bringing picnic tables out, these terrible people for whom everything was an entertainment. Someone, noticing her up there, began to wave.

*   *

*   *   *

*   *

When the phone rang a minute later, as my mother's footsteps receded down the hall toward the elevators, I thought it was Mrs. Fitzpatrick again, calling to say that *she* would come by, that there was no reason for Barbara to disturb herself; but instead, as I lifted the receiver, waiting for these red, candied words, I heard that voice that I loved, tearing apart the world:

Georgie, my father said. *When I bring you here one day to look at every-*

*thing, to look down with me on the earth, golden with atmosphere, my progress will
be like a map of the moon, with all its obscure geographies as essential to each other
as the organs of the human body.*

*The moon is an organism, I think sometimes—but one without life. It is an
ecology of solitude, where everything lies in relation to the world mounting on the
horizon. I've known such places before—such lonely stations. I've known them in a
distant, refracted form, when I used to call home from roadside pay phones in
Pennsylvania or Michigan, a map clutched in my hand, near the exit for some wet-
lands. It is a comfort to me that those grassy fields, those lifting clouds of finches, might
have, even just in memory, some taint of this land, because then, perhaps, the opposite, too, might be true. And when, one day, I show you this place; when we unfold
together this great, silent map, we'll follow, you and I, my footsteps in all of their
necessity. A kind of necessity exists in our wildest dreams—if you will believe that—*

His voice tipped back into noise, and for a moment I thought I'd lost
him, but then our connection welled up again with a start:

*Damn it—Georgie, I'm sorry—but will someone please get that jackass
Barnes out of there.*

I glanced outside and discovered Lyle placing a Red Cross blanket
over the back of one of the astronauts. I was coming to understand the
term "public figure," booted around so loosely, in this large man whose
gestures were always performed so they might be viewed and judged
accurately from outer space.

*I apologize if I startled you. It's just that people might leave otherwise. They
might just pack up and go back to their lives, and then we could all—*he fell silent,
newly distracted—*Why blankets in the summer? What does he want, anyway?
He's just making things worse—*

"He's running for district representative," I said, "with you," producing a long silence in which there was little to do but follow the
unwanted politician on his rounds. We watched tablecloths hump and
settle, people busily firing up their grills and heating pads, preparing
those beige and brown foods so popular at cookouts.

As I looked, I saw Lyle pause, glance around, and catch sight of Bob
Nightly loitering nearby, hands occupied as always, when not clamped
around a pretzel or some other greasy food, in scribbling notes in his
maniacally small hand. The pair had scented each other.

It was as when, in the public lavatories of this melting pot of ours, a jackbooted logger and an environmentalist step up simultaneously to the same urinal bank, side by side, and are both confounded in their efforts to micturate by the proximity of their natural foes: though neither man would, literally speaking, devour the other, they are in fact both competing for the same precious resource—feeding off the teat of the same big timber, or big government, or big spotted owl, or what have you—and so have entered a primitive state of fight or flight, hackles rising, urethras contracting. So it was with these men.

If you feel yourself rise up against Mr. Nightly; if you—like myself—want to strike him at times, long to maul Mr. Nightly as the logger longs to maul his urinary companion, believing that no good could ever come from him, please, hold your readied hand. Don't be like so many children or lovers or friends of great and small men alike who carry on secondhand political or sporting quarrels through loyalty alone, until the field is a dog run of anachronistic armies unleashed by private wars. Mr. Nightly had done us no harm yet and, even with hindsight, we can see that he is a man more to be pitied than condemned.

None of which was really on my mind at the moment, though, because something else, probably obvious to you, had occurred to me in the substance of my father's outburst.

"Then you *are* watching us," I said, searching for a ghostly sliver of moon in the sky.

Through a thicket of astral noise his voice emerged: *I'm going to write a book about us one day, Georgie. About you, and me.*

"Will Mom be in the book, too?" I asked.

Of course.

"Who else will be in the book?"

Everyone—everyone, Georgie.

Lulled by the burn of space, I imagined this book, like a map of the moon, no doubt, filled with that necessity he'd spoken of. Below, Mr. Nightly reached into his back pocket and peeled out bills to give to one of the recumbent astronauts. He placed the money in the gleaming and gloved hand.

"What kind of book will it be?" I asked.

The kind of book you might have written, he said. *It will be your book.*

I watched the teeming, multicolored crowd of men and women, dazed and baffled by the rays of the sun, waiting for dark to come so they could turn their telescopes to the new crescent in the sky and hunt for their hero. Here and there they clustered around the astronauts, reading to them, introducing their children to these fallen warriors.

One of the Apollo men—the one to which Bob had given the money—stumbled back after visiting a nearby bodega, a grocery bag in his billowy arm. He handed Bob a packet of snacks, then reached inside the bag again and withdrew two cans of beer and a straw for himself. Bob broke into the snacks, and they stood together, man and astronaut, as Bob licked his fingers and, realizing the plight of his fellow, took the straw out of its wrapper and handed it to the silvery mitt.

When my father spoke again, his voice had fallen to nearly a whisper:

There are men, Georgie, who have failed in everything they set their minds to. Your mother thinks of me as such a man, but that's neither here nor there. The great danger for men such as these—and I think Bob Nightly is among their numbers— is that, failing the fertility of their own modest offerings to the world, they grow cynical of all offerings.

Such men will perpetuate a circus for the sake of circus alone, and if they cannot star well in their fellow man's destiny, star ill.

I believe at times, he said, static moving in—a great arching wave, perhaps the ripple through space of a distant and dying sun—*that Mr. Nightly will become my dark star on earth.*

His voice faded, was almost gone.

"Will Mr. Nightly," I asked, "be in my book?"

Yes, Georgie—his voice dissolving—*I'm afraid there's no other way.*

SIXTEEN

Unlikely Allies

That's how his voice always arrived to me—tearing apart the world—although I've heard it said that such is the way with the voices of great men or women: in them, we hear ourselves, but as if they are more ourselves than we, and we their faint echo.

It was of this—or some distant corollary thereof—that Doris Fitzpatrick was thinking, Neil Armstrong's words ringing in her head, seeming to float—to fly there, even—drawing her up with him on a great current of humanity, beneath which the promontories and valleys of our aspirations and sufferings assumed an almost pastoral repose. And more: he seemed to say that our very place is among the clouds, or perhaps even in that sky of skies, among the stars. She gazed up, wondering that we didn't all follow him, didn't quit our jobs, lay down our earthly possessions, spread our long-neglected wings, and . . .

And then she smiled to herself.

She was up to her elbows in chicken, a sweet cold working into her wrists; but there was everyone down at the potluck in the court tonight, and from all Doris knew astronauts sounded like big eaters.

The morning had kind of gotten away. She hoped Barbara was taking her time coming over, because she had to finish cleaning everything for the marinade, and Angie had been no help whatsoever, spending her early hours in the bedroom on another one of her crying jags. When she'd given her the chocolates, the girl just up and ran out. It was sad, Doris reflected, stretching out a wing from the eviscerated bird until she

saw—my God—this one had a four-foot wingspan. All this business—
that poor man.

The knock at the door, as always, came too soon. She shouted for
Barbara to let herself in, and then directed her to the kitchen, calling, "I
had a wonderful dream last night. I've been dying to tell you all morning."

Barbara's face appeared in the doorway, wrapped in shawl and sunglasses.

"I was at a cookout—like this thing tonight, you know. Me and you
were talking to Lyle, and eating shrimp cocktail."

"Oh?" my mother said, removing her sunglasses and sitting down at
the kitchen table.

"They were the kind you have to peel. I don't even remember what
we were talking about, but you noticed after a bit one of the shrimp was
tough peeling, you know—"

Barbara indicated that she did.

"And then I looked and saw it wasn't a shrimp at all. It was a little
astronaut. You had his helmet half off. There were a bunch of them
mixed in."

"Had I eaten one already?" she asked.

"That's what I wanted to ask you, but I woke up, you see— Would
you mind getting the fridge?"

Barbara came over and held the door while Doris jostled the bowl
inside. Staring into the large, mostly empty refrigerator, she recalled that
Doris had had several children, who'd grown up and gone away; that
she'd been married once. The fridge was undoubtedly a relic of that more
capacious life.

And right then, Barbara decided that she liked Doris. She'd wanted
to, as soon as she'd hung up the phone and put her jacket on; but it was
looking inside the emptiness of the woman's refrigerator that made
the difference. It was a peculiarity of my mother's that she could vacil-
late between extremes of opinion about a person, based entirely on
minute impressions of kinship; and while she still would have charac-
terized Doris as a harebrain, she thought of many people she liked in
this way. The markers, she'd realized long ago, which indicate our feelings for people have more to do with reaching for the same spaghetti

sauce in a supermarket aisle than with our actual opinions about one another.

"How's your daughter?"

"Oh, she had a fit and went out."

Not relishing the thought of meeting her here, after an already trying day, Barbara was relieved the girl was gone.

"Was it because of me?" she asked.

"Don't bother yourself," Doris said, waving her hands as she hurried about, putting things in the dishwasher. "She's just upset about them coming back from the moon without Jerry."

"Georgie doesn't even realize," my mother confided. "I don't think he knows what this means. Instead, he's made up this fantasy where his father calls on the phone to talk to him while I'm at work."

"How wonderful—I didn't know they had telephones on the moon."

"They do not."

"Well, I'm sure it's more fun than the tantrums . . . it's all so dramatic." Doris sighed as Barbara tried in vain to imagine how it could be otherwise. "But I guess I shouldn't be so hard on her. I suppose she's no worse than the other kids these days—they just don't appreciate things.

"Why, it's like when she first told me about herself and Jerry—she couldn't believe I was surprised. 'Surprised?' I said, thinking that was pretty rich. And she said, 'You think I'm not good enough, don't you?'— as if it was anything to get some ape to jump on top of her—no slur on your husband, of course."

Doris went over to the stove and poured hot water for both of them from a kettle. Barbara observed that the kitchen here was identical to her own, but that the glacial passage of three children through these walls had scraped the finish off the orange and brown appliances, the gold-flecked Formica counters. "They think they know better than you," Mrs. Fitzpatrick said. "They think they just understand everything about everything—including yourself.

"She has no idea how lucky she is," the woman added sadly, again momentarily alarming my mother, who watched Doris slowly lift a cup of tea—her cracked, full lips recoiling almost imperceptibly from the heat. "She thinks this was just coming down the pike."

"Does she still think Jerry's alive?" Barbara ventured after a moment.

"Of course." Doris waved. "I mean, if he wasn't, that changes everything, doesn't it?"

"To be honest with you," Barbara said, "I don't entertain any such hopes."

She wasn't surprised when Mrs. Fitzpatrick extended one of her large, pink paws across the table. "Barbara—it's important—" Doris began, but my mother wasn't having any of it.

"No," she replied, gripping Doris's hand. "It's important to be realistic. I'm not doing myself any favors by clinging to some idiotic belief Jerry has sustained himself up there for a week and a half on ten hours of oxygen. I just wish everyone would wake up to that."

There was a moment of silence in which Barbara realized she was still holding her new friend's hand, and released it. Doris, however, as if enlivened by that touch, pressed a bit closer across the table. The buzz of an electric clock both excited and warned against intimacy. "What do you think of Lyle Barnes?" she asked suddenly, her eye twinkling.

"Lyle? Lyle's fine—that's the way he always is," Barbara said, thinking the woman was perhaps, like Kitty, concerned about his morals or sanity.

"I think he's sweet on you," Doris whispered, pursing her lips.

My mother flushed. Hadn't they just been discussing her husband, likely a dead man? Still, she found that, exactly because Doris was so much of a harebrain, it was difficult to take offense. "He's just *like* that— it has nothing to do with me."

"Maybe so, but I think he's a highroller," Doris admitted, reaching for her tea again.

"If you mean he's the sort to hang fuzzy dice from his rearview"— Barbara laughed—"then I think you have him nicely." She wondered afterward if this wouldn't describe Doris, too.

*   *

*   *   *

*   *

Had we asked, I'm confident Angie would have entirely agreed with my mother's assessments of both Lyle and her own mother—for in ways she was a lot like Barbara Finch; though had we posed *that* conviction to the girl, or had someone, for instance, asked why she didn't drop by our house anymore, Angie would likely have acted as she did that afternoon with Bob Nightly—suddenly turning a pair of scorching blue eyes upon the unfortunate journalist, her voice becoming quiet and hard, with just a hint of invitation:

"Look," she'd explained, taking a long drag off her cigarette, "I like you, Bob, so I'm going to give you a friendly tip about your friend Mrs. Finch: the woman's a dried-up prig"—crossing her arms over her chest—"Though I guess," she went on, noticing Mr. Nightly was paying more attention to his fountain pen, "it's not like anyone really *is* asking, are they?"

It was true that hers was an unpopular sentiment in Magnolia Court, and Angie preferred, understandably, to spend her off-hours away from both Doris and my mother; which meant, given the limited scope of our world, she could usually be found in the rear parking lot, where the Winnebagos and the more recent arrivals had set up camp. Once Angie was there, Doris couldn't monitor her from the apartment window, and among these people she could smoke and enjoy, undiminished, the celebrity of her acquaintance with the Finch family.

Bob, perhaps not unrelatedly, was also frequently discovered in the parking lot these days. The journalist, notebook in hand, had buttonholed the girl in the shade of an Airstream, and she was ribbing him, without caring particularly, about the transparency of his conversational motives: "Didn't mean to sidetrack you from your research."

"No—not at all," Bob replied with a grin, donning his glasses. "You're just lucky that Barnes character keeps hanging around. If he'd step outside that apartment for more than five minutes, the leech, I'd go there myself and ask my questions."

He flipped through the small spiral binder scratched full of microscopic script. "You *wrote* all that?" she said of the words he rapidly shielded from sight. "Bob, you're such a geek."

"Oh, but remember—you thought Jerry Finch was a geek, too," he reminded her, scribbling.

"He was—you both were. But you still *are*," she said, crouching by the wheel well and picking a stick up off the ground. "Though at least you're not doing that Vietnam trip anymore. You know, when you'd come to class, all dressed in your uniform—"

"All right . . . I admit, it was obsessive."

Angie rifled through an anthill with her probe. She smiled to herself, recalling the days when Bob Nightly—Mr. Nightly—had been one of her middle school teachers, before she departed for the larger, more worldly Ernest B. Crawford High. He'd never seemed like a happy man—no, never happy—but with a peculiar intensity, even then, which prevented people from treating him as the unhappy are generally treated behind those pimply walls. There was something in his demeanor that warned against ridicule.

It was, of course, the Vietnam thing—she and her fellow students imagined that Nightly's intensity arose from years spent in the jungle, killing, endlessly killing as he trampled through rank and steaming underbrush. She'd witnessed the way he lit up whenever anyone questioned his fascination with the war—a topic not generally taught concurrently with History 105, *The Cradle of Our Nation.*

"Of course it's relevant," she could still hear him barking at Mary Magdaniels, pressing his droopy mustache to his face as he paced the room in a pair of fatigues resembling ladies' bloomers. The girl had, perhaps unwisely, questioned the persistence of the Vietnam theme during the sixteenth and seventeenth centuries. "The Vietnam War is *the* American drama of the twentieth century—but it's no less a lens through which to see all our nation's historical desires, our most debased and glorious longings; it offers to the voyeur of history more of a window into American consciousness than even the Civil War, let alone World War II." He waved his hand as if this last conflagration was little more than an intramural softball game.

"Mr. Nightly," Oliver Baskerville called out, "Mr. Nightly. Mr. Finch said that the *Apollo moon landing* was the American drama of the twentieth century. Do you have any comment on that, sir?"

Oliver was a boy whose place in the front rows of classrooms was a sort of hommage to professors everywhere, and his question was meant only to elicit the sound of his master's voice, no more. But the shriek of unfurling vinyl as Bob yanked down the map of the Mekong Delta left total silence in its wake.

"Baskerville," Mr. Nightly said quietly, pressing his glasses to his face so his eyes swam among greasy fingerprints. "Was that Jerry Finch you said? Our own Jeremiah Finch? Mr. Finch, the *earth* science teacher"— he emphasized, bringing his hand down with a slap on a pupil's desk— "who likely believes the earth is a satellite of the *moon*?"

He raised his eyes to the heavens. Oliver coughed weakly. "Point taken, sir."

"Angeline Fitzpatrick," Nightly called suddenly to the blond girl at the back of the room, her eyes dawdling out the window. "You have homeroom with Jerry, no? Care to offer any of your homeroom-spun wisdom?"

"What?" she said, dragging herself from some fantastic, romantic embrace.

"What is your opinion, Ms. Fitzpatrick, about the state of Mr. Finch's sanity?"

"Well—I think he's not getting laid often enough, Mr. Nightly," the girl suggested to the class's delight. "You can tell, you know, from the way he rubs his hands together when he talks."

Looking back now, Angie longed to believe that the girl who'd spoken those words was someone other than herself. She was sure Bob had his regrets—they'd both been so shallow—and she wondered if the teacher cum journalist was perhaps, at the moment, dwelling on similar failings. It was, she reassured herself, only the Vietnam thing that made her want to talk that way—about Jerry, of all people—to Mr. Nightly; made Bob seem, at the time, despite all the mantlings of authority, like a mad dog you could tease because it was chained up behind the fence of academia. Only recently had she discovered, through some casual remark he let fall, that Nightly's military career had been spent as an army corps news correspondent, generally more behind desks than behind enemy lines. She looked over at him, where he leaned against the aluminum vehicle, still scribbling in his tiny, manic hand.

"You're making that clippity-clappity sound," Bob said, glancing up, "that you make whenever you've hitched yourself to an idea."

"I was just thinking of Jerry. I mean—what is it, do you think, about astronauts?"

"What is what?" he asked, scribbling to a halt.

"You know—is it the danger? The adventure? What makes them so different from . . . well . . . like, middle school teachers?"

Nightly knocked his pen against his notepad. "I've thought about this myself," he admitted, suddenly earnest—and it is something amazing about astronauts, this earnestness they bring out in the most ironic souls. "No, really," he added, as if sensing her mistrust. "It seems to me there are few men in this world like the astronaut, who've simply done as they pleased, from when they were children with the simple desire to walk in the stars. Astronauts have never had to give up such things, you see. They've never had to lay aside their toys. With everyone else, we've had our first dreams broken, and all we can do now is look at them from the outside. But your astronauts, I suppose, will never know that feeling. They are always *inside* the dream."

She looked at him doubtfully, and then a smile spread across her face. "Sort of like Lyle, huh? You know, with *you* always on the *outside.*"

"That's right," he growled, "trample on my sincerity." Though in fact he wasn't angry. Lyle was a sort of pet topic for them.

"His head's so far up his ass you can see hair behind his molars."

"He's a force for blindness in the world," Bob agreed, humor creeping back into his voice.

"He's a whole ass farm," she suggested.

"No doubt, the man's a rural type," he acquiesced, picturing that calm, cheerful face with a shudder. "It's the smugness that gets me . . ."

The two were silent a moment, each cherishing her or his own hated Lyle Barnes.

"You know what?" Angie asked after a suitable pause.

Bob's face bespoke his question.

"I think Lyle's a cop," she whispered.

The journalist laughed. He took out his pipe and tamped it out before fumbling in his pockets for a pinch of tobacco.

"Or if he's not a cop, he's working for the cops," Angie persisted as

he continued chuckling. "Oh, you know what? Fuck you, you little baboon," she added, half-smiling, grinding out her cigarette.

When Bob's chuckle had receded to a dry cough, he said, "What on earth put that idea in your noodle?"

Lighting another cigarette, she stared at him, as if to determine whether he was a worthy confidant.

"Early in the morning," she said slowly, "on that same day he showed up at Jerry's, in the rain, I'd gone to the police station—the radio'd been stolen from my mom's car—and I remember noticing this guy—Barnes—walking up the steps to the station."

She glanced at Bob to see if he was listening and, although he wasn't writing anything down, he seemed to be paying her more than half of his attention, so she went on.

"He was going in while I was going out and, though I'd never seen him before, I remember thinking, Now that's a worried man. But the point is, what was he *doing* there on his first day in town? Is that the first place you'd go in a new town?" She shook her head at the memory. "When he showed up at Jerry's around lunchtime, it creeped me out. I mean, do you think he's FBI?" she asked, with a teenager's native loathing for and fascination with all forms of secret service. "Is he with intelligence?"

"More like counterintelligence," Bob said, reloading his pipe. It wasn't his way to let someone know when a tip was a tip, but he had to admit, he was interested. He even found he liked the man a bit better, now he might have some sides to him.

"He has out-of-town plates." The journalist shrugged, stroking his mustache with ink-stained fingers. "Cops probably gave him a speeding ticket. They need donations, I'm told, for the new Little League stadium. And who knows—maybe the poor man had *his* radio stolen.

"But say," he murmured, looking at his watch, "I don't mean to change the subject, but what are you bringing to this cookout thing? Because I'm not much of a cook myself, and even as we speak I suspect your mother's poring over the *Ladies' Home Journal*"—which was true, or at least very nearly so, although the other part, the first part, about the stadium, wasn't, in fact, what he believed at all: Bob Nightly believed in conspiracies.

SEVENTEEN

Looking Glass

We've been invited," Barbara said that evening, "to have dinner tonight with Mrs. Fitzpatrick—Doris—at the cookout."

I watched her fiddle with a stack of letters on the stand by the door, jangle her keys, and tap her foot; but I saw she was pleased. She was trying not to seem too pleased. "I don't know—what do you think? I mean, we *should* go, shouldn't we?"

She'd come home a few minutes before, turned off the television, and opened the curtains. Orange light, reflected off the opposite face of the asterisk, fell dull and slanted into the room, and for a moment she just stood, staring at my father's dilapidated chair, the gentle dapple of time and wear on the beige, wall-to-wall carpet, the glint of a silver picture frame on a bookshelf. Without waiting for an answer, she vanished into the bedroom, emerging a few minutes later in a short dress decorated with brown and yellow lozenges. She found me in the kitchen, my hand around the Jerry Finch that was posed like a tiny angel on the windowsill, gazing down at the maze of tables near the center of which Doris grappled with the grill of a barbecue.

"Well, come on then," Barbara said. "Put something on your feet."

I looked at her, then back to the swarming vignette of old and young, anchored periodically in its turbulence by great-bellied men in baseball hats stoking fires, calling hoarsely to one another. Smoke swirled and hissed beneath their hands, each master of the grill accompanied by some smaller apprentice, or by a woman, hand braced painfully to her back or

side, cigarette at the ready, bestowing a hawkish glance now and then on the badminton net near the front gate, at which terrifying and animal-headed children played.

"Well, come on," she coaxed. "You can't just stay up here all day."

It was only a few hours ago I'd gotten off the phone with my father and, as was always the case when we spoke, the world I'd returned to was a strange and unaccountable place. I gazed at it with fresh eyes—my father's, to be exact—finding it difficult not to hear the echo of his concerns and frustrations with Lyle and Nightly, with the presence of all these people in our backyard, whenever I turned my eye to them, as *he* no doubt was doing, from so much higher above.

If I must parse for you my feelings upon emerging as we did a few minutes later into that thick smell of meat and fire where voices cackled and rattled, I would say they were made up of two separate fears. The first I'd tasted weeks ago, on the day of the moon landing, when it seemed I must dissolve in this solution of sweaty hands and smiling eyes, just as surely as my name, through repetition, had dissolved into meaninglessness in the mouth of the crowd.

There was within me now, however, a new and contradictory fear—call it a presentiment—that, far from threatening personal dissolution, this mad world was merely a reflected and refracted version of myself. I was perhaps young for such self-conscious solipsism, but the idea of the book proposed by my father had lodged in my mind, and I couldn't help but see each of these people gathered around my home as a character, some purposeful creation of my anxieties. After all, wasn't the wildness surrounding me exactly a world in which childhood fears and passions had been allowed to assume adult proportions? Wasn't it that terrifying moment, experienced by so many impressionable children at the circus, when the interior world of heightened sensation becomes incarnate, lurching up with the force of a clown head on a spring?

As we made our way to Mrs. Fitzpatrick's table—a feat of diplomacy in itself—I asked in a low voice: "Why are they all like this?"

"Who?" Barbara asked. "Like what?"

"Why," I said, retiring before the fourth or fifth offering of candied apples, "why are they all like cartoons?"

She glanced down at me with mingled amusement and satisfaction. "That's the way it always is, at first," she said quietly, perhaps thinking of Doris. "People are cartoons when you meet them. Then, after a while, they're just not—or you don't notice anymore—I'm not sure it matters. After all," she teased, "you were one once, too. And who knows, maybe you still are."

The problem certainly didn't seem to preoccupy anyone else. Instead, I was coming to realize that for these frightening but in fact perfectly ordinary people around me, who'd never met an astronaut before, this evening would prove abundant beyond their wildest dreams. For even if it was love and loyalty alone for my father that compelled the astronauts to continue wearing their suits, it was obvious that most people, particularly the children, were simply delighted by the chance to see spacemen *in costume*. There was already a crowd three and four deep around Buzz Aldrin, Cud Wilson, and Gary Sprine, who'd seated themselves together with Angie, Bob, and the incumbent district representative, David Cabot, and his platinum-headed wife, Charlene. The press, at the request of Lyle and the Magnolia Court security, had withdrawn for the evening, and the resulting respite, together with a bit of rest on solid ground, had calmed the Apollo men considerably since morning.

One question, however, while repeated only every now and again, well meaningly, and in the way all questions are posed to celebrity—that is, personally, and as if for the first time—threw upon each astronaut in turn a harrowed light:

"What happened up there?"—a question probably meant to let each man tell *his* story; a question that no doubt weighed most upon Buzz and Neil but that, to each of them, whether at mission control during those terrible days and nights, or upon the very fields of the moon, searching among the shadows for the shadow of a man, became, through the convolutions of troubled minds, What might *I* have done differently? A question to which, possibly for the first time in the lives of these young men, there was no satisfying answer.

Perhaps thirty picnic benches were fanned around these astronauts and our neighboring table, where Neil and Flek Davis had sat down together with Doris, Lyle, my mother, and me, introducing themselves again and asking if we minded their company. Mrs. Fitzpatrick placed her hand in the ruffles of her red blouse, watching with patriotic reverence as the men tried to accommodate themselves to the furniture we offered.

"I hope we haven't already spoiled our welcome, Mrs. Finch," Neil said. "We must have been a real trial to you this morning, after everything . . ."

Barbara brushed the thought aside. The arrival of the astronauts in the wee hours seemed a distant moment in which no one had been thinking clearly—she hoped they felt the same way.

Meanwhile, Kitty, Tom, Fauna, and Fauna's little brother, Baker, had dragged their table up next door. The Shanks were, I'm sure, there only out of consideration for Barbara, but even Kitty greeted the politician good-naturedly. While they were all arranging themselves, she got my mother's attention and gestured quietly across the table to her husband. "Tom gave me quite a tongue-lashing," she whispered, "when I told him what I said to you this morning."

The man in a pale green sweater who smiled at both of them hardly seemed capable of disturbing a cricket, but Barbara still protested, "Now shame on you, Tom—if it was anyone's fault it was my own," even as Kitty dismissed the possibility. "It's beside the point is what I mean. You being oppressed by your troubles, and me getting you all worked up—I owe you an apology," she said firmly; though that idea seemed only doubly oppressive. There were too many people apologizing, Barbara felt, given what they did and didn't know.

An uncomfortable silence followed at our table, in which even Fauna participated. The girl had obviously been dressed against her will for this occasion, and her eyes caught at mine, directing my attention to the elaborate collar and long sleeves of her dress, more suited to a church function than to a barbecue. Cautiously, as if we were wartime spies relaying secret code across a crowded room, I raised the Jerry Finch above the edge of the table; and while she seemed to take little notice, immediately looking away, a quiet absorption came over her, and our silence at once became conspiratorial.

When Lyle finally cleared his throat, announcing, "It's a beautiful night," the statement seemed so incongruous we were taken aback. After a moment, however, Kitty conceded that things could look a whole lot worse—which was true.

The magnolia leaves shimmered in the dusk. Jalapeño-shaped Christmas lights twinkled over the gates to the visitors' parking lot, and distant music from disparate locations melded into a single sound, spangled with recurrent glints of laughter. Despite a further tense moment in which Angie refused to join her mother at our table—pointing out, rightly enough, that there was no room—it was very much the sort of utopia Lyle dreamed of, and liked to believe existed, in Magnolia Court. And I admit that, for a brief time that evening, I, too, saw something of what this world meant to him. The Sterns, Dave Moscowitz, the Barnstables—people I'd met only once or twice, those I'd offered cookies to one distant rainy night—gave me kind glances and winks of encouragement. Watching a little girl kiss the visor of an astronaut, turning from side to side to take in the welter of faces, I felt perhaps I'd overreacted when I first arrived. The voice of this multitude, only a moment before so terrifying, seemed velvety now, something that melted into the breezy temperament of the night; the only blemish in these contemplations occurring when my attention was drawn to Bob Nightly, laughing behind me like a seal. I watched him as he drew a handkerchief from his pocket, dabbing his eyes while addressing himself to Cud and Sprine:

"It is a wild and forbidding place, I'm sure," he said, tipping his head back to stare at the moon's first, faint impression. "A battleground of sorts. And I know your terror, Cud—believe me, and forgive my laughter. Perhaps you think I have no familiarity with such things, but I've seen the moon cast its glamour upon men so they run howling through the jungle." Laying aside his pipe and glancing around with a calculated carelessness, he asked, "Are you boys, perhaps, familiar with the Nam?"

The men nodded their helmets. They were exhausted and bewildered by the events of the last week, and though Neil had convinced them that the best thing would be to spend time among ordinary people, I'm not sure that Bob Nightly was precisely the sort of person Armstrong had in mind. Fortunately, they were rescued from any impending lecture by the flight commander himself, rising and tapping on his glass with a spoon. A hush fell, and the great man began to speak:

"Good people of Ashtrakan," he said, voice echoing in the enclosure of the court. "I'm sure you're all hungry, and I realize that this has been a trying day for each of us. I just want to remind everyone of why we're here, gathered together tonight, on this earth.

"It's a rare treat for myself and my fellow astronauts to spend time among folk like you, and we're grateful for the hospitality you've shown. I'd like to apologize again to everyone—Mrs. Finch, to you especially—for our behavior this morning. We were distraught at the loss of our companion, and acted without professionalism.

"But more to the point, I think all of us—you and I—feel an identical and keen distress tonight, and I believe that if we have any hope of saving Jerry Finch—husband, father, astronaut, friend—we must act decisively. We mustn't be quiet about our love, or allow complacency to dampen our voices. The clock is ticking, and I admit," he said, turning his entire body from side to side to catch everyone's eye, "that I'm afraid for him. We need a new launch, good people, before it's too late."

There was a long surge of applause, and he waved several times, settling back into his chair. Lyle wiped his eyes, and Barbara reached out a hand and thanked the astronaut; but there was also, had anyone delved deeper, an undercurrent.

Certainly, it wasn't to be found in the face of Mr. Armstrong, a man of few currents, regarding us all with the smile of heartbreak and necessity we each recognized from our own finest hours—eyes sharp, brow compressed beneath mountainous thoughts and reciprocated gratitude—but I realized, despite the brief unity I'd felt with the crowd a moment before, that I'd immediately tuned my attention to this subterranean fault. Was there not something tentative in the way Representative Cabot met the astronaut's gaze with his own? Was this very gathering not, by my father's own lights, the seed of disaster, or at least of pointless delay—even if sown by the most loving hand?

There *had* been, I thought, a nearly insignificant pause, a moment of reflection, before the applause began. Bob Nightly glanced down at his plate, self-consciously stroking his mustaches. Kitty exchanged rapid glances with her husband. And as Barbara reached out her hand to the astronaut, I saw the confusion in the gesture—the desire to show gratitude warring with a nearly equal urge to scream out that this was insanity, a festival of denial. I waited, tense with the possibility that this current, so close to the surface, would suddenly announce itself—I'm sure if Barbara had said anything, Kitty was prepared to ask some difficult questions but, failing such a sign, Mrs. Shank held her peace and allowed herself only, "Pretty words, Mr. Armstrong," to which the astronaut bowed.

I chose this moment to attract Fauna's attention, kicking her lightly under the table; miscalculating, however, I instead struck Flek in the shin and looked down hurriedly into my plate, pretending to be immersed in the intricacies of potato salad and Frito pie.

My mother, meanwhile, eyes glazing with frustration, had withdrawn from the proceedings. I imagine she saw no hope at this time in contradicting Neil about the need for continued missions to the moon, and for a moment, amidst all these people, she'd slipped into loneliness again, glancing away across the court when she heard Lyle say, "True words, Mr. Armstrong—truer words were never said."

Up until this point, Lyle had sat quietly, just listening to Neil. The astronaut had been Jerry's greatest friend in those final days and, sensing that they shared so much affection for the same man, Lyle must have intuited—though he would never have said as much—that his own finer qualities would be mirrored in Mr. Armstrong, the way lovers of the same man or woman often find not only elements of the loved one but echoes of themselves as well when they chance to observe their rivals. It made him uncomfortable, but only momentarily. He leaned across the table in the aftermath of the astronaut's speech, mentioning his own father, the senior congressman from Michigan, alluding to the fact that he himself had recently entered politics, and promising to use all his "political might" to help carry on the search.

"I'm a native of Wapakoneta, Ohio, myself," Neil said, wrinkling his nose as if scenting something. "Class of '62. We were the Wapakoneta Prairie Dogs. If I'm not mistaken, we used to play you boys in regionals."

"That's right—I played for the Sarsaparilla Gorillas. I thought you looked like a linebacker in all that gear—"

Barbara, feeling bored and nostalgic, watched the men talking. You give two men nothing at all but a shred of goodwill, she was thinking, as Neil showed the politician the mess of hoses and valves that constituted his suit. It took him, he was explaining, twenty minutes, assisted, to climb into and out of the thing. "You get used to it—asking someone to 'zip me up,'" he said, glancing at her with a smile. "Though of course, here on earth, all this engineering doesn't do a damn bit of good—"

"Oh, I bet the cooling system's nice on a hot night," Barbara suggested.

"It's a lifesaver," Neil agreed; but then, at the thought of lifesaving, he fell silent.

At this awkward juncture, I endeavored a second time to get Fauna's attention, though once more I succeeded only in prodding Flek up from his chair with a whispered, "Well *damn* me—" at which my mother, realizing what was going on, hissed, "What's gotten in to you tonight? Can't you just behave yourself for an hour?"

Lyle winked across the table. Neil looked respectfully aside. Finally catching Fauna's eye, I raised the Jerry Finch doll into view once again and indicated we should slip away.

At a distance from our table, by the front door to her building, an elderly Italian man ran an ice cart—a stainless-steel box under a yellow umbrella, hand-painted with the blue words MOON ICE. We crouched in the shelter of his kiosk, beneath the translucent slab from which he shaved pale cones infused with colors from a line of bottles, a transistor radio at his side concealing our conversation from prying ears. Holding out the Jerry Finch, I watched as Fauna's hand closed around the slight, nearly delicate doll.

I don't know what I expected, but I think I assumed her reaction would take the form of excitement—the same mad excitement I felt in the air all around me that night, as if at the proximity of my father. Instead, a glassy sadness entered her eye.

"What is it?" I asked.

Her voice caught when she tried to speak, though she smiled weakly to show it was OK. "It just looks so much like him," she said at last. "I mean, look at his hair."

It was, as I said, a small doll, nearly half an inch shorter than Neil's towering four inches, painted with the sloppy details such toys normally contain, so that the eye color—a shade of murky brown—didn't fall quite on the eyes themselves. I had to admit, however, that the same casualness with which the brown and gray had been daubed high inside the clear, plastic helmet, did provide a fairly good representation of the thin, wild thatch my mother had worked so hard to control.

"And his clothes," she suggested, as I noted once more the swatch of red where my father's collar would be. I hadn't realized at first what this might refer to, but knowing, as I did, that each detail in the doll was there to convey some aspect of Jerry Finchness to a child, I'd decided that this must be a hasty allusion to his red plaid shirts—very symbol of his humble, earthly origins. One could even make out, poking from a flannel pocket, his reading glasses—glasses he'd incidentally left behind, on earth, but no matter. It was, I reflected again, appropriate to my father, the sloppiness with which these details were applied, mirror of his own dishevelment.

Fauna stifled a sob. "And his face—how can you stand to look at it?" she said as, for the first time, I began to feel disturbed. Even as I noticed the lips of the doll, frozen in my father's shy, apologetic smile, even as I perceived the slouch lent to the shoulders, I suspected that all of these things were deliberate appeals to a certain caricature of my father that could be dabbed on any face, any body. It was a version, I couldn't help but feel, that many people would be as happy to accept as the original. Looking more carefully now, I realized that the heads of all of these dolls—each of the various NASA astronauts—were likely made of identical nubs of molded plastic and had only been detailed with different colors depending on the crew member.

As she opened her mouth to say something more—likely to draw my attention to some further perceived trace of realism—I grabbed the Jerry Finch from her hand, commenting, "They've never even met my dad, whoever made this. Even most of *these* people"—meaning the court— "never met him. What do they know about Jerry Finch?"

She stared after the doll, obviously disappointed.

"I wish they'd all go home, so he can come back," I said. "Because he would, you know, if everyone wasn't watching." Though when I saw how she held her eyes away from me, I added, "*You* still believe he's coming home, don't you?"

Her gaze drifted to the doll's face, then fell. "Let's not talk about this, Georgie."

"But what if he's already here," I hinted, looking up at the horizon of rooftops and house lights above which the glow of the city dissolved into a fine net of stars. "You saw the note on the window—what if he's not *on* the moon anymore?"

She sat down silently, and I, sitting too, wrapped my arms around my knees, the doll clamped loosely in one damp fist.

"It's my fault," she said at last. "Georgie, you're not going to like this, but your father didn't write that note in the greenhouse." I must have begun to smile, because she said hastily, "No—it's true, I wrote it myself. I wrote it on the glass, while I was waiting for you. It *seemed* like a good idea. . . . I thought it would help until he came back, but . . . it doesn't look like he's coming back now, I guess."

This was, I admit, something of a blow. I looked at the tiny plastic man, face and feet jutting out on either side of my hand. I thought of the Russian soccer player, armless, helpless, and recalled Louis's Jerry Finch, melted down by the Russians, destroyed or saved in a thousand tiny scenarios around the country every day. Suddenly I wondered how these lumps of plastic had ever meant anything to me.

"That's what you wanted to talk about, wasn't it?" she asked and, when I didn't answer, "You know, he *can't* come back to earth, now the astronauts are all here. He can't just walk home from the moon. And you can't keep pretending he has his own rocket ship or something."

"Well, he might," I said. "He might have retro-rockets—he might have a parachute—he might have stowed away, in the payload where you keep rocks and things." But the words were childish, and I felt foolish saying them. "What do you know, anyway?" I griped, feeling ridiculous. "You're just saying what your mom would say."

For a while we sat without looking at each other, the old Italian man singing tunelessly along with his radio, until, after a few minutes, between my hostility and the new dress her mother had made her wear, Fauna grew uncomfortable and stood back up.

"Sure, go on—just leave now," I muttered, adding, "I don't care—who cares if he hasn't made it back yet. He'll come back when he's ready. He told me, you know—"

"Georgie—"

"Honest," I repeated, standing up beside her. "He told me—he called."

Once more, face-to-face, I sought her eyes, perhaps believing she might discover in my own gaze the depths of my sincerity. I expected, I suppose, that, as she'd done once before, she would relent and again admit to me that secret and shared belief I felt even my mother must have, deep down—she'd admit to the allure of space. I waited, watching those eyes flicker with possibility; but instead, she simply looked past me, and I saw only the dull fires and lanterns of the night reflected there. Remembering the doll in my hand, suddenly disgusted with everything, with myself, I hurled it against the thick glass doors of the building behind us—Fauna's building—where it bounced into the bushes. It was a violent gesture and, even if born of impotent rage, it must have been frightening to her, because she ran from me.

I was just awakening from this fury, detecting the first, faint chords of remorse, when I heard a voice call my name: "*Geor-gie,*" it said, "*Geor-gie*—" And I turned to find Angie, holding a red cone of shaved ice, standing beside the ice cart. She was smiling, amused, and she continued to watch me, biting into the frozen mound as she pushed up the sleeves of her sweatshirt.

"I didn't mean to sneak up on you," she said, teeth nibbling. "Take after your dad, don't you, you little heartbreaker?"

I was so startled, I was momentarily speechless before, surprising myself again, I said, "You don't know anything about my father." The night had turned into a fun-house mirror in which I could discern that no one had ever treated me with anything but gentle ridicule. Angie, my mother, even Fauna—none of them had ever believed a word I'd said.

"Actually, I know quite a lot, I think—even biblically speaking," she replied. "Still getting your phone calls, aren't you?"

I wondered how much of our conversation she'd overheard, and when she came up and tousled my hair, I shied away without answering.

"Don't be mad, Georgie—I thought you'd *miss* me. I'd come visit you, you know, but I can't. And hey," she added, "if anyone should be mad, it's me—I should be jealous of *you*." She smiled, offering me a taste of ice smelling of cherries and frost. "I'm stuck at home with my cow-of-a-mom, and no one ever calls. I *wish* he would call me."

For a moment I thought she might be serious, but of course she wasn't. In the reflection of the dark glass doors I saw us: myself, the skinny boy who came up only to her chest; Angie, hair in a rope down her back, rocking on her heels, one hand in the pocket of her jeans.

"Why *should* I tell you?" I blustered. "You won't believe me. No matter what I say, no one ever believes." I turned away from her, to the mirror door of Fauna's apartment building. "You had your chance. *You* can't speak to him. He calls *my* house, to speak to *me,* because he knows when I'm at home. He's watching—he's probably watching us right now, but it doesn't make any difference. *You* don't care. You don't even believe."

She'd half-knelt—I realized I was speaking very loudly—and gently took both my arms in her hands. The radio behind us played something slow and waltzlike, the old Italian man murmured the words to a song I didn't know. There was laughter in the distance. A solitary astronaut lumbered through the dark, light falling from his body.

"Is there anything that would make you believe?" I asked without turning; but she shook her head. Just behind me, I could smell her hair.

I don't believe I've ever really told you how beautiful she was. She wasn't grown up yet, and she still had a little softness to her face, a rounded profile, her nose that button shape she hated—she used to sit beside me watching TV, pulling on the tip to make it grow. Only in the gentle slant of her eyes—her father's, I knew, from the photo in her house of a tall, uniformed man—the dawdling line of her mouth, budded but not yet blown like her mother's, could I see what she'd look like, all grown up. She straddled those worlds that summer, wanting to leave her childhood behind but constructing, like everyone her age, fantasies from the very material of that preadult world, as if it would never end. However much she wanted to leave, she would keep doing that—building a wonderful childlike adulthood for herself—until someone came along and destroyed the last of it.

"I want him to tell me," she said, her voice wistful, suddenly older. "I want him to tell *me,* just like you say he tells you. I mean, that's it, isn't it?—the whole thing about waiting for him to come back. It's about wanting the thing that can't happen, but wanting it because *he told you.* It's what everyone wants, I guess, but won't admit," she said, fumbling for her cigarettes. She knocked one out of the pack and lit it behind her small fingers. "Without that, it all looks pretty fucking lame, doesn't it?"

I watched myself reflected in the doorway, small beside her, my face floating in the glass above the weak fluorescent lights of the lobby, the elevators with their tiny red numbers rising and falling. Like my father, I thought: hair a bit awry—a dome of straight, brown hair blown over itself. The very ghost of my father now: chin weak, the white tips of my upper teeth showing in a slightly open mouth, ears a bit large. And my eyes—only my eyes, like Angie's, more serious, older—heavy and dark like my brows.

The girl's words fell through me. She wasn't really talking to me anyway and, like myself, she could only address the hypothetical person who might listen. "I couldn't live that way. I just couldn't live like that— like Mom: realistic, reasonable, as small as you can possibly be. For Christ's sake, don't let anyone know you're alive."

My mother's words—my father's really, transformed—returned: "If your father didn't exist, Georgie, someone would have to invent him." As, equally, if I didn't exist, I knew someone would simply invent me. When I thought about it, it didn't even matter if I existed—I would be reinvented by everyone I met, everyone who didn't believe me. Who said it first? *To be is to be believed.*

I understood, then, why Angie could never believe in a Jerry Finch who wouldn't call *her* on the phone. I understood this so clearly at that moment—how everything I felt myself to be or believed to be true was nothing to her, that I was nothing but what others believed I was.

And in myself, I understood, I was nothing at all.

*　　　*

*　　　*　　　*

*　　　*

Through the pangs and tinsel of this night, Bob Nightly had suffered his own little epiphany and, his mind inflamed, had been searching high and low for nearly an hour now for Angie Fitzpatrick, little suspecting he might have found her crouched behind an ice cart with a little boy. He'd wanted to ask about Lyle again—or, if he hadn't decided this in so many words, it was at least true that what she'd told him about Lyle had, for hours now, been the one lamp illuminating all his thoughts. Bob was the kind of man who couldn't let something alone and, with a few drinks in him, the mask of the world inevitably began to slip from the face of his eternal adversary, to whom we'll simply refer here as the Great Dragon. He could almost feel it in the air tonight—the presence, somewhere nearby, like the scorpion beside Orion, of the Dragon of some tyrannic deception, some untruth. Lyle Barnes was certainly not this Dragon— Bob knew that much—but he was part of the mask, of that he was sure.

The politician, for his part, was blissfully unaware of these attentions. He'd struck up a conversation with Kitty Shank while her husband was talking to Neil Armstrong, and he was having a great time—it was perhaps the one occasion she'd allowed him to tease her.

"I just can't help feeling you've still got reservations about me," he hinted, when she complimented him on his standing in the polls. "Don't you, Mrs. Shank?" he asked, something impish in his eye. The night felt good, and he was supremely in his element, a friend to one and all.

"I'm not sure I know what you're talking about," she said, her accent deepening as her mood lightened. She'd drunk a little wine—a great rarity—and her evasion was playful rather than forbidding.

"Oh, I just wonder sometimes whether you believe I'm entirely on the level," he replied, eyes turning down modestly to the table. "I guess I don't really know if I have your vote, is what I mean."

Nightly, lingering nearby, approached the table where Lyle and Kitty were talking, his face swathed in the thick, red look of alcohol—a concentration, when he glanced at Barbara, seeming to reside not on her face but slightly in front of it. He'd recently begun wearing a green, checked cap; this, taken together with his green professor's jacket with the suede patches at the elbows, and the pipe he'd lit as he strolled the court, gave him a likeness that Lyle was the first to point out: "You're quite the leprechaun tonight, aren't you, Bob?" He was meaning to be friendly, no doubt, but met with a cold glare.

"Mr. Armstrong," Nightly said, extending his hand for the astronaut to shake. "Bob Nightly, journalist." He peered around and noted, "Barb, Kitty . . . Barnes." He was carrying a beer, and after he was done shaking hands, he toasted Neil with the can. This kind of thing had been going on all evening. The rest of the table raised their glasses automatically, except for Lyle, who was looking for something to drink.

"Here you go," Bob said, seeing his plight and starting to pour off some beer.

"Oh, thanks, but no thanks—is there any OJ left?" Lyle asked, looking around, placing his hand over his cup as a trickle ran onto his fingers. Barbara laughed, and Kitty remarked quietly to Tom, "He's drunk."

Bob was sensitive to such things—he often detected a smile on the face of the world, a mocking smile he caught if he turned just quickly enough, as if it had always been there, waiting to erupt on his own mother's breast, just below the nipple.

"Oh, come off it Barnes," he growled, his face, if possible, growing more sanguine. "Don't be such a piece of wood—" And right then, whatever levity was in the air evaporated. Lyle, good humored until that moment, appeared to remember something, and Barbara stopped laughing.

"What did you say?" she asked.

"He heard me." Bob gestured at Lyle with his can. Glancing between them, Neil was trying to decide if this was a joke when Kitty rose slightly in her seat. "The man doesn't drink," she said in a low voice, surprised to find herself defending Barnes but disturbed by the little green man's tone. "Is there something you don't understand about that, Mr. Nightly?"

"I guess I don't *understand* men like you, Barnes," he said, standing as tall as he could, still directing himself exclusively to the politician. "But we've all got our secrets, don't we?"

To his credit, he was brave. He was looking for his Dragon, and if it turned to fight he would be there: he would stab at it until it turned, and then he would stab at it until it died.

Lyle, however, only watched the journalist, face gone surprisingly inscrutable. Whatever had crossed his mind a moment before left him either sunk in thought or above wrangling with a drunken man. He placed his hand upon Kitty's in a gesture of forbearance.

And perhaps it was this gesture, or perhaps it was the sudden feeling that all eyes—as they were—were upon him, that finally had some effect upon Bob Nightly. He took his beer can up from the table and finished it in silence.

"Armstrong," he said, tipping his hat as he took his leave. "Everyone—Barb—sorry if I . . . said anything."

It was another bad patch—and I don't mean to give the impression that bad feelings prevailed throughout the evening, but there were patches, an undercurrent.

Disaster, though, was at the periphery this night. Barbara watched as people got up, one by one, to go to the back of the court, huddling around their telescopes to stare at the narrow slip of the moon. She could hear Neil describing possible scenarios involving her husband, the noises of agreement or surprise made by the stargazers. Her son had vanished someplace with Fauna; Kitty had grown tired and gone back home with Tom; and Angie—she was just relieved the girl hadn't stayed. During the few moments she'd stood at the table, Barbara had found her eyes drawn so persistently to Angie's midriff, she thought it incredible, in retrospect, that no one except Doris had taken any notice. It was only the two women now, alone.

"Why don't you tell me what happened to *your* husband?" she asked suddenly, pouring herself another glass of wine.

For a moment Mrs. Fitzpatrick seemed not to hear, then she waved away the offending idea. "I don't want to talk about *that* . . ."

"Of course, if you're uncomfortable—but I mean, you know all about my family. Everyone knows about my family," Barbara reflected.

Doris sighed. "It's different. I'm sure you don't *really* want to know—"

"But I do," she said, and it was true.

Mrs. Fitzpatrick rolled her eyes, then nodded her head. "Well, the short of it is, he died in a plane crash."

Barbara put out her hand, and the large, red-haired woman took it. She remembered the pictures of Mr. Fitzpatrick in uniform decorating the Fitzpatrick home. It was a terrible war, she thought to herself, asking, "How old was Angie?"

"Tiny, not even two—it was a long time ago, now—nearly fifteen years. Sean, our oldest, was just eight."

"Before the war?" Barbara said, somewhat surprised.

"Vietnam? Heavens, yes."

"Where was he going?" she asked, beginning to see it hadn't been what she imagined.

"Nowhere," Doris said. "I mean, it's not like they really 'go' any-where. They just go around and around. Or straight up—often it was just straight up." She glanced over and saw Barbara didn't understand. "You knew he was a test pilot, didn't you?" And then, realizing, "I'm sorry—I thought everyone knew that. I guess it was kind of a big deal back then—they were like movie stars. I still think of them as movie stars."

Doris paused and thought this over, resting her face on a broad, soft hand as she looked out across the court: warm, full of cozy groups of people and their telescopes. "He used to call his plane the steel go-cart. It was back when they just flew *planes*—nothing fancy—but he wanted to be . . . well, you know . . ."

Barbara continued to look at her blankly, though somewhere back in the darkened chamber of her mind, a light had already switched on.

Doris leaned closer. She was wearing false lashes, the lids of her eyes blue iridescent. "He wanted to be an astronaut. It's why we came down here. It's why I married him," she admitted after a moment, perhaps to herself.

EIGHTEEN

The Stain

I've since heard the August 14 potluck described as the last occasion of true goodwill in the court; and though it was, as I've mentioned, an evening already alloyed with darker currents of emotion, one had only to go outside a week later to understand how anyone could find in that night the swan song of better times, and discover that the breathless anticipation of the first days, when the astronauts had just returned from space and anything still seemed possible, had given way to a general breathlessness, a paralysis of urgency. Spacemen and anxious patriots waited in the halls, lurked in the elevators, and puttered in the lobby. Even the Sterns, always selfless and kind, needed something now besides their Scrabble and magazines. It wasn't that they needed anything *from* Barbara, but they wanted to tell her of their hopes and beliefs about her husband—why she was fighting the good fight, waiting so patiently.

They'd begun to notice things, too, terrifying things.

"That Fitzpatrick girl," Mrs. Stern exclaimed on one occasion, adjusting her hand as her husband deliberated on his discard options. "You know, Mrs. Finch, I'm not the sort to speculate, but she's really letting herself go. She used to be such a slip of a girl, and now she's getting so thick, you know, around the middle—"

"Just like her mother." Mr. Stern threw in with his card.

"You have such a lovely figure, Mrs. Finch, and of course I notice she doesn't come by anymore," she said, taking up her husband's discard with awful majesty. "So it's only natural we should start to wonder now, if maybe the girl isn't jealous." She turned her kind, old face up from the table and held open the door at the fourth floor with a yellowed claw.

It was after a particularly grueling such ride that Barbara deemed it better not to go out at all. Certainly, there were times when a little congress with the world was unavoidable, but otherwise she decided the cornflower walls and beige carpet of the apartment must become, for the time being, the entire world for her little family.

In the hall, photographs of her husband sealed in glass mirrored this newly immured state, and even the television, obsessed as it was with the lost astronaut, began to seem like an organ of her inner life. Still, if Jerry's face continued to haunt network news, it did so dimly now, his name, if Barbara wasn't mistaken, already shrined in that special cellophane of regrets that surround those dead we've never personally known. Perhaps the nation truly mourned never having made more than a passing glance at Jerry Finch in its hurried history but, whatever the depth of the nation's sorrows, his family, furtively photographed, was displayed nightly now in his stead. Viewed from without during these days, I can understand how Barbara might have appeared, as one anchorman put it, as elusive as her husband: with the curtains drawn, unable to speak her mind publicly, she'd turned inward; methodically, out of the prying eyes of the court, she'd begun to clean her home of any trace of space.

She approached the task not with cruelty but with the instincts of a survivor, and it gave her actions, for the first time in nearly a month, a purposeful air Lyle sensed immediately when he stopped by. "What's—ah—what's this all about?" he murmured, loosening his tie, watching her take down the photographs of her husband's helmeted face lining the kitchen hall. "Getting the place all spic-and-span for the big man. . . ?" His voice trailed away when he saw the books on astronomy and astrophysics thrown one on top of another in paper bags.

Barbara had been dreading his visit, expecting that the politician would try to discover what was going on; that she'd then need either to have it out, or worse, not to have it out. But Lyle, too, no longer seemed the same.

"Is Georgie around?" he asked, looking away after watching her for a moment, silently. "I thought maybe he'd like to have a peek at the moon together, you know, with the old 5300."

"He's over at Kitty's," Barbara explained, adding with a wry smile, "By the sound of it, he had some apologizing to do after the potluck." Glancing at the politician, however—whatever her feelings on Lyle's reticence, or the continued use of the telescope, when he now merely turned and gazed out the kitchen window—she felt as if she'd deprived him of some vital happiness. It was the continuation of a process that she'd noticed before but that had perceptibly accelerated: he looked older, spoke less frequently, and lacked his accustomed easiness. She wondered if the last month's events had acted as caustically on his life as upon hers.

It was, though, in the person of Mr. Nightly that Barbara noted the most extraordinary change, even if the precise difference was more difficult to pin down. Also wasting no time in apologizing for his behavior at the cookout, he at first seemed to have swallowed his pride and returned to making house calls, notepad in hand, ready to talk shop. "There's rancor in all this cleanliness" would be a typical comment as he settled on Jerry's chair, watching her chip away at the stars peppering the ceiling. "Which is to say, you've taken on the classic role of housewife, but in the true sense of the word: as a woman married to her home."

After such an observation, he'd often jot his thoughts down, with emendations, reading them back aloud and carrying on with himself something like a genial conversation. It wasn't long, however, before it became clear that, far from adopting a more humble attitude, he'd grown emboldened by Lyle's recent timidity and, sensing the politician had a stake in Jerry's physical return which he, and even Barbara, did not, the journalist would sometimes bait Lyle mercilessly if they found themselves in the apartment together.

"It's a kind of Godot thing, don't you think, Barnes? All this standing around with nothing to show." He'd put his pipe in his mouth and take it out, unlit, as he wasn't allowed to smoke in the house. "But I suppose we can make do with or without him. Isn't that right, Barbara?"

"That's right, Bob," she replied, forcing him to rise so she could stand on the chair to reach a last few celestial refugees.

Nightly put the pipe back in his mouth, shrugging his indifference. He was becoming stronger, it seemed, as everything else fell apart. It was reflected in his dress—he'd had his jacket refurbished—and in the general sense that he found himself increasingly charming, frequently leaving his cap behind to furnish himself with reasons for coming by later in the afternoon. More and more, if he arrived and found Lyle gone, or on occasions when he'd actually driven him out, he would evangelize against the politician.

"I'm not necessarily saying I suspect his motives," I recall him complaining on one occasion to Neil, who'd arrived that day just in time to see Lyle beating a hasty retreat. "It's just that everything's a referendum with Barnes. 'The People of Ashtrakan County this,' 'The Citizens of America that,' 'My Friends in the Larger Titusville Area,'" he grumbled. "It's all politics with the man. He's got the soul of a hamster—"

Neil had suffered, on this particular morning, a failure in the cooling plant of his PLSS pack. He'd been in the house for more than an hour now, listening to Nightly's griping, and between the heat and the whining we can probably infer the reason he lost his temper and brought the reporter up short.

"Lyle," said Neil, narrowing his eyes and turning his weathered face this way and that in his helmet, "is a hawk of a man." He tapped the side of his visor. "He has a keenness of vision, and he cuts a sharp figure in this world. He can coast a long way without appreciable effort, with the most delicate adjustments, because his true element is the current of public opinion, if that's what you mean, Bob."

Armstrong was a gentle and unassuming man whose love of the human race derived, it's been said, from near total incomprehension of its functions. Jerry Finch had been for him, briefly, a possible key to the human heart, but now that this possibility was gone, he'd reverted to his longtime habit of likening people to various birds—a habit that had greatly endeared him to the lost astronaut, but was also, more immediately, a mark of his ignorance of human sociology.

Bob, who understood Lyle was more of a jay—a raucous opportunist—held his peace.

"A tenacious man and a true man of his flock," Neil continued, squinting methodically but forgetting that hawks are not flocking birds. "I applaud him, and I believe that we all have something to learn from his longevity—a long-distance flier. I'm sure that he'll weather this winter."

Surprised at his tone, Barbara looked up at the astronaut and noticed, inside his helmet, beads of sweat starting on his face. "Are you all right?" she asked.

"It's nothing," he assured her, sitting down. "A minor systems failure." Glancing at Nightly, he added, "Sorry if I snapped at you, Bob—it was uncalled for. I guess I need to take it easy for a while, at least until Buzz makes some repairs. I just wish," he said, grasping awkwardly over his shoulder at the pack, "I wish this miter valve . . ."

Drawing near, Barbara hovered at the back of the suit for a moment, unable to see what he meant. She recalled something else, however, about the locking rings on the helmet.

"You know," she suggested, reaching around the suit's neck, "if you just took this off for a minute—" But she'd barely touched the stiff Mylar fabric at his shoulder when she found herself nearly thrown to the floor as Neil lurched to his feet.

"Whoa there, tiger," Bob remarked, taking his pipe from his mouth. He'd seen this happen before, down in the court, when a helpful and sympathetic person—usually elderly, him- or herself acutely aware of the heat—tried to assist an "overdressed" astronaut.

"Damn it—I'm sorry," Neil said, offering his hand. "Barb—truly—it was reflex"—trying to laugh it off—"you might call it a principle thing"—glancing sheepishly from face to face—Nightly was certainly amused—though a moment later, obviously flustered, the astronaut excused himself and left.

"A man of *principle*," Nightly commented dryly when the flight commander had closed the door. "In other words, a man without humor in a world without honor.

"Which reminds me," the journalist continued, pretending to find something interesting on the bookshelf, denuded of books, "I've been doing a little research, and there's someone you're quite close to, Barb, who I'm afraid hasn't been entirely straight with us."

Barbara's heart fluttered to a stop. It was exactly the moment she'd dreaded since that awful phone call from Doris Fitzpatrick, so long ago. She blushed, thinking of her husband, and what she could say to defend her own conduct—her conspicuous silence, at least—in all this. Bob, stealing a glance and detecting the blush, misinterpreted her embarrassment.

"I see we understand each other. Perhaps you've grown fond of him—but you simply must come to terms with the fact that the man is a criminal."

"Mr. Nightly, you come in here, swinging that word around—"

"I followed him yesterday morning, Barbara, to his parole officer."

"Well," she said, sitting down as she rethought the situation.

"Look," he continued. "I know what I've done may strike you as cruel—it won't be the first time I've been so misunderstood—but it's for his own good. We can at least agree about that."

"Oh, but can we?" she said, hoping to throw a little more light on the subject.

"Barbara . . . dear Barbara," Bob said, turning decisively from the empty bookshelf, finally giving her what she wanted. "He's running for office on your husband's good name."

And whatever she was prepared to say blew out of her head.

Barbara knew she *should* feel badly for Lyle, but the truth was, she was simply overjoyed that it wasn't her husband's—and thus, inevitably, her own—sordid past being dragged up on the block. She only hoped that by the time Angie was undeniably, scandalously pregnant, this circus—of which Bob Nightly was a card-carrying member—would have struck its tents and moved on from Magnolia Court. So while she did feel a pang of sympathy for Mr. Barnes, her voice sounded complacent enough when she said, "Yes, I suppose you're right," grateful that she wouldn't have to pretend to feeling too badly now.

"Think of it like this, Barb: if he's going into politics—the big leagues—whose name is he wearing around town, like a coat? Even *on* his coat, if I'm not mistaken." He ruminated before answering himself: "That's right—your husband's"—pointing at her with his pipe—"your husband the national hero. Now think of Eisenhower, Barb. Is that what you want here? Do you want your husband's memory bogging down in a mire of questionable associations and allegations when this all comes to light? And it will," he jabbed again, nearly chuckling at the thought.

"Don't get me wrong—I like Barnes. He's a swell guy, I'm sure, but we can't have him fouling up the works and making a scandal of your husband's memory. I'm sure things are tough enough as they stand."

Barbara nodded at the mere thought of an investigation. She stared at Bob, afraid of something in his homely face, the profile with its long nose, the forehead clenched in a thoughtful knot under the checked cap; she would have been surprised to know that at this moment, in the midst of his triumph, Bob in fact felt nearly fond of Lyle: the man was more faulty, and vulnerable, than he'd ever believed, and for once he didn't entirely relish the idea of destroying him.

"What did Lyle do?" she asked.

"Lyle?"

"Yes, what did he serve time for?"

Bob took the unlit pipe out of his mouth and leaned toward her.

"Murder," he whispered.

"Murder?" she breathed.

He put the pipe back in his mouth and laughed. "Actually, I have no idea. What does it matter, anyway? It's not the crime itself, Barb, it's the stain."

NINETEEN

A Place to Sleep

The side streets around Magnolia Court are dark and empty at night, broad slabs hung with heat through which headlamps and salsa music periodically sweep, tiny worlds that close behind themselves like zippers.

A block away, Lyle could see someone was messing with his car. It happened sometimes, after dark—kids. They never saw fit to take anything, just bust a window and fuck up the seats. It was depressing.

"Hey," he shouted, breaking into a stiff run.

The kids glanced up—Cubans, he thought, as they took off in a crackle of Spanish. Two of the taller ones hesitated, checked him out, then parked themselves on the hood.

"What's your hurry?" one of them said, getting up as Lyle reached the car.

They wore white tank tops, slicked-back hair, tattoos of Catholic derivation. They weren't a gang—they wore gangland theatrically, excitedly, like people with something to prove. After all, anyone can *say* they're a gang. When he hit the first one in the jaw, the fabric of the suit bound up around his arm and his fist hurt like hell, but he felt a bone break somewhere inside the kid, and they both fled into the dark.

The driver's-side window was smashed. There was beer spilled on his garment bag, which he brought outside and shook off. In a few years, he thought, they'd all have guns and life would be that much harder. He threw his jacket into the back and loosened his tie. He felt dirty, but he'd have a shower in the morning at the Y. The kids had generously left a few unopened cans in the passenger seat, and he grasped one and held the cold metal to his hand.

Sometimes Lyle thought about leaving, but he put the idea out of his head.

"You just have to do something for a while, lose yourself in it until everything blows over," the senator from Michigan had told his son when Lyle was forced to leave the state in disgrace. He gave his boy that look—the earnest look—because this was a question of *sacrifice:* not pulling the family down in the wake of one's own personal disasters.

And now here he was, fine except he was worried about money— he had a few hundred dollars to hold him until Jerry got back. And he needed to do laundry.

A car went by, a slight shudder in the street, and then a redoubling of the heat, the silent whisper of palms. There wasn't much to be done about the jail time thing getting out. All you *could* do with a situation like this was minimize the damage. He thought briefly of Bob, for whom he had no hard feelings—Lyle saw what the man meant about Jerry and keeping his name clean; but what Bob didn't understand was that, when Jerry got back, none of this would matter. Finch had that kind of power—he could destroy the past.

The moon slipped quietly into the sky. It warmed the heart. It was right that it was waxing again—not much now, but it could only get larger, clearer, calmer. This would all come to an end—all this confusion. He wondered how many people already knew about his eighteen months in Jackson State, but whenever he tried to say something about it, the words sounded like excuses.

Barbara knew—he could tell from the way she looked at him these days. She reminded him of past, happier incarnations of himself. He thought of running over the perfect grass with the nippled pigskin ball nestled under his arm and the white increments beneath him, his feet covering them as if he was growing larger every moment, his hand reaching forward into the future. You could become anything at a moment like that—you could understand how a man could walk on the moon when a dozen men couldn't prevent you from crossing a little grass field if you wanted it that badly. It was what made him want to grasp Neil's hand whenever he saw him—he wanted to catch his eye for just a moment and say, That was what I meant. What you did on the moon, when I felt like I could grow into another man, that was it.

Barbara didn't really believe in such things—he knew that—but what hurt now, tilting the seat back and pressing his swollen knuckles against the perspiring can, was the fear that she could see he didn't entirely believe it for himself anymore. Lyle Barnes wasn't used to thinking things he couldn't say out loud, and this was that kind of thing. He couldn't tell Neil—it would be like saying, "I don't believe in *you*." And he couldn't say it to Barbara, because it was as good as saying, I don't believe he's ever coming home. She had enough doubts as it was, the poor woman.

Sliding down the seat, he rubbed at the window so the moon came through good and sharp. He thought of Neil again, when they had met at the potluck a week ago.

"You're a hawk, Mr. Barnes, an albatross," the astronaut told him, extending a Mylar hand. Lyle liked him immediately.

He'd even invited the flight commander to the car a couple times, pushing the passenger seat back so the astronaut could climb in with his PLSS pack. They had sat together and watched the moon come up through the windshield, like at a drive-in movie.

"So this is your ship," Neil said, his voice like a radio transmission from beyond the earth.

Lyle swept an old pair of trousers out of view. "That's right. She's got 200,000 miles, nearly."

The astronaut smiled. "You keep on, Lyle—just 50,000 to go. It's beautiful at the end, those last few miles falling toward the moon. The way Jerry used to talk about those white shores was enough to make you weep."

For a few seconds, sitting in the car now, alone, he could hardly breathe—it was a terrible moment, the thought of what he wanted to say sweeping through him as if no one would ever set foot on the moon again. As if the whole human race was ebbing back and we'd have to tell our children stories about a world foreclosed to them, that they wouldn't even comprehend. He wanted to be held by someone, even if that some-one couldn't understand. He'd never thought of kids before these weeks with Georgie, but, pounding lightly on the dashboard with his good hand, he found he wanted to be held by his own faulty and unborn chil-dren. They wouldn't know what he meant, these children he could only imagine as small incarnations of himself, but they would understand him.

And somehow this, in itself, was soothing, because it was much larger than Lyle Barnes alone. It was a world of longing that couldn't even recognize the things it wanted anymore, and it made him feel a part of something, like whales hunted out deep in the ocean, as he pushed his shoes off and stuck his hand out the broken window in a quiet wave—the good night he gave every night to the moon before he closed his eyes.

TWENTY

Grand Hotel Part II

In his dark room, the traveler, too, rests his eyes and listens to the machinery of the Grand Hotel: pang of elevator chains, interminable digression of ducts, the insomnia of distant engines. Sometimes, from the water world of the hall, he overhears the passage of the night staff collecting shoes or bearing messages and, opening the door a little, he beckons until they approach, faces wide and staring. They are immaculately dressed in the regalia of the hotel, these people, but they are children—literally. When he tips them, they fix him with those liquid agates, then steal like mice through the corridors and stairs. Only after the last patter has died away does he peer again through his window, up among the waves.

We may imagine his glance cast on the shore, a silver shoal of minnows crinkling in the starlight. He blinks at the sky arranged above the sand, the bright brand of the moon, and he thinks about the face there, always gazing down over the earth, hidden and revealed like a face glimpsed through the chink in a door, now opening, now closing upon some darkened room contained behind the night.

He remembers being told, when quite small, that there is a sense in which every moon is the face of a different man, so the moon shades from life to life from month to month and night to night. A cloud passes before the satellite, and he waits, watching the submerged likeness for that clear celestial face to reappear; but then, with the first shiver of sleep, his eye strays among the constellations to the fold of a figure eight, bioluminescent and strange, opening in the deep.

If he's not mistaken, it's grown larger since yesterday—since the sun first went down that very evening, in fact. Even last week, when he stared at it, he might have believed he was watching a distant carnival—a fairground of stars, each with a tiny voice, each as large and alive as if drawn by the hand of a child—and the longer he stares, the nearer it seems, until he feels that, if he just stared for long enough, it would fill all his dreams.

TWENTY-ONE

Open Secrets

The dog days of August wore on and, as hangovers fade, and then the memories of hangovers, so, too, did the novelty of astronauts. It wasn't a conscious callousness that obscured them from our eyes, they simply became ubiquitous: lumbering, useless-looking, something one stumbled upon asleep in the halls, newspaper spread over their white bodies, hands held up to visors to keep out the light.

The poverty of their days was taken by most to be an extension of the loyalty they felt toward Jerry Finch; and it was no surprise that men closeted in space suits had little interest in small talk. We would be wrong, however, if we failed to acknowledge that this lack of social graces hadn't begun to erode their public standing as the days passed and their behavior, ceasing to seem remarkable, became merely disappointing. It was a feeling probably best expressed by Angie when she complained, "After you talk to them for a while, they don't even seem that cool any-more—just weird."

Certainly they were still handsome, sharp-eyed, and aglow with the aura of daredevils. But they hadn't seen a movie since 1970, they didn't know any bands, they weren't aware of current events, political activities happening at home or abroad—nearly anything that might have furnished two well-meaning people with conversation.

Even Lyle Barnes rapidly exhausted his supply of conversational topics once his stock of lunar lore was played out. If asked, all of the Apollo men would say they had wives and most, children, too. They could supply photos of these people, together with images of their cars and the sunken living rooms of their suburban ranch homes. They could easily be convinced to join someone for a drink. Any closer inspection, however, revealed little experience with the world except as a place they'd once passed through and in which they might spend future training-related engagements.

Only Bob Nightly had remained fascinated, and was now often found brooding at nearby bars or in the back lot with these sullen and grieving men, asking questions that rekindled each to a consciousness that guttered and went out nearly as it was lit.

At first glance, with his pipe and professor's jacket, his unathletic frame, Nightly was the last man one would expect to keep the company of astronauts; but to understand what made Jerry Finch tick, he felt he had to begin among his brethren as much as with his family, and Nightly's deep sympathies for America's forgotten soldiers meant he instinctively spoke their language. He won the respect of these solitary, inscrutable men with his unflinching loyalty to their plight, perhaps, more than anything, convincing them that they *had* a plight—that something had been taken from them, of which Jerry Finch was the physical sign.

You may find, in reading this work, the comparison between astronaut and war veteran uncomfortable, but if the lives of the former seem purely glamorous to you, not to be counted among things easily forgotten, consider how few astronauts you, yourself, can name. Do you, honestly, remember any of these men besides Neil Armstrong? Buzz Aldrin? This, I suppose, is what they all already knew.

By the week following their arrival, the astronauts were becoming like landlocked sailors, or the veterans in the hills of North America, growing taciturn as they watched the eyes of the nation drift from this pivotal event in their lives toward other dramas. The astronauts saw bitterly that, while the hopes of their country had for a while beat within their bodies, the nation was fickle, and had drawn its hopes toward new men and deeds, different organs of desire. Despite the increasing distance between themselves and the members of North Court, they found it harder than ever to leave, because it was only there, among the few dozen men and women awaiting some closure to the Jerry Finch tragedy, that they felt any sense of home.

Neil was the sole member of the *Apollo 19* team to reach outside this tiny circle. He spent little time with his compatriots, instead coming by the Finch apartment to relay news of his talks with senators and congressmen. While he was always polite, like an old southern gentleman in his worn and crumpled suit, Barbara found him a disturbing presence; as it turned out, she wasn't the only one taken aback by his visits: Doris, too, had formed a few ideas.

"Barbara, do you know who's sweet on you now?" I recall the woman asking, the sound of an electric blender roaring into the phone in the background.

"I'm really not considering my potential admirers at this stage in the game," Mrs. Finch admonished, disliking this kind of talk and feeling, not without reason, that it was a little out of place; but in her mind she made a glance again toward Lyle, and then, possibly, there was Bob.

Doris waited until she was sure her friend was done speaking, and then said, "Neil Armstrong."

"Neil?" Barbara repeated.

"Armstrong."

"The astronaut?"

"A real astronaut," Doris opined, delight deepening her voice. "Not to say Jerry wasn't," she added, "but, you know, he's really the real thing."

"Well," Barbara said, beginning to form a few conceptions in her mind.

"Well," Doris repeated.

The idea, once presented, was, in fact, hard to shake. During the succeeding days she examined her encounters with the flight commander, and what light this new information threw on his courtly behavior.

Barbara's conversations with Doris also led to broader considerations than the activities of Neil Armstrong alone. Having voiced her conviction that her husband was unquestionably dead, she found herself increasingly disturbed by the situation outside her window: at a time when it should have been clear to any sane person that there was nothing left to do, the actions of these spacemen appeared more and more unhinged.

Across the court, for example, she'd discovered that one solitary astronaut was holding vigil in the windows of an empty apartment. When she entered the kitchen she would see him there, as if he'd waited hours, rising to meet her in the dark of his rooms. Neil, unable to account for the man among the numbers of *Apollo 19*, conjectured that he might be from a previous expedition, traumatized by the recent disaster. It was true that several members of past Apollo missions had broken down in recent weeks, driven from quiet lives by the articulation of their own worst nightmares on the pages of the nation's newspapers. After years of repatriation into the productive workforce of America, these men had donned their space suits once again and taken to the proverbial hills.

In the evening, as she and Georgie made dinner and the reflected light of sunset died from the windows around Magnolia Court, this reclusive astronaut's pale and bulbous form grew in the glass like a laboratory culture of the country's sickness. Curious and repulsed, they drew the blinds and peeked out at the man dressed in a billowy, silver suit, motionless in his room, looking back. Neil offered to intervene and speak to the rogue but, made shy by Doris's suggestion, Barbara politely declined. She felt herself drawing away from this stoic and good-hearted man, wondering if the conjectures of North Court as a whole hadn't followed Mrs. Fitzpatrick's, sliding so easily from her husband's death to her own future romantic prospects. Neil, for his part, continued to drop by the apartment, as unaffected by these quiet currents—imaginary or otherwise—as one would expect a man to be who'd sealed himself inside a plastic suit.

*   *

*   *   *

*   *

It shouldn't come as any surprise that there'd been, for some time, a slow attrition of what the patriots in the court described as day-trippers: high school kids, hippies in the throes of acid revelation, vacationers who'd read a magazine article about that quintessentially American family, the Finches, and wanted to have a peek on their drive down to Orlando. They were easily spotted, these pasty latecomers with clothes unscathed by sun, smoke, and rain; they were enthusiastic, ambitious, talked a great deal about right and wrong; but they were also, inevitably, the first to leave. This was, after all, summer—tiny, nine-volt-powered fans built into the visors of hats did little to cut the trembling heat, and the days left a relentless, peeling tan on those who chose to remain.

On one such airless morning, however, the court awakened to find a paper banner large enough to read from fifty yards—perhaps from space—affixed to the lobby doors of the Finches' building. Eyes were bleary, few were even conscious when Kitty had appeared in her rose red sarong, marching through the crowd clasping their first mugs of coffee; before any of the assembly had time to react beyond the release of many great, trembling yawns, she'd taped to the glass this message reading, in its entirety: GO HOME.

There was a distant murmur. Even if the words were generously interpreted to refer to Jerry Finch—a man who, after all, they *wanted* to come home—the diction, the tone, seemed wrong.

It's unclear how long the banner might have remained unmolested, an object of conjecture, had Lyle Barnes, emerging several minutes later from his white Impala with a box of donuts, not entered the court, quickly sized up the situation, and strode directly toward the posting, hand outstretched. His muscular arm, however, terror of football fields past, never reached its goal.

"None of your nonsense today, Mr. Barnes," Kitty scolded, thrusting him aside. "Go home if you aren't half as big a fool as these half-wits following you."

The crowd, feeling itself abused, stirred ominously, and Lyle, unaccustomed to physical confrontations with women, stepped back a pace. He was, truth be told, tired—he'd slept badly and his hand was still swollen—but he tried his best to treat the situation as the misunderstanding it no doubt was.

"Everyone just take a deep breath," the politician began, wondering what his father had done, faced with potentially volatile detractors. "I'm sure we're just having a little problem with translation. Kitty, if you wouldn't mind—why don't you tell us what this is all about?"

She glared at him before applying more tape to the poster, saying only: "You know what this is about."

Not entirely satisfied, he glanced quizzically at his fellow patriots. Thank God the cameras weren't here yet.

"Well, there's one thing I *do* know, and that's that this isn't about you or me, Mrs. Shank—I think we can both agree on that," he said, his eyes resting on the faces of David Moscowitz and Joan Nutrino, massage therapist from distant Oakland. "The lessons of the past weeks are bigger, I suspect, than any of our personal dramas and, frankly, I've been humbled"—judicious murmuring all around—"and believe we can all agree that this is about Jerry, about everything he stands for. So why don't we start by putting away our munitions, so to speak."

Kitty half-turned. She'd picked up a large, closed umbrella from where it leaned against the glass and now hefted this piece of rain apparel something like a sword. She had, however, other sorts of munitions in mind.

I'd like to direct the reader to an old adage—a few words that gave Mrs. Shank pause: that to tell a secret is to shake the whole structure of secrecy. As if to say that the entire collective of secrets were bricks in a dam together, and on every secret we feel the pressure of a world that runs on knowledge, like a weight of water at the back of the mind. It was very much what Barbara Finch felt the night before, as she leaned across the sofa toward Kitty, speaking in a low voice, though the two of them were alone.

Nothing about Lyle had prompted her to do this—Barbara was, you might say, instead impelled by every other secret in her life that she couldn't, at that moment, tell; or, if this seems too easy, consider that she increasingly feared herself to be a person without confidences, without even the ability to explain her inner life to another because the pages of it were overrun by passages marked not merely confidential but classified. She probably hoped obscurely that, like a war in the springtime of a presidency, a single, sensational confidence might drive before it all doubts and equivocations about her fittingness to be, if not president, then at least a friend.

"Kitty," she began when Georgie had left the room to go to bed, "I'm afraid you may have been right, all along, about Lyle Barnes."

"What do you mean?" Mrs. Shank asked, coming alert after what had seemed like a sleepy evening.

"I just found out, myself . . . but I guess Mr. Barnes has been—or technically still is—on parole. It even seems he might have done time," she admitted to Kitty's ever-widening expression.

"I know, I know—I told you he was all grown up, but nobody told me about this until *yesterday.*"

Mrs. Shank, wincing, thought back to the potluck, when she'd last seen Lyle—had she actually stood up and defended him?—her eyes growing wider, until she said very evenly, "What's Mr. Barnes in trouble for?"

"It's not like he talks about it," Barbara explained, watching Kitty's face and beginning to wish she'd held her tongue. "I don't know—maybe it's not even true."

At this Mrs. Shank only folded her fingers together. "Thank you, Barbara—that must have been tough." The words reached the other woman like a slap. "I admit I imagined a few things, but . . . it's enough to make you sort of mad. I'm trying to bring up *children* here, for Christ's sake."

It was with this in mind, in the wee hours, that she'd stolen quietly from her husband's side, slipping down the hall to Fauna and Baker's room. By the yellow glow of a night-light, she watched her daughter's lashes flutter as the girl pulled herself deeper under the covers, toward some nocturnal treasure. Baker had thrown off his blankets and lay with his small fist to his mouth, the sound of his breath like lace over the night sounds of traffic, the thin rattle of an air conditioner. Very quietly, she took magic markers and a roll of construction paper from Fauna's desk. Careful not to wake them, she kissed the girl and boy and went into the living room.

For the next hour, she squatted in the dark, drawing letters as large as dinner plates. It was hard to see the colors, but the shapes grew clear as she filled them in, using a new marker whenever the last ran dry; and when the first light picked out the toys where they lay on the floor, she lifted up the sign and silently left the house.

"What Jerry Finch stood for, Mr. Barnes, you living-in-the-past fool—and that means all of you," she growled, straightening her sarong and gazing at the crowd with the air of a radical reformer in a degenerate institution. "Let's have a show of hands out there: who here really believes—*believes*—that Mr. Jerry Finch is coming back from the moon?"

There were a rustling and some gentle stirrings, but although several people placed their hands on top of their heads, after a moment seeming to scratch their scalps or necks while looking away, there were no sure hand motions.

Lyle, understanding the voting habits of his country and, more important, understanding that at play here was a subtle combination of phraseology and the Newtonian principle of the conservation of energy, made a countersuggestion. "All right—no one get excited—let me clarify what Mrs. Shank is asking: How many of those here believe that Jerry Finch, the astronaut, is dead?"

The crowd repeated its vague motions, and he turned and nodded to her with his reproving and reasonable face.

High above, in her kitchen window, Barbara had already realized what was about to occur. And if her voice contained any irritation when her son pointed out Bob Nightly, emerging notebook in hand from the crowd, it was likely because she felt herself to be, in no small part, responsible. "Well," she muttered, "here we go, Georgie. I'm sure we'll have everything cleared up nicely, now."

The journalist had appeared from a little gantlet of astronauts who'd dragged a refrigerator box into one corner of the court, where the Apollo men slept like diseased kittens in a dense mass of reflective bedding. He himself had stopped going home at all and camped nearby, in a military officer's tent that Buzz sometimes shared with him. Curiously, Neil Armstrong—usually found camping with members of the older Winnebago crowd—was nowhere to be seen on this particular day.

Nightly took in the developing situation with a grim shake of the head. Having something on Barnes had been better than a handle, but since this morning's row first penetrated the walls of his tent, he'd gradually admitted to himself that he was perhaps no longer so alone in his possession of certain information regarding the politician.

"Let me pose another question to our audience," Kitty was saying, tightening her sarong and turning to Lyle. "You people seem to have a very fine opinion of our Mr. Barnes. He's just the cat's meow to you, isn't he, Florence Evangelina?" she asked as the woman so addressed hid behind a large, red hat and the politician began to look unwell.

"So, I guess I should get a show of hands on how many people out there know that Mr. Barnes here is on probation? Or what about who knows that Mr. Barnes just got out of the *lockup* for—Well, Lyle, why don't you tell everyone about it *yourself*?"

Halfway through he'd closed his eyes, but he could hear the terrible stillness that spread through the crowd. Sooner or later, he'd always told himself—but hadn't really thought, or allowed himself to think, it would happen *this* way. Lyle had cherished the prospect of a gentle reckoning, some wrinkled hand resting on his shoulder as he told the story, his own story, with regret, but without shame. In his mind, it always took place in the context of Jerry's return, in the general amnesty of that moment. When he opened his eyes, everyone was watching him.

He lingered tenderly on the features of the Barnstables—Clyde had his cap in his hand and a dying look on his face; there was that nice older man with all the grandkids, Eddy Cabeza; just yesterday, they'd been discussing kiddie pools together. In everyone's eyes was the question—he heard it shouted out loud, once—"Is it *true*?" And then, as the silence continued ruthlessly to enlarge the moment, that look—the look his mother had given him three months ago, before he left the state in disgrace, when she murmured, *Oh, Lyle*.

"Jerry once asked me," he said, clearing his throat and hunting for his words among the faces, "whether I'd ever been afraid of the earth . . ." Beside him, Bob stepped up and forked his glasses carefully into place. There were flashbulbs going now as members of the press arrived.

"Shut up, Lyle," he said quietly.

The politician broke off, seemed to sag within his bluebird-colored suit, and Nightly, giving the crowd and cameras a cursory glance, turned his attention to Kitty. "You're quite the bully," he sneered, "aren't you, Mrs. Shank?"

She was a little surprised to find Nightly taking Lyle's side and, more, she was off balance. Staring straight at Lyle as she denounced him, rather than feeling a good, solid blow, like punching an ox—the exaltation we might fondly imagine accompanies a just act—she felt instead that she'd slapped a child. All the same, her dander was up, and behind the jeweled points of her glasses, her eyes sparked. "What do you want?" she asked contemptuously.

"Your disdain for these people is touching," Nightly replied, surprising her again. "You think you can just pack everyone off with your little cries of Shame, shame—your Go Home signs. I'm shocked at the narrowness of the teleology."

Turning to the crowd of patriots gaping at the silent Barnes, he said, "Mrs. Shank has obviously begun to treat this gathering"—he swirled his hands in front of him to garner some visual interest—"as the thing it truly is: a protest"—glancing at Lyle, who wasn't looking at anyone now—"Because we are a protest, a resistance, a certain residue that cannot be erased—"

"Oh, you're so full of shit, Bob Nightly," Kitty said. But even she flinched when the journalist screeched: "Don't interrupt me!"

There was a scrambling, brittle sound as the astronauts, obviously agitated, stirred at the back of the crowd. "Easy, boys," Nightly added. "Easy."

He could sense the patriots' mistrust. Their eyes stole over the faces of the ragged spacemen, looking for the clean, piercing features of Neil Armstrong. He may have been the one man able to bring these disparate parties to the bargaining table, who might have spoken a common tongue with all of them, but on this particular morning he was nowhere to be found and, instead, things escalated.

"I'm talking about whisking things under the rug," Nightly resumed, feeling around for his pipe. "The big guy, treading on the small guy." He motioned curiously to the hulking politician. "Culpability—that's what I'm talking about."

"Lyle," someone shouted, "is it *true*?"

"I would have told you," the politician confessed unhappily. "I wanted to—but how do you tell someone"—his brows clouded—"and what does it *matter*? It isn't about me, or you—"

"We know, we know—it's bigger than all of us," Kitty said. "Plain craziness. Don't you people have jobs and families and such? Something to do besides stand around all day, eat hot dogs, and wait for nothing?"

The crowd shuffled its feet. "Nothing, Mrs. Shank?" Bob replied darkly. "Quite the contrary: we are here to protest the abandonment not just of one man but of all these good men"—his hand ranged over the astronauts—"who this country has used and thrown away. Sure, they're no longer the children of grace they once were, but are they to blame for this? Are they not victims, too," he asked, now turning to the crowd, "just as you are, yourselves?"

A noise like the buzzing of bees was coming from the crowd's pink throat. The crowd glanced behind itself at the astronauts, feeling both guilty and scornful, its murmuring shifting up several whole tones, as voices often do when asking questions.

Bob saw the astronauts' discomfort and called to them, "Come forward, all of you," while Lyle, beginning to revive, gently parted the patriots and signaled to the cameras.

"I made a promise to Jerry," he told the Apollo crew in a faint but rising voice, holding out his hand to each spaceman, "that we would humanize this country as he has humanized space. We are keeping that promise today."

The bulbs were popping. The astronauts stood ranged opposite Kitty, and for a moment Mrs. Shank waited braced with raised umbrella. A charge was imminent, and sure, she reasoned, she might be able to beat back these shiftless Apollo men—but how would that look to the eyes of the world: a strong, healthy woman thrashing a handful of beleaguered astronauts?

Quickly, as the first Mylar gloves groped for her weapon, she retied her sarong and dashed out of the way, chugging up the field to the left of the advancing line, shouting, "All right then—everyone who's had enough of this foolishness, get off your behinds. You there, Mr. Pollen," she called, using her now open umbrella as a shield and grasping hands, diving into the crowd for some of the older and more sensible participants. "Mrs. Shrubsburry, Mr. Almondine—you there. Don't you hide from me, Florence Evangelina." There was a tearing noise—perhaps it was Kitty's poster being ripped from the wall—but the most visible effect was that nearly half the patriots were borne off around her to the far end of the court, where she turned and harangued the remainder.

"I see, Henry Petite—don't think I haven't noticed. Olive Duboise—come on now. No one wants you here—I don't, the Finch family doesn't. If Jerry Finch was alive, he'd tell you all to *go home* and get on with your lives."

Bob Nightly, meanwhile, feeling outmaneuvered, was moment by moment shaping anew his vision of the crisis. "There's no use running from the truth. Those who stand by us today are here to witness for Jerry, for Cud Wilson, for all of these brave souls—" He gestured toward the astronauts who, winded from their charge, stood wide-eyed amidst the pandemonium. They wanted to help. They'd been trained, as much as any fireman or policeman is trained, to help. But now they saw that even the patriots who'd remained looked back at them as if they were sad monsters.

Perhaps it was simply a variation on what had seemed to Bob, until now, to be exactly the astronaut's glory: that while everyone else had been broken from their first and brightest designs, their original loves, and could only look in on these things from the outside, these men had never known an outside—they existed solely in that world of primal dreams. For although such a state of edenic splendor might seem glorious, for everyone else there is a choice: one can spend the rest of one's life fruitlessly craving each first, unattainable impulse, or one can come eventually to love the land of exile; to see those pristine strivings as naïve, childish—even as things to be a bit despised.

Buzz Aldrin stared up at the Finches' window as Nightly bellowed and Lyle soothed; and, in her kitchen, Barbara turned away again, herding Georgie from the room. The debate would rage through the day and into the night, but already the end result was clear. An irreparable break had occurred, and those who remained in the court would no longer be the loose collection of Parrot Heads, Philatelists, and Elvis fans who believed in Jerry Finch as children believe in the goodness of balloons. A sense of wrong had crept into the patriots, and even late, when it was dark and everything was silent, you could hear the crowd breathing shallowly out in the court, licking its wounds.

*   *

*   *   *

*   *

It was nearly 2:00 A.M. when the sounds of acrimony finally died out. Up in the apartment, Barbara and Georgie slept fitfully, dreaming fever dreams that opened invisibly out of their beds and onto other worlds, dreams so permeable that the next morning, when they woke to the pounding of astronauts on the front door, resolute but still weak from time spent in space, they at first turned over and tried to go back to sleep.

As Barbara later recalled, there were four of them when she opened the door, pouring into the hall, taking up every inch with their bulky suits.

"Mrs. Finch," they cried, rattling the hoses and tubes that abounded on their equipment like ghostly chains, "help us." They pressed in on all sides, saying, "Look at us, Mrs. Finch—look what's become of us," though when Barbara stared into their eyes, she saw they'd become strangers, domestic animals reverted to a feral state. She screamed and ran as, down below, in the court, the crowd stared up at the window, watching horrified as she cowered at the far end of the kitchen.

"Go home," she cried, searching in vain for Neil's face among the Apollo men, "go on, all of you. You can't do anything here. Just go back to your families—go back to the moon," she sobbed at last, unable to make any impression.

For a moment, half asleep and panicked, watching from the doorway, Georgie thought she was going to throw herself down on the riveted crowd. Nearly blind with fear, he was shouting at the padded men, beating their silvery sides with his fists; and perhaps it was this tiny rain of blows, or perhaps it was the sudden awareness that it was a telescope—a gigantic steel telescope—she'd interposed between herself and the astronauts, that roused Buzz Aldrin to consciousness.

Distraught as he was, Georgie perceived the change in the Apollo man and paused in his onslaught. The scene in the kitchen loomed reflected in Mr. Aldrin's visor.

"Gentlemen of space," the astronaut appealed, eyes wild in his helmet as his fellows turned, the title like a lash to them. "Look at your-selves—look what's become of us."

The crazed men stared at one another, abashed. Their suits were rumpled and dirty, stuck with bottle caps. Their faces were harrowed, weathered now not by the fractions and astronomies of space but by grief.

"Do you realize what it means," he continued, "when you leave a man behind, up there, alone?

"He may never come home, but he will never leave us."

Cud Wilson looked away, eyes bright with helplessness, and Barbara stared at a little silver moon buggy on the floor, ashamed that her family and its personal dramas had so destroyed these men. Imagine how much worse, then, for Georgie, who could at any moment have said the words that would lift this nightmare, and give the world its true form again. It's possible that if he'd told everything he knew, right then, the further di-sasters that were to overtake them may have been softened, but we'll never know. He was afraid—afraid for these astronauts, but more afraid to disturb the deep waters of the dream they'd been cast into, a sea wash-ing the shores of earth and moon alike.

It was as if they were all dreaming, his father the thing they dreamed together. Jerry was coming back home now, through this shared narcolepsy—he'd said as much on the phone—and though Georgie couldn't articulate it at the time, his greatest fear—greater than his fear of and for these poor men and their crumbling lives—was that if the dreamers were to awake, they would awake to a world without his father.

TWENTY-TWO

The Moon Indoors

This was the day Georgie admitted—or, if you prefer, re-admitted—his mother to the secret world that is the substance of this narrative: that he was, in fact, still receiving phone calls from the moon; that Jerry Finch had been watching them, enviously, like a child behind a playground fence; that the lost astronaut was laying plans to return home—perhaps had already begun the implacable journey; that he'd never been lost, only hiding; and that he loved them both, dearly.

The words, of course, written here as they tumbled, without justification and with little prelude, sounded like nothing more than the hysterical denials of a bereaved nine-year-old. At the moment, though, without the comforting and enlightening perspective afforded us by time, he couldn't understand how she withstood his disclosures so calmly, and then, with no more than a kiss to the top of his head, instructed him to remain at home while she went out.

It was nearly dark by then. The astronauts had left hours before to resume their vigil in the court, and Georgie had been helping her pack boxes of books—all his father's space books, books on telescopes, and the neglected books on ornithology. She'd be back, she told him, in a few minutes. He should expect a surprise.

He had anticipated many reactions, positive and negative, to his disclosure, but nothing the boy had envisioned could be carried out with such composure—one might even say indifference—as his mother had just demonstrated. As he stared around the barren apartment, however, these gloomy thoughts were ceded to a contrary and dawning idea: because wasn't it possible, he reasoned, that she'd departed with the sole intention of bringing his father home?

There are occasions in life when we discover that our own admission is all that is required to achieve our desire—as when we kiss someone for the first time, and they return our kiss, and we feel the difficulty was only imagined, self-created, and that we were always both the lock and the key. The thought of his father's return, as if a reward for the very truth he'd courageously revealed, was just such a denouement; and slowly at first, but with a growing, electric vigor, he galloped through the house, from room to room, trailing his hands over the bare wallpaper, spinning under the chipped canopy of the ceiling, panting exhausted at last on the plush carpet in the living room, the surface that had once been, beneath his fingers, the very silt of the moon.

Lying on his back, head whirling the way it did when his father spun him out through space, he was thinking of the grip of those soft, nearly effeminate hands when the phone rang. And, for the first time, he was neither bored nor excited by its promise but simply afraid.

You must understand that, at this moment, a call from the moon would have meant that Jerry was no further along on his journey than he'd been at the start; that in fact his journey hadn't even begun. The boy lay very still, hoping the phone would stop, but it didn't, and after a dozen rings he got up, and lifted it to his ear.

Georgie, the voice said, crashing like surf on a shore, the undertow, the endless recession of space all around. *Georgie, they're nearly gone now. It's breaking apart, as it had to. As the astronauts have given up, these people, too, will give up and move on.*

"Mom's gone to get you," the boy said breathlessly. "Can you see her coming?" He imagined his father's great, sad eye holding her wherever she walked.

I've been watching her, Georgie. She is going out—but not to find me. He waited a moment, silent. *She's wonderful, you know—your mother. I suppose you must. She was wearing her dress with the blue lozenges. She had her sunglasses on, and she walked right through all those people, looking neither right nor left, like a star.* There was a soft, shaggy pause. *You've become,* he said, *the things in life I revere.*

Static ate into the line. *It was long ago when I thought I could explain what I've done. I called you—I called and called—but there was no one home. I wanted to ask again: What does she say, when she says my name?*

Georgie would have spared that great, sad voice, but he wanted to hear some vindication; he wanted his father to show him the moon, laid out in all its necessity. "She says you're a coward," he whispered. "She says you're the most cowardly man she's ever known."

They listened together to the static crackling and splashing over itself.

Go to the window, Georgie, his father said, *and look outside.*

Carrying the handset, he went to the little window set in the blue wall of the kitchen, with the moon climbing large and stained among the antennas and water towers of the building across the court. It was enormous, set above the glimmer of yellow apartments, the throb of television light.

The last life of the day was spending itself, and it was a tender and beautiful world. A woman leaned from her window, beating a rug against the brick facade in a galaxy of dust; there were children running down, down past the windows of a stairwell; a father and son hunched on a balcony over a small telescope, the stars reflected in their eyes; behind glass, the silhouette of a man—or rather, that astronaut, again—peered from an apartment across the way, into the night. Space rose up like a storm on the end of the line. And then his father drew in his breath, and the line was nearly quiet.

Look at the moon, he said, and the static flared like a struck match. *Look at the moon in all its splendor,* and the boy did, watching its edges ripple as it cleared the dense horizon of the earth's atmosphere and towered into the clean night. *Now, look at me, Georgie. Do you see me there?*

His father waited patiently as Georgie examined the beautiful globe. And he said, "Yes," of the bland, silver face.

Let that be our secret then.

There was a patch of silence, an expanse like black ice, broken only by the sound of Jerry's breath. Only a man who's run out of oxygen in a cold and dark place, far from another living creature, could breathe that way. He seemed to be thinking.

You told me once you'd been studying our telescope—the Zeiss, he said at last. *I want you to do something for me.*

I need your help, Georgie. I think it will make the difference.

*　　　　*

*　　　*　　　*

*　　　*

When his mother arrived home half an hour later, she was carrying two shopping bags. Taking off her coat, moving aside the coffee table, and setting the bags on the living room floor, she ceremoniously lifted from the brown paper two cans of cream-white paint, a small can of gloss high-white, a roller, a tray, paintbrushes, and a plastic tarp.

"We're painting the house," she said, "you and me. And you can have any job you like: walls, edging round the windows, bookcases, ceilings— it's yours for the asking."

Together, they regarded the assortment of tools.

"If I could afford it," she told him, "we'd pack the car, sell this little trap, and leave Florida tomorrow"—though if the boy had any thoughts about this, he remained silent, so she went on: "When everything clears up and the government's done with its investigation, we'll get some money from them and your father's job at the school, and then you can pick a place—we can play spin-the-globe like they do in movies, and you can pick any place you want in the whole country, anywhere—and we'll go there and forget about what happened here. I know that's not sup- posed to be what I tell you to do—forget it—but I don't think there's anything left to learn here and, frankly, I'd like to forget it all myself."

They looked at the tools again as she spread them on the tarp, and he reached tentatively and picked up a small brush—the smallest. It was, perhaps, a mark of confidence in his father's return, a mild protest against his mother. Still, she was relieved he'd done anything.

"What we'll do for now is change *this* place," she told him. "It will be like living someplace new." She added hopefully: "I think we both need to do it for ourselves—" Although he detected in her voice the level control of terror, and suspected that she'd rehearsed these words on the way home, that his secret had only made her more determined to eradicate his father's memory.

"We'll begin," she said, looking around and pushing her hair back with a nervous flick of the wrist, "by throwing away the things we won't need in our new life." And Georgie knew exactly what these things would be.

Together, they carried down to the dumpster at the rear of the building his father's books and papers, his photographs, his memorabilia. They brought his clothing down in bags, his shoes by the pair. Only the telescope, silhouetted in the kitchen window, was left untouched at Georgie's insistence. They did these things furtively, using the stairs to avoid detection, but needn't have bothered: no one saw, and no one paid attention—the Sterns had picked up their table and thermoses that morning and left the elevator, returning to other, truer grandchildren; the court was exhausted, humped in its tents, its beleaguered ranks considering what they'd done wrong and who their tormentors were.

Isolated in their home, Barbara and Georgie spent the rest of the day, and the next day, too, painting. They covered the wallpaper, the chips that were once glow-in-the-dark stars, the cracks and stains and shapes on the walls like the faces of angels and devils Georgie had come to know as well as the freckles on his arms. Barbara rolled over the shadows where photographs had once hung, and together they patched the scrapes where crazed astronauts had gouged the walls with their gloves.

As the paint filled the rooms with an edible smell, like cake, Barbara began to feel as if she was coming through to the other side of something. On the third day she had the old beige carpet pulled up, and men in coveralls appeared and unrolled blue fields. When they put the furniture back, the pieces looked lost in the new terrain.

"I can *breathe* again here," she said, walking slowly from room to room as if to test this assertion. Even Georgie seemed pleased. He drove behind her on his hands and knees, rolling the tiny lunar buggy, inhaling the carpet.

Amidst all this activity, he'd nearly forgotten what his father had asked him to do over the phone; he had, however, at least ensured that the telescope, necessary to Jerry's plans, hadn't been thrown away. The 5300 was the last trace of Jerry Finch in the house, creating under its sheet something like a shrine, although when Barbara found her boy lingering there, hands under the cloth on the bright controls, she'd send him back to the living room to arrange furniture or replace window fittings. Several days passed before Georgie began to put his father's plan into effect.

It was evening, and he was gazing toward the swollen three-quarter moon through the viewfinder, when there was a soft knock at the door.

"Excuse me," came a muffled voice through the wood, "Mrs. Finch, Georgie—it's me, Neil. Mind if I come in for a minute?"

She looked through the peephole, and there he was, in the flesh, his face peering back from within his helmet.

"Where on earth have *you* been hiding?" she said, opening the door; but before she could ask him anything more, he began walking unsteadily through the rooms, reaching out to stroke the brilliant new surfaces with his silver hands.

"Have you ever touched the wall of Copernicus?" he asked after a moment.

"I'm sorry?"

"The crater—Copernicus?" he said, though, shaking his head, he added, "It was whiteness I was thinking of—the whiteness of Copernicus, Barbara. But, of course, Copernicus is on the moon."

They strolled through the kitchen and then into the living room, Neil bobbing this way and that, maneuvering carefully so he didn't scrape the paint in the hall with his PLSS.

"Who did the trim?" he asked, indicating the windows.

"That's me," Georgie told him.

"You're a feather from your father—a swallow, a man who attends to small things." Pulling back the curtains a hair, he peered outside.

Barbara, who'd been watching him curiously until now, recognized in this gesture something quite familiar to herself. She was so surprised, it took her several seconds to find her voice. "You're *hiding*," she said, "aren't you?"

"Not exactly—I've just been out of town recently, though I saw what happened on the news. I'm sorry about all that . . . craziness the other day. Are you all right?"

She shrugged. It really wasn't a question of being "all right" at this point; but before she could respond, there was another knock on the door. Stealing down the hall, she pressed her face to the peephole. Someone rang the bell once, twice. They listened until footsteps moved away.

"It's poor Lyle," she said, quietly returning and laying her hand on Georgie's head. "He comes almost every day, but I can't let him in—it would break his heart to see this," she explained, motioning to the utterly changed apartment.

"You know," Neil mused, "it's hard to share in someone's good prospects when you have none yourself. And I admire Lyle for that—his selflessness."

"It's terrible, isn't it," Barbara said. "I wonder what he did. I mean about the jail thing."

"He killed someone, back in Michigan. It was an accident, but that wouldn't change the way a man like Barnes feels."

"How do you know? That he killed someone—"

"I asked him," Neil said. "When I got back last night, I went to visit him, and he told me. He was in a wreck, I guess—drunk, and it was dark. The woman went into a coma before she died. It sounded awful." Barbara and Georgie listened in silence, as surprised by this recitation of facts coming from Neil—ordinarily so removed from the world—as by the events themselves. Neil sighed into his helmet. "And then, after his sentence was up, he left the state, feeling his presence would be a black eye to his father—the senator, you know. His father's a hard kind of man."

"He's very loyal, isn't he?" Barbara asked, a bit appalled.

"Lyle feels awful, about everything. He'd change his life if he could—and I'd help him," Neil said, "but I'm afraid I won't be around much longer." His face wrinkled like a leather glove cast in deep thought. She glanced at him from out of her reverie.

"Actually, this is what I came to speak with you about. I wanted to tell you both I'll be leaving again in a couple days—"

Barbara began to object that the astronaut had only just returned, but he held up a hand. "I've been meeting with the boys in Washington—quietly, you know—and they want to send another mission, to collect Jerry."

Neil glanced at Barbara, who accepted this in silence. "I don't like to think about it, I guess, but I suppose I have been hiding. I haven't seen anyone since I got back to town except Lyle, and you." She tried to imagine Neil in his puffy space suit sneaking through the halls of the complex, unseen; the astronaut, however, was obviously not endeavoring to paint an amusing picture. "Maybe I was wrong to come back to earth to begin with: I just feel as if I have no purpose here. I can't do anything, even for my own crew, and it makes me feel . . . I have to admit, it makes me feel like a bit of a coward. It's why I went to Washington. I don't think I'll see things any differently until I can return to the moon, and bring Jerry home." Looking at them both, he smiled sadly. "I need closure on this—the whole country does."

There was a short pause before Barbara replied, "The country will be fine, Neil—don't make this any harder for yourself." And when he made some rumbling protest, she interrupted. "Look at the TV. Look anyplace else but here. I'm sorry, but no one cares anymore—just those people out there"—she waved to the window—"and a few congressmen, looking for an election-year issue."

The astronaut sank down on the edge of a chair, and Barbara, taking the sofa opposite him, continued. "I'm not trying to be unkind, and you really mustn't tell me *not to give up hope,* because I'll brain the next person who utters those words. My husband is dead. And . . . I think there's something about Jerry you should know. Maybe I should tell everyone—I probably should have told everyone weeks ago—but I'll at least tell you: my husband didn't exactly get *lost* on the moon."

Her words surprised Georgie as much as they must have alarmed Neil. Not that the boy didn't know that his father's disappearance had been no accident but, with a surge, he wondered if his mother, in fact, secretly believed all the things he'd told her—everything she'd seemed to dismiss.

"You've idolized my husband—everyone has," she said, finding it hard to continue. Barbara glanced at her son—it was a look of remarkable warmth for such sharp, black eyes; eyes, I remind you, which always looked twice, two differing ways, as if offering alternatives. She was waiting, it seemed, and at that moment Georgie thought, perhaps erroneously, that she wanted him to speak up. She took a deep breath, those eyes flashing out at the astronaut poised on his chair; and during that interval of suspension, his father's truth, too large for a single small boy to hold, flooded in.

"Mr. Armstrong," he blurted, "my dad's been calling the house," overriding a stream of apologies from Barbara. "He's watching us from the moon, and he calls, all the time. Just a few days ago he called"—struggling from her grasp as she repeated, "I'm sorry—the strain, you can imagine"—though Neil, hunkering on the carpet to look the boy in the eye, only asked, "What did Jerry say to you, son?" as Barbara's voice receded to a distant fretting, like a storm driving outside, against the windows. For Neil Armstrong, like Georgie, was a person who believed that Jerry Finch might accomplish anything.

"I'll show you," the little boy said. "I'll show you what he said."

The moonlight was so bright outside that night, it looked like phosphorous spread on the ground. Georgie told them to stay in the living room and went into the bathroom then to pick up his mother's hand mirror—flat on one side, convex on the other. They watched him parade past with this object, toward the kitchen, and Barbara shrugged and mumbled something to Neil, who turned his helmet and body slowly to follow her son.

The 5300 had been motoring along quietly, keeping time with the moon's track across the sky. With some difficulty, Georgie had repositioned it an hour ago according to his father's instructions, to take advantage of an effect previously unnoticed but quite clear now that he was standing free of the telescope: when the lens is focused upon a bright celestial object, the captured and magnified image—providing wonderful and detailed illumination to an eye applied directly to the viewfinder—if unobstructed, is transmitted through the eyepiece as a condensed and narrow ray of light, much like that beamed from a film projector. Pointed at the moon, with lunar filter removed, as it was now, such a large lens conveys a beam that is nearly blinding; and, focused further by the eyepiece, due to its orientation, this beam was at the moment projected like a filament down the hall, coming to rest against the wall that ran between the living room and the front door. It burned there, a little leprous patch beside the coat rack—tiny upside-down and reversed incarnation of the satellite. If you had squatted very close and stared, you could have made out the corrugated lunar surface, rocks and diminutive footprints; with a magnifying glass or microscope it might have been possible to discover individual grains of sand.

The boy had in one hand the mirror, and in the other a pair of his father's reading glasses, used so often by his mother that she'd neglected to throw them out. It was the concert of these two objects that he relied upon to complete the experiment, representing, as his father had indicated, a kind of mystical optic union.

Holding the glasses close to the wall, inching them forward until he'd intercepted the telescope's ray of light, he slid the convex side of the mirror into place behind the spectacles, where the now magnified image blurred.

At first, Georgie was simply dazzled. A gaunt, streaming light shone into his eyes, and for several seconds the world seared with spots as he adjusted his grip on his tools. It was necessary to move the mirror back from the glasses so that the projected image grew larger and dimmer, and could then be magnified many times. The sensation was one of juggling an invisible object, aligning this patch of light with mirror and lens in a reversal of the telescopic process, an unpacking of the moon's microscopic contents. Finally, however, he succeeded in grasping the bright reflection there as between two tongs and, by gently moving his hands, first one and then the other, managed to steer the image, enormous now, down the hall and into the darkened living room, where the adults awaited the illumination. Upon the bare white walls slid the lunar backdrop, shimmering with space, nestling in the bookshelves, clinging to the profile of the upright piano, impregnating the folds of the drapes. The woolly blue floor swam suddenly with dusty shapes and the footprints of long-departed men. It was as if they'd been transported a quarter million miles and stood at the floor of some ancient lunar mare, kicking up silt, feeling the pelt of Lilliputian meteors; but if Jerry Finch had hoped a shift of scenery would bring his wife closer to him, would perhaps give her a greater understanding for his predicament, he'd completely miscalculated.

The most immediate effect was that Neil, ordinarily calm and self-possessed, grasped frantically at the valves of his suit, trying to initiate a flow of oxygen from his life-support backpack before the vacuum of space ripped the air from his lungs. The earthbound astronauts had long forgone the use of their suits' breathing apparatus, as they would have done when sealed safely inside the space capsule, receiving oxygen feeds from the ship; however, they'd trained incalculable times for a moment precisely like *this*—the instant when some chance event rips open the seal between a regulated atmosphere and the sucking wind of space. Neil must have felt that the vacuum, never far off, had without warning opened wide to extinguish this fragile bubble of life. It was an astronaut's worst nightmare.

For a few seconds he was entirely absorbed in adjusting various hoses, bobbing on the fresh carpet as he opened the necessary feed systems. The reflected light played over his body, a single footprint projected onto his chest like a coat of arms. What he did next, however, came as a total surprise.

Georgie watched from the end of the hall, mirror and spectacles in hand, as the astronaut grasped his mother's waist and pulled her to him, and then, with a mighty grunt, tore one of the auxiliary hoses from the emergency oxygen purge system, placing this streaming conveyor of life against her mouth. Holding Barbara tightly in his arms, he dragged her, protesting, out of the living room and into the bathroom, where he closed and locked the door, presumably to try to restore pressure in this secondary, sealed chamber.

The boy squatted for an instant, frozen and consumed by the heroic act Neil was engaged in; but slowly the sense of the fiasco he'd made of his father's already desperate plan overwhelmed him, and he let the mirror and glasses sink to the floor, the living room lapse into darkness again. It was as if he'd shone this light into some dark corner of the human soul and found a hidden scenario of insanity and gallantry taking place inside. He felt ill.

Imagine with what trepidation he went down the hall, hearing all the while what seemed to be his mother's hysterical sobbing coming from beyond the bathroom door. With no idea of how to undo what he'd done, he knocked until he heard the lock disengage.

She was sitting in the dark on the edge of the tub, bent nearly doubled. Neil was perched on the toilet, the expression on his face invisible from where Georgie stood. But he saw when his mother sat up that, while her face was shiny with tears, she was laughing. Neil held the oxygen purge hose in his hand, gushing into the room, and periodically he murmured, "Mrs. Finch—Barbara—I apologize. There wasn't a moment to be lost—" while she continued to laugh, grabbing the hose now and then and spraying his helmet.

When she'd gained some composure, she gave Georgie a stern look, but it melted almost immediately.

"Neil Armstrong," Barbara said, wiping her eyes, "Commander Neil Armstrong? I'd like to thank you for saving my life," although as soon as the words were out of her mouth, she lost it again. "No, I mean that," she sputtered as he stood, blushing. "I'm sorry—"

"I'm afraid you have me at a disadvantage, Mrs. Finch."

"No, not at all, Neil," she said. "Not one bit." Her laughter subsided to a smile as she reached for her boy, and he slipped into her arms. "But I've offended you, and you were so gallant—don't you think he was terribly gallant?" she said to Georgie.

"He's an astronaut," the boy pointed out.

"Yes—I suppose he is," she said, turning back to him. "I forget that at times," she mused, beginning to smile and stopping herself. "Let me make it up to you, Neil—my ungrateful reception of your earth-shattering kindness." He covered his visor with one large mitt. "At the least, let me invite you over for supper. What do you say?"

He continued to cower behind the glove, but as they walked him to the door she asked, "What are you doing tomorrow?" already sure that he was doing absolutely nothing. "Because you're not going to tell me you'd rather spend the evening in a pup tent eating that baby food you all live on." She snorted again, once, unable to help herself, then apologized. Before he went out, she took one of his large, silver hands. "You're coming over, aren't you? Come at nine. I think it's best we do something latish, so Georgie doesn't put you through the wringer again."

"I feel a bit ashamed of myself just now," he admitted, as she kissed him on the faceplate.

And when he was gone and she'd closed the door, she broke down laughing all over. It was something she hadn't done in a while—perhaps she was afraid to stop. They stood in the hall, staring into the dark living room, scene of Neil's tribulations.

"That man saved my life," she said in a stagy whisper.

TWENTY-THREE

A Man upon a Breeze

Were we, that night, floating high above the court, to glance into the windows of the Fitzpatrick living room—facing, exactly as the Finches' living room, across a narrow wedge of air and light upon nothing but more living rooms—we would have caught a strange reflection of the scene we'd just departed: an oblique view of Doris where she knelt on the carpet in the hall outside her bathroom. She was talking through the door to her daughter, who sat with arms wrapped around knees, up on the toilet, her mother's words coming through as something indistinct—a voice from a cloud.

"My poor dear," the voice said, "my poor thing," hateful because the girl recognized the voice for what it was: she'd heard it before, and knew that this was the voice which visited affliction and the afflicted in their season; a terrible, unreasoning angel come down to pray for her. And while her triumphs would always remain invisible to the angel, it would be there, a soothing crush of poverty, whenever she fell. For weeks the voice had haunted Barbara Finch, who didn't know what it was; now it had come back to Angie Fitzpatrick—no succor against disaster, but disaster's secret face.

"You dear, you dear you," it said from so far above her, trying the door. No one locked in the only bathroom of an apartment truly desires solitude, and the angel knew as much; which is why, although it got up and left, it returned after a minute.

"Please, open up dear," the angel said again. "I want to show you something."

Outside in the hall, Doris had a shoe box of photographs in her lap and, waiting for some reply, she began to go through them, exploring the little paper packets of film and negatives. There was no sound from within the bathroom, and little organizing principle to the box. She opened the packs, one by one, and shuffled through photos, wondering what her daughter had meant when she said she'd *seen* Jerry Finch.

The court was such a circus of roaming astronauts and angry patriots—was it possible, she asked, Angie had mistaken Cud or Sprine, for instance, for Jerry? It was certainly understandable; but it seemed this had been the wrong question.

The silence behind the door renewed, though in truth it hadn't been the question so much as the tone—the tone of that voice—that reminded Angie of something she herself had said just the day before, when she'd laughed with Bob over the idea of Georgie and his phone calls. "From the moon?" He'd chuckled. "Really. Why, that's wonderful." To which she'd replied, "Isn't it? But, you know, Georgie's full of stuff like that— you even half-believe him, sometimes," at which point they'd broken into fresh hilarity.

Only at night did the splendor of her days recede entirely to a mirage of adulthood, evaporating at the sound of her mother's voice; and now, alone with the awful angel, Angie gritted her teeth as she became, inevitably, a child once more, cast into the sandbox of lunar fairy tales.

After a while, still without any response, Doris found the photo she'd been thinking of—one of few from this long ago, black and white, small and nubbly-edged—stuck to the back of another picture. Ungumming it the best she could, she passed it under the door.

"What are you *doing*?" she heard Angie say. "Jesus Christ—stop *sticking* things under there." But a moment later she heard her rise and retrieve the photo.

"Don't tear it up, dear—I don't have the negatives anymore," she reminded the girl.

There was a tense silence. Doris was relieved not to hear ripping paper and the terse flush of the toilet she'd received when she tried an hour ago to pass Angie a note.

"That was the summer I met Ryan, your dad," she said of the picture of a young woman standing against a split-rail fence, neck craned to see something off to one side. Angie already possessed a vague notion of what her mother had looked like back then, but she was still struck by how closely they had once resembled each other, Doris and herself; it was quite remarkable to see her mother slender, with a nearly boyish figure, and a quickness to her expression, as if her face was incapable of not betraying the fresh and animate mind beneath. She was wearing a striped, close-fitting shirt—a sort of leotard—and what looked like riding pants.

"I didn't know you rode horses," Angie murmured into the wood of the door, turning the photo over to read the date.

"That's how I met him. He was on a horse—there was a horse farm near where I lived—and he was visiting and stopped to talk to me by the roadside. I was seventeen."

Doris felt through the pictures again. She was so glad she'd remembered this box. It was like placing her hand on a sunlit window, wonderful to be alive, opening these packages. After a few moments, she found another photograph, this one more recent, of herself with a tiny baby— it was Sean, Angie knew, picking up the picture—cradled in a blanket in her mother's arms. There was a man's sinewy hand, her father's no doubt, just touching the blanket, his shadow cast upon the both of them. Her mother was looking up, into the camera, face vibrant with minute, reflected delight.

"I was eighteen—just before we left for Florida. I think Ryan was already admitted to the program for experimental fliers, and we moved down, close to here, just a few weeks after."

As Angie gazed at her father's marvelous young hand, all etched with blond, Doris rustled in the box and found a third photo, this time in color. Her hair had been nearly strawberry back then. She was at the beach in this one, in Florida, with two kids: Sean pulling at her hand, while James, probably not even two, crawled naked after a Labrador retriever that lay in the sand nearby. She still had a wonderful figure, lusher, heavier in the bust, but so beautiful—a sort of bombshell in her black one-piece. She was laughing, tanned, starting to get up to follow Sean as she looked conspiringly at the camera. Even now she wanted to say it: Wasn't I beautiful? But she didn't, and she struggled for a moment to forget the thought had crossed her mind.

"I'd be twenty-one there, twenty-two," she said, passing the photograph beneath the door. "It's Pablo Beach. Do you recognize it?"

Angie nodded silently. Her mother's voice contained a nearly religious reverence for these pictures slipped timidly into the room beside the bath mat, fascinating and hauntingly intimate because she'd never seen them—or she'd seen them so long ago, they were no more than déjà vus. The sky was a child's sky made of construction paper, and it looked as if they'd been cut out from somewhere—Massachusetts, she supposed—and placed on top.

There was a picture of herself in her mother's arms, suddenly part of the world, her father, half in uniform, lounging beside them with a cigarette, face nearly concealed by smoke as he said something. Her mother was perhaps twenty-five then, and they were all with another couple Angie didn't remember, on a bleached stucco deck overlooking the sea. James squatted on the ground with a black-haired boy, playing with a red toy car. The sun and time had drawn the color out of everything but the car and her mother's hair. Despite the animation in the faces, there was a stillness, the sense that they'd paused at the sound of a distant noise whose meaning wasn't yet clear.

"Who are those people?" Angie asked, looking at the man next to her father, also half in uniform, leaning forward with his bright, clean-shaven face full of light.

"They were friends of ours—Marge and Andy. He was a flier, too. They were part of the same rocket-plane team, him and your dad."

Angie heard Doris rustling, and this time she passed a photo beneath the door that the girl recognized. She didn't remember the day—she was perhaps two, two and a half—but she'd seen the picture before, of her mother together with her and her brothers. Doris was seated, and Angie was sitting on her mother's lap in a tiny dress, her brothers standing beside her. Everyone was neatly turned out in short sleeves: backs straight, squarely facing the camera, each with the same blue eyes—an exotic daub of glaze placed on their different faces—and yet every face was lifeless. No one was smiling. They seemed more determined than happy, and her mother, only twenty-seven, twenty-eight, had lost some spark. Her face looked soft, vacant; there was the palpable sense that life had been sucked out of the picture. He'd hit the ground at over five hundred miles per hour. You could tell, just looking at them, that nothing was left. It was hard to pull herself away—this belonged to Angie, more than anything else, perhaps—but she did. "I know what you're trying to do," she said quietly. "So stop it. What you're thinking now is all about you—it's all about things that happened to *you*."

Her mother, Angie knew, had simply divided her life down the middle when her husband died. Doris Fitzpatrick loved very deeply, and if her husband had no life, she would gladly give him half of hers. Everyone had done this in Angie's family—her brothers, for their part, were in the air force; they had all cut their lives in two, except for herself. Only Angie, never having really known her father, had been selfish enough to remain completely alive.

"This is fifteen years ago," she said aloud, feeling, once again, the tenderness of the angel on the other side of the door, who wanted the smallest world for her, a tiny world in which she couldn't fail—in which no one could possibly fail, because there were no stakes; in which every sentence would always begin with the words "It's a shame . . ." the complicit smile, unimpeachable and inescapable. Whenever she stepped outside of that world, the angel would be waiting back at the gates to welcome her home from her disasters. The angel was, after all, only half alive—it couldn't accompany her, and it half-envied the living.

"Everything that's happening now," she said, "is happening to *me*."

"I know," the voice from the other side of the door murmured. "I thought the same thing once, I'm sure, but no one ever explained—I just wanted to explain."

She waited for her mother to say more. There was the tread of feet down the hall; and then, after a moment, she heard her coming back, carrying something which rustled stiffly against the walls.

"Please, open the door," Doris said, but the girl didn't. Angie knelt on the bathroom floor, the pictures gone, all pushed back again, except the first, of her mother leaning on the fence.

"I want you to have something."

They waited on either side of the door, her mother holding a dress made of stiff silk, as if preserving within itself its own atmosphere—the perfect dress in which to capture an astronaut. It was the dress in which her mother, after all, had captured hers.

"I want you to have this," Doris said to the door, feeling the cloth under her fingers; and she knew it like her own skin, although it was, of course, not her skin anymore.

TWENTY-FOUR

The Secret Night School

It was nine the next night when Neil Armstrong knocked. Kitty had come by an hour before, taking Georgie back with her for a sleepover, and the astronaut found Barbara just lighting candles on the narrow table in the kitchen, the yellow flame opening and enveloping them, Barbara's face dimpling with surprise as she noticed the astronaut's suit had reacquired its sheen—the glass in his visor now clear, sparkling, his jaw clean-shaven. Neil saw her watching him, touched and a little amused, and he smiled, too.

"It's the shave, isn't it?" he said. "I had some help from Buzz, because—well, you remember, we can't get these things off by ourselves," he explained, tapping on the side of his helmet.

Pulling back a stool for him to sit, she asked, "So, you do, sometimes, take off the suits?"

"It's a balance we have to strike, Barb—I see it as a kind of sacrifice."

"Isn't it rather a lot to sacrifice?" she asked from the stove, spooning out lasagna while he fumbled with the armature of a corkscrew and a bottle of red wine. They watched as he slowly withdrew the cork between his mitts and then laughed together, a bit embarrassed.

"Cheers," he said, pouring into the stem glasses. Barbara sat down, following his actions as one watches the cautious advances of a child. She was beginning to wonder if perhaps this wouldn't be more awkward than she'd imagined.

"Well, isn't it?" she repeated, the rasp of knife on plate slicing the room. Neil reached forward and lifted his wine, glass clacking gently against visor as he sipped through his straw.

"Don't we all make sacrifices?" he asked and then, perhaps feeling that the mood was becoming too somber, added, "Maybe I'm not choosing my words well. It's not about sacrifice, after all—it's what we're sacrificing *for*. God"—he breathed, a deep hush inside his helmet—"I love this world. I've never known much of it, but it's more beautiful to me every day. It's probably getting to spend time here again, with such wonderful people. I feel so grateful for the chance, even under the circumstances." Neil hesitated.

"I'd like to thank you, Barbara," he said, raising his glass. "You look beautiful tonight, too."

She wore a black, strapless dress that hadn't appeared in public for years. Once, long ago, up by the Michigan shore, she'd bought it for a party, and she was flattered it still fit in a different state, in her different life. Suspended from her ears were ruby pendants given to her by her mother as a wedding present, around her neck a thin gold chain. She was conscious of wanting to look beautiful in a way she usually didn't, as if for a few hours she was standing in for all the charms of the earth. Normally this would have made the entire situation, with its attendant rules and subtexts, ridiculous, but tonight she didn't care.

"It's just an old thing," she protested, beginning to eat and hoping to bury the embarrassing interlude, until she noticed his hands were idle. He glanced down bashfully at his plate, the candles playing across his visor.

"I should have thought," she apologized, realizing that, although he'd cut his food up, he couldn't eat anything that couldn't be squeezed through a tube or straw.

"Don't worry about it. Happens all the time, you know—I really hardly notice any more. And to tell the truth, I got a bite to eat before I came over."

"A bite?" she said.

"Well, you know, it was tube food."

"Do you ever miss using your teeth?" she asked.

"Sometimes . . ." he began, but his voice trailed away. He shook his head. "It's just one of those things, Barb."

Suddenly the night seemed so serious again. Maybe there was something she could say to lighten it up, but she realized she didn't want that: she wanted him to talk about things he didn't say to everyone else down in the court, at press conferences, corporate inspirational meetings.

"Do you ever think you might have done things differently?" she asked, wanting to precipitate this confidence. "Not about *Apollo 19*, but—I mean—you weren't always—"

"Sometimes," he said, "I see I could have done things another way. I think meeting your husband meant a lot—when I knew Jerry, and what he had in his life, I thought maybe I could have done something else. Something like that."

"Please—don't think about my husband, Neil. There's nothing we can do for him."

"Your husband," the astronaut replied firmly, and then again, hoarsely, "husband"—a high, quavering sound like a kite over the prairie. "It's that I want to remember him," he said at last. "We all wanted to be like him, with his wonderful life."

She placed her cutlery down. "I know you feel like you owe Jerry so much, but it wasn't that Jerry *did* anything that anyone else wouldn't have done for you and your crew, Neil. It could have been anyone—it could have been you—"

"But it wasn't," Neil said in a soft voice, the room swimming in his visor. "I've been on the moon, and nothing changes there. You don't change the moon, it just changes you." She saw her own face reflected, the dark line of her bangs, all that white neck, before he tilted his helmet down.

"Barbara," he said, without looking up. Was it a question? Barbara? She felt herself stand, and come around the table. She wanted to comfort him—that's all she wanted to do right then, whether for him or for herself—but her hand met cold Mylar and drew back.

Neil was perched on a stool, leaned forward slightly to balance the PLSS backpack, with its communications and telemetry gear, oxygen and water tanks, fans, pumps, lithium hydroxide canister for the removal of carbon dioxide, and batteries; plus the oxygen purge system—neatly repaired since the night before—with its backup supply of necessities.

For a moment her fingers hovered close to his sleeve, and then she went behind him and laid her hands on his shoulders, around the towering life-support apparatus, her fingers sliding up against the curve of his visor. Neil's hands jerked toward hers, protectively, then came slowly down to rest again on the table.

"Neil," she said, "I'm going to take this off now."

She hesitated, unsure if he would resist, but when he didn't, she wrapped her hands around the joint between his helmet and the body of the suit—it looked as if she meant to strangle him—and twisted the lock-lock as it's called, the secondary lock keeping the locking ring in place. Releasing the locking ring proper, she rotated the broad neck seal with both hands until, with a rushing noise, the helmet came free, and she lifted it cautiously above his head. Underneath, like a wet suit, Neil wore the hood of the liquid-cooled garment, or LCG, covering everything but his face. He turned toward her as she came and stood in front of him. He hadn't turned his head independently from his body in a long time, and the sensation was disorienting. He was about to speak, but she placed her hand to his lips. He felt as if he hadn't known the touch of another person in years.

The stomach and lower chest of the suit are where water, oxygen, and communications hoses and cables lead from the PLSS into the suit itself. Pulling back the dustcover sheaths, she firmly twisted each locking ring to release the hoses, which now curled away from his body. She came around behind him again, and he shut his eyes as she unlocked the straps that secured the PLSS to his back. Bracing herself against the weight of the life-support system—120 pounds including the OPS when fully charged—she eased it gently to the ground.

Neil sat back, hands still resting in front of him on the table. His heart beat so quickly it made his eyes flutter. What was happening now was exactly the kind of thing he'd been warned about over and over during training, worse even than the embarrassing near disaster of the night before. This was, in every sense, a full breach. In a real-life scenario, in any oxygenless environment, he would die within seconds. He had to forget everything he'd ever learned: a life-absorbing faith was required, of the sort one normally bequeaths only to a copilot. He breathed deeply as she undid the straps on either side of the suit and then, coming around, released the locking rings holding his gloves in place.

"Neil," she said, laying her small hands over his, "I'm going to take these off."

With infinite care she pulled them free, folding and placing them on the table, beside his knife and fork. He looked at them once, then closed his eyes again, feeling the raw bite of the wood beneath his fingers.

"Ouch," he said, knowing it was childish, touching all the things laid out around him, his arms still assuming the broad, muscle-bound arcs imposed by the stiff outer layer of the suit. He touched the cool sides of the wineglass, dipped his fingers inside, and tasted. By candlelight his hands looked ruddy and alert with life..

He felt her hands around the sides of the suit again, and then she was standing before him, her fingers moving down the front of the outer garment, unlatching the chains of Velcro and zippers and titanium locks that kept the suit closed and impervious to the lunar vacuum. He looked at the Mylar springing open down his chest, and held his breath. When she was done, she helped him stand, and the suit buckled from around him, over the chair. Stepping free of it, they both stood by the dinner table, the ghostly outline of a silver man laid out where he'd been sitting a moment before. He turned to her.

Neil was wearing only the LCG—the final, inner garment, like a pair of long johns embedded with a fine network of plastic tubes circulating coolant water close to the skin before it's pumped out and routed past the feedwater, which, in its turn, deep in the machinery of the PLSS, draws off body heat in an exchange coil that sublimates out into space. Standing beside this elegant woman in her slim, black dress, he might have been a deep-sea diver, still separated from her by worlds, although closer now than ever.

Very slowly, he ran a hand through her hair. "It's so soft," he said aloud, comparing it to all the kinds of feathers he'd read about; to the moon's dust, those fine beds of rubbed glass. He felt the smoothness of her ears, the earrings there, cold, metallic, and stony. She felt his hands travel her throat, then down the sides of her dress.

Over their shoulders, out the window, the moon swam in a lapidary sky, its light falling through the room, revealing everything unrevealed by candles. Had they looked, they would have seen the yellowed orb pearling above the antennas of the building across the court as it had so many times before, the facade silhouetted so that the eye was drawn to all the windows awake in the night, and then to an unlit window on the fifth floor, where a bulbous form pressed to the glass, aluminized suit shining. After a moment the figure could be seen to turn away and fumble into the darkness of the room, as if imagining it might have been seen. And it was then that the phone began to ring. It was ringing in the little kitchen as the candles winked out, one by one. It rang and rang, at first brightly, then urgently, and finally as an endless entreaty, without inflection, but no one picked up.

TWENTY-FIVE

Grand Hotel Part III

At night, when the sea turns cavernous and cold, the traveler grows restless, his room becomes a prison; but then he reminds himself that he's waited for this hour all day, glancing out the window from time to time as it grew dark, and the room threw its lamps more heavily against the glass.

I'd been over everything there with an insomniac care: the overstuffed furniture pricked with tiny flowers and twined vegetation; the bathroom with its gilded mirrors that grasp a person from all sides like monstrous pinchers; the credenza by the door on which half a sandwich lay—something unfinished from an adventure outside last night, into the strange, holiday air. There were paintings on the walls—paintings of the sea, or perhaps the lake—real oils. I'd pressed my face toward them to smell the paint but naturally couldn't smell anything inside the suit but myself. I hardly went out anymore—there was usually some child passing in the hall, and for a quarter tip they'd bring back whatever I needed. No one had to see my face. No one had to know my name. And even when I did go out, it wasn't as if anyone recognized me. I was just another astronaut. Who could tell us apart?

It was the same each evening. I would take the braided satin cord and draw the curtains wide, so that for a moment, to someone outside on the chill bed of the lake, my body would appear full and silvery like a reflected moon in the window, room burning around me; and then, this accomplished, I'd bound slowly into the recesses of the chamber for the

wall switch, extinguishing the lights, plunging the entire room into darkness as now, through the sympathetic rising and falling of two worlds on
opposite beams of a scale, the outside, revealed for me by its own peculiar luminaries, flared into life.

There, below on the silt floor, would be the encampment of North
Court, the fires and tents among the denuded magnolias. Across the
court, mirror of the Grand Hotel, was a redbrick asterisk hived with yellow light. I didn't need to count floors or windows anymore—I knew
exactly where to look.

There was always the shape of the telescope—bent, veiled head. And
tonight, there was Barbara, moving by the stove. I watched as she walked
from the room into the hall, responding to an invisible summons of the
house, and returned bringing, of all things, an astronaut—my own
reflected self—into the kitchen. It's always hard to tell astronauts apart
from a distance, even for an astronaut, and I looked for telltale signs.

There was, however, before I could determine anything about this
person projected like a dream into my home, a knock on my door, there
in the Grand Hotel. I sat up, no doubt with an expression of bald surprise. When a traveler is at home, a knock can be a multitude of things,
good or bad; but seated by the window, I found the possibilities both far
more immense and totally without allure. I hadn't ordered room service,
hadn't asked anyone to come by. The knock was what knocks are to
houses in the country, far from human habitation in the middle of the
night: you may expect only complete surprises. There is simply nothing
else left. And I was so careful now, on such a narrow road, I didn't want
surprises.

The knock returned. I got up, crossing the room with weightless
strides, and toggled on the light, squinting to place my eye to the peephole. For a moment I caught my breath, remembering this face from
another life.

"Jerry?" a voice said, teasing, young.

"I can hear you in there," the voice insisted despite my silence.
"Jerry—I know it's you. Just open *up*."

There was nothing to do. I opened the door and peered across the
chain.

"Angie," I said after a moment, and we regarded each other, I and the young, blond woman—she couldn't be more than sixteen, I remember remembering—out in the hall. As if through some misplaced act of memory, she was dressed in a blue ball gown, sleeveless and shiny with buttons of pearl, her hands gloved in blue to the elbow.

"*Room* service," she said, and then, smiling, "Hey—aren't you even going to ask me *in?*"

I closed the door and unchained it. When I opened it again, she slipped inside, saying, "Wow, look at you," reaching to touch my visor with her hand. She glanced around. "I've never been in these apartments—pretty swanky." Her nose wrinkled.

"Did Georgie tell you?" I asked.

"Georgie? No one knows . . . but me. I figured it out all by myself, talking to Fauna." I knew who Fauna was—she lived down the hall. Had I asked her to go to the store? Maybe I'd asked her little brother. It was hard to keep track, all those silent exchanges and money slipped under the door, and you never actually looked anyone in the eye. "How long have you been back?" she said half reproachfully. "Weren't you going to drop by and see me, Jerry?"

"No one's supposed to come here," I told her, aware that I wasn't answering her question, that there was something unfriendly in my tone and, for the first time, she looked confused. She'd undoubtedly hoped for a different welcome. "I haven't come back, yet," I added. "I'm still on my way. It's very difficult."

"Oh," she said, nodding and looking around again, "well, we're all waiting for you, you know, to come back." When I thought of what was perhaps going through her mind, I relented a little, and tried to smile. It must have looked ghastly. She'd never talked to this incarnation of Jerry Finch, who didn't want to explain or share anything—a man who feels he has to be very quiet or someone might notice he's alive.

"What's the matter with you?" she asked; and then, regretting her choice of words, she sat down on the bed. "Is it your wife? Because you shouldn't be afraid of Barbara—I told her, I told her about everything. And I told her to leave us the fuck alone." She nodded her head at the imaginary woman. "Mind if I smoke?"

I retreated back to the window, closed the curtains, and perched in the chair. "I did," she said, and I saw her face take on that deep inner sufficiency of cats' faces, my wife become small and inconsequential to her.

The suit I wore was stuffy and uncomfortable. I felt like the beleaguered hero of an English war tragedy—something with silent men smoking in parlors, feeling the starch in their uniforms. It was in the nature of this particular tragedy that Angie wouldn't know—or wouldn't want to believe—that I'd had two lives, like a spy, and that these lives were converging on me now, like trains, both hopelessly large—either one easily capable of crushing me. Because she didn't know, she took things too easily: I didn't like how Barbara's name rolled off her tongue. I wondered if words meant the same things to her, this girl whose life had seemed, just a couple of months ago, so full of the tumult of youth. I couldn't believe I'd made such an impression; but then again, she'd certainly left a mark on me.

"What were you doing?" she asked.

"Watching my wife."

The light in the room was yellow. Her hands seemed yellow. She said, "I'm having your baby."

Which was terrifying. I looked at her from deep inside the space suit, as far back as I could go. Such wild, aggressive words. "What am I supposed to say to you?" I said, crumbling. She was so much younger than I remembered. "I know you came expecting all kinds of things from me—all kinds of magic moments—but I can't do that." I was horrified when her face didn't change. I wondered if it was stuck and thought, God, I've done this to her—but I couldn't do anything with that now. "Do you think there's *anything* I can do? Can't you see, I can't do anything? I can't do anything at all." I kept my voice level, however, and stood, curled slightly against the weight of the pack. I was thinking of the other astronaut—the one in my home, so like myself.

"Who is that, in my house?" I asked, and she shrugged. It was cold in the room. I asked her if she was cold, but she didn't answer. The conversation was moving, she could feel, away from herself, as if she were incidental. And, at some level, she must have felt it was a waste of time being caught up in talk about someone else, who wasn't either of us. This was an us thing to her. The whole mess—all these people, the astronauts—was about us in the end, about her and about Jerry Finch. I seemed to have forgotten that.

"Is it Neil?" I asked, fingering the curtain.

"Probably," she said, getting up from the bed and looking at me sharply—I could see her reflection in the little corner of glass I'd uncovered. She knew I wanted to push back the drapes again and look out. She'd been so happy when yesterday, standing in the court, looking opposite my family's apartment, she'd figured out I was here, right under her nose—or just above her head. Nightly was there, twisting her ear with his stupid theories. Angie had been thinking about something Fauna told her a few days before, and she'd just looked over his shoulder and discovered my window. It was like Bob fell off the face of the earth.

I realized, even then, that I was behaving badly, if that means anything under the circumstances. I owed her some explanation, I felt, if not of everything then at least of what was happening now. But I'd never been good at explaining.

"I want," I said, trying to measure my voice, "to be small, the smallest thing. That's what I have to do, Angie, if you can understand. If I could be a flower, or a mouse— I could be a fly, and I could come back slowly into this world. I could grow like a weed in a crack in the road, and no one would see me, and I would reach back into my life, invisible, unremarked. I could be a fly on the wall of my own life, and she wouldn't hurt me," I said, as the girl watched in disbelief. "She wouldn't raise a hand, and I'd be something growing, flourishing."

Angie flushed as I'd seen her do only amidst her family. "Listen to you," she murmured. Even Jerry Finch now—even I—the one person who she thought could understand, who hadn't succumbed to the twin adult diseases of complacent selfishness and indifference—even I seemed content to let everything roll on as if nothing had happened between us. She looked at me, standing at the window, my hand on the curtain. "You're out of your mind," she said, because perhaps that seemed better than the alternative.

"No. I'm not crazy. It's the most ordinary thing, to want what I want.

I could be anyone else, and I could let myself in and out of my life so carelessly. To be that astronaut, over there, in my home—"

"Is it because I'm too young for you?" she shrilled. But what was the point of discussing that? She closed her eyes as I sat down, leaving her to hover in the room, untethered, wondering if she came back, another time—perhaps this was a bad time.

"I'm sorry I can't help you," I said, feeling relieved. "I know you're disappointed."

And after a moment of standing by the bed, allowing the insult of the whole thing to grow in her—as if she was superfluous—she reached into the bodice of her gown and threw a piece of paper down on the twisted covers.

"Read this," she said, "when you have the chance." I'd discover, later, that it was my letter to her—the one copied out so long ago in these chronicles—written on the eve of my journey. At the time, however, I did nothing, and she crossed the room, slamming open the door.

"Please," I said to this usher in my tiny, personal movie, as I prepared to open the curtain, "could you turn off the light on your way out?"

She hesitated, a burning point at the periphery of my vision, then flipped the switch, her shadow standing in a long incandescent rectangle across the floor, perhaps waiting for me to call her back, thinking that I must, but I didn't. Instead, I drew the curtain open, and the apartment building across the court flooded the room with its cells of light.

I saw the kitchen aglow with candles. Barbara, in a black dress, was doing something with her hands. It took a moment to discern that she was lifting the helmet from an astronaut.

And as if it was myself there, I saw the helmet rise and reveal the hood of the LCG, all happening in slow motion, as if it wasn't happening at all. I watched my wife take the gloves off the astronaut and lay them on the table, and I watched him touching everything—touching her—as in a dream in which I saw myself rise up, up, and some kind hand blessed me; as when I first became an astronaut, that day I received the notice in the mail that I'd won the contest: *Gentlemen of Space*. The astronaut turned a little in the light, and the thought entered me, chill and awakening, that it was Neil, not I, knighted now by this soft, feminine hand. It could be anyone's hand at all, really—only that some great hope is bestowed in the intimate touch of another; and I knew it would not touch me again, ever. And then, the man so blessed turned away and was for a moment, once more, any astronaut, my own mirror.

I watched them together, my wife and this man—this astronaut peeling off his space suit—who, for a moment, I might mistake for me; and as if from a dream, fitfully, I would awaken to the realization that I was alone in this room in the Grand Hotel, sinking now and then back into the dream of being the thing I watched, then grasping with submerged panic that the little room across the court was impossibly far away, and I had not made it back, after all. It's one of the first things an astronaut learns, while still leaping in the training harnesses: that you will always require another, you will always need a second person to get you into or out of your suit—to make you an astronaut or place you back in the world—as a knight, a Gentleman sir, requires the gesture, the blessing hand of a queen. I watched the woman across the court raise her arms to release her dress, his hands joining hers and guiding them into some blind opposite of flight.

I was leaning forward in the overstuffed Second Empire chair, feeling the weight of my PLSS pack, wanting to squeeze out a pain that rested in my lungs, when I realized by the light cast through the doorway that the girl who'd come to see me hadn't yet left the room. I wasn't alone. The moment when I'd wanted to show her my whole world, because it seemed more wonderful than anyone could imagine, hinged back sadly from itself to reveal a tableau of the last eight weeks. As I was then, I'd become unimaginable to myself now.

"Please," I said, half-turning, holding my gloved hand against the window, "don't look in there. That's my life." But she was shutting the door already, quietly, embarrassed to have seen so much. She didn't say a word, no longer angry with me. She had, if you must know, misunderstood one last time.

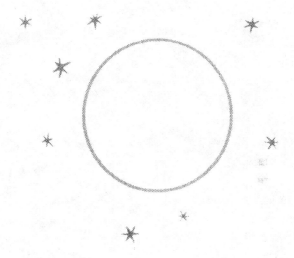

TWENTY-SIX

Night of the Mind

The moon was nearly full—one of those moons so close, you can't really tell; so big in the sky, it cast everything into cold, blue tones, as if world and satellite were part of a continuous landscape—as if the moon rose and set upon itself.

Someone riding the thermals over the court, listening in on conversations inside and outside the redbrick stars, would have been struck by the multitude of voices murmuring a single theme in different registers, inversions, variations, as if all singing a hymn to one man. Brooding above the earth, such an observer might have remarked a brightness down between the buildings—not the pallid shine of satellites but a flickering, lurid glow. He might have watched when the night came on and people set up their telescopes, as someone lit a fire—a very large fire—and he would have perceived that the gentle denomination that had pitched its tents at the nativity of this summer had mostly departed, leaving the crass newcomer, the beleaguered hanger-on, to feed the flames with the magnolias and wooden picnic benches from kinder times. An observer high in the wind would have seen Neil and Barbara peering out her kitchen window, faces drawn tense by reflected firelight. Our fellow traveler would have heard the phone ringing endlessly until she unplugged it and they stood together in the gaunt silence.

You might still wonder about Barbara Finch—my wife: who she was, what she really believed. Much earlier I asserted, perhaps too glibly, that I could see with her eyes, travel the back roads of her mind as if the countryside was my own; but I admit to you, she remains at some level indecipherable and prior to my thoughts, like another grammar. I do know, however, that it was a great relief to her that night when she finally told Neil about her husband, the fugitive from two worlds. He took the news with equanimity, after a moment sinking into a seat by the kitchen table.

"You look like you need a drink," she suggested, opening the freezer.

"I didn't know—" he began, still seeming to believe this was somehow his fault, but she wouldn't allow it.

"About Jerry's problem? Of course you didn't. My husband never told you. He never told me either, so here," she said, handing him a vodka tonic. "Drink up."

He took the glass without looking. "They won't send a mission," he murmured, "when this stuff about Angie breaks—"

"That's just fine," she said after a long swallow. "If Jerry wants to be the man on the moon, let him"; though she hesitated before suggesting, "Maybe he didn't want to come back. And anyway—it's not really possible at this point, is it?"

"My expectations," the flight commander replied, "have never been entirely reasonable."

A surge of voices below drew their glances out the window. The astronauts, goaded by a handful of spectators, were trying to roll a cruiser that had pulled up beside the gates, lights throbbing and dyeing the night.

"You can't stop worrying about him, Neil, can you?"

"It's just—I feel like a bit of a third wheel—" There was a quiet, detonated sound as the squad car toppled on its side, a section of metal fence collapsing into the parking lot.

You see, these people—Barbara and her astronaut—had a sense of this night's finality. They knew that if, somehow, Jerry Finch did return, it was over—the moment for something lasting between them past. Of course, you might point out, it was infinitely more likely they would never see Jerry Finch—would never see me, I should say—again. But Neil recognized, even in this, that the window between himself and Barbara was closing. He looked at the table across the kitchen, where his space suit lay. If Jerry never returned, the whole world that had become his—space, the moon, and its servants—would all, he knew, fade to nothing for Barbara. Just looking now at the suit, glowing in the dark, made him shiver. He walked across the room and picked it up. "I'm getting rid of this," he said. "I can't look at it anymore."

Which is why, in the middle of the night, he went down to the green dumpster at the rear of the building and laid the suit among the bags of trash and the boxes containing the last of my worldly remains. He sat there for a long time, hearing the garbled warnings of police in the distance, staring at the moon as he'd done with Lyle Barnes, and thinking of a lost astronaut dying out of two worlds at once.

It was while Neil was putting the last of his former life to rest that Kitty came by Barbara's apartment, disguised in a yellow raincoat. She'd tried for hours to sleep, but despite the fact that her home didn't face onto North Court, she'd been continuously roused by the commotion. Finally throwing the covers off, she'd come outside, sure she'd find Barbara, so much closer to the action, awake.

"It's lost its mind out there," she remarked, putting down her hood as she came in. "I mean, if I were you, I'd think seriously about taking a few days and going someplace. Or haven't you noticed?" She smiled at her agitated friend. "Ever been to the Keys, Barbara? They're lovely. Go to the Keys—go to Disney World for all it matters. Just get out of here."

It was then that Kitty noted the fancy spread on the kitchen table.

"Hope I haven't barged in on anything," she murmured of the straw jutting from a wineglass.

Watching the woman's eyes, Barbara gave up on any possibility of extricating herself. "I don't even know where to start," she said, throwing down the last of her drink, smiling as Mrs. Shank wheeled into the living room to compose herself.

"All I'm saying," Kitty added from her seat on the couch, "is if you ever thought about travel, this might be a good time—" And she was still talking, musing aloud about the state of things, when Neil Armstrong appeared in the doorway.

"It's just full of surprises around here," she said, glancing at the bathrobe he was dressed in, the pair of slacks and a shirt he carried over one arm, fished from the trash. The robe, Kitty saw, putting a few things together, wasn't a gentleman's.

There was the brief whoop of sirens below as Barbara emerged from the kitchen. Kitty cleared her throat. "Penny for your thoughts, Mr. Armstrong."

He glanced at her, then at the clothes in his hands. "To be honest," he said, sitting on the edge of Jerry's chair and standing back up, uncomfortably, "I'm worried about Lyle. I'm not blaming anything on you, Mrs. Shank—but Barbara told me what happened, and I just don't think you understand Lyle very well. This is his whole life down there."

"Oh, the man's crazy—that's all," she said placidly, to which Neil replied, "At the moment, I don't see what any of us have to be proud of."

Kitty gazed at the discouraged astronaut. "Welcome back, Mr. Armstrong." She nodded, pushing her glasses down on her nose. "I appreciate how you feel—I really do—but something you should understand, as a returning citizen of our planet, is that guys like Lyle—well, let's just say they're survivors.

"Now," she said, raising a hand to ward off objections, "I don't want you to think I mean anything nasty by that. What I *do* mean, though, is that Mr. Barnes has a powerful imagination—he's almost as good as Jerry that way—and if he doesn't make it to Congress, you can rest assured he'll make his kingdom out of a barbecue shack or *whatever* his next hobby happens to be. Which is fine with me—*just* as long as I don't have to live in it.

"No," Kitty concluded with a shake of the head, "I'm not worried about Lyle. And I'm not worried about you, neither, Mr. Armstrong—at least not anymore." Then she furrowed her brow, looking down in the court where the crowd hunched around the flames and Nightly stood in the door of his tent, firelight playing in his glasses.

"It's everyone else that has me worried now."

*　　　*

*　　　*　　　*

*　　　*

Bob Nightly's tent would glow eerily throughout those small hours, as alone he evolved his final theory on the Apollo mission. He hadn't mentioned this theory to the astronauts or even, for that matter, to Angie Fitzpatrick, although it was, once again and much to his surprise, this sixteen-year-old girl who'd inspired him.

Only the night before, he'd stood beside the tent with her, explaining his plans and goals—how there were rumors out of Washington that Neil Armstrong had swept through the Capitol, rumors of succeeding lunar missions. No, he assured her, shaking his head sagely, the nation hadn't yet forgotten the moon; in fact, wasn't there room, yet, for a man to make that leap from space into politics? Hadn't John Glenn just entered the Senate last year? And, true, while Nightly himself wasn't by any stretch of the imagination an astronaut—for he *was* thinking of himself—he saw his own affinities with space as something with perhaps broader appeal: wasn't his cause the abandonment of the very astronaut in the human race?

Nightly paused for breath. By the waning light, patriots were setting up their telescopes, a touch of defiance in the way they adjusted their clock drives and aligned their viewfinders. They all seemed to feel as they imagined their hero felt—like a fugitive from an indifferent law.

He'd glanced at Angie and, finding her preoccupied, followed her eyes to a window—the Finch family window—from which Barbara peered, face pale and vague with distance. Bob wondered if Angie had heard a word he'd said when she murmured, "Bob, you're a perceptive guy. What do *you* make of Barbara Finch?"

"I suppose I like Barbara—I like her quite a bit," he replied, feeling in his pockets for a pipe. "We understand each other, you might say."

"Everyone seems pretty taken in by her."

"She's an abstract woman, if that's what you mean. Many people in her position would have lost their heads by now, but she—both of us, I suppose—are practical people. We're survivors."

For a moment they stared up together until, realizing that there were a dozen other onlookers standing among the tents, also studying Barbara's window, Angie chanced to turn and look across the court, into the windows of the building opposite.

Bob picked up his thoughts where he'd left off: "If only we had more media attention," he said, stimulating his brow with the ham of his hand, "things would feel a lot less tenuous. It's just that a man like me can't charm the cameras—at least not like Barnes." The politician, or ex-politician, had been conspicuously absent, lately.

"Don't laugh, Angie, but at times I think I could use the man. Something I've come to realize about myself is that people don't listen to me." He shook his head in self-sympathy. "Sure, they might listen to my ideas, but I'm a whole other matter—it's a hard thing to find out about oneself, but it's true: I'll always be the man they hate, because I'm right."

Taking off his glasses now, alone, Bob recollected that the girl had excused herself immediately afterward. He wondered if he'd sounded arrogant to her—she'd remarked to him in parting how he'd make a fine *dad* one day—though he had to admit, when he really considered his new theory, he seemed arrogant even to himself.

He'd accidentally stumbled upon the theory that afternoon, examining the record of phone calls traced into and out of the Finch apartment. As he would later explain in *The Secret Night School,* he'd made friends in the Ashtrakan municipal police department while investigating Lyle's parole status, and with the aid of a few well-placed twenties—his curiosity spurred by Angie's comments—Bob had determined with some certainty that the Finches' home line *had* received a series of calls during precisely those times jokingly cited by the girl as occasions for Jerry's moon correspondence. He'd forgotten in the rush of discovery how she'd got wind of these calls, but what he did know for sure was that they were placed from *within* the United States, and that it was apparent to him upon closer scrutiny, that their various points of origin made up a recognizable constellation, bearing the unmistakable stamp of Jerry Finch.

Which is a roundabout way of saying that Bob Nightly now maintained, if only to himself, that, far from getting lost on the moon, Jerry Finch had never left the earth.

As you can imagine, surrounded as he was by astronauts with whom I'd spent months of training, two of whom had lived for days with me *in* the space capsule, he was reluctant to publicize his theory. How, for example, would Buzz Aldrin respond to the idea that there had never been an *Apollo 19* mission? That while Neil Armstrong, NASA, the newspapers and television stations, history books, and the president of the United States took the mission to be as substantial as the moon itself, Mr. Nightly, in his infinite wisdom, declined?

Years, in fact, would go by before he'd publish his ideas, by this time illustrating his theory with detailed diagrams of my supposed progress across America, eyewitness accounts from hayseed towns, and questionable photographs culled from minimart security cameras in such places as Fawn Hill, Texas; Lakeside, Utah; and Greening, Michigan—all of which locales, Bob was pleased to indicate, had furnished me, on previous cross-country trips, with opportunities for bird-watching.

But leaving aside the fact that every Apollo launch, from the first, has been dogged by fanatical skeptics who view the entire space project as a hoax, there are two points in regard to Mr. Nightly's assertions to which I'd draw your attention before we lay aside his book once and for all: the first being that while his account, as *The New York Times* yawned, made "provocative" reading, the reviewer lost no time in remarking that our intrepid author, after a five-year investigation, not only had failed to isolate these phone calls entirely from the numerous inquiries placed by fans to the Finches' home but also wanted so much as a hair of the man he claimed spent three weeks merely emptying dimes into Midwest pay phones.

And *that* aside—granted even that such a possibility be taken seriously—if someone had fabricated these men in space suits who lay sleeping at his feet, not to mention the very events that had flooded his television all summer and kept him camped in the mud for the last two weeks, had effectively written the master narrative, complete with major characters, for nine months of American history, his theorizing could lead him only to all sorts of questions about the very nature of reality—about his own substance—which, needless to say, it did not. Robert Nightly was left merely with an odd sensation, as if he'd awoke one morning to find that none of his clothes fit him anymore.

But we must leave Bob now to pay a final call in our flight through the August night, peering again into the Fitzpatricks' apartment, where mother and daughter sat across the living room from each other, nothing to intervene between them on this occasion except a carafe of weak coffee. They'd been talking ever since Angie arrived home, and just fallen silent—awkwardly so.

"If I tell you something," Angie said after a moment, "you have to promise not to tell anyone, no matter *who* you think should know."

And so it was that she brought Doris to the little kitchen window, very much like the one in Barbara's apartment. Above the red face of the firelit crowd, at a diagonal across the court, was the central building in the complex, and she counted up stories on one arm of the asterisk, and then across, until she came to a dark casement on the fifth floor.

"There," she said. "Do you see the window above the blue Christmas lights? The one with no lights at all?"

"OK—"

"I want you to watch that window."

Doris leaned forward and placed her face to the glass, and for a moment they both stood staring out into the night.

"Oh," she said suddenly. "Something's inside, isn't there?"

"No, Mom. I'm making you look at an *empty* window."

"But why?" she said, turning, and then she looked back again with a smile. "Right."

One might have imagined it, at first, this motion—a change that was little more than the deepening we sometimes perceive in a person's eyes—but the next instant she cried out: "Oh, did you see that? It's so . . . weird."

"Isn't it."

"What do you think it is?"

"What does it look like?"

Doris pressed herself to the glass again—it gave her a shiver, this business, like being with a girl her own age, or, rather, like being a girl again.

"A snowman?" she teased.

"Oh, come on . . ."

"It's an astronaut, isn't it?"

"It's Jerry," Angie said. "That's how I found him."

Even after being told who it was, Doris felt that the shape in the window could have been any of the Apollo men. Still, there was something in her daughter's expression that checked her from saying as much.

"How'd he get here? On earth, I mean."

Angie didn't know, and her mother returned to the glass, squinting to make out any detail in the bland, white form.

"Why doesn't he come down?" she asked.

"He's frightened, I think, of the attention."

"Oh—men," Doris said, waving her hand.

"And he's afraid of his wife."

"Of Barbara? Yes, I suppose someone should tell her"—starting as the girl grasped her arm.

"You promised me—"

"But it's a sort of miracle, her husband coming back—"

"No," Angie hissed, pulling her from the window, "you *promised*."

The two stared at each other, nearly eye to eye.

"Please," Doris said, Angie's grip on her arm giving way, "try not to be so dramatical." In the last twenty-four hours, Mrs. Fitzpatrick had begun to feel, for the first time in years, that there was some affection, some shared adventure between them. It was appalling how thin this was.

"I don't understand"—she sighed, looking to where the astronaut pressed like breath against the glass—"how you can treat *me* like your own worst enemy—"

"Maybe it's because"—Angie rounded on her—"you don't listen. Sometimes I think Bob Nightly's a better listener."

With a stifled exclamation, Doris turned from the window to the fridge, rummaging inside. And even after Angie had walked out of the kitchen and down the hall, she could hear her carping, "What does *that* mean? What is *that* supposed to mean?" But there was no point, the girl knew, in explaining what she'd seen from the window across the way. Instead, a thought came to Angie of something like a story—perhaps a story from a book she'd read as a child—about a boy in whom no one believed, who one day, for no other reason than this, had simply disappeared. Though she tried to remember the boy's name, she found she couldn't, and finally she reflected that it didn't matter what her mother believed or listened to at all.

If her mother saw Barbara as a friend, to the rest of Magnolia Court, Mrs. Finch had become as distant and reclusive as any astronaut. To turn the court against her now would take little—only that little, Angie knew, would have to come from someone besides herself, someone above reproach.

TWENTY-SEVEN

The Mask

In the dream, Bob Nightly was alone in the back of an open limousine, like the one in which the astronauts had so recently ridden from Cape Canaveral through the streets of Ashtrakan. He was standing, waving, the street's length barricaded by police, lined with a somber crowd that regarded him intently, but lifelessly, until he realized they weren't regarding him at all. Examining his surroundings more carefully, he saw they were simply cardboard cutouts pasted above the curb, even the police just two-dimensional props.

Still, Bob continued to wave. And he was waving, watching the inert crowd as the car coasted, until, glancing down in front of himself at the driver, he noticed that the man at the wheel was wearing an astronaut's suit. His face wasn't visible, directed forward and helmeted as it was, and Bob was wondering who the astronaut could be, reaching out his hand to tap him on the shoulder, when with a start he saw that his own arm was encased in Mylar, his hand in a bulky, white mitt. He glanced up to see that the crowd, seeming to realize his situation at the same moment, was now coming to life. And then he awoke.

There was a voice calling his name—a high, sweet voice he recognized as Angie Fitzpatrick's. He wasn't surprised to find her standing outside the tent when he emerged into the miasma of the court—it had happened before—and his eyes just grazed her face as he checked his watch. Four in the afternoon—the day already blown—though it had been, he reflected, a late night. If Nightly was momentarily indifferent to

Angie's presence, it was only because he was focused on this vision he'd had, eclipsing the obscure dawdlings of sixteen-year-old girls. His dream, he felt, was part of a larger picture.

The entire drama—the Jerry Finch Episode, as he called it now—so pressed down on him he could barely sleep. He didn't entirely understand what was happening anymore, but he felt he was in possession of a vast, strange secret—something like a child's idea of a treasure map. He couldn't show it to anyone until he'd deciphered the precise whereabouts of the treasure, but even failing that, it filled him with a sense of power and purpose.

His state of absorption did obscure certain details, however—at the moment preventing his noticing, for instance, Angie's evening dress: puffy, strapless, and better suited to a junior prom than to this carcass of a campground, a ravaged caricature of the suburbia these people knew. It depressed him to wake up to these scenes of carnage, the deterioration of conditions like a collective memory of dank morning-after misgivings.

"And how are you today, Miss Fitzpatrick?" he asked. "Busy as a bee I see"—before he considered her dress, at last, and suggested—"You have plans, perhaps?"

"I'm going to swing by Barbara's later. Want to come along?"

He disregarded the question, assuming it was sarcastic, but was surprised when after a moment she said, "You know, she doesn't *want* Jerry to come back."

"It's entirely possible," Bob agreed, ruffling her hair. "Given the disruption she's already suffered in her life, her husband's resurrection, at this moment, would be as traumatic as the appearance of a ghost."

"You think he's dead," she said, "don't you?"

"Dead," he replied with a smile, "is a strong word. Some things, you know, become more powerful after death. Take Christianity—" And Nightly would have explained that Jerry's particularity wasn't important here—like most heroes, he'd no political or social ideals of his own, he was merely a point of cathexis; but he glimpsed the bulk of Lyle Barnes emerging through the wrecked gates of the court. Spotting Angie and Bob, Lyle waved, veering toward them as he raised his chin to the day and grappled with his tie.

"Morning." He grinned, arriving and shaking hands. Nightly noted he'd donned over his button-down shirt a denim jacket with velvet letters reading: LYLE BARNES AND JERRY FINCH—GETTING US BACK ON TRACK. He seemed too old for it, like a rock star on a revival tour; still, Bob had to grant the man was resilient. He seemed even cheerful, and a familiar twinkle, the old pleasure of just being alive that once seemed always to pink his cheeks, flashed in his eye as he said, "Who's the lucky fellow, Angie? What's the dress about?"

Ignoring him, she asked, "Have you guys seen Neil around?"

"Bet he's at Barb's," Lyle replied, undeterred. "I was just heading there myself to see if she needs anything."

"Oh," Angie added quickly, "I'm sure Neil's already taken care of Barbara's needs."

Bob glanced at her—she didn't seem entirely right this afternoon—but before he could comment, he noticed the Barnstables and Buzz Aldrin approaching.

Buzz held a megaphone in his hand. He'd been circulating since the dawn hours, "Doing promo for the softball game," he explained. The announcements had commenced shortly after Nightly fell asleep, and each time the astronaut's amplified voice jerked the reporter awake, he cursed him together with Barnes, who'd suggested that a few acts of community service might be useful in repairing the Apollo crew's tarnished image.

"Say, Armstrong's not at NASA HQ?" he asked Buzz, who shook his head and, hefting the megaphone, called, "Paging Neil Armstrong—paging Mr. Armstrong."

Bob couldn't tell if the astronaut meant to be amusing, but that was the thing about astronauts: they acted so on the level, it was hard to know if they weren't being straight with you. Absorbed in this question of transparency and belief, Nightly found himself, however, distracted yet again by Angie.

"Armstrong?" the girl was saying. "Lyle's right—he's probably *still* at Barbara's." And though he was about to say something to her, she turned from him suddenly, a determined look on her face—quite remarkable, really, as if she might cry. Angie, too, not surprisingly, was wrapped up in questions of belief. And while such questions have pursued all of our players, with Angie, perhaps, there was a difference.

She owned, to begin with, a secret so perfect that even Nightly—who craved secrets as other men crave air or love—would never have believed it had she simply offered it to him, gratis. In itself, this was not so unusual; nor was the fact that no one at all would have believed her had she openly accused Barbara Finch of adultery, let alone unveiled her other, more dramatic piece of news. There was, however, one person, besides Jerry Finch, whom everyone *would* believe, who knew the truth about Barbara as well as she did, and who she knew would speak that truth, even if it meant his own destruction. It's often hard to imagine, but there are people for whom truth makes their very bones: they cannot help but describe it. Bob Nightly, not being such a person, and not understanding what was happening in Angie's mind, could only look on.

"I just came from Barb's," he heard Janet Barnstable telling Lyle, "and there was no one but a gentleman from the school board—young fellow. He must have come by for lunch."

"Bob, is it true," someone was suddenly saying at his elbow—it was Clyde, face freckly and credulous—"is it really true NASA's sending a rescue mission this week?"

Nightly gritted his teeth. There was pressure in the air, he could feel it, and he heard the words rolling out of his mouth as if they were not his own, but merely one voice among the six or seven he was trying to monitor: "That would be the thing for the Agency boys to do," he said. "A scrap to throw to the media—the caring government, the Good Father rescues the good father—not that they expect to really *find* him. It won't be necessary. The point is, NASA's found its golden goose for a while. They can send up two or even three missions, though of course the most important thing is another few years of funding, more rock collecting, et cetera."

Clyde, as ill-informed as ever, was opening his mouth—no doubt to divulge a charming bit of platitude picked up from Barnes—when Nightly heard Janet, beside him, comment, "Why, there he is now, that school board fellow I just told you about."

The man in question was making his way toward them, and at first, finding him to be a large and athletic person, Nightly assumed, contrary to what Janet maintained, that he was someone sent from NASA regarding the rescue mission. When the stranger was about twenty feet away, however, Buzz let out a strangled yelp.

"Holy Jesus," the astronaut said, "Neil—you're exposing yourself!" as with a start they realized that the individual approaching them in slacks and a short-sleeved oxford shirt—all a bit small—was Neil Armstrong. Having learned to see his face clasped inside the terrarium of a helmet, they found him nearly unrecognizable today, as if Santa Claus had turned up one season in evening clothes.

A few people stared. Across the court, an astronaut had awakened from his bed in the refrigerator box. In slow motion, he kept looking, pointing, and then turning back and shaking his companions.

When Neil arrived, Buzz cautiously touched a glove to his face. "How'd you get it off?" he asked, a thought flashing through his mind as, growing visibly pale, he whispered, "Was there a flaw in the design? An error of some sort?"

"No—no such thing," Neil assured him, voice crisp now it was free of his helmet. "It was a pure act of nature, as a bird emerges from the nest."

"And I imagine," Angie commented dryly, "Barbara Finch keeps her nest as warm as the next bird."

Despite himself, Bob gave a start; Neil's face, save a scant, leathery wrinkling around the eyes, didn't change. He said, "Careful there, young lady."

"I'll be as careful as I like," she replied, bringing every other discussion to a halt. "I never thought you, Mr. Armstrong, could sink so low— and after you said you loved him."

Neil's eyes swept the faces all around. The astronauts were approaching, bleary and alarmed; when they bounded up, they looked for some help or explanation, but no one could offer any. Perceiving the tremble of doubt and curiosity, Neil returned his attention to the girl. "I do love Jerry Finch. There's no one in this court today, I'd hope, who wouldn't tell you the same. Is there something you mean to say to me, Miss Fitzpatrick?"

And though she'd opened her mouth to speak, the words died on her lips.

Perhaps it will strike you as ridiculous when I say that she'd staked all her hopes on this man—a man whose corroboration would mean his own confession—but understand: people thought of astronauts as their own polygraph tests, and she'd assumed Neil would furnish her most damning witness, even against himself. The situation, until this moment, had been exactly what she'd wanted—if she'd dreamed of exposing Barbara in front of everyone as an ice queen, capable of abandoning her husband exactly when he needed her most, Neil's testimony would have buried the woman.

The flight commander's blue eyes, however, firm and bright as buttons, betrayed no intention of telling anything; or, worse, seemed to dare her with the terrible possibility he'd lie. It was a threat that may seem trivial twenty-five years later, inured as we are to duplicity, but Neil was challenging her to ruin something that she—that everyone there that day—had always held to be perfect. If he chose to carry this all the way, no one would believe her, no matter what she said. The thought was desolating.

"You aren't an astronaut," she managed to get out, feeling the attention of the crowd upon her like sweat, the moment in which she might have destroyed Barbara in the eyes of the nation, in the eyes of her husband, passing, nearly gone.

"That's right, Miss Fitzpatrick," he replied, "not anymore."

A flurry of voices swept the patriots. The Apollo men all began talking at once, at first quietly, but then in a growing cloud of radio, a hiss of numerology; all except Buzz Aldrin, whose voice rose above his comrades': "What about the rescue mission? What about Jerry?"

"Jerry Finch is dead," Neil replied, his certainty damning, as even Buzz gave in to the frenzy of emergency recompression, the astronauts fumbling with their gear, turning valves, grasping hoses. It was a frantic moment of activity that Neil recognized for what it was: he'd done it himself, only two days before.

"You're not an astronaut," the girl repeated, turning to Bob, who regarded her as he might a contagious person.

"Angie," the journalist appealed, "don't be a fool"—though before he could say another word, she'd buried her face inside his jacket, sobbing. Reluctantly, he allowed his hands to support her as he turned to Lyle, staring at Nightly as if slapped.

"Sure," Bob stammered, "he's dead—the man's dead"—as Lyle continued to stare, appalled. "Oh come off it, Barnes, he's been in outer space with just a helmet and a pair of boots for two weeks—" But he broke off when Angie began murmuring into his chest, "Don't be mad, Bob. I was going to tell you—I was going to—" spoken quietly, on the verge of tears. "It was him, and her, you know—*doing it,*" her voice coming in gasps, but in tones that to Nightly's ears contained the distinct cadence of nightmare. "And of course, Jerry ran away—how could he—live with such a *bitch*?"

"How do you know this?" he said, nose quivering.

"I saw it," she stuttered.

"But *how*—how did you see?" Bob asked, noticing Lyle was watching him—it was as private as an ice rink around here.

"What?" he said to the stunned politician. "What do you want now?"

Lyle had been certain, until thirty seconds ago, that, regardless of difference of opinion, he himself among everyone—save, perhaps, Kitty—was most lacking in faith. Like most true believers, he'd taken faith as a baseline, assuming his own lapses to be deviations from a norm rather than recessions from extravagance. This confession of desertion, by Neil of all people, plunged him into confusion. A murmur went up from the faithful, their questioning eyes upon him as he turned to the former astronaut.

"I'm sorry," Neil said.

Lyle shook his head and croaked, "Where's your suit?"

"I don't do that anymore, Lyle."

"But where is it?" he insisted, as if this was all he could think to say; and when Neil didn't answer, he lumbered away, through the pale mass of faces.

In the ensuing silence, a caesura in which Angie hoped everyone would now turn to her, people, instead, looked anywhere else. She stood there like a fool in her borrowed dress, watching Janet come and lay her head on Neil's shoulder, the girl's eyes following the former astronaut, allowing her last hopes to drain away as he, too, moved off through the crowd, vanishing through the doors of our building. And it was at this moment—no one, I assure you, was more surprised than myself—that she heard a voice beside her: low, gruff, but speaking to *her*, asking something of *her*. It was Bob Nightly.

"Go on," he said, wrenching the megaphone from Buzz's hand, "say it, whatever it is."

He didn't look at her—he couldn't bring himself to do that—but he could smell a secret, and he was the sort of man—a grammarian more than a historian—who believes all secrets true, in that there is no secret *nothing*. He felt the Dragon, at this moment, coiled among the crowd; and while he didn't know what Angie might say, he understood that unless someone said something, the entire show—this marvelous blueprint with all its potentials—would dissolve, the mask would never fall. He held out the megaphone to her like a giant, yellow toy, watching with rapt horror as she closed her eyes, raised the device to her lips, and cried: "I'm having his baby."

The court filled with the shriek of feedback and a bewildered silence. The pronoun was vague. She held the megaphone away until the whine dulled to a tone. "Jerry," she said above the face of the consternated crowd. "I want you to know we all love you—how much I love you."

"I'm going to have it," Angie repeated as the crowd bleated in a large, confused voice. "I'm going to have our baby, like you'd have wanted. And I'm going to call it Georgie—if it's a boy, I guess," she said, speaking to the crowd now. "Like our names, you know, together: Jerry, Angie."

"My God," Barbara muttered up in the apartment, turning to Neil as he stole in to stand beside her at the window. "Did she say Georgie? But what a ridiculous name for a child."

"I hope he's just like you," Angie added softly, resting her hand on her belly. "I know he'll have your eyes," she murmured, though this last comment turned out to be too much for these people already having trouble with the idea of an astronaut sleeping with a minor. A married astronaut.

"What's the idea here?" someone heckled.

"What's the meaning of this?" another hooted.

Realizing what was happening, Nightly took the megaphone from her. He knew these people wanted something tangible, and accordingly he drew from his pocket a piece of paper—it was, in truth, an oily bag that had once contained snacks, but he waved it admonishingly. "We have evidence everyone—this is *real,*" and the patriots fell back, cowed by the authority in his tone. He returned the megaphone to the girl.

"Jerry?" she said quietly, her breath too loud under amplification. "Jerry, I know you're watching me, and I need you to come down now."

Angie stared out at the court, the waning day. For a moment the air was quiet except for the yammer of a few precocious crickets, the far-off honk of cars. The patriots, the press, residents of Magnolia Court, Barbara Finch in her little window—everyone looked at the young woman in blue, hair done in a braid.

"Jerry," she repeated. "Sometimes I think about that game we played before you left, when you'd come home from space camp—the one where you'd spin me around the apartment, and I'd imagine all the wonderful things I'd fill the moon with. Remember?

"I thought of a lot of stuff," she said, pausing as if the quantity of things astonished her; as if the moon was a supermarket—shelf after shelf, aisle after aisle of dreams. "I've been adding things to the list, every day."

The simplicity of her words touched some, and several people followed her gaze over their shoulders, perhaps believing the astronaut might have made it partway down from the moon and was hanging, suspended, nearby. It was an unusually large moon, just risen in the bleached evening sky over the central apartment building.

"I need you to bring some of those things back now."

Silence, whether pregnant or empty, returned. The crowd blinked and a lawn chair creaked. In the expanding moment, she began: "You are the father of this baby—" but broke off, staring ahead.

Nightly came forward and took the megaphone again from her hand. "People," he intoned, motioning vaguely with the oily bag. "People of Ashtrakan, Florida, America. We have a petition here, signed by several members of our community, in which it is alleged"—the crowd repeated the word in a confused din—"that on the night of June 27, shortly before his flight from the earth—in which said space exploration I assert he was deliberately fleeing from and deceiving the American people—"

The words rose in volume as they proceeded, sending a quiver through the assembly—"after sleeping with a minor, a felony offense in the state of Florida"—before the crowd grunted once again, interrupting in a hundred voices: "This is a put-on." "You liar." "She's not pregnant—I'm more pregnant."

Angie withstood the heckling, waiting for Jerry to appear or even give a sign. Clearly, the crowd wanted a spectacle, and the thought of someone on the moon not only looking down on them but looking down with the derisive air of an escaped criminal just made matters worse, as if they might be, themselves, the spectacle.

"Hey, baby, I'm an astronaut," a man shouted, standing on a chair and making a lewd gesture as people nearby burst into laughter. "Wanna go for a ride on my rocket?"

Watching the progress of events from her kitchen, Barbara was momentarily buoyed. She wanted, I'm sure, the most demeaning end for this little scrap who intended to ride her husband's failure to fame, who saw the entire fiasco as some dance enacted around herself; and she smiled, looking through her window—or at least, from a distance, that's how she appeared. Whatever slender gravity she'd once exercised over the court, she was now a minor planet, her face a distant fury cupped in the evening sky, its features written, as we so often discover those of the truly powerless to be, all the more vindictively.

Doris Fitzpatrick had just emerged from her building, drawn outside by the voice of her daughter. Maybe she saw this smile or, more likely, she'd simply grown incensed at the ridicule heaped on Angie for something that was, after all, no matter for ridicule. Making her way to the front of the crowd, she placed her hands on the girl's shoulders. "Angie dear," she murmured as her child tore from her arms into Nightly's. She blinked at the onlookers, the cold moon molting in the sky. It was all very confused.

The journalist didn't look at Mrs. Fitzpatrick, but she caught the high, lonely disdain in those magnified eyes peering out from behind Angie's golden hair, her daughter perhaps the only thing this disdain failed to take in. She felt it upon herself, as if she was no different from any of these people, and she looked away from him, watching the crowd surge. She saw a wild look on the face of a young woman, someone with a feather in her hair who, like her daughter, wanted to believe. Perhaps she realized, right then, that if Jerry Finch refused to appear, if he never came home, the situation was merely squalid.

"Get down from there," she shouted at the man standing on the chair—he'd taken his shirt off now—but no one seemed to hear. She went over to Nightly and grabbed the megaphone. "Get out of there, you—sit down," she bellowed, turning very pink, false lashes battering incongruously on a face unexpectedly fierce.

The crowd muttered, but she persevered, scolding the man on the chair until he acquiesced. And then, when the jeers subsided to a prickly quiet, she pointed across the court to the central building. "Are you all through ogling my daughter? Do you want something to look at? Well look over there." She pointed to the darkened windows of an apartment on the fifth floor. "Look, goddamnit," she said as people wavered. "There's your astronaut."

The crowd, following her indications, was baffled; they glanced at her, then at the windows again, unsure which she meant, or if she meant a window at all. In the gathering dusk, they found themselves staring at tiny, lit rooms from which terrified families stared back. And then, as they looked, they saw ghostly in the glass of one dark room, visible only because momentarily in motion, the pale blur of something withdrawing into dimness—the globular shine of a Mylar suit, a great, round helmet. It was gone for a few seconds, then reemerged like an apparition from the murk of the apartment, looking down on the crowd. A woman fainted; a gasp threaded the night.

"It's him, it's him," the crowd screamed, as Doris said into the megaphone, "Mr. Finch, would you *please* come down." But the specter sank back into the dark, and when she spoke again, her voice contained an undeniable twang of irritation: "I think we've all had quite enough games, Mr. Finch. *Jerry Finch.*"

There was a breath, then a cry: "You bastard!"

"Child molester!" came another voice.

"Monster!"—as suddenly, the astronauts, who'd looked on in amazement, stubble-faced and ghastly inside their suits, began roaring. The crowd converged around them.

"Look what you've done to these good men," someone crowed. "You coward," someone else shouted. "You liar!"

Barbara and Neil stepped back from their window. They listened to the chants go up, the tromp of riot police filing through twilit boulevards outside the court.

"Come on, let's get out of here," she murmured at last, heading into her bedroom for a suitcase.

The ex-astronaut followed in a daze, though when he stood beside her at her dresser, he suddenly remembered. "Should I give Kitty a call? I mean, about . . . about—" But she only turned back to her packing, throwing over her shoulder that look of benign incomprehension, the one we so commonly bestow upon children.

Down in the court, Nightly's eyes fell slowly from the fifth-floor window. "Were you ever going to tell me?" he murmured to Angie, wiping his glasses on his sleeve. "Didn't you want to tell me?" And then something hardened in his voice: "Which room is he in? Which one?"

"What room, dear?" her mother repeated as the girl shook them both off.

There are photos from this moment you might be familiar with: Angie's tearstained face, eyes that could barely see for the lights of the press, lurching toward her like an insect. I've been accused, myself, of being the cause of those tears; and I've been called pitiless by Mr. Nightly; but I ask you, where was the pity in this groping and grasping, these men and women who wanted to tear her open to find a number?

"Which room?" Nightly whispered again, noticing something flashing in the glove she held up against the great, multifaceted eye of the evening news. And then, the next instant, she fled.

Is it any wonder? She heard Nightly shout her name, once, with the belated sense of his mistake; she heard her mother's soft reproach and then the press, lumbering behind with its "Miss Fitzpatrick, Miss Fitzpatrick." Still, she knew she could never look back: from the moment she said the number, everything would be out of her control, though in truth it all already seemed that way. For something begun so wonderfully, her romance had become everyone else's to do with as they saw fit. She could barely remember what she might have wanted for herself; or whatever it was, it seemed to belong to another person now. Her thoughts, however, were exploded by a hail of rubber bullets and a volley of tear gas.

Mr. Nightly would later, in *The Secret Night School,* blame the girl's flight, and the chaos that followed, largely upon himself and his sense of betrayal, momentarily blinding him to his deeper feelings and responsibilities. He had not, he claimed, realized until this moment the resistance he would face from both friends and foes; and worse, he'd underestimated the cunning of his adversaries: for, seizing on the turmoil within the ranks of patriots, riot police had entered the apartment complex through South Court and set up a bunker in the lobby of the central building. Beneath the barrage of riot guns, he watched the court retreat behind tents and folding chairs as masked troopers leered like the faces of Halloween animals from half-open doors, indifferent to everything save the astronauts creeping through clouds of tear gas, grappling with those officers foolish enough to make a sally onto the grounds. Like giant, white hounds, the spacemen roamed, deflecting rubber rounds and hurling their foes through the air.

Bob continued calling to Angie, stumbling through milling refugees as he followed the blue dress, voice inaudible even to himself in the confusion. He'd made a terrible mistake, he realized—if he'd hoped she might ever come to trust him, his intentions a moment ago must have seemed brutally selfish. And then, as he advanced through the stinging smoke toward the blue apparition, upright and luminous in the dense air like a watermark in the night, a rubber round caught him in the back and threw him to the ground. His glasses were loose, gone, but he continued to crawl toward the glowing bell of blue, shouting, "Get down! Get down!"

He was moving painfully along a rut in the dirt, gunfire, the moans and cries of the wounded and terrified all around. The air smelled of napalm, and he felt in the moist heat the print of other days he'd hoped gone forever. Perhaps Nightly imagined it, but he thought he heard his name—it *seemed* like his name—called in that young, high voice that just a few hours before, in a kinder world, had slipped through the door of his tent. Face raw and incomplete, the world blurred beyond recognition, he could only continue crawling, though when he at last arrived at a little cul-de-sac of tents, the place he thought he might find her, there was nothing there but a single blue glove.

Something shimmered in the glove's fingers and, nearly blind as he was, he brought it close to his face. A brass circle depended from a key: a shape—perhaps a starfish or an asterisk—stamped above the number 535.

For a moment he hunched, sleeve to mouth, the key clutched in his hand as he surveyed the carnage for a sign of the girl. One of the Apollo men was briefly on fire, then rolling on the ground. Bob could tell from the proximity of their megaphones that the law had been driven back to the confines of the lobby, but it was only a matter of time until they overpowered the handful of astronauts, and the crowd would be entirely at their mercy.

Obviously these servants of the state of Florida were in league with the fugitive spaceman. It was beyond coincidence, he reflected sadly, all this activity here and now, the police guarding the very building Jerry Finch had holed up in. Once the muscular arm of the federal government asserted itself—he could hear choppers honing in the distance—there was little a small band of unarmed people could do. Already the media were being cordoned off by Secret Service in the boulevards beyond Magnolia Court. We were over the wall, behind the looking glass—some such moment had occurred, and Bob was on the point of cutting his losses and clearing out before they started the general lockdown. He was staring at the key—like a key to an old hotel room—so preoccupied that at first he barely heard the noise: a distant scraping and squealing coming from toward the front gate. It sounded like a tank, he thought absently as, squinting through a tear in the smoke, he glimpsed riot police running, diving out of the way, and an instant later a pale four-door sedan roared into the court. There was, he saw, getting to his feet, an astronaut inside, helmet battering against the windshield as he tried to steer with his padded arms.

The car slithered into the midst of the patriots, scattering everything in its path, fishtailing directly toward him until it bottomed out a few feet away. The astronaut stuck his helmet through the driver's side window, disconnected wires and tubes everywhere.

"My God," someone said, "it's Lyle Barnes—" And he realized they were right.

"Where's Jerry?" Lyle asked.

"What?" Nightly shouted beneath the now redoubled vigor of gunfire. "Jerry? He's up there." He pointed to the embattled building towering through the smoke.

Together they looked at the emplacement of riot police, then at the key Bob still held, twisting gently in his hand; Lyle counted up floors in the central building.

"Get in," the politician said in the martial voice of a football coach. "You—all you guys," he said to Cud and Buzz, ambling up beside the car, "inside."

And then, turning the engine over and pointing it at the glass doors of the lobby, as the front window blew out and the voice of the police rose in a shrill scream to the sky, he ramped the car right through the entrance into the foyer of the Grand Hotel, sending the riot police packing.

*   *
*   *   *
*   *

Coming to amidst the moans of his companions, under cover of a small electrical fire, Lyle kicked open his door and staggered from the car. Everything was covered in glass, as if a chandelier had exploded. At a distance he still heard the sound of the cops, but it all seemed to be taking place in another room, having little to do with him. At first, he imagined it was raining inside, though he quickly realized he was walking in the torrent of sprinklers, the tile beneath his feet slick and buckled; and he pressed on across the lobby toward the banister of a staircase, into the dim, upward spiral of steps. Several times he stopped to wipe the visor of his helmet with the back of his arm, and once, turning at the third-floor landing to look behind him, he found the ragged column of his friends close behind, waving him on. He would have liked to have brought Neil, Barbara, Angie—everyone he knew—but he'd brought everyone he could.

Contrary to what Nightly later claimed, Lyle Barnes's decision to don a space suit recovered from the trash had been both considered and reasoned, based not just on the suit's ability—even in a half-assembled state—to repel hostile atmospheres but also on the soothing impression he hoped to make on Jerry Finch, a man, after all, only recently returned from space. And while it wasn't clear to him how the missing astronaut had traveled so far back toward his home, what seemed important, at that moment, was to see this man he'd staked his life upon, and have him restore a semblance of truth and order to the universe. If Lyle Barnes had struggled up from a scandalous past upon the shoulders of fresh disasters, he needed someone now to tell him he'd done no wrong. He'd certainly never meant to, and it might even be said he'd done the best he could. Once, it would have been possible for Barbara or Neil to have told him as much, but although he had failed in everything he set out to do, there was one man he'd never disgraced himself to: he'd been with Jerry Finch, all the way.

Lyle stopped one last time as he gained the fifth-floor landing, his eyes meeting Nightly's, a floor below. No one would ever know how near he'd come to abandoning the journalist out there in the mud, dangling his key in his hand. Lumbering on, toward the room, he was glad he hadn't.

Perhaps it was simply that Lyle loved people—all kinds of people—and might have felt as much for anyone. Looking back, however, on the journalist's harried expression, Lyle saw something—something more than even what he'd discovered in the faces of these astronauts who , loved Jerry Finch as a comrade they'd give their lives for but who perhaps didn't love him with that deeper love we have for those who will, despite our own best wishes, finally elude us. It was a love not unlike the love we feel for our own children, Lyle may have reflected; though had he reflected upon anything now, he might have conceded that Bob Nightly probably never loved anyone very much, if for no other reason than that he loved above all else a thing he called *the truth*. How much happier the man who loves both men and truths—and how Bob wanted to, right then, panting up the stairs. How he hated Jerry Finch; but how he would have loved to awaken, as if from a nightmare, to that lost astronaut, to the great man Jerry Finch might have been.

Nightly watched Lyle and the Apollo men surge ahead, stopping to catch his breath as they rounded the fifth floor. He had no idea that any tenderness had been shed upon him as he ascended the stairs; he felt only the fire-alarm sprinklers, finding the halls, when he reached them, like cloud banks, an extension of the smoke and tear gas below.

As it turned out, by the time the journalist arrived on the floor, the politician had already reached Room 535. Without waiting for the key, or even trying the knob on the door, he'd thrown his padded shoulder against it with all his strength, the wood splintering at the hinges, falling in like a plank upon which he was served into the dark. Lumbering up behind him, the astronauts shuffled to a stop and stared into the doorway through which he'd vanished, so black in the room that they couldn't see him when he climbed to his feet and called in a hoarse voice, "Jerry? Jerry, it's me—it's Lyle."

Everything was muted except the blue outline of a window. He called out again, but there was no response, and he was just reaching around for the light switch when a brilliant beam settled over everything, so startling he screamed and footsteps clattered in retreat down the hall. A helicopter, he realized, was roaring outside the window, its floodlight trained upon him. He tried to put it from his mind and concentrate.

It was an old place he was in, dingy, torn up and soaked, the hard light showing all the seams. At first it appeared to be empty: there was an unmade bed, a chair and a telephone pulled up close to the window. The room, however, was L-shaped, and around the corner he heard running water.

In an alcove to the right, he found a counter and sink beneath a brown, scaly mirror. The splashing sound came through the bathroom door. He heard the others calling to him out in the hall, but if there was something terrible here, he didn't want anyone to see. Reaching his hand out, he twisted the knob.

Surging water wrenched the door wide, though he held on struggling until the flood released his knees. Against the back wall a white tub, copper stained, spigots gushing, poured out across the floor. He waded in and turned off the taps, and then his eyes roved the green prism of water, falling at last among yellow tiles, hoping here, of all places, not to find his hero, observing with relief that while there was a bar of soap, an old towel now wrapped around his space shoes, undulating with the last liquid current, the room was empty, a conversation that had forgotten its own thread, a cartoon world, pedaling over empty space.

Stumbling from the bathroom, he stopped and stared down into the court through his reflection in the window. The helicopter continued to track him in its light, a voice from inside the steel nose barking commands, a kaleidoscope of words. He heard the name Jerry Finch repeated, insistent, and realized that they were talking to him. He was in Neil's suit, but they couldn't tell the difference; and it made him sad—the knowledge that soon everything would be in the hands of such people. There were explosive flashes, sirens. Something was missing, and the phone was ringing. The men were shouting for him out in the hall, and he was looking at this little, black rotary-dial phone ringing cheerfully in a pool of water on the carpet.

"Hello?" he said, picking it up and talking into a rushing, trickling static like the recession of a wave. "Hello?"

*   *

*   *   *

*   *

Had we that night found ourselves outside, suspended fifty feet above the court, the room would have seemed cut from the same gaunt fire that burns each object to its shadow on the daylit surface of the moon. It was the livid light of sodium, something one could nearly smell in the helicopter, where the crew crouched, trying to determine why the astronaut was on the phone, why there was no ground support—where the hell was ground support?—before the pilot banked the craft up, sharply, to reapproach the facade.

Out in the hall, Bob Nightly climbed to his feet. It seemed as if noise was being mangled into light just beyond the doorway, and he kept raising his hand to his empty face to find his glasses, afraid some physical violence awaited him in the room. He would have to go inside, he knew, looking around at his companions, visors brilliant and reflecting. They were waiting for him.

As the room went suddenly dark, he tented his jacket over his head and hurried through the door, the astronauts behind. He found Lyle dimly silhouetted by a window, beyond which a helicopter loomed, bearing slowly around in the air, shaking everything.

"Lyle," he shouted to the man in a space suit, coming up beside him as the politician put down the receiver of a telephone. "What are you doing?"

Lyle turned, eyes gazing out from deep within the helmet. "It was Jerry," he said in a hoarse voice.

"What?" Bob shouted.

"It was Jerry Finch," Lyle repeated.

High above, they made out the helicopter, angling back toward them, while below, in the court, frightened people milled. The police and National Guard were closing in, cherry-tops shifting the magnolias with color. Lyle saw two children running, stopping to look up at the window.

"Is that Georgie?" he asked the journalist, still digesting the politician's last remarks.

"What?" Bob shouted, the helicopter bearing down on them so they were plunged in broiling light. "Did you say Jerry was on the phone?"

Lyle's answer was lost in the roar of the chopper; and though Nightly found the calm in Lyle's face appalling, he instinctively kept close to the politician in his protective suit, as if he might find at his side some larger shelter.

"What?" the journalist repeated.

"This is a terrible night," Lyle said, shielding his face from the light, "for children to be out. It's a dangerous night—"

"You said you talked to Jerry," Bob howled as the helicopter began its monologue again, adding, "What are they doing? Why don't they leave us alone?"

"They think I'm Jerry Finch," Lyle said, squinting out the window. "They think I'm an astronaut."

For a moment, the two men stood together, Bob staring into nothing, Lyle looking down into the court.

"Do you see them, though?" Lyle said during an interlude in the warnings and announcements, indicating the two children again. "Do you see Georgie, running by those tents?"

Bob followed his hand, but only for an instant. "I can't see a thing," he confessed, pointing at his own eyes. "Who are you looking at?"

"Georgie," Lyle returned.

"Who?" Bob said. "Jerry?"

"No," Lyle corrected him, "Barbara's son—Georgie." And though they tried their best to understand each other, going back and forth in this way, something at last seemed to occur to the politician—something that made him stop, and stare around the room as a man might do if he believed he was running out of air. All at once, he blundered past, not looking at anyone, not even Mrs. Shank, with whom he nearly collided in the doorway. She'd heard the fire alarms and come to see what was going on; it had been, incidentally, the moment in which the children slipped out, racing down the back stairwell into the night.

Lavender umbrella held up against the sprinklers, Kitty examined the astronauts slumped on the bed in the flat white floodlight. The moment had passed—wherever Jerry was tonight, that much was clear. She watched as Nightly stumbled in and out of the bathroom, face stunned with commonplace, saying, "What did you see, boys? Did anyone see anything? Where are you going?" But it was to be the last that she, or anyone, saw of these heroes, for even as Bob spoke, the Apollo crew stood and streamed sadly from the room, obviously feeling there was nothing else to be done here, little to be hoped for, and that perhaps none of it—the good or the bad—had ever been true.

And what happened to these men, each with a face so carefully made—children of our country's fond imaginings? What became of them, wandering unnoticed from Magnolia Court, past the police barricades, reporters with their pastel suits and notepads, the mild eye of the nation? When they left Kitty Shank's eyes, our own eyes, where would they go?

Would they be put away, like dolls in their boxes, words in the grain silo of language, some to be taken out in fifty years, some in a thousand some never again? All given only a face, now, and a sin or a grace?

Bob went to the window and picked up the phone, trying to get a dial tone as he gazed over the madness playing out in the court, feeling he'd been drawn into this more than he planned.

"What was Lyle talking about?" he asked Kitty, half-turning. "Did you hear him? He kept talking about Barbara's son"—though Kitty only shrugged, irritably, as if to say it was much too late, now, to play games. She left him there, in the drizzle.

Alone, water running down his back, he wondered how it could just end in an empty room, little more to go on than at the beginning. Hadn't he approached this with as much integrity as—no, with more integrity than—anyone? Hadn't he been a friend to these astronauts?

But he wasn't thinking of astronauts. He was thinking of Angie Fitzpatrick, wherever she was. Hadn't he been good to her?—though, in truth, hadn't he always meant to do better?

In a week, he supposed, he'd return to his old job at the school. He pictured the desks laid in rows, a class full of faces he'd never seen before and, at the end of the year, he'd never see again. He already knew what he'd teach: he would teach the war. And he knew what their expressions would contain on that first day—all those children: it was the fascinated look of dread the survivors of the *Titanic* must have worn, crowded in their lifeboats, watching the grand ship slip under the sea. Florida kids—they weren't like him, or any of the adults, born elsewhere, migrated to this paradise. They'd never known a fall; they'd never known snow slanting into the ocean. They were born into a world so new, and already so old.

Epilogue

Sometimes, eyes closed, head beneath the covers, I think of that little room up there on the moon—the enviro-tent—starlight filtering down over silent beds of green, those small lives growing quiet and unseen, and I imagine among them my father's sleeping face.

Sometimes it even seems to me that I've been there myself, but this is, of course, impossible: that humid chamber I recall, presided over by a twinkling sky, can be only the greenhouse—the greenhouse to which I'd run so long ago, in which our story began, and where at last I concealed myself that chaotic summer night, heart pounding, seeing upon the gravel path before my eyes the booted feet of an astronaut. It comes back now like a dream in which I am always on the verge of rising, for that is how I felt, crouched beside Fauna, having fled through the dark to hesitate for what seemed like a lifetime on the brink of revelation or discovery—as if I might still be waiting there in that room today, wondering: What if this was my father?

There are those of you likely coming forward with reasoned and intelligent arguments to the contrary, but rest assured: reason alone is a pointless cruelty, and while I admittedly felt then much as I did weeks before, cowering with Fauna and the Cousins, believing that the figure of Mr. Pebbles, standing poised above us, was Jerry Finch—imagine: there was in the greenhouse not twenty feet away an astronaut; his breath came and went in the room like the waves of a dry sea. As the seconds passed, I knew that if I didn't see his face, if I hung back in the dark, I would always believe that my father had returned this night to the moon in despair, having come all this way, yet still unable to find me.

As quietly as I could, I crept toward the aisle, navigating the crawl space beneath the tables. And though by the time I'd reached the edge of my dark shelter the room had fallen silent, I was unperturbed. When the sound of breathing was renewed, very cautiously, I stood.

A little light fell through the roof, showing me the silhouette of the astronaut a few yards away, leaning against a table, resting. His face was obscured, set deep within his helmet, but his voice was distinct when he said: "Georgie—please, don't run." My hopes mounted before he added, "It's me—it's Lyle."

Coming closer as I stared at the impassive visor, he admitted, "I was beginning to wonder if I was imagining things—I was even beginning"— he spoke more softly—"to wonder if I lost you, if I might never see you again. It's hard to explain—" Then something seemed to occur to him and he asked: "Were you running away from me?"

Concealing my disappointment, I lied. "No, no—I came in here to play—" My words were followed by the scramblings of a little girl emerging from beneath a table, behind me: "We came in here to play"— as Fauna removed from the pockets of her shorts two dolls: her Neil Armstrong and my Jerry Finch.

Lyle watched intently from inside his space suit; reaching up, per- haps to straighten his hair, his hand collided with glass; and then, grop- ing around his head, he twisted and wrenched at the locking ring of his helmet—only half-sealed—grappling with it until the headgear came loose, and he set it on a table. His face appeared small and surprised in the vast, circular collar. Balancing against the weight of the PLSS pack, he crouched beside me, saying, "I've been wondering a lot, lately."

"Me too," I replied with a certain false cheerfulness, embarrassed by his earnest gaze. "Uncle Lyle," I asked as he continued to stare, "did you find my dad?"

I saw a dozen things crowd into his face, but Lyle Barnes was never a man to speak what wasn't on his mind: "I talked to him," he admitted modestly, "on the phone."

And at these words, I felt something go weak inside.

"On the phone," I repeated, one of his sooty gloves resting upon my shoulder.

"Your father told me he was afraid for you tonight—especially tonight. He asked me to find you. It was the strangest thing, too, because when I looked out the window there you were, just running through North Court, in the middle of everything."

I don't know what Lyle expected me to say. I wanted to be happy— I wanted to be happy for him—but instead I was disappointed: my father had called someone besides myself. And while a few weeks ago this announcement would have meant everything, I confess my father's absence and my solitary knowledge of him had grown into what felt like a tenderness that lay between us.

"He said he wanted you to know he'd always be watching," Lyle continued, voice sinking. "He's watching—I'm sure he's watching you even now."

The politician fell silent. I know we both understood what this meant: these weren't the words of a returning hero. They weren't the words of a returning man at all; and somehow, the knowledge that he'd failed to come home this night made him seem further away than ever. I felt Lyle's eyes upon me, but I couldn't look at him. Instead I stared, numbed, as Fauna approached the table and placed the dolls upon this surface strewn with potting soil. Evidently disturbed by our conversation, perhaps even now doubting my father had ever called either of us, she began quietly playing.

The toy astronauts bobbed upon a great field sparkling with mica and round chunks of vermiculite, their motions those silent and momentous strides I often imagined such men might make in space. I heard her speaking above them, the *pssht* of radio communications, the vaguery of a conversation about nothing, invented as it went along:

"This is Neil Armstrong to Jerry Finch—*pssht*. This is Neil Armstrong—*pssht*. Are you reading me, Jerry?"

She fussed with Neil's helmet, then held him up again.

"Neil Armstrong to Jerry Finch—*pssht*—over. The oxygen tanks are nearly empty. We have instructions from mission control to leave at oh-nine-hundred hours—*pssht*. This will be our last radio communication."

Outside, a breeze pressed against the greenhouse, rumbling the glass. As if they were the receiving mechanism for an antique radio, she readjusted her grip on the dolls.

"If there's anything you need, Jerry—" Fauna hesitated, the astronauts regarding each other in silence. "If there's anything, you know, because it could be a while—

"Or if there's something you want to say, to everyone back home . . ."

I watched as a frown of disappointment or concentration crept into her features. Clearly she knew only half of this conversation—the same conversation we'd all tried to complete for ourselves, I imagine, ever since, beginning with Barbara, one by one over the last weeks, we'd decided Jerry Finch wasn't returning. I found myself listening with her for the voice of my father—that old stage voice of his, culled from Westerns—until she suddenly turned to me.

"I'm sorry," she said. "I'm so sorry—"

I suppose she thought she'd hurt me.

But I could see now that no one—not even young Louis Cousin—had really meant any harm. Like anyone who has made that inhuman journey from private person to public persona, Jerry belonged to all of us—and, consequently, it would be nearly impossible to damage him without doing some damage to ourselves.

I gently took the Jerry Finch from her hand. The doll felt warm, slightly damp. There was a place on the helmet where travel time in someone's pocket had worn away the silver enamel. Placing my chin on the table, I gazed over the dusty shoulders to where Neil Armstrong loomed across the unfocused field. My father's voice, when it came, sounded amazingly clear, like a voice inside the mind:

Can you imagine, he said, a deep intake of breath filling the greenhouse, *what this place—Magnolia Court—was like, once? I'd guess it's hard to conceive it was ever otherwise than it is now, but I'm speaking not of ancient times, only of months—less than a year gone by—when it was a place of its own; before people like myself went to the moon, and the moon was just a fable, a sort of Shangri-la whose lights glittered on the horizon at night.*

There was the slightest pause, and then Fauna nudged the Neil Armstrong forward, cheeks dimpling as she stared at the doll in my hand

and replied, "I was born in such a place, Jerry—a quiet place—a little town in Ohio."

I wish, Neil, you might have seen the court when it, too, was a quiet place. I'm sure you can imagine a man like myself—an ordinary man—might be happy there.

By which I do not mean that Magnolia Court was particularly wondrous— only that the faded bricks, the worn gleam of elevator buttons, the damp smell of the halls became, after a time, things that one could believe wondrous, as a child believes—because they contain the whole world. It was a place where an ordinary man might be happy forever, when he loved the woman he was married to, and when, though he had no children of his own, he was a teacher, surrounded by children every day.

As my father spoke, Lyle had risen and drawn closer, on his face a look I hadn't seen since we'd combed together, with a telescope, the fabled shores of the moon. If I'd had another doll then, I'd have given it to him, but it was easy to imagine that, dressed in his space suit, he was content to pretend he walked with us now upon a darkened mare, and that the disparity in the sizes of the astronauts was merely a product of the great distance that lay between us. He might at that moment have stood upon the rim of Copernicus and listened to a conversation echoing across some lunar basin:

It is of this Magnolia Court that no longer exists, my father was saying, *that I wish you to think tonight. I want us all to gather in this departed place, one last time, because I want you to imagine that this man we are speaking of—not a bad man, as I said, but an ordinary man—might, intending no harm at all, come one day to ruin this world. And I want you to imagine that in the ruin he brought upon himself and his home, that he lost his wife, who once loved him, and that he had even, perhaps, wrecked the life of a young girl, a former student—someone who had, it seemed, mistakenly admired him.*

It amazed me that a person might accomplish all this without meaning to destroy anything. There must have been, I glimpsed, an instant when, gazing into this young person's eyes, he thought he might embrace worlds; where he could see the wishes of a girl as if she was made of glass, and he saw there, inside of her, himself. My father, however, continued:

At first I know this seemed to him entirely a nightmare—a dark sleep from which he would awake. And afterward, relying upon time and love's habits, you would be right to believe that he'd hoped he might repair his home—he might one day make his way back. But these hopes, he said to our continued silence, *were short-lived: they could only be dashed when the man learned that the girl was pregnant.*

A door, he understood, had closed upon a whole region of his life. And still, even if he could now never again teach, even if his wife would never again have him, there was this: he dreamed of the birth of his child—a boy as he conceived, having been a boy, once, himself. At night, in strange rooms, he often pictured him, playing against the wall of his closed eyes—a little boy who became with the passing weeks and months the one person who even in the man's worst moments might see everything, yet could understand, and believe in him.

Jerry drew in a deep breath, and for a while there was only the sound of his breathing—a careful, meticulous sound—as if he was breathing for all of us.

But despite everything that I've related, despite the way his mind doted upon this child, as the weeks became months, and finally years peeling away one after another; as he awoke to his own face in the mirrors of so many strange rooms, he understood one last thing: that he would never actually meet this boy, would never know him, because he was afraid, and he could not go back to the world he loved, where people no longer believed in him.

There is only this, then, that remains for us having come this far, Jerry said, his voice withdrawing to a whisper before it welled back across 250,000 miles. *Our disasters, they say, are unequal. As there are small disasters in which a single life might drown, there are also great disasters, magnificent ones, capable of swallowing lesser catastrophes, so that even our nightmares come to seem slight in the welter of these grand failures.*

I imagined a star generations might wish upon, a flag beneath which an entire country might rally—this special kind of disaster, this very special kind: the disaster of which we've probably each, at some time, secretly dreamed.

You see, he said as if divining my thoughts, face swimming in the shadows of his helmet—that face we knew so intimately from television, always turning away, just as someone calls his name—*I've been trying to imagine the disaster we would require for people to believe again in this man. I am, after all, the last man on the moon, and I think about him all the time.*

We listened to the silence that followed, a faint sound, like air escaping into space and, realizing I was gripping the little doll painfully, I relaxed my fingers, watching Fauna, across from me, do the same. We were both, I know, startled when Lyle said, "Maybe this man you're talking about shouldn't come home." Looking up, I found the politician staring at the tiny figure in my hand.

"The man I remember," he continued quietly, "loved the world more than anyone I ever met. He was the sort of a man who would have gone to the ends of the earth, even beyond—he told me, once—for the ones he loved. But this man you want me to believe in—who'd leave a child alone, on a dark night, because he was ashamed?

"I'm sorry," he finished, undoing the Velcro on the backs of his gloves. "I'm sorry, but I can't believe in him."

We watched as he took off his mitts and laid them on the table. He didn't even glance at my father when Jerry Finch answered, gently: *You don't need to believe in him at all, Lyle.*

And when there was no reply, Jerry Finch inched forward until he stood before those silver gloves like the wrecks of satellites. *You only need to believe in this little boy. You only have to believe in Georgie.*

It's not that I'd change your mind, my father told the politician, *I agree with everything you've said. Yet I know that this man does love the world, more than perhaps anyone. At night he dreams of it; during the day it burns beneath his eyes; and though it's so far away, now—or perhaps because it is so far from him— he sees the world in the smallest detail, as if he might touch it with his hand. He sees the world as he never knew it before, when it was his.*

It might seem like enough to you, to make a man cross 250,000 miles—but it isn't. In the end, it is only as if he dreams that someone loves him, though even here, I think sometimes that someone must be dreaming of me, or I would have gone out, like a little flame, long ago. I only need this one little boy, you see, to look up in the sky on summer nights and think of me; yet even if Georgie believes—even if he always believes—someone, too, has to believe in him. As I sit here, so far away, I've come to see that someone has to believe in each of us.

It's like a chain—a long thread through the dark—when I imagine such a thing. I feel at times as if I'm waiting up here for the day the links grow taut, again, in my hands; and while I also feel that if I was to look too closely at everything I've described, it would seem impossible, let us instead think of these things as precarious, my father said.

As precarious, you might say, as a paper chain. Sometimes, I even think of them as a book—though there was only a kind of helpless fury in the politician's face as he looked up.

"I believe in Georgie. I've always *believed*—just like I believed in everything." His rage rose as he spoke, and heard his own words, and saw us, watching; but it didn't last. We were afraid of him, alone in that little room, and I don't think he could bear such a thing. The anger passed back out of his features, until he added, almost as an afterthought: "But who's going to believe in *me*?"

It was a question for which my father had no answer.

Having arrived in Florida as something of a fugitive, having placed all his hopes in Jerry Finch, Lyle Barnes would have found little consolation in knowing that at this moment the lost astronaut did feel for him, but only helplessly, as a fellow fugitive. My father's mind had no doubt gone out to those words of our president—that humblest of men—who on a distant day, full of boundless optimism, so wisely, even prophetically, suggested that space travel, after all, had only ever been about people. It was so easy, at times, to forget.

I was gazing up into Lyle's face—our eyes, meeting and finding in each other the same familiar and beloved eyes that we always thought we knew, wavering and already turning away—when Fauna lifted her tiny, plastic doll once again onto that star-strewn table.

"*I* believe in you, Lyle Barnes," she said, raising Neil's hand in a gesture of greeting or farewell—I couldn't tell you which—and crossing those vermiculite fields in great, weightless strides. I don't know if she spoke for herself, but it hardly mattered as we watched her recede across the darkened room, until she reached the door, turning before she went home. "I will always believe in you."

We gazed up, then, at the stars pressed gently against the roof of the greenhouse, that field of tiny voices ringing the face in the sky. Perhaps even tonight my father is there, as he told me he would be, watching, although it seems as the years go by and we become more and more alike, my father and I, that perhaps this man I imagine looking down over my progress on earth, from the moon, is in fact by now made up more of my dreams than of my memories. Perhaps he's discovered something much the same about myself.

There will be people—and I hope you are not among their number—who misunderstand me. There are so many soft hearts in the world, it's a delicate place to walk. No one knew this better than my father, and perhaps this was why he promised to show me his maps, and was in the end unable.

I haven't meant to be cruel to anyone, not even poor Mr. Nightly, whose books few, besides myself I suppose, read anymore. I frequently imagined while writing this that I was singing a lullaby to all these people who loved one another too poorly—everyone figured in the Jerry Finch story, and others unnamed. I think I've loved each of them as much as they should be—as much as they could stand. They are all sleeping now, and in their dreams, when they meet my father, they'll remember that there was something they'd always meant to tell him: all of them loved him, once, with that hoarse love and, as if whispering to myself, I've given it all to a little boy I never knew. I would make you all good, if I could.

Acknowledgments

I would like to thank Miah Arnold, Greg Lichtenberg, Iain McDonald, Adam Tibbs, Cathy Wagner, and Rebecca Wolff for their advice and willingness to read *Gentlemen of Space* in all its various incarnations. Many thanks must also go to my agent, Bill Clegg, for his support and cama-raderie, and to my editor at The Free Press, Amy Scheibe, who got it from the first. Finally, I am indebted to the following sources for astro-nautical, astronomical, and telescopic information: *The Summer Stargazer* by Robert Clairborne, *The Peterson Field Guide to the Stars and Planets,* Fourth Edition, *Seeing and Believing* by Richard Panek, and the online archives of NASA lunar material at http://history.nasa.gov

ABOUT THE AUTHOR

Ira Sher's short fiction has been published in the *Chicago Review, The Gettysburg Review,* and broadcast on *This American Life.* He has been a finalist for the Pushcart Prize and Best American Mystery Stories. He lives in New York City.

Printed in the United States
By Bookmasters